LIFE WITH SWAN

Also by Paul West

FICTION

Terrestrials
Sporting with Amaryllis
The Tent of Orange Mist
Love's Mansion
The Women of Whitechapel and Jack the Ripper
Lord Byron's Doctor
The Place in Flowers Where Pollen Rests
The Universe, and Other Fictions
Rat Man of Paris
The Very Rich Hours of Count von Stauffenberg
Gala
Colonel Mint
Caliban's Filibuster
Bela Lugosi's White Christmas
I'm Expecting to Live Quite Soon
Alley Jaggers
Tenement of Clay

NONFICTION

My Mother's Music
A Stroke of Genius
Sheer Fiction—Volumes I, II, III
Portable People
Out of My Depths: A Swimmer in the Universe
Words for a Deaf Daughter
I, Said the Sparrow
The Wine of Absurdity
The Snow Leopard
The Modern Novel
Byron and the Spoiler's Art
James Ensor

PAUL WEST

LIFE WITH SWAN

A NOVEL

THE OVERLOOK PRESS
Woodstock & New York

First published in paperback in the United States in 2001 by
The Overlook Press, Peter Mayer Publishers, Inc.
Lewis Hollow Road
Woodstock, NY 12498
www.overlookpress.com

Library of Congress Cataloging-in-Publication Data

West, Paul.
Life with swan / Paul West.
p. cm.
1. Novelists—Fiction. 2. Women poets—Fiction. 3. Women naturalists—Fiction. 4. Astronomers—Fiction. 5. Friendship—Fiction. I. Title.
PS3573.E8247 L52001 813'.54—dc21 00-051563

Manufactured in the United States of America
ISBN 1-58567-123-1
1 3 5 7 9 8 6 4 2

For Diane

LIFE WITH SWAN

Must I stay tangled in that lively hair?
—Theodore Roethke, "The Swan"

ONE

A puberty ago, I watched from my office window one afternoon as she descended into baking sunlight on the library steps in a Spanish-looking straw hat (Eton boating style), drape-swinging her legs in polychrome-striped bell-bottoms, behind her the terminal moraine of black hair that set her out from the crowd since she was ten. Lissom, bosomy, elegant, she marched down the Mall with an involuntary swagger, caressing a book, Heidegger no doubt or *The Psychoanalysis of Fire;* in those days, I recall, she was into books on silence and also well into her maturity as a poet: her last teens. It is hard to imagine how excellent her work was, her poetry at least. Without uttering a word, she had figured in some class I held on twentieth-century British fiction, but always looking volumes and, in winter this, sealed off from the world in black sou'wester and oilskins. A huge raven perched on the back of the class, she had a look of profound astuteness, coming to me to ask if I would read her poems only after a six-semester wait. But I had read them already in campus magazines and been astounded by the real thing. Finally, when I got to review her first book, I wrote that she was the best living lyric poet. There again, having noted her quality, I perfected her at once, I the fugitive from the courtly love of the Middle Ages, the johnnies or the johns who thought nothing sensual was good unless it contained a decisive mental component. Not a shuddering orgasm quite, but a shuddering one that incorporated also a perfected image of itself, hence a goad to even sharper shudders. In a way they were right, those old-style courtiers, knowing that, once the orgasm was over and the makings rendered back up to God, Nature, or biology, its perfected image hung on, a neuter rhapsody, a stained-glass window arranged on a dangling penis. The more you mentalized, the more you got to keep as part of authentic memory. She, of course, had an easier row to hoe with silence, one of the cult words in those years; with perfection I was out of my depths, but the craving never went away; with silence she could always practice it in the back row while the rest of the class chattered itself to death.

When, some other day, she came sauntering past the liquor store, where I happened to be stocking up on Scotch (a bottle a day kept angina away), she looked even more sensual and not because the clerks in there, once having seen her, began as a team to stick out and withdraw at demented speed the tongues with which they yearned to taste her. Their mouths wobbled, their saliva ran, their chops lolled with fatigue before she heaved those flanks out of sight, still walking in the voluptuous amble she had learned from Spanish movies maybe, or Silvana Mangano, or even her chocolate-noshing mother. I, I kept my tongue to myself but imagined it becoming sarcastic once I had quelled the day's shakes, once I had decided she was imperfect enough to warrant my intervention. Would I read her poems? I did and sent them off to an editor in New York, informing her this was the best poetry I had seen since Dylan Thomas and what were they going to do about it?

So the girl turns up with her degree, all that hair screwed into a huge thick chewable bell-rope, truly a hirsute weapon, a containment of fluid substance, ideal (almost perfect) for grabbing her by, to swing her around or to hold her back when she tried in a panic to leave, screaming Ah, the Sixties. She was twenty-two, mentally a good thirty-five, with an odd habit of breaking into

German (she could quote Rilke by the yard). She stayed for over a month, one day offering to wear a blond wig just for variety's sake, but I was too besotted with the avalanche of black curls she claimed she inherited from her Mongolian ancestors, though I, ecumenical to the last, said she looked Greek, Italian, Persian, your sultry enchantress fresh from one of those dashed-off Byron poems about Albanian women. Her mother, she said, when we were well into our talk, was always saying how drab she was when just born, not only jaundiced but with a wicklike protuberance vertically bisecting her forehead. This was the kind of propaganda you expect of a doting mama who all the time means the opposite of what she says. With a daughter that gorgeous you can say anything which deprecates; but such was not this mom's way with a girl who turned out to be a whizz at languages and writing, inscribing poems on her hands and wrists.

I could see now why she had been silent in class, convinced that all the other students were brighter than she, why she responded to praise with diffident incredulity even though she knew her competence. Her identity was a myth she needed to believe in, but she backed down from it, which made her easy meat for almost anyone who wanted to shove her into a role. She had even, I gathered from a series of swift pawnbroking allusions, been married, to no purpose, and had been made responsible for the couple's debts on the marriage's dissolution. She had played another desperate hand in a psychic gambling game of her own and had lost. She might just as well have joined a zoo, become a sky diver, borrowed five million dollars to found a restaurant that poisoned. She was unaccustomed to affection, had come up with the term affectopath for herself and was willing to live by it, saddled by a label rather than fondled by a man. She held her liquor well (gin, I think) and showed remarkable capacity for intellectual talk at a level far above the rumination in her poems, which tended to be vignettes or cameos. She felt most at home with anthropologists, she said, because they were willing to take people as they found them.

I had been up in the attic at the rickety manure-tainted table I worked on. Imagine. I had resolved to drink myself to death on schedule, yet not before I had written and arranged for the publication of all that remained for me to say, though doubtless (as I feared) continuous drinking might commit me to topics unanticipated, creeping up on me during delirium and demanding their day on the page. The means of ending things prolonged them. Then came Ariada, whom I soon began to call other names such as Pi and Honey; I felt that calling her by her given names was like sending out Christmas cards emblazoned with the push-out adhesive gold angels that came in the box. Refusing to affix them gave me some freedom of action in the world of heraldry, and so with her names. For a long time she was mainly Pi, but once she had become Swan she was always that, beautifully dubbed, I thought, for her gracious golondrina walk. Even to call her Ariada while looking back feels awry; who *was* that early she?

I had acquired a sensitive, though I did not know it, and of all men I was the least qualified to deal with her problems, with her various modes: overwilling, mortally wounded, catatonic, exuberant rodomontade. It took me a good twenty years to get the hang of what was going on inside her, though she showed a consistently sweet nature, a silken gratitude for trifles, an ebullient charm, that told me she was the winsomest girl in the world, B.A. The big thing was to deal with her gently, never to shout or grumble, and I was hardly the man for that, with a so-called Irish temper simmering ever beneath the façade of delicate reserve.

TWO

Clouds of glory tear themselves to pieces from the outside in. I have never been able to love someone or something without making the object of my affections perfect, as if, I suppose, nothing was ever good enough for me, as if I had within me, also rending itself, some capacity to perfect denied the creator of all things. In fact, the attempt to perfect was a tribute; the loved person would always be a paragon, the loved object would always be flawless. It was as if even my infatuations rotted within from ego, but not really. I needed to worship whom and what I loved.

That was how great religions began, with a simple act of homage converted into obsequious addiction. I hoped, as the years went by, to rid myself of so slavish a habit, learning at last to settle for human values; but the yearning has never gone away, not yet anyway, and I perfect Ariada Mencken, whom I dub Swan, as I did my mother, coming up with two goddesses instead of a mama and a spouse. Perhaps the hurly-burly of everyday affection is not for me, but instead the absolute of idolatry, a heavy burden because the worry of it allows me no tolerance: if I don't get perfection I don't want anything, anyone. This means I am a *manqué* of some kind, a monk who missed his vocation, a mystic who mislaid his universe. I must be the last of those who practice courtly love, honoring not the person or the thing but the grail.

Harsher commentators on me than I would say I tend to sentimentalize even the universe, which is bad enough, especially if you are at all informed; but to deal with a grown woman, into whose affections you have insinuated yourself for years, as if you had played together as children, is worse. "Crush" comes again to hand, hand to mouth: he who has a crush is helpless, sweeping his victuals into his mouth with a flat hand wiped across the plate he holds between his lips. Gorging out. As Adolf Hitler did. Or I am like a spy who, broken and wretched, wanders into a village grocery and tries to obtain marmalade and corned beef on credit, hinting perhaps that he would trough on the latter all week and save the marmalade for a weekend blowout, all the time knowing that once paid in a few days' time after doing a few days' stint in the bookstore he will reenter the little shop whose bell goes ping-clang and ask for peaches and caviar. He is a cur who has read Proust. He too has this rotten vision of the perfectible, an ideal that, at times, must rack the Creator who has given the leopard too small a heart or the human a swallowing mechanism too close to that for breathing. Inured to praise, from me at least, my Swan gets on with life, lauded to death by her swain, but hardly put out if I forget to extoll her; she has acquired such impetus she needs no extra shove. I realize of course that all my verbal maneuvers add up to self-praise for having found her; but self-praise, they say, is no recommendation.

I idolize memory because it never quite obliges us, always remains, even if only half a percent, its own thing, which makes a perfectly imperfect emblem of it, from our own point of view at least. I have made up songs about my Swan, which I sing to her in passable baritone, and she endures them, yielding a half-smile anyway as I intone:

Where is that Swan?
Where can she be?
Where *can* that Swan have gone?

When I cannot find her, that is. She never sings back, though she has an exquisite soprano (touch of Rosa Ponselle); she knows my elvish ways and does not fight them, resigned to the fact that I am an *expressive*, outmouthing person, prone to tunes.

It should surprise no one that my fetishes matched her obsessions. I, the man who flew to Miami with a ream of best bond typing paper in order to soften it up for the assault (so it wouldn't fight back), the one who felt his life worthwhile so long as he was writing good fiction, dovetailed with her, whose vice was taking advice, whose main yearning was not to be yammered at, dragooned, manhandled, jeered at, abused for being born. *Quel* mess it promised to be; she tossed a homemade life belt to a drowning man and, with maximum tact, suggested he use it. If I wanted to stay up until dawn drinking, shouting at the TV set, or rambling, she stayed with me, Lady Philosophy come to roost, and if I wanted to go to Jamaica to bake the ethyl out of my skin she went with me, no complaints, although on the eve of one such trip waking me at 3 A.M. to ask the time. She didn't want us to miss our plane. Something so tender from those years makes me heave; in spite of everything, she was heaven's gift to an ailing man. She regarded her function as catalytic, always the discreet helper, even while writing poems that made custard dolts of all other poets writing. She was perched on some visionary edge, wobbling maybe, but unable to fall off. She even agreed to pick up my Scotch for me from the liquor store, seeing that I was too ashamed, and this held true even when I switched to cognac because, as I claimed, Scotch no longer had any effect. I should have been her muse, but she was mine instead.

Astonishing to me, but commonplace to her, she played violin and guitar, taking her proficiency at both as something easy and natural as breathing. Perhaps she played so well, with educated brio, because music dangled and was dandled on the fringe of poetry. As a child she had swung on the doorknobs of rooms, improvising poems above what she regarded as appalling depths.

Asking her to demonstrate this on the doors of the not very sturdy house I rented was asking for trouble, but I did so, and she mimicked it, clasping the knobs hard but without abandoning her body to its weight. She heaved to and fro, smiling as I envied her agility. In her time she had played squash and cricket, daughter of a gifted baseballer. She belonged on the prow of a ship. When I attempted the same feat, the knob tore out of the panel with a grating crunch and fell to the floor. End of games. For once I had amused her, I who usually made her wince or look away, what with my Celtic temper and so on. The music that really bonded us together, though, was not that which she played, even if it induced in me an ecstasy of direct address, like a poem dedicated to me or a prolonged, unpercussive kiss. During those long boozy nights we listened to, mainly, Shostakovich and Vaughan Williams, some Hindemith and Brahms: not what you might call daring fodder. I was advancing, however, and she got me into Scriabin and some other composers right for my outlandish tastes. Set for incessant repeat, the record player ground on through the night and she lay there on the rug like a small factory in my arms, nodding and rocking, sometimes dozing, but ever-present in the meniscus of sleep or the pericardium of delight; I had only to stir my incompetent bulk (once that of a professional jock), twice her weight and twice her age, and she would stir, peer at weakening night or triumphant dawn and ask if we needed breakfast. I had learned by then never to try to live without music; the instant I did, my life went awry. I had grown up in the house of a music teacher and concert pianist, so a house without music seemed barren. I had even, to her dismay, arrived at the point of being unable to watch *Combat* or *Route 66* without having music playing at the same time, as if to mute the crassness or to flavor the banality. Worse, with both music playing and TV blaring, I read the books I received monthly for review from *The Washington Argo*, income from which improved the pittance I got for teaching. Each Saturday, to her amazed horror, I "read" five novels in three hours, having chosen them from a parcel of twenty or so, and then wrote the review in another hour. Ever since then (and my time for reviewing has become severely limited), I regarded Saturday as an almost religious tantrum, whose echoes and latterday vibrations I can quell only by listening to the afternoon opera on the radio. I hate most opera, but I find it a useful antidote, countering one abuse of language with another.

"Why bother?" she asked with tender pedantry. "What's it worth?"

I told her it brought a couple of hundred extra dollars a month and, the real benefit, infuriated my colleagues as well as the authors of the novels I reviewed. "But the real boon," I explained, "is the education I get. I was in their offices one day and somebody held up a translation and asked if I might be interested in reviewing it. Indeed, in such translated novels in general." I said yes, and from then on I taught myself comparative literature in translation for some twenty years, at the same time amassing a fair library of contemporary European or Latin American fiction in translation. "Nobody else wanted to do it; they thought it was a bore and a waste of time, as if French or Spanish novels had anything to do with anything." There I was, as they no doubt thought, like the condemned man licking his lips at the sight of the gallows, giving a sheepish grin at the hangman. That awkward problem had gone by the board because a sucker had shown up. Amazing. What they didn't know was that writing those little essays was an artistic discipline I had learned as an undergraduate.

About the same time as we sprawled on the rug, listening to scratchy 78s I had brought from Canada, we evolved special ways of talking to each other. Each was the other's child: she had had no nurturing to speak of, I had had almost no adult manhood. When we lay on the floor in the direct sun intensified by glass, we called it *spanieling.* I was in the presence of that ineffable miracle, a young woman in full flower, delighted to be where she was, and in fact belated in this state, coming into it from the last stages of puberty. That distant and obscure marriage of hers had been a mere kindergarten bauble, erased by one sunset or a good bubble bath, and she had reverted to who she had been before it, before *before*. It was all new, like one of those books of blank pages the beauty of whose binding readies you for something more velvet than a vacancy. She was growing up with appetitive innocence before my eyes, almost as if she had been entrusted to me by some force wafting at random through the universe, at last able to bring her justice and love. Or so I thought. But no one applauds the tenor for clearing his throat, or the soprano for gargling. We blundered about in joyful unanimity, she making many more concessions than I. *Victim of the Molecule* she called her first book, unpublished, alas, but now she had moved along and the molecule was her patron saint. She thought about the planets all day and wrote copious odes to them, deleting as many lines as not. She was inspired.

In these first months I, rather than she (I told her little about it and rarely played the music pertaining to it), fixed on the music of paradisal occasions, drifting from Delius's *The Walk to the Paradise Garden* to any one of four versions of *Pelléas et Mélisande* (Debussy, Fauré, Schoenberg, and Sibelius). I was into finical impressionism and she into sweaty Romantics. We overlapped, but not entirely; I cared more for French flutes than she did, and she for certain timbres of the male voice. Later we found Villa-Lobos and adopted him as the perfect composer, easing Richard Strauss into second place—*Metamorphosen*, his seamless dirge, had taken us over. What a musical couple we were, rather than a literary one; writing was work, and hard, whereas music had to it something of the flying carpet and the magic cave of Ali Baba. There in a decrepit house on a noisy street we trysted and dreamed.

Not long before, the borough had moved in and cut down all the trees on that street, even though students had roosted in them to save them, in vain. Students occupied an annex behind us, forever revving the engines of secondhand cars, but we endured them, even when they blocked in her little Volkswagen. Off she buzzed to class while I incompetently tried to clean the three stories of the house in her honor.

One day around Christmas, we were absentmindedly helping ourselves to a box of candy canes, red and white sugar sticks supposedly evocative of Christmas shepherds' crooks. These were wrapped in the softest, most clinging form of cellophane that clung to your fingers long after you had finished sucking and licking. Was it surface tension or some weak electrical force that made the pieces of cellophane cling thus? As you seized hold, it bonded to the seizing hand, and on and on, which meant that, so long as you tried to free your hand of it, it clung. It sounded almost like an account of love that, where you least expected it, held fast, reminding you with a faint stroke that it was there, attached in the least demanding way. Wherever I thought my Swan was not, she was, and I found my merest yearnings being intercepted by a mood of genial anticipation. I was swathed in the tenderest of linings, invisibly wrapped up, as never in many years. Our love was working well, keeping us warm and calm, yet without, I thought, any assist from shepherds tending sheep, unless we were sheep ourselves. A timely image, to be sure, it told us we had reached a plateau of sorts on which to repine and spaniel: one we had no doubt earned, sealed up in a coiled transparency of our own devising. We had been reborn and like dumb, dazzled animals were licking away the fragments of birth-sac, maybe even eating them.

Such were the images of delicious peace that came without our having tried that hard to bring them into being. We bred them, exhaled them, flicked them off our shoulders like so much angelic excelsior. Someone, now jubilantly forgotten, had spoken of obnoxious things, imaging them as a vampire bat on a string under your Christmas tree, but we failed to "twig" it, both of the opinion that the bat has a tender, neurotic face, is a nuzzler rather than a slasher, and could take a dose of gentle care. It all depended on how much you knew of bats, who to me had always looked raw and unhouseled, rubbed raw by prejudice, hypersensitive to the merest contact. In after years, Swan would write a long piece rehabilitating bats, and she received many letters from people newly converted who were going to build bathouses to invite them in. It was only a matter, I thought back then (swamped by images of angels and cherubs), of installing the bat as yet another desirable Christmas face, to be affixed to letters and parcels in a mood of lenient euphoria, knowing the recipient would respond to the contents in the noblest manner possible, as if the parcel said What possible dislike could you form for anything postal emblazoned with a bat? It is nonetheless a quest worth pursuing hard; prejudice rarely dies, and the bat's reputation as a bloodsucker et cetera does not yield easily to kinder views. To us, all creatures great and small were bright and beautiful. Such were the rosy spectacles of romance.

One should always make the most of greenhorn ecstasy; it never lasts, and, although one can never predict the day when the rot sets in, come it will, disguised as a difference in taste, a fit of indigestion, a side effect of high humidity. There are cynical experts on romanticism who counsel one to switch from one young inamorata to another in the nick of time. To be sure, the candid, ingratiating ways of the nubile girl hardly ever show up in the performance of the incipient matron, who always knows what she wants you to be, even if it kills you. Universities ought to teach courses in this: the phases of love or something such, especially warning women that their tenure of bliss is short, especially since nothing is odder than juvenile mannerisms crossing the face of a woman over forty, her career draped over her shoulder like a fresh lion skin. If it is true that, for the university teacher, he or she gets older while the students remain the same age, it is also true that men remain the same age while women merely get older. Men's habits and mannerisms remain those of a twenty-year-old, which is no doubt reprehensible; but young women are pleasing because nature wants them impregnated right off, whereas nature, at least as I understand it, cares not a tittle whether the sperm comes from a youth or an ancient drone. Man bears nothing but the planned obsolescence of the female. To hell with all cynics; one should blunder ahead without counting the cost.

THREE

Winter has always produced in me a searing depression others attribute to lack of sunlight, but I blame lack of warmth, lack of color. Alas for me, most of the people I know at all intimately adore snow and cold. Winter, they say, briskens them up. I say it brings into play all kinds of puritanical obsessions (pain promotes brainpower) and I fall like an addict on anyone who longs for pink sand, blue skies, and palm trees, never mind how much vulgarity goes with them. We come from a different country of the mind, a remote Bermuda as the poet says, and we twitch at the touch of frost, needing nothing Siberian but the bower of tropic bliss. Much as we may hate to sweat, we proffer the meat of our faces to the broiling sun and feel it searching through our sinuses for golden contraband.

Hence I say, as now, safely ensconced in Silver Sands, Jamaica, we found the restaurant closed in that resort hosted by a Yorkshireman, but managed to trough well on a huge canned ham we had somehow wangled through Jamaican customs. It was a bit greasy and sinewy, but adequate with some powdered potato mixed into hot water. Eventually we would try the local delicacy (chicken necks), fit fuel for vultures only, but the resort's restaurant never opened. In its stead came a local woman, Millicent, who cooked red snapper for us in the mouse-infested villa while we played improvisatory games on the patio, at our best reinventing Scrabble with little squares of lettered cardboard (the object was to tie). It was there that, confronted with Swan's bigtoes freed of their scarlet enamel, I inscribed them both with the symbol *pi*, thus devising a nickname that stuck for ever, abiding even the arrival of Swan, with which it runs neck and neck to this day. How did that tropical, definitive conversation go?

"Why Pi?"

"For being constant and unrepeating."

"Why not write it out in full then?"

"Not as cabalistic."

She accepted that for the time being, but with a stricken smile that said she had been branded and didn't quite approve. It also rhymed with Hi, I told her, eliciting little response. She knew the name would wear off her as off the toenails, and then she would come up with the next one. That nicknames eked one out, she knew already; her etymology was outstanding, and it was her idea that we allow into the mellow exchanges of our Scrabble the ancient versions of words, such as *waeps* for *wasp*. In a game designed for ties, there was a literally endless supply of play-enhancing maneuvers consecrated to stalemate. For several years we held on to that rudimentary cardboard kit, but eventually set it free to cascade through the pandemonium of garbage and bought several routine sets we tossed together in a plastic bag, scrabbling for novelty. *Rare japanesqued stools* was the last phrase I remember (hers in the end). Our rules were rubbery, our ties romantic. Each was the other's ally. Silver Sands was far from the best place for a weeklong assignation—even the shallows were full of shards—but we made the best of it. Our photographs from that time show us wistfully young, overheated, guileless, and aflow with delight.

In those days she did not have the winter cough she has now; she pooh-poohs my suggestion that she adapts to winter no better than I, who do not even cough, though my sinuses dribble from December to May. Frankly, I do not like weather, but dote on air conditioners and heaters that do not rumble or hiss, go chink-chink or whirl with an invisible propeller. Severe cold, severe heat, I the radical abominate both, and I understand why Richard Nixon in the White House first had a roaring fire built, then put on the air-conditioning full blast. Swan and I have evolved over the years a host of tender rituals that ease us from one day to the next, she sometimes unable to make her muscles relax and therefore calling on me for an Iceberg: "A big hairy white block of ice," I whisper, "is sliding down your front from your upper chest, fresh from the frigid Arctic." That usually does it. As for me, when I wake too early, as often, she will plant the tiny Panasonic radio by my ear, playing the only station it brings in, a classical outlet with too much news. With luck, I get to sleep again, especially if steered by Delius or Finzi; for some ten years I have kept this radio by my typewriter, listening to the one station, at which the frequency selector has jammed. How fitting, how time-saving. She cannot pee and I can't sleep. It was almost always thus, and the trick, I guess, is to revel in the symphony of disability, the mental limp.

This is how the idea of perfection widens itself, not so much that you can stand almost anything and revel in it, but that you allow yourself, and your dear ones, to rattle and wobble a bit. It is all a matter of internal stance, of riding the waves and squeezing the boils, so that the internal sense of integrity rides free of its physical basis. Cousin to the stiff upper lip, the stoicism of Seneca, the dumb ox of Hemingway, even Lawrence of Arabia's "the trick is not to mind," this girding of the brain, this overall calm harks back to such movies as *Journey's End* or Rebecca West's *The Return of the Soldier*, to the most refined and obstinate performances of Celia Johnson, that British exemplum of sangfroid taking vows in icy hotel rooms, looking into the heart of war and remaining unscarred, reserving herself for the future of one much endangered man. It has to do with possession of your worst, accommodating your warts into the choice idyll of your—as if you were a postage stamp—most honored watermarks. Part of its excellence resides in one's not being able to make it clear what this quality is, but it abides if you husband it right, graduating, as I suppose I had to, into a complex version of taking the rough with the smooth—not as easy as it sounds, but worth attempting in the thick of things. Comes a steel crash as the jackboots of the mind come to attention and then relax. You have tried to make sense of yourself once again, for a moment, and that is always enough. To go farther, you need your Swan.

Predictably the poet and the novelist invented special ways of talking to each other, from an early word "flaff," which meant pointlessness raised to exponential maximum, to "mrok," which denoted a plaintive cry often uttered when one of us was alone in the house, just hoping with that cry to find the other. People we concocted included two pedantic Frenchmen, devised to liven up the sound of English: Auguste Mrok (descendant of *mrok*) and Jean-Louis Grandquel. We avoided developing their attributes; they were just names to say at inappropriate moments. *Hand* became *handle*, of course, and *breakfast breaklefast*, *mouthwash mousewash*, and *lens lensness*. Not major deformations, these, they revealed our affection for words as we found them, but nonetheless evinced our desire to leave a little mark on them, as with *shelbst* for self, *schluffy* for *sleep*, and *Carsonienses* for the Carson show. One especially fond reference we abbreviated to A.C.H.M., often written Achmed, commemorating the tiniest mouse we had ever seen, in a botanical garden in St. Louis: A Certain Harvest Mouse, a phrase we would sometimes emit simultaneously, to the dismay of others. Sometimes Pi was Trout (we never eat trout) and sometimes I, or HB, was Rabbit. Our intimate bestiary also included stuffed animals from panther to pregnant sheep (Sheep with Lamb), many lions and seals. Our totemism gave us a private world as secret as that of Cockney rhyming slang, but also a new angle on the world we wrote about, which was that of other folk. Quite often, in carpet slippers, she walked on top of my feet as I padded slowly backward and we let out a noise we had linked to the roseate spoonbill exquisitely depicted in watercolors in the laboratory waiting room at the local hospital: *Clack-clack-clack-clack*, we went, together being a bird that stepped in and out of tidal pools. Anyone overhearing this racket seemed dismayed, whereas anyone catching a glimpse of a kiss imposed on the corner of the mouth followed by the phrase "Consider yourself wrenned" was merely mystified, having observed a first wren-kiss. The wren, a perky hostile little bird that skimmed like a military support jet over lawns and gardens, appealed to us because we also knew of a high-wing monoplane (actually a converted Cessna) called a Wren which had hen's teeth on top of its wings and could take off *across* a runway, so efficient were its slow-flight qualities, though we had heard it was almost impossible to get out of a spin. One of our Christmas songs went like this, never overheard until now:

> Khyber Khyber Khyber Pass,
> If you want a splendiferous Christlemas,
> Get on to your most secret self
> That enigmatic red elf,
> Who in the night so quietly spoken
> May bring you an extra token.
> There's one big thing about a Khyber:
> You can't outwit or bribe her.
> Be nice to her ad infinitum
> And you may receive an extra item.
> Until next year, just be your shelbst
> And await the renaissance of that red elf.

Untidy, incoherent, and unworked upon, this doggerel vented our seasonal exuberance of spirit, and you would have to know that, of all present-givers and -wrappers, Swan is the supremest, working throughout the year to find and wrap gifts for her closest friends, from chocolate alligators to exquisitely crafted tiny suitcases that hold business cards in leather. Reconnoitering the stores wherever her work takes her, she doesn't so much shop for Christmas as reexamine the world of phenomena in case there is something she might have missed. Her glistening browns, that have scrutinized Amazon rain forest and the ice massifs of Antarctica, are just as much at home at Henri Bendel's and Saks. She is fascinated by human inventiveness, so she pores over counters, asks countless questions, calls manufacturers, writes to catalogue compilers, and ends up with something unheard of, later on making her loved ones gasp at the ingenuity and resolve that have gone into the gifts. My favorite among my own, I think, is still the pen-sized microscope that lets me squinny even as I am traveling, although a certain purple bathrobe held my affection long after it developed holes and tears: it was my first gift from her, handed me like a prize after an especially arduous trip from Europe. Truly, her gifts are benisons to make the recipients feel a little bit out of this world, almost as if a faith healer tapped them. I would have expected no less from the inventor of the rhyming riddle that sometimes goes, assuming the form of a spurious question: "How many islets does a broncheyelet on Pontius Pilate's islet—?" The answer is always "Three." Other words topple into this dire puzzle, from *pilot* to *Bali Hilet*, without changing the answer.

The sense of beauty overwhelmed her from the first, natural or artificial, and she surrounded herself with artifacts and photographs, always eclectic, never predictable, in much the same fashion I always needed to surround myself with music—more than literature, paintings, gorgeous interiors. Much to her disdain I once said I would be happy in a tea chest if the music were good enough. I am a more transcendent soul than she, I suppose; I live inside my head, though my senses are as tuned in as hers. I am willing to try to see the glory behind and beneath the horror, even to the extent of providing the glory myself, whereas she dotes on surfaces, loading a room with flowers, for instance, which I enjoy almost as much as I do classical music.

* * *

Seen in a group of other young women, Swan seems the most animated of them, smiles more and giggles loudest, whereas Janine's smiles last longest of them all, Fallon has the highest-pitched voice, and Celia the quietest one. Watching them as a mere male, I have always felt that women tune in to a dimension denied us men, which makes them gurgle and giggle as if little matters but fun. It is not what they say that animates them, but what they animate by what they leave unsaid, honoring something out of sight, a mucous membrane or a mishap with blood. Something like what men sometimes imply when they talk about sport, but more atavistic. Women in flux, I think, always fluctuating, are more open to suasion, readier to intuit someone else's mind. Women's talk seems more intended, more purposeful, with none of the poised laid-back chatter men go in for, so when I watch Swan launch into something in a female group I see mannerisms and ploys she never tries on me: she becomes a teeny bit the eternal female who knows a good deal about the ephemeral, the expendable, or, to crudify the idea, paper knickers, baby caca, and the appeal of men's butts. Men in such groups appear to flounder, never going at the right speed, never rising to that celestial hold on the transitory, as if words themselves could rise from the things they denote and waft off into the stratosphere, their work done forever. With other women, women go into overdrive, whereas men attempt power-ploys languidly. The only times I have seen men hold an almost female conversation have been Edmundo Javès the Mexican novelist holding court with David Rough, his friend, and Napoleon Tarot, the editor, with Macdonald Bethlehem, a short-story writer now dead. The degree of nimble give and take in these conversaziones amazed me, and especially such overheard morsels as "Don't forget to get me that prize now" and "Not once does he use the verb *to be*." Literary mayhem, this, impregnable as jade.

Early on, her tenderness for life astounded me, I who had grown up among a rough crowd and gone on to a crowd of genteel ruffians in which I at last learned how to assert myself "like a man," which was to say with astute brutishness. Swan revered life for its utter mysteriousness in everyone she met, discerning even in me the sensitive novelist and willing to coax me out into the open, to be less cerebral and more emotional, most of all in my work. This calling, as I regard it, has seen her through many crises, but the unique miracle of her days has been the way she grew up whole and harmless, ever alert to discern in people their potential and then to have them achieve it. An enabler from the outset, she swallowed the misery of many, listening to them and counseling as if she had never had anything but a gentle, pensive upbringing. It was like having faith in atoms, over and above the ills to which people's personalities were heir. Her view of others was unconventionally religious, as if compassion were a reflex and had only to be shown to people to have them willing to accept it. Never mawkish about this, she recognized its presence in her, yet only when forced, told that she had this selfless gift inherited not from her parents but from members of the family she never knew about. Or, harassed young, she deduced its necessity from circumstances, born the custodian of some bright impetus easily lost and wasted. All this went on in her mind before she was twenty, but I saw it in action as she took charge of me, urged me to quit drinking, to desist from pondering violence (its historical version, anyway). What interested me most was the difference between historical and ontological trauma: what happened to you, born when you were, and what was the quality of your existence from peristalsis to heartbeat whether or not you were at that instant subject to historical forces. She never approved of this distinction, but she took much pleasure in citing it to make me squirm, so I assumed a piece of her enjoyed it and thought it had merit. I wondered about the person who, to test the distinction, lived an entire life indoors, was never bombed, arrested, mugged, or called for jury duty: the Indoor Person attuned to her/his seeping, gurgling body. I was always after the bodily resonance of people, wondering if they knew what their existence was like.

Yet there was this other side to us both; we worked hard at being phrasemakers, doing our best never to do what had already been done, but then resorted to extravagant verbal fun in order to unwind, embracing the silly, harping on the frivolous and the trivial, just to give the mind a sedative waltz. When we drove, she sang Childe ballads in a peerless croon I shall hear and love to my dying day, and I reciprocated with initially improvised songs (or Latin American–style *piropos* of extravagant praise) that soon became permanent formulas, as much part of an outing as her Childe ballads:

> She has a more than silky smile,
> With eyes like dark brown chocolate drops
> Into which we plun—n—g—ge
> And Cliffs of Dover whiteness to her teeth,
> Above and beneath.

FOUR

You do not have to know someone very long before deciding whether or not you both need a telescope. We sent for ours, dickering about what kind, and settled back to wait, in the meantime growling at the skies we would soon open up. Our motto from this time was "Tell dope, send scope," from Altoona actually. We made many phone calls to ascertain when it would arrive, and how, and how many would be required to lift a twelve-inch catadioptric with all its trimmings. When it at last showed up, the entire street came out to watch as two New Brunswickian UPS men staggered up the broken concrete of the walk with a pale blue trunk much like that given to an officer in the military: easily big enough for a corpse, should the mind run that way. It took a week to get the telescope put together and fixed up, and then another week of chilly early fall nights to get it working, with the electrical drive purring away beneath our hands. The sky was there all right, and so were the stars, the golden oldies exactly where the Starfinder book said they would be. Thus began, on a whim, one of our lasting obsessions, mine especially. With such a vast and inviting canopy it had always seemed to us trivial to write about humanity as if the stars and the galaxies weren't there, as most writers did. As science popularizers kept saying, all anyone needed to become an amateur astronomer was a pair of binoculars. We, on the other hand, were already an observatory, not quite up to doing star photographs but soon finding our way about along the Milky Way, of which I soon began making a model in the basement, five feet long, one wide, on supermarket bag stretched over a balsa-wood frame (for lightness). Our star obsession clinched something romantic in our everyday behavior; the panoply matched our day-to-day closeness. Swan soon developed a serious yearning to become an astronaut (the first poet into space) and I, building in the basement and peering skyward every night in a thermal germ-suit, soon became afflicted with astral hunger. Planets did not lure me as stars did; I liked the big, explosive stuff, its enigmatic origins, the whole idea that the universe had a diameter and an age. The most fascinating paradox of all came from a lecture on campus, when Isaac Asimov told how at some time all matter was present at one point: all of everything, he said. But, if so, if all space was in this original bolus, he said, *where* was the bolus? There was as yet no *where* for it to be in. My mind drowned happily in this conceptual morass. We were in training, though we did not know it, for some space adventures of an uncommon sort, far beyond the compact vision afforded by the telescope. We were going to become involved with cutting-edge astronomers and go with them on their quests, though not into space, of course. Nonetheless, Swan applied to the space program and began filling out the forms they sent her. She would be among the first of the few.

Being together so much, and preoccupied by the process of falling for each other a different fraction per day in the mutual osmosis of love, we sometimes felt we had been taken over by a metaphor. Far from star-crossed lovers, we were cosmic ones; there was this enormous addendum fastened to our diurnal busyness. The starstuff was up there, in plain view, and we, starstuff also, were down here plotting our course, perhaps even our historicity. It was deeply moving to be at one about this, hand in hand but also mind in mind, involuntarily even in the daylight looking upward as if for celestial confirmation. Of course the Sun was a star; I had never quite considered it that way, and I was delighted it looked so close, just another of those bright points I could tune in with the telescope each night. My mind and senses rejoiced in such variable focusing, the near and the far, the far and the near. We had become heirs to some huge caravansary that hardly changed over a human lifespan, and there was something reassuring about such relative permanence, especially when on certain nights the stars appeared to be buzzing and fuming, full of flash and energy, seeming so close, so neighborly. I have never lost the initial thrill of it all, have always felt the urge to situate my characters in a cosmic setting, maybe to ennoble and aggrandize them, maybe just to give them their fair share of magic. All this time, Swan was writing her *Solar System.*

At some point I took the trouble to establish what sort of relationship I had tugged my Swan from, only to discover that she had one principal female friend, Hermione, a vivacious blonde who had actually been enrolled in my Shakespeare class, which I delivered to some five hundred unlucky souls in an underground auditorium lined with slate. The acoustics were superb. So Hermione had already heard me hold forth on *Titus Andronicus,* my way of doing things over fifteen weeks being to start with a good play such as *Macbeth* and slowly go downhill until the end of semester, declining through *All's Well* to the aforementioned *Titus,* which had in it such costive lines as "Enter Lavinia ravished." Hermione and Swan, until recently, had made a habit of going around town dressed like out-of-work actresses and talking wildly in stores until thrown out for frivolity. I actually remembered seeing them, two mighty attractive hussies as I thought at the time, conversing wildly over marmalade and corned beef in Burt's Dairyette, whence the tolerant Lee Burt did not evict them, himself fascinated by the pair and no doubt wondering if he was going to see a flash of leg, moss, and maidenhair. I too, like a snake hypnotized by two mongooses, lurked there, pondering what devilish things they might be persuaded to do in a class. Yet the moment passed; I went out with my cans of chili, my block of frozen haddock, and a loaf of Wonder bread. Odd that Hermione had not recognized me, but in those days I wore shades and thus gained a reputation for doing drugs. Swan I did not know as she had not yet been in my British Fiction class. The arrangement was odd, I thought, as I recognized her friend, little realizing it was the other girl who would invade my life. Had we met on that day, a Sunday, we might have been able to spend even longer together. If only I had taught British Fiction before Shakespeare, or at the same time. Then I would have identified both as students of mine and urged them away to Darjeeling up the road. Now, however, my link to the two was more respectable, though not much, and clearly I would not be dealing with them as a pair.

My friends thought I was crazy even to remember such events and to mull them over. "You've done all right as it is," Asa Humanas told me, he our august Rare Book Librarian. "Don't go and make a mess of something else. What are you going to do if the other girl wants to make it a threesome? As in the realm of ideas, certain formulas reign and then yield to their successors; if no successors appear, then the next phase is the first phase in parody. Do you see?" I did not, nor ever had. He had this habit of making a perfectly lucid statement and then capping it, exemplifying it, incomprehensibly. I grappled with his notion, but got nowhere at all. He was the raven that croaked *if only*. "No," I told him, "it's not that kind of an affair anyway. We're stuck on each other. The girlfriend's an excrescence. She goes her own way." I couldn't help wondering what I had got myself into, though, recruiting an Amazon, even one into astronomy and poetry, for my caravan. It was a matter of keeping Hermione at bay and Swan within reach.

If I shed a cautionary, nostalgic tear now and then while reciting the onset of our (by now quarter-of-a-century) affair, I owe it to the vulgar contrast between my initial desires and the grave rather public life we undertook together. A willful romantic had embarked on a serious relationship he was ill equipped for, as Swan soon found out. Having been almost extinguished by a distant deadlocked marriage, I was no candidate for weddings. Beautiful intellectual high-minded Swan was a diversion for me on the road to hell, much as some philosopher said a woman's pudendum was a place in which to languish comfortably while awaiting death. To her enormous credit she possessed a divine adaptability so generous and expert that she accepted me much as I was, trying only to make me give up liquor and my doctor-phobia. While a certain colleague up in the English Department (he of the attractive, feline wife whose demure purr egged us on) was at department meetings busily deploring my late-rising habits to a mostly indifferent faculty, Swan said live and let live; above all, let sleep. She had seen my good side and was content to fertilize and groom it, finding in me one whose emotional growth like her own had been scarred. What an unholy bond that was, a salient truce between ex-prisoners, likely to bring them both a double dose of grief, yet just possibly the source of a healing union. On I went, getting up so late I could not even make a 4 P.M. class.

As long as I live, I will chew on the guilt of not having responded to her tenderness with something similar. She was in many ways an open book, vulnerable and tempting like a sunny ample valley witnessed from an icy upland, almost a Ganges Delta seen from the Matterhorn. I exaggerate, but the simile reveals my chagrin. I could have done better, recognizing that, when she uttered the word *harsh* (her mild complaint when I said something tactless or wounding), she was giving me all kinds of chances. A precious experiment in life had been placed in my hands, and I was not, sometimes, showing even the tact of a market gardener. She who had suffered so much had this extraordinary honorable gentility to her, something worth adoring instead of being taken for granted as a humbled adjustment. It was no use saying I was not myself; I was. And who knows what self one is from day to day, year to year, rather than a mess of psychotic confetti? No, she was regal, serene, lavishly young, and here she was unwilling to run away without trying to mend me, as if I were the worst-done-by specimen on the planet, worthier of rest and rehabilitation than she herself. I wince when I think how kind and understanding I could have been to her instead of reading her work with a bark. What I told her about style was correct, I imagine, but the bringer of bliss deserved a nicer tutor. Only much later did I realize she had all along the mentality of the healer: the wounded surgeon. She had all the makings of psychiatry, learned raw in the woods of night.

I recur to Asa Humanas in this narrative as often as I do because of what he himself was going through at that time. As I was gaining, he was losing. It was almost inconceivable to think that his cellist wife Giselle was leaving him, she who had fallen out of the bedroom window as a child and had developed an eye twitch that never affected her virtuoso playing. But they had come to some Rubicon of the heart, unable to discuss their problems even, and the terminal day had arrived on which, alone at home, she had selected his favorite books from all over the house (alphabetized titles ascended from the ground floor through two others—Aesop below, Zola in the attic with the bats) and had stacked them into his side of their queen-sized bed. He did not return to the house until late that night, having had on his plate a meeting of the Pigskin University literary club, so when he arrived he made tea, shaved against an early rising on the morrow, peered briefly at the Late Show (he a movie buff), and went to bed. Or tried to, finding the space taken. She was asleep in her half, and no help; apparently he tried several times to mount the mass or to split the herd, shoving books aside in order to lie down, but there were just too many, so he went back downstairs and napped on the couch in the living room, swathed in bath towels. This eviction marked a watershed in his life, to be sure, affecting his eating habits, his mode of speech, his selection of metaphor, and indeed his attitude to friends. If his home were a grave, he had been disinterred from it. If it were a library, he had been banned from the stacks. If it were home sweet home, the sweetness had gone out. What upset him most, since he had been dreading the external signs of a definitive break, was that his books were now out of order and would have to be reshelved. Giselle the pupil of Boulanger had cocked a snoot at his system, mangling its neatness to say a final thing, after which, ironically, she hung on to see what he would do. His retort was to leave his half of the bed full of books, never again to consult those particular volumes, and carry on as if nothing had happened. One friend had suggested to him, not entirely seriously, that he procure a horse's head and leave that in her half of the bed, bleeding and reeking, but the solution had something of movieola about it and did not appeal to Asa the moviegoer. Instead, he left the half-full bed to her and began to sharpen up his commentary on his friends' private lives, informing me that I was too old for Swan, whom he liked enormously, and that it would be in her interests to sever the relationship now before it became painful and disproportionate. He was no doubt right, but I spurned his advice out of pique and selfishness, also because you do not, do you, so to speak, accept racing tips from one whose horse has broken half its legs?

Nonetheless he opined, and to Swan's face, except that she was keeping her powder dry, willing to listen but not to answer.

"You two," he said in his swift-chatter way, "you're asking for it. It's not so visible now, but you're from different generations. He'll become impossible sooner than you, it goes without saying. He's bad enough, ornery enough, now, and he's going to get worse. It comes from his having been a professional sportsman" (he intended my cricketing career, long over). "The violence required will find another outlet, mark my words. It already shows up in his expressionistic metaphors."

"It sure does," said Giselle who was passing through the room with books in her arms, maybe to choke the toilets or to jam the upstairs windows open.

"Come on, Asa," Swan was saying. "He's not that bad. All you have to do to appease him is agree with him. He likes to have things his own way." It was humiliating to be postmortemed thus, or vivisected, by one's intimates, and made me vow, unsuccessfully, to keep Swan and Asa apart. They could discuss me behind my back, but not to my face. Who were they anyway to censure me who had never voiced critique of them? I had a young face, a strong body, a lively mind; I would be good till ninety at least, so what was he talking about? He was attributing his own decline to others, just for a librarian's idea of fun. But lovers are impetuous, going their own reckless way heedless of sage advice and, as at Asa's, dramatic instances from life lived. Very much on our side were Lou Vielis, anthropologist, a Vienna-educated Swiss who filled his house with birds and spears, forever returning from some unknown country with horrifying artifacts he showed the IRS, together with receipts printed and scrawled in indecipherable letters.

"Where there's a will—" he drawled.

"There's an Ann Hathaway." Swan was being pert, a role she enjoyed; if she had been a boxer, people would have marveled at her hand speed. Only the other day I had been saying about Madame de Scudéry "she wrote with her brother," and Swan said "why not with her hand?" This could be unnerving from second to second, at Swan speed as I called it, but I began to regard it as yet another of our eccentricities: hers, anyway. It was so odd to be odd, hard to know when surrounded by the likes of Asa, Giselle, and Lou, who all lived verbally for the moment, meaning they rejoiced holily in words. Swan had her allies all right, even among those who thought she ought to bail out of an unpromising relationship with a self-engrossed sybarite notorious for philandering and being late for class. How odd, I thought, that my detractors fixed on my late rising rather than on my lateness to class, as if they spurned the fun I must have been having in bed, fully erect with who knew how many moistened girls. It was the pleasure principle that irked them.

"You make a lovely couple," Lou was saying, his simplest

utterance in years. "Somehow you epitomize the symbiosis to be lusted after. That's a compliment."

Taken as such, it hardly added to our luster, which came from within. In any case, how came it that everyone we knew had an opinion, as if we even contemplated splitting up? Where had they found such a notion? Had we asked? Had our mien, as old-fashioned writers used to say, given us away? Did my guilt show, my sense that already I was not giving the generous, indulgent Swan a fair deal? Did entomologists' wives stuff one half of the bed with butterflies or spiders? Did the wives of physicists rig lasers beneath the coverlet? Giselle, an original head to be sure, would be depriving the neighborhood of some elegant pranks. Perhaps she could be talked into staying, just for the havoc she raised, with her erudite stammer, her frontal insults, and of course her ways with beds and books. Asa, I thought, would have been just as happy to keep her on the premises for simple circus; he had reached the point of nihilistic glee at anything bad that happened to him, regarding himself, in the modern way, as raw material. In the long run, he said on several occasions, with wistful finality, it was just a matter of getting through your assigned portion. Life was no more than that, and perhaps no less. I could see in company, however, how well Swan manipulated men, confounding them with wit and looks and that gorgeous pelvis. They didn't know where to look next while agreeing with her. Where, their looks said, did *he* get this nonpareil, worthy of someone more attentive? Has his luck at last changed? Is he going to too?

One way of establishing if a relationship had really taken root in the eyes of observers, or connoisseurs of the underground, was to contrive to be invited to one of Gloria Gluckstein's parties, not so much parties as tours of inspection. The lady in question would spend the evening asking salient questions of both the couple and her other guests. It was a kind of viva voce examination done with the mind sheathed in rubber gloves. Gloria herself, married to Frank Foxpasta, whose name she had not taken, fancied herself as a matchmaker, though her tendency to benign gossip had undone as many unions as she had blessed. But an indicator she was, like turmeric, and in our case she made no bones about it, hooting on our arrival that, ages ago, she had introduced us to each other, and she held fast to this monopolistic, wholly wrong assumption to the end.

"Don't you remember?" she said. "Of course you don't. You were too engrossed in each other to notice. It was the night of the jazz trio, when Frank played trombone, Delray Pepp played piano, and Don Weldon the Benny Goodman clarinet. Lovers rarely attend to the circumstances of their initial bliss." Was she hoping to get into one of those strained compendia of records, for having pandered nonstop, or was she hoping for fame through aphorism? "Come in, darlings," she said loudly, "and join the throng. You know everybody." We probably did, but without joy; most of these people, sixty all told, spent their weekdays expounding in the most elementary way, with huge assists from critical tomes, on the simplest texts in literature, simplifying them still further until, say, *Candide* or Benjamin Franklin's *Autobiography* fell in front of students like a bunch of teething rings. Sophisticated conversation did not happen here, but gossip reports, assessments of cough, estimates of weight. It was your typical faculty party, hardly the context for an affair of the heart, though it was possible that a genuine affair, afflicted with the usual measure of sublimity and delusion, might thrive in such a gritty context merely to assert itself against an alien and destructive element amid which most things died a natural death, mocked and chiseled in the course of an evening. Those whose marriages were on the rocks came here to have the rocks sharpened while Gloria went from group to group invisibly recording phrases in her lethal mind for use later on. Romantics went elsewhere, to drive-ins and burger joints, as is the American way; but faculty, even faculty dating waitresses, came here for Gloria to give them the once-over, like elephants getting a first whiff of the graveyard. And that did it, of course, in that no passion or crush could survive the gathering's tendency to pawnbroke and mock. Not only that: on worse occasions, one in particular, I had made a fool of myself and had thus achieved instant acceptance as a serious spirit; having had too much to drink before even arriving, I felt a strong urge to vomit, and Frank Foxpasta, an expert reader of signs, ever ready to haruspicate or scry, at once rammed a pale brown mixing bowl beneath my chin, catching much of the overflow. It was all part of the service, of the sophisticated obeisance that Gloria and Frank had made their own. An early-retired professor of trumpet, bugle, and trombone, Frank had gone into real estate with a colossal loan from the bank, thus outdoing his Chinese rivals; he got a bigger loan because his eyes were the right shape and he had stuck to his guns throughout the integration wars, maintaining firmly that local barbers should not admit blacks to their emporiums, not even to shave them bald as if for jail or the Marines. Together, Frank and Gloria had squandered hundreds of decent impulses, not theirs but other people's, left out to dry in their presence. Slowly they moved through the throng, attuning themselves, clipping and knackering, until two hours later they had upset what was left of honor in their guests, having ridiculed and teased almost everybody into a paroxysm of self-scorn. It was an interesting process if you cared to watch Gloria in the act of overhearing and, from time to time, butting her left breast hard against her victims to knock them to their senses. She could do this because the breast was a prosthesis, some said of gunmetal or chain mail, polished in its nest, and maybe radioactive as well. One of her direst jokes was that, if a Jew had chain mail, she called it Chaim mail, after an Israeli statesman.

To put it more generously, Gloria and Frank had a taste for the bizarre; bizarre themselves, they were collectors and contributors, as able to classify people as Linnaeus the Swede the phenomena of nature. Surely, within this hunger lurked a love of people in all their oddity, a dedication to the mystery and panoply of the human race, crammed as it had to be into a provincial test tube in the ambit of a dark university. Once, no doubt, they had been lovers, though now they were Fates, norns, sibyls. They had to be dealt with in their own terms or they would not converse. That night, Gloria took one look at us and pronounced the truth: "*I* introduced you two. Now you're going to save each other." She hardly knew Swan, but that was typical: she presumed her way in, making an initial grand gesture of hyperbolical arrogance and then retreated from it over the years until she seemed almost diffidently shy. You got it in the chops to begin with as she steamrollered aside all pretense of formality or discretion on the newcomer's part.

"I guess we've been anointed," I told Swan, who grunted.

"Well, we've been approved of," she said. "When does the holy oil come out and the watery sign of the cross grace the brow?" Had I been Gloria, I would not have messed with Swan, who was too sarcastic for her, for anyone, without ever losing her gentleness and poise. It was all, for Swan, an exercise of the mind in its own right, a series of verbal challenges she could not refuse, hurting no one but taking nobody on trust.

So we circulated, in the shabby shamble you were reduced to by Gloria's furry carpet roughed up by too many guests, making polite conversation to those we could not avoid, and actually catching sight of Hermione Mackintosh on the arm of somebody in uniform, Army perhaps. Tall, blond, aloof, she saw us not and left early, en route to an even hotter event. I had never seen her at one of Gloria's dos before, and I wondered if she had been invited to give evidence, to testify and leave, under military escort. How did Gloria know her? I at once abandoned the thought, realizing that any attempt to extract something logical from Gloria's behavior was doomed; she would have found a truer destiny in the German or Japanese Foreign Office in the 1930s, say, and was really wasted in a small university town, one of its few soirée-givers. Once there had been a rival set, run by the wife of a microbiologist called Eckermann, a charming couple, but Gloria had taken them over and fused the tribes, ever eager to mix departments, or to invite endearing students from the amorphous body of some thirty thousand, but mainly concerned to expand her zoo by gobbling up competitors. If she kept lists with evaluations I have no idea. No doubt all the lowdown was in her head, where it kept her sweet in between soirées. She was really an epistemologist at heart, eager for information, but also a tyrant, a Saturn who devoured her offspring. She had, so the rumor went, two lovely daughters who never came near her, although their hugely enlarged photographs adorned the piano, reminding us oddly of Ava Gardner and Gene Tierney. Were the photos fakes, at least of the daughters? Why not have photos of women unknown to the general populace? Or baby pictures of almost anyone? This uningenious attempt to pass muster disturbed me alone, as far as I could tell, and I never failed to inquire about the two lovely daughters, who always seemed to be passing through Singapore or Calcutta in their business as couriers. One always wondered, especially about Gloria, whose many tall tales included one about the actress Agnes Morehead. Once, in Saks, Gloria found herself standing at the counter beside a handsome, red-haired blue-eyed woman of imposing personality. "You must be Agnes Morehead," Gloria said. "And you," Morehead is supposed to have said, "must be Gloria Gluckstein." Frank had fewer pretensions, but he stuck by what he believed in. He was my landlord for a lengthy period, hence the almost prurient interest he and she took in my private life, not that they wanted me married off; they just wanted my sexual expenditure curtailed, spread less far and wide. Frank's great gift was for lasagne, most of all for a little group of favorites he gathered around him on Friday nights, when we watched boxing on TV. His lasagna dishes were deep and burly, loaded with sausage and hamburger meat, but also, as he proudly insisted, sugared to taste. No Italian food, he claimed, was genuine without a tablespoon or two of sugar. Hence one who loved boxing, as I always did, much to Swan's disgust, also developed a sweet tooth. But so what? We went home groaning with distension, as if we ourselves had been pummeled in the ring. What was left over he fried up, with extra sugar until he had on his hands almost a dessert, ironically padded with meat. It would have done no harm to smear all over it, as he often did, clotted cream, just to vex the diner into trying to establish what variety of dish it was.

Some of us, no doubt the cruder ones, were regulars at Friday night boxing for lasagna, a vulgar enough event; but when Gloria took charge, staging a peripheral event of highfalutin gentility, Frank's boxing cronies and acolytes took a backseat, in particular when an Italian-sounding pal of hers, Tommaso Phammon, came and read from his latest novel, or rather his latest manuscript, for his effusions were rarely published. A different class of folk attended these soirées, I excluded since my works were somewhat barbaric by comparison and always had against them their bearing what for academe was the mark of Cain: publication or a signed contract. That was enough to damn you in the eyes of the literary virgins who clustered around Gloria on Wednesday evenings to drink champagne and to coo. To his credit, Frank avoided these gatherings and went to discuss real estate at the local hotel with his Chinese competitors. Phammon was the only reader, as far as I know, and what he read was wholesome, genteel, and hearty. God knows what Gloria and her friends found in what he wrote: perhaps some counterpoint to the grossness of her behavior at weekends when the scum came past her portcullis and aired their underwear.

FIVE

What a glory Gloria was in that smug, Republican town where a radical such as I was as rare as a diabetic dandelion. I was always being "reported," to whoever was in power, for belittling the town or the university, and subsequently chided for lack of tact. Look here, this isn't Manhattan, you know: that kind of cackle. After one chairman had gone, a senior secretary who had much the same views as I handed me a comment he had written: "Of all our members of faculty, he is the one least capable of being institutionalized." I roared at this gem from a pinkie, at first hoping he meant I wasn't fit for a lunatic asylum, then realizing he meant I'd never be a company man. How right he was, the dear old poop, hoping that perhaps I'd learn to behave myself. In the Air Force I had seen and sabotaged dozens like him. You could see them coming, writ in hand, and the only way was to apply a little fiction to them to see their heads revolve and their brains implode. Once he became perturbed because a Greek student had accused some members of the department of having carnal knowledge of her; his was one of the names. He had her shipped home to Athens as fast as possible, as if Nausicaa had sprung up from the sand and nipped him in the ass.

It is an axiom in this life, and no doubt in the next, that people of fastidious taste have ugly habits, and vice versa; you have to make your choice according to which—the ugly or the fastidious—you put first, though it must be possible to meld the two. Perhaps that was what Gloria aimed at, roping in weirdos of all kinds to create a complex human landscape out of damozels and bullfrogs. Swan and I wondered time and again at our crescent love, a serious and doughty growth in so rabid and contemptuous a place. I recollected Androcles and the lion and the way he gently tugged the thorn from its paw in the very arena. Clearly, to be a success in life, one had to make the mind accede to violent contrasts; we were the exquisite blue flower of Novalis sprung from the rank byre of a drying cow turd, a cow patch on the way to paradise. It felt like that, certainly, as we doted and canoodled, easily at peace in each other's presence, with all antagonism switched off, all untoward words and motions banned, only compatible overtures left to us wherever we spanieled or stood, practicing our eyelid kiss. God Almighty must have sent our acerb context to us to make us feel grateful and to warn us to take good care of blessings bestowed; there might have been a nightmare to come. As it was, the only cloud on our horizon, if that, was Swan's obliging herself to decide between going off to Peru, to help earthquake victims, and Africa, to suck on the Hemingway mystique and overtouted scenery, or between either of those and somewhere's MFA degree, which might or might not confirm her in her vocation as poet.

It must have been discussions of Africa that brought into being our games with the panther, although we became somewhat confused about the animal's habitat. Certainly Africa got us into the right frame of mind. For years I had been in the habit (I the late sleeper) of dozing on the mattress with a sheet wrapped loincloth-style around me while emitting a faint pretended snore, not to any audience for audience there was none, but to surround myself with convincing ambience: if I made the right noises, I would float away to some land both aboriginal and permissive. I would become a domesticated savage. So, on occasion,

I purred and growled, imagining myself almost any predatory feline. It was a far cry from the prose I was writing upstairs in the attic; I was pitting boundless, animal freedom against the hunched, contained manufacture of elegant sentences. A more civilized being than I would not have bothered, but would no doubt have played some violent games of squash, tennis, or pelota, with gratifying results as the heart returned to average speed. I, however, needed some kind of primitive immersion: the tiger drenched from swimming in the Bay of Bengal, the lion made itchy by dust from the veldt, the panther pestered by stinging flies. It was as if I needed an accompanist from a world so primitive I dared not write about it. Such was the overture upon which, almost unintentionally, Swan and I began to build, becoming more and more ingenious the longer we stayed blissfully together. In no time, but of course only over months, we evolved a game or sport that had me dozing and purring in my habitual solitary fantasy, sometimes heaving a haunch or flailing a paw in unwitting unconscious exertion, merely to stretch, no signal intended. Remember how a sleeping house will creak and snap, at deep play with itself? I would pretend to awaken, then go back to sleep with a contented snarl, having noticed nothing, certainly not the presence of the nude with the black mane. On I slept, with a slight quiver and a half-cough, but with no eye opening. After more rasps and a purr rather more vociferous than usual, I would open an eye, then another, as unable to see as a newborn, but working myself up gradually into quasi-paroxysm. During this, Swan lay there paralyzed with mock-panic, waiting the full gaze of the monster she was lying with, even as he felt around with an arm and a paw without trying hard, however, to see anything because he knew nothing was there. But, as I became a fraction more aware of my surroundings, I opened an eye wider, ostentatiously looking away from my companion, who now pretended to shudder with fear, knowing the instant of discovery was at hand. I protracted the wake-up process a few extra seconds, now adding a moan and a slight impending roar to my vocal act, and then, suddenly, my eyes opened wide, I saw the other creature stranded there and, even as she screamed, I roared and seized her for the prolonged kiss we ended with. This bit of drama we came to dub the kissel-panther, whose waking moments ended in giggles. There was nothing African about it, but much lovers' folderol. It was magical because unseen by others. Our Africa was not east of the Americas, south of Europe, but central in a grown-up nursery appropriated by adults. Perhaps this was how the real Africa died from her tableau of intentions, mocked into irrelevance by a couple of inaccurate, erotic bestiarists. Perhaps we played the game once too often for her to take Africa seriously. Then, somehow, succoring earthquake victims in Peru seemed beside the point and belated. Only the Master of Fine Arts remained, much to my relief; had she gone traipsing off to Africa or Peru, I would no doubt never have seen her again. She would have vanished behind a veil of noble motives. All the same, even while she was ruling out two of her options, she located and took lessons from a fellow in town who described himself as a former mercenary. She learned from him to throw knives, how to fight with a knife, how to fire that most inaccurate weapon the pistol, and judo. In a weak moment I thought she was learning these arts in order to give me the coup de grâce, which my colleagues pronounced coup de gras as if it were a pâté; but I dismissed the thought and understood that learning these things was her way of doing obeisance to the course not taken, the help not given. *Art* had chosen her, as it had taken me in my teens, its thumbs on my Adam's apple: a sickness unto death, an obsession like a fire in the belly, no holds barred.

There was only one discussion about Africa, in the course of which I mentioned Sartre's advice, or lack of it, to a young Frenchman who, during World War Two, was trying to decide between family and escaping to England to join the Free French. Sartre didn't tell him what to do because he *knew* what he was going to do, and he was right. Or so he said. I tried this line on

Swan, who had been genuinely looking for guidance, and she gave me a look compounded of derision and disappointment. To my mind, she was heavily committed to writing, and going to Peru or Africa would eventually seem to her a kind of self-betrayal.

"You're leaving it to me, then," Swan said dejectedly. "Harsh."

"For the thrill of deciding your own life."

"It's bound to affect you, one way or the other."

"But only too much," I told her, "if I've had a hand in the decision. Whatever you do, I'll back you up. What could be more cordial than that?" She winced and turned away from me.

There were cliché versions of all the embraces she proposed, so was there anything of which a cliché version did not exist? I could not think of any. My colleagues included one man of affable demeanor, a bit brusque in a genteel way, huge and pear-shaped (bulky end down), who cultivated orchids in a natty greenhouse of his own design and spent the rest of the time playing piano. He had evolved, I thought, an almost unique lifestyle, not least because he had hired a live-in chunk of Brunswickian woman to monitor the orchids. A bibliographer of some standing, he sported a pencil-thin mustache that resembled an anorexic leech. I used to think him debonair and rather well-bred until I heard about his habit of breaking toilet seats with his four-hundred-pound physique, including a mahogany one from the sixteenth century that had withstood thousands of bottoms for so long until he at last, for the first time, sat himself down, and the seat split. This was in England, where he was a guest at the Oxfordshire home of a don who sat in his garden with a candy jar full of aspirins, munching them by the handful as wasps flew formation drill around him. He was the scholar-critic who said he kept all his correspondence with scholars and burned that with writers. He knew what was what, all right. Both of these men had been genial to me, but as they aged they became peevish and obtuse, unhappy to see me prospering in the uncouth terrain of the novel, and I began to identify the clichés of the lifestyle that hovered about them, like lepers in waiting. Did I know no original people at all?

Swan told me she had applied to four MFA programs in poetry and would go wherever she was accepted, if anywhere; failing that, she would plump for Africa. What a cliché was there! I could hardly choke for almost throwing up at the evoked thoughts: green hills, Kilimanjaro (what was the leopard doing at that altitude?), *bwana*, pride and joy, elephants knocking trees over, mambas hurling themselves, tsetse flies stinging cattle, Kenyan Brits living the Anglo life with servants galore. Did she really want that, or would she end up in some dump such as Angola or Nigeria? I tried to put Africa aside and go back to my sticky attic table, where a ream of softened bond awaited my worst excesses. Once Swan had decided, we could discuss the whole thing to death. *She* was unique, but some of her enterprises were not and would get in the way of her poetry. On the other hand, as the saying went, you could not destroy a poet, or indeed any full-blooded creative person; whatever came their way was grist for the creative mill. I had found this to be true in my own life, even to the point, perhaps, of looking for appalling situations to get into, just for the kick-start they would give me. Please crucify me, but leave my typewriter at the foot of the cross. That kind of uniqueness preyed on my mind and set it racing. Was that why I agreed to teach Shakespeare and fiction-writing, Modern British Fiction and Lord Byron, ever alert for an experience so degrading it had, simply had, to generate some priceless piece of prose to hang on to? When would I cease fawning on horrors?

Every now and then came one of those days of synthesis when the jigsaw of your life fits together and you can see the wood in spite of the trees, sure then that your projects relate to mighty tectonic planes of experience, not splinters and fragments. It is then that we become bolder than usual, saying to ourselves, for example, my way of writing fiction goes against the current American fashion, or my way of teaching defies the present cult.

This is when the Zeitgeist has descended, filling one's being with purposeful ecstasy, steering one from maudlin fussing-around to a goal as clear as a white lighthouse against a murky sea. Then you go for it, heaving all kinds of detritus away from you, instructing yourself—with a shovelful of misgiving and shame—that this is precisely the purposefulness that Heidegger the Nazi thought he saw in Ancient Greece: not dabbling, not shuffling, not doodling, but fully roped to the armada of yourself. Swan was fondling some such concept, no longer staying limber and receptive for the poem of the occasional inspired day, but putting all she did, no matter how little, in the context of some program, some quest. It was for this, I said, that people educate themselves. The educational process exists to help us make sense of life, not the other way around. Which parents are going to cough up twenty thousand dollars a year so that their child can acquire a deeper sense of the fertile muddle, and a reverence for it?

Still interested in grouping, I fantasized what would happen if the orchid man, Pendennis Cleveland, alienated *his* wife, the pink-chopped and unobtrusive Hedwig, and decided that of course she would fill his half of the bed with orchids. If the bad thing happened to a chairman, or head, of English, his wife would fill his half of the bed with the rest of the department. What, I asked my Swan, would *she* do? "Oh, I would spend my last dollar filling your half with bottles of Scotch to help you drink yourself to death that much faster." She was a loyal, reckless amour, my Swan, whom, if I had met her much earlier, I would have taken to my bosom like a long-awaited drug, and I would have had no career at all, done no studies, made no effort, but would have stayed her swain, her churl, her lickspittle. She was just too good, ever showing that smooth, adroit demeanor; she would sometimes wear her blond wig to the movies, entering blond, leaving brunette, creating how much muddle I never knew. Contrasted with some of my more peripheral colleagues, this was empirical reliability. Rabinowicz, who collaborated with

Weber, our authority on military history, on detective novels according to the Dodd Mead formula (one crisis every ten pages), used to look wearily at me and bark "You're confused!" I never answered this; he smelled bad and I left his presence as fast as I could. Then there was Pfeitz, an expert on something or other, who whenever he saw me raised his umbrella in a Nazi salute and said "*Heil.*" He was the only colleague who ran a ménage à trois, at least with humans. Students admired him for his insatiability and his explanation: "For some men, one woman is just not enough." The whole faculty wondered how they did it. Then there was our token black, De Vrees, from Princeton, sometime head of graduate studies, who when he finally left to go to Yale abandoned behind him several steel lockers full of unanswered graduate studies mail. Everyone said he was a nice man and he kept on reminiscing about the Salzburg seminars, the last place he had done any work. Twa Twa, his wife, not so nice, made the mistake of reading a little autobiography I had published to some degree of success, and aired far and wide her view that, if you happened to be so unlucky as to be born into the bottom class, you should not celebrate the fact. She was a member of that new breed, the Gorky snob. Confronted with all such, and there are scores more meriting three lines, my *vita nuova* with Swan *was* like having a new life, certainly a double one, an idyll among the high camp of the language reservation called Department. It might have been Deportment too. We were lynxes who had escaped their cages.

Time and again we talked about how seriously we were taking our affair whereas all else struck us as trivial buffoonery. This was no doubt arrogant on our part, but we could not rid ourselves of the notion that we were the only serious people in town. Or was it that, within their shells of silliness, all the others were every bit as serious as we were and had serious thoughts about themselves? And did they find us as silly as we found them? No, it could not be: their daftness began on the outside and went right through, you could tell that a mile off. How came it then that we had been singled out for this exercise in intense, undeviating, rhapsodic, mutual, unprecedented infatuation? What had we done right, and when? Thinking along these lines was akin to behaving like the needlewoman who, repairing an old shirt, scratches an itchy eye with a scissors in hand and thus cuts her eye open without thinking. We could injure ourselves, each other, by being so abstracted from the world at large, by calling each other "Buns" and "Cuddleskin" in high-camp euphoria. There was some danger, wasn't there, in so abstruse a love. We felt Chaucerian, at once frivolous and dead serious, each watching the other watch him or her self. It was like being in a pavane or in a sedan chair. There was no weather, no time. There was no furniture beyond flesh and bone. There was no sun, no ice, no vegetation. We thrived in a vacancy created by all the species of beings who had decamped, unable to match us in a dozen different areas. She was the only one of her kind, the *hapax legomenon* of her race (this a phrase she herself had actually produced in the throes of some blissfully amicable argument). To lose her would be criminal, an affront to the world's plenty.

So on we went, teasing each other out, plumbing unsuspected depths and attitudes, the first known coelacanth encountering the first known navanax on the ocean floor in pitch darkness. Everyone had advice for us, of course, since it was an interfering kind of town, and prophecy galore, but we took all that in good part, safe behind our barricade of codewords and undetected glances. We lived in a private dimension, light-years away from Palgrove our Oxford don murmuring "Edit a Shakespeare text, my boy, no one wants novels nowadays" and Gimblett the snoop whose presence still bulked large, murmuring after invading my mailbox and opening the packages, "Don't review this one, darling, it's trash." All these people, so zealous about affairs so commonplace, were mere blades of grass; the meadow they composed was idyllic, but we flew over it at mind speed, or rather our shadow cruised it, flying evenly over each and every corrugation like a contoured fluid. There was no time to pause.

We soared ahead toward whatever, fingers linked, our bodies twisted to enable us to exchange itinerant kisses. From time to time we set down to discuss gorillas' habit of fouling their own nests and actually eating their own dung, none of which troubled her much, though I could tell that Africa was waning. What if none of the MFA schools accepted her? Unthinkable, not with that portfolio of hers, at once majestic and racy. Myself, I would have handed her the degree on reading it, no need for further study, just go out into the literary world and prevail, over the heads of the pedestrians only once heard from, if ever, and never heard from again. Peru was a goner already, Africa had dwindled, so my unconscious mind began to grapple with an academe of elsewhere, just as vacuous no doubt, and spiteful, costive, miserly. She would find out what I did not think worth passing on to her. All she would have to be was good, and the vultures would begin to gather, ever ready to strip out the intestines of a poem.

Nonetheless, a girl who is ready for Africa is ready for anything. As she herself said, she had been running with a rough crew of anthropologists who often got themselves into dangerous fixes in foreign parts and had to beat their way free. These were the people who carried guns and knives and practiced judo in Spanish-speaking ghettos, people from whom she had learned something narrow, but way below her level of wit, which would have had no suitable target or audience on such trips. Would I have gone? No, but I was willing to commute to whichever campus might take her in. I lamented that, owing to slow motion at Harper and Row, she did not have an already published book of poems to be her portfolio: a premature golden egg.

It struck me then that up to now I had spent little time kissing. Oh, there had been the usual connections, of course, but relatively little of that tender holding and inhaling without which love in life is a mere scamper. Swan and I spent hour upon hour with our faces close together, appointed to wear out proximity as an hypnotic device. In this way we discovered an almost digestive quietness related to a peace that, certainly passing all human understanding, supplied a fragrant bank on which to rest, as in some old poems and plays. There was a gift of mutual immersion I had never known before, requiring no training and no motive, but only the sublime sink into liquid homage. This sounds grandiose, but it was humble and uncontrived, possibly the natural condition of the soul, with, in its modern incarnation, huge petals from some unimaginable amaryllis piled high on horizontal eyelids, several inches deep, then a foot, then six feet, twenty, a hundred, all the way into the sky, a towering skyscraper of petals, undulating and flexing but never falling, there for the wind to bend. Some such experience in which acute vulnerability met singular physics. In a word, we held together, in all the versions of that phrase, coming to a halt in life, surrendering all volition like a flag catching fire and slowly blowing away to all points. The key to such experience, of course, was how our awareness of it fed back into the experience itself: perceived, it became different, but the difference fed into the original, not merely disarming us, quite ridding us of any self-consciousness but also inviting us into a further and presumably infinite extension of what was happening. Always perceived, and ever changing, it could never exhaust itself or us, but went on changing as in the creation of Nature itself, becoming—here my imagination paddles with delight in gorgeous concepts—planetary, alkaline, juridical, spherically geometric, anally complete. It would no more go into words than into lips, this ravishing sotto voce union that might have wafted from the entanglement of two aliens on the run, all veils and cube roots, unseeable and incapable of being addressed. One flails around in the hinterland of any such experience, always trying to banish crude approximations: being converted into an angel, lifted off Earth into weightless sublimity, dying without ever believing it and with a brain alive enough to worry. If only we had had some readymade handle other than "love," but we did not and hence were condemned—some condemnation!—to the choked suburb of meanings, where the tumult of defining haunted each word in every language. All the same, we had a hint, a glimpse, a tang of infinity, at least as far as humans may know it, and we surrendered to it as if we knew what it was other than chaos yawning wide, wider, yawn without end. That all this could come from four lips touched in a mood akin to weariness (delight enervates) astounded us and kept us quiet when we might well have replighted our troth noisily.

SIX

Ah," said John Johnson to me a good ten years before I met Swan, he the brother of actress Celia, "it's no use getting into all that old romanticism." Bad advice, I thought at the time, not what you wanted from your first literary agent, never mind how statuesque and much-watched his sister was, especially when standing next to a naval officer with four gold stripes on his sleeve. I was being given the old-boy runaround, the code for stiff upper-lippers; I had paid my dues to Zola and Dreiser, of course, but Byron and Faulkner had formed me, and he was glad enough when I wrote a critical study of the former and then a first novel based on the latter. He sold them both with chaste gusto. Romance soon melted into romanticism, being merely a phase, a mode, whereas romanticism imagined hotly and proclaimed the subjective's license to perform. I remembered shingles that read "B.A. (Failed) Calcutta." Well, this one read something indecipherable, perhaps letters on fire from a Bower of Bliss that had fallen into the Inferno. There was no polity, no protocol. You made it up as you went along, bound by no public code save that of language, and even that somewhat bent. Inward rhapsody took over, communicable or not. Your mind widened you. There would be a Swan or there would not; and, if no Swan, you imagined one and got on with the chore of ministering to your own bliss. All those medieval knights howling in towers for unreachable love had not reached the stage of self-supply. Odd how often imagination, lively on show, failed in private.

All very well, says the man in the street, it's mighty ethereal (if he knows the word); doesn't anything as low-down and dirty as an oiled sausage enter into your daily goings-on? *Didn't* it? It might have slackened off now, but in the heyday of erotic fervor wasn't there just a bit of sex? The man in the street usually ends up as the man under the bed, an heir to squeals and bellows, the proud custodian of creaking springs and vented breath. To answer him would restate the obvious. Of course, I would say: Do you think we were a couple of pool balls? The only information he needs is that this was the one area that overlapped with predecessors, lust being the lowest common denominator. It is like asking Did we eat, did we read, did we exhale? He shall not be the fly on the wall, but the fly on the bedspread stunned and tipped into the toilet.

One day, after we had been to the grocery, we left the empty bags on the kitchen floor, and I, wandering about in the small hours, entered the kitchen without putting on the light. Crash I went into the first of several brown-paper bags with a sound of drums, a hollow and flimsy timpany, as stunned as if someone had fired a gun near my ear. Sex was that kind of commotion in the elemental life, almost always taking me by surprise as the gathering seepage of desire shaped anew an old destiny that started a heave in the loins. One would not have thought the body had so much energy to spend, so much inclination, but there it was, the metronome beat of the hormones, hardly part of one's identity but body's daily bread. One could spend a lifetime, or an entire puberty, on the fact of a vagina that clamps you tight and squeezes, nay milks you like a farmhand's palm; but I will not, for these are the generic mysteries of togetherness, whereas the pensive impromptus that accompany the act have unique appeal, not always quite one's own of course, but sufficiently original to outlast the barrage of coupling consummated without words.

"So, how's the nooky?" It might have been Asa asking in a slack moment, instantly regretting it, only to be told that all aspects of our relationship (hated word) were A-1, even down to which oil we cooked in. We did not so much kiss and tell as kiss and kiss. "Good in the sack?" someone else asked, jocularly preying on us until we cracked. Indeed, I think that had been Hermione, her old friend, whom she still saw for tea some afternoons. Swan reported the question with good-humored disdain. Life was going on in the old way. I wondered about the distinction between women and men. Did women discuss these basic plumbing matters among themselves, or go the way of decorum, offering a smile and a gesture? Men, in my experience, never got around to it beyond an occasional swift, impersonal allusion; they only talked this way about the women they had *not* slept with, or slept with no more. Unless, of course, like my friend York, best described as an anthropological novelist, you wanted to enliven a whole chapter with improvisatory cunnilingus in the course of writing which you manifested a copious knowledge of tropical fruits. York appears not at all because he had not yet swum into my ken, but was away at Yale luxuriating in his fellowship and ruining girls. I may be wrong, but men, who have a reputation for blabbing, don't blab much, and women, I guess (I have never been able to get a straight answer), discuss things in gynecological detail, simply out of respect for the hydraulics they have been gifted with. A man will readily talk about keeping his penis wet, but has little to offer about where it shall go, which rainstorm or lagoon. I yield to wider experience. To Simenon, who fucked himself to death and got little of it into deathless prose. He kept his public mouth shut, apart from boasting, as men will (I'm approaching a hundred, a thousand, fifty thousand). He would have kept score mentally, I guess, had there been an apparatus up top to do it with. Is it, was it, in the old days of trial and error, like trying to count up one's colds or nosebleeds? I stress the element *count*, conceding any number of saliences from tupping as such: how she did this or that, and how one received it. Education has a thousand morsels on its plate. Somewhere, sooner or later, arrives the ghost of perfection, and now the body's tremor joins that of the mind. You slide the landscape under a woman even while she is talking about something else—thus York, who has kept it wet almost like a deity showering a planet. Myself, I doubt very much if a woman is ever surprised into sex, since her approach to it tends to be global, holistic, whereas a male, yes, he can screw absentmindedly since his fundamental approach has to do with a safety valve and a piston: no more than that. If a woman strolls into the landscape of desire, she knows it, even if her mind is merely on strawberries or perfume, Rimbaud or mutual funds. Men can come and go without ever deserting an idée fixe. Thus Asa, the bed-evicted, philosophizing about a house whose books remained alphabetized.

Deep in my gut there would develop a cold vacancy into which, at least in theory, a new experience could fit, though none ever did, and the sensation amounted to something eerily suggested in the phrase *a goose walked over my grave*. I had this same sensation now, not because I was clearly going to spend the next few years of life with my Swan, none of whose expert and exotic moves I knew by heart. That was not it. I sensed the imminence of something dreadful or splendid on the level of ideas or ordeals, and I knew I would be demanded of, perhaps more than ever before. Had she felt the same? Not at all, although she now felt strongly that some writing school was going to accept her; Africa, at least for now, and Peru, had blown away like burned paper. I confided my uneasiness, the spooky feelings in my stomach, but she pooh-poohed them, saying I did not eat enough, that I had a case of the butterflies because the book I was writing hadn't gone well of late. There was a drug, I knew, that professors with butterflies took before they went on the platform, and then they were uncannily peaceful; all they had to do next was taper off from the drug. I needed no drug but one of those Macbethian foretellings, by witches or other prescient beings, just to get me straight. Yet the cold sensation would not go away, and I concluded I was being haunted by the future, if such a thing could be. Some rooms went cold when you entered them, even if you were not superstitious.

The same sensation came back several times during the next few days. Things began to happen swiftly, and they proved demoralizing even though we had known about some of them. Swan was going away to work for *Literary Digest* in Manhattan, just for the autumn, and I was going to visit my mother in England. Things were falling apart even though, dawdling lovers that we were, we had hoped circumstance would somehow drift away from us and leave us be forever. No such luck: she was already committed to an apartment in Whitestone (in which, she would discover, the furniture was sheathed in see-through plastic, and there was a place next door that sold marvelous pound cake). Once more, sleepless as ever on that transatlantic route, I would ogle the rising sun soon after midnight and feel, in the joy of reunion, the remorse of having been away. The external world, of whose frivolity and indifference we had been only too aware, was making inroads upon us. Then Coriolis University accepted her into the MFA Poetry program, though by that time none of the other schools had replied. She accepted, and I felt the beating of reptilian wings, tearing us apart for a season of obligations. Much as, together for long timeless and sometimes mealless days, we had felt diminished back to childhood, we now felt accelerated into maturity, obliged to live conventionally. To see her at all I would have to commute; I taught little, whereas she would be carrying a heavy load and more or less required to remain on the premises. It felt grievous. We wished we could enjoy the boons of society without having to shoulder its wheel.

"Harsh," she sighed. "All this all at once."

"Africa would have been much worse," I said, trying to put a brave face on things. "Imagine how we'd have felt."

"Damn Africa," she said. "Damn futurity."

"It will damn itself," I told her. "It always does. It's the nature of futurity."

"We never seem to have any control," she said with an aimless swing at the ceiling. "Why?"

"Because we want too damned much."

If she agreed, she did not say. Life once again was enlisting us in its demented relay races, heedless of love; the human body, as Emerson said, can be nourished by any food, even boiled grass and the broth of shoes, so the human mind can be fed by any knowledge, or indeed any form of motion, quiver, twitch. If only we had learned to remain absolutely still, say in a swoon of delight, hidden away in the attic, wrapped in a rug, we might successfully have severed ourselves from society; but no, there was some force undiscovered by physicists that drew us out into a noxious spiral and gave us, in the end, other things than the ones we really wanted: books instead of rapt, wordless communion, money instead of exquisite affinity, safety instead of aerobatic fondling. We would encounter it again, this centrifugal impetus that cheapened and aborted, appealing to our egos and annulling our hearts, and try as we would we could never outstrip it and vanish into the pledgeless continuum we yearned to inhabit. Wanting less, we would have been happy, but, quite happy, we found that happiness somehow fortified our ambitions. In the old days, as after some torrid affair that merely left the house reeking of estrus and sweat, I would retreat to the smelly table in the attic, shut the world out, and get on with work. She, more gregarious than I, was capable of just that, but unwilling to make the surrender implicit in any such act. Now, however, our sense of separation and abandonment was working in a vaster zone in which huge slices of the planet shut us off from each other, and being alone meant being lonely. I cursed the Ivy League, the MFA program, the Finger Lakes, even her first book (which had clearly got her in), and wondered if I should try for a teaching position at Coriolis, not that I had heard of any vacancy. There just had to be a better way of selling each other down the river after so beatific a season. We started wailing and squealing, altering the register to personalize it and transform the sounds into an Indian love-call special to us. We had bungled our private lives. I cursed Asa, whose kindness had procured her first job for her through his contacts at *Literary Digest*, but cursing was helpless rant, changed nothing and, though I had little notion of this at the time, boosted my blood pressure (extra headaches, a sense of distension, tightness felt in the eyes, pinging sounds in my ears, and muscle pains in the back of my neck, all of which I attributed to hangover). I told her I was going to train my mind by reading the *Vita Nuova*, of which I had an unopened paperback, and she responded instantly, as she would, saying that we should read the book together, side by side, with our heads touching, and say certain passages out loud (she had already read it once). Yet I, I was thinking of the *Inferno*, with some relevance remembering T. S. Eliot's rendering of the famous lines about Paolo and Francesca. Several times, as they read about Lancelot, their eyes met and their faces flushed until a certain moment at which "the fond smile was kissed by such a lover, he, who shall never be divided from me, kissed my mouth all trembling." When I think of all the kisses in literature, that one wins for instancing the high dream.

She was moved, and silent.

I too was moved, and silenced by memory.

What had I said to her?

Perhaps we would not read the *Vita Nuova* after all, though the title was appropriate to us; the book would only make us feel worse, would divide us even more: another ocean, another section torn from the map. So we kept on saying, more or less in concert, *La bocca mi bacio tutto tremante*, since we were both literary buffs and had some smattering of Italian.

It was fun to attitudinize in the shade of Paolo and Francesca, riding to new heights of tenderness. We felt quite allegorical, as if Dante had had us in mind too. The notion of lovers separated by life yet united by a book had stylish charm and consoled us somewhat, at least until I began to wonder about the wholesome visage of the entire thing. Consider all the sinners in Hell. Dante's treatment of these two was the tenderest, no doubt because their sin, so-called, was excess of physical passion, meriting light punishment (and some risk of overcrowding). The Carnal, as they are called, spin and drift through an atmosphere made murky by their passion, impelled by a gale. The truth was, as I ascertained after looking up Paolo and Francesca with the zeal of someone hunting the lowdown on a treasured relative who might have left a will, that in 1275 Giovanni Malatesta of Rimini, sometimes known as Giovanni the Lame, a somewhat Byronic hero, made a marriage of convenience with Francesca, daughter of Guido da Polenta of Ravenna. So far, quite neat. But, when Francesca arrived in Rimini, she began an affair with Giovanni's younger brother Paolo, who was not lame. This was why Francesca was damned in the second circle of Hell, a condition later evoked with torrential force by Tchaikovsky in his *Francesca da Rimini;* she had so soon changed from Francesca da Ravenna to Francesca da Rimini. The composer seems not to have noticed the illicit quality of this amour, certainly not in the tender section suggesting innocence, in the clarinet heard against plucked strings. Then hell takes over again. Paolo, it seems, already had two daughters of his own, but his affair with Francesca continued for many years, until Giovanni happened upon them in Francesca's bedroom and killed them both. Small wonder that, to disguise the naked erotics of this story, there grew up a legend that Paolo had been sent by Giovanni as a proxy; Francesca supposed he was the real bridegroom and returned his embraces. A lovely twist, but Dante says nothing of the kind, and, although various other whitewashings have appeared, or euphemistic readings (for example, their love is so pure it transcends Hell itself), Dante's version remains: contemplating each other in Hell only makes them feel worse (than if, say, they had been separated), and their bodies, now become mere ashen aftermaths, pain them as bitter reminders. There is no desire left, only a forced proximity.

Chastening as this version was, the story charmed us, or rather the quality of the writing did. Hell seemed remote from us, unless it was Coriolis's savage winter climate (why had she not applied to somewhere in Florida?). An odd thing I discovered was that, while Dante was writing his long poem, Giovanni Malatesta was still alive, poor Giovanni the cuckold, though Dante had already assigned him to the first ring of the last circle for dastardly acts against his kindred. Some tabloid quality, invading this sex idyll, made me smile, especially at Dante's jumping the gun. How enterprising of him to make reservations in Hell for his contemporaries; the twentieth century would have kept him busy until the end of his life, and I thought I might end up doing the same except I had no Hell available to me, my own idea of that region being Milton's: why this is Hell, nor am I out of it. If only we had been smacking our lips over something as crude as *The Story of O*, we might have been closer to perdition, but our fixing on Paolo and Francesca, in the traditional mood of innocence vindicated, only served to prove our wholesomeness and prancing good taste. How often people read history as they wish it to be, and how often works culled from historical events end up being read with a huge slant. One despairs of ever getting the truth across about anything. Dante amazed me with his nigh-newspaperman's grasp of contemporary scandal and theological destiny. He was a muckraker and a secret travel agent, an absolutist whose system had a place for everybody. Now, on reflection, I shivered a little when I thought of Paolo and Francesca, for whom Dante made no apologies. Their gentlest passages together sharpened the pain of their ultimate fate, and one could only wince at his remorselessness.

"Screw *them*," Swan whispered. "This is us. Nobody's going to pigeonhole *us*. After all, the book Dante said they were reading together, about Lancelot, was actually pornography. He's a didactic old nerd, isn't he? I vote we nuke him." She took the

Inferno in one hand and slid it behind a cushion, where it lay unretrieved for the next several months; I rarely vacuumed the house, and when I did the cheap machine made a noise of a gasoline-powered model plane, so I rushed my chore and let sleeping books lie. I nonetheless admired Dante's use of compartments, his superb sense of cemetery, his knack with labels, his exquisite awareness of the different types and degrees of sin. Reading in a news report that, in the 1990s, sodomy had become the rage in Rome, the in thing, I felt I was reading Dante, and that Dante was there, on the spot, taking notes on you know whom. Perhaps that was his great feat: to make you feel he was observing you, stylus in hand, wondering which of his slots to sign you up for in a world as tidy as that of the census-taker.

Something else bothered me, quite remote from Dante and the poem he himself entitled *The Comedy of Dante Alighieri*. Swan had repeatedly urged me to speak more quietly in public places. I did not hear too well how far my sotto voce carried; what I thought was a thistledown murmur turned out to be, she said, a huge stage whisper that made people turn around. I was shocked, wondering how deaf I had become. How many secrets had I given away in restaurants and cinemas, thinking I was being conspiratorial when I was broadcasting. Perhaps, secretly as somebody in the *Inferno*, I was looking for punishment, airing secrets in hope of the whip. Her plea for secrecy and hush affected me deeply inasmuch as I was not the person I had thought I was. Was I, then, also rough and coarse and boastful and cruel? How little self-knowledge did I truly have? Was she, over the next few years, going to modify me until I had no personality at all? It was a marginal, trivial fear, but one I sometimes allowed to roam through my mind like a mad three-headed dog, eyes red, its beard greased with phlegm. If she cured me of being, oh, a loudmouth and a blabbermouth, would it not be easier to cure me of other traits? It was like thinking you know how you sound to other people, and then hearing your voice without the intervention of the bone that has deformed it all these years.

That was a shock too, but I had first heard the difference when I was twenty and recorded some of my poems. Not a bad voice, I thought of the one on the recording; if anything better, with more timbre, more dark browns. Swan thought so too, but it took me years to adjust my mind to the thought that, whenever I spoke, it was the "other" voice that hearers heard. Now it would take me just as long to quieten down lest I blab. Somehow, I thought, Dante and this voice problem were linked, and the clue was delusion: no one wanted the actual story of Paolo and Francesca, any more than I wanted to know the truth about my own voice—and what had been the truth since my voice broke. I asked her. "You pro*ject*," she said calmly. "It's all that public speaking. You put a column of air behind every whisper without knowing it. And, coupled with your unceasing candor, my treasure, you're something of a liability." That said, I had of course nothing to say in return.

You no sooner say something is over and done with than it rears up again. The *Inferno*, I had thought, was safely marooned behind the couch, a cathedral for woodlice and ants, but out it came in conversation like the three-legged hirsute elephant you are determined not to think about.

"Imagine that old Dante Alighieri," she said. "An old toot."

"Meaning a male whore," I said, ready to find a new topic.

"If you like," she said. "He's always rapping somebody over the knuckles. He's always got something in store for almost anybody. He wants perfect behavior. I don't think he felt much sympathy for P. and F., even if he did write the *Vita Nuova*. He only got sentimental to sharpen the tooth of blame. He's a sadist, really."

"Well, we nuked him, along with Galsworthy, Sir Walter Scott, Sir Philip Sidney, *Beowulf*, Somerset Maugham, Simenon, and a hundred more. We'll never consult him again."

"Oh," she said pithily, "I'm just pissed off because I'm leaving; and you too. We organized it all very badly. It's going to be months. Painful, infuriating, pointless. Shall I chuck the job and the MFA?" Indeed not, I told her, this was a lovely chance for her torpedo to get launched. Both were.

"So you do think I have a future and it's not all downhill from here?" Genuine tears in her already shiny brown eyes.

I held her close, doing my best to look forward to when the wound would heal.

Our dealings with each other in those days were buoyant and euphoric; nothing, we thought, would go amiss, and even being parted was a merely temporary snag that would sweeten reunion. We waltzed from mood to mood, capping each with a smart-ass line, her best one being something at once musical, lugubrious, and witty in a predatory way: "After many a summer dies the *Schwann.*" My own best is hardly worth reporting, but we did manage to score verbal victories over vicissitude (and to alliterate as well!) without exerting our brains too much. It was the phase of an affair when no one heeds colds, but plunges willy-nilly into the cold climate of a partner's viruses, heedless of drip, cough, and sneeze. Indeed, there was something intimately voluptuous about infecting each other with invisible life-forms, almost as if we had taken too much to heart Donne's bracing poem about the flea. Prudence in these matters would come later, when the first flush had yielded to the second flush, and so on until love had become a well-tended castle with a portcullis and all kinds of prophylactic taboos. Depression, sadness, however, we passed from one to the other with connoisseurs' casualness, having ample reason to feel low. Parting was not death, as the tradition had it, but a form of premature loneliness that mechanical means such as the telephone could not quite dispatch. There was nothing like murmuring in each other's ears, with the possibility of instant replay if something sounded bad. Speed of response was paramount. We wanted to be more efficient, almost capable of mind reading, impatient with the conventional means of colloquial exchange. Presumably Paolo and Francesca, stuck in Hell, drove each other batty by merely conversing, such were the memories of the ecstasy in which they had adulterously begun. One of their penalties was not to want to talk with each other ever again: nothing with the lascivious dripping pink tongue at all. We had decided to nuke them, but they kept intruding into our thoughts, which was perhaps what Dante intended; he had meant to inject into all spontaneous amour the desperate chance of love in excess, for which you entered the second circle. Surely, we thought, no amount of intense marital love got you skewered, it was only adultery that got you into trouble. After all, the boredom of the uxorious was legendary; surely nobody would enter the second circle for *too much* marital devotion. It was hard to tell, but we strengthened our conviction that no theologian should come near our obeisances, whether accomplished with a lubricant or with a frozen lip fresh from winter's clamp.

Even packing split us up, though we did it only a few hundred yards apart. She had her stuff and I had mine, and she was abandoning her now virtually unused apartment, given over to Hermione and their cats. The day came and went, neither of us able to speak, but she was soon sending me little packets of Dino cigarillos disguised as socks and hankies, at least on the green customs slip. My mother and I watched TV westerns and reminisced about the old days, which didn't seem very distant to me. Letters reminded me what gorgeous, emphatic, cuneiform handwriting she had, and I discovered that, especially when apart, one can develop a fixation on somebody's penmanship, each whorl and curlicue embodying a caress. Most people's handwriting left me cold, and in the dark as well (I a poor decipherer), but hers blazed forth from the paper often in royal blue, an unmistakable network of signs and symbols that sang across space and tweaked the tail of time. I kept all her candid, generous letters, reading and rereading them with a fanatic's thoroughness, hunting an innuendo I had missed, or parallels only now calling out to each other in bewitching reciprocity. Her writing was much like her poetry: Nerudian frontal pageantry, saying "I am very much right here behind it." Some folk got so little of themselves into their handwriting that they wrote in order to vanish before their own eyes, allowing no space in their o's and e's and a's, flattening everything as if penmanship were camouflage. Well, *her* boldly drawn letters loomed large in two dimensions, each commensurate with the others, and the overall effect was of a lovingly inscribed tablet. If this was the conduit of poetic thinking, then she honored it, fusing elegance with pith, telling the reader there was more here than met the eye—if only you would go back over the lines, you would discover implicit treasures galore, all for you.

Absence may make the heart grow fonder (it did for us), but it also makes the mind grow wiser, even if only for a short time. Distanced, so to speak, from the intense burn of togetherness, I began to contemplate the exact nature of our affair, feeling both jubilant and lost. Compared, I thought, to our friends, we were eccentric people, bent on stylish originality, determined to get each sentence right before moving on to the next, whatever the cost. So this to some extent disqualified us for rational judgments about everyday living. We made noises and assumed stances that others did not and would not even have contemplated. Perhaps we were too eccentric to be able to tell each other anything. My own theory is that creative people live under such bizarre pressures they cannot live as other people do, cannot conduct themselves in a conventional way. Besides, their minds are forever on something abstruse, something that imagination by its very nature has created without making it present to the empirical senses. We were histrionic, we had been told so. People expected it of us because we were effusive, showy, not determined to be different but willing to let all of our differentness come through. Eccentrics, I thought as I tried to soldier on through her absence, serve a useful purpose: one at least. They remind people of where the center is, if they care to be reminded. This is not to say that eccentrics should be manufactured in quantity, but they should be there in all kinds of society to enliven the woof. Swan and I by no means held the record for supermarket smooching or movie-necking, but we did our fair share of these things, and one-on-the-other's foot walking came included, like wren-kissing and rhyming duets sung to populate an empty-sounding house. We never tried to be so-called normal but when separated (as I now realized) went through the same old motions in the abstract and sang the same songs. It was passing strange to be marooned with the ghost of your own performances, rehearsing them with nobody there (except my mother, who did not attend that closely or dismissed what she witnessed as *American* behavior). True, we had photographs and mementoes, then letters after a brief interval, and the phone, but the experience was still one in a test tube. I had heard of men who traveled with an inflatable woman, whom they seriously laid in a motel or even in a bedroom in a friend's house, bringing to the act a huge bonus of imaginative stimulus. Well, what I needed was no rubber woman but someone, something, more like what used to be called in the old days "the madonna of the sleeping cars," the madonna of the wagons-lits. That made the problem more ethereal than ever. It could be solved only in imagination, in a trance in which nostalgia talked to nostalgia, I talking to a she who wondered how I was coping, and vice versa. We had had no practice at this, of course, and might never become proficient; but I recognized almost from the first that solving the problem of loneliness was akin to that of writing a novel, the major trick of which is to have a sufficiently personable, adroit voice; otherwise all is lost, and the novel degenerates, as so many do, into railroad timetable, sociological survey, census count. The novel depends on a trick of throwing your voice, and not just on behalf of your characters; no, the bulk of the work lies in presentation, accouchement, depiction done in the manner of a ringmaster doing voice-over. Such was the challenge of narrating my own loneliness as if to her and then imagining, somewhere in the atelier of imagination, the ballet of our eccentricity in which we sometimes fell or stumbled. We were an ellipse, with two centers, so that the ellipse contained two circles based on the same two points. What we found in the ellipse but not in the twin circles was that eccentric superplus: the kisses that missed, the embraces that enclosed nothing, the sighs that never arrived, the inhalations that had no target, the quickening heartbeat that had no provocation, the exploring toe that had nowhere to go. It was marvelous in a way to be deprived of so much, but not such a bad compensation to have at least the style, the bearing, that was preliminary to all happy oddness. The main thing, however, was to keep in practice, perhaps adding to the repertoire a new caress, an innovative phrase, to be tried out three thousand miles away in the near future. In a way, eccentricity sealed us in, making us unavailable to people who comported themselves in a predictable fashion, and whose antics added up to no more than a day in the life of a year.

Because of all this, the eccentric person seemed to me utterly private, enclosed in a behavior so blatant as to deflect the observer from what truly lay within, which I had always presumed was high seriousness, a career-long devotion to the artistic in its highest range. You can, in some countries, go around saying such things, and you will not be ridiculed; but in other countries you keep such sentiments to yourself lest you interrupt the commercial dream of millions of yahoos. That is why eccentrics, presumably folk who have been flung from the spinning center (or who have flung themselves thence), rarely boast of knowing better than anyone where the center is. Or centers plural inasmuch as the eccentric's orbit is elliptical, as proposed earlier. There is another point, however: creative people such as Swan and I tend to have more intellectual energy than others, and this spare energy gets into our behavior, indeed into the way we interact with uncreative people, who then walk away murmuring "He does come it a bit, doesn't he?" Well, screw them, we want *Lebensraum* for oddities, the right to practice peculiarity, and this of course relates us to all kinds of other extraordinary unconventional people. This is to say that your creative person, poet or novelist, tends to be marginal, because thought so, but in fact craves the center as a place from which to start drawing radiants. This means, I suppose, that the helplessly creative person must not be economical but profuse, always capable of wasting, of throwing something away and starting again because our creative act goes on all the time, not during Sunday afternoon picnics only or at an assigned hour. Silkworms squeeze silk out of their rear ends, and creative eccentrics secrete it from their heads.

So there she was, over there in Whitestone or Manhattan, earning her daily bread, actually writing little reviews of books to come, harnessed to the trade for a pittance, and wondering why she had to live among plastic-sheathed furniture, as if she were permanently dirty, she who washed her enormous hair each day. All that would soon be over and then she would zoom off to the Finger Lakes in her red Beetle, poems on her lips, titles of books lisping in her ears: to a new life, in which I did not figure and would only through interruption as she tried to pass muster with people who, even if they could not find anything wrong, felt obliged to criticize and carp. The more I saw of academe the more I began to respect newspapers; teaching I began to see as an inspired mode of hand-holding, which was easy for me as I had never had anyone teach me novel-writing, only the straight and narrow of English and French literature. What a blessing that had been. Always I dealt with the dead, who did not mind what I thought about them. I was free to make my mistake and do my pillaging, whereas Swan, obliged to swim in a lake of egomaniacs all hot to trot, would encounter personal problems even while discussing texture.

SEVEN

Another way I had of keeping in touch with Swan was through a certain book I had picked up at JFK en route to London, the last copy on the rack and somewhat battered. The Coriolis astronomer Raoul Bunsen had gone through I. I. Shklovsky's treatise *Intelligence in Space* and popularized it, fattening and augmenting, sometimes with new illustrations. I was unsure if this kind of thing had dignity, but I decided it would justify itself if it made the Russian easier to fathom; Russian books on complex matters tended to feel like basalt. Bunsen was already making a name for himself as one who understood science and could pitch it acceptably to such ignoramuses as me. Little did I know where this vicarious interest of mine would land me; it certainly helped to make contact with one of the lively minds she might encounter up at Coriolis. I even embarked on reading some books by members of the English department. I was still the youth I used to be, reading Malraux and Bernanos and Gide when I was supposed to be ploughing through Hardy, Cowper, and Sidney. What was my defensive aphorism from my teens? He who has rebellious taste will come to grief, but through the front door. Actually, the figures in the Shklovsky-Bunsen book occupied me more than the text, especially the photograph (on matte paper, therefore not as seductive as it might have been) of Stefan's Quintet, a quintet of stars in which one was streaking away from the group. Somewhere in this arrangement, I thought, a literary form announced itself, and I fondly conjectured four narratives all joining forces, so to speak, and one misfit departing the company at speed even though, seen from the front, it maintained its place. Constellations were a gross cheat, weren't they, valid as patterns or outlines only as seen from Earth, without depth. A computer would easily reveal the lie, showing things as they seemed from other perspectives; the shapes would be very different, even the Big Dipper. So there was arbitrariness and relativity to welcome here; things were not as cut and dried as I used to think, and there was Frank Deck's marvelous equation with which to calculate the chances of there being intelligent life out there. A trapdoor swung open as my world increased and I suddenly thought how Swan and I had a massive backdrop against which to relish each other. She already had a constellation, Cygnus, named for her, which was more than a head start; but surely we could do better than that, handing her a Stefan's Quintet out of the universe's nameless largesse. She would not be studying astronomy, or so I thought; but she would be under that umbrella of cosmic bravura, excited by incessant discovery. I had seen Bunsen on TV, in his rapture quoting the worst of Swinburne, but speaking of the Milky Way and other galaxies as of things exquisite and familiar, made of the same stuff as we. His version of the human setting was more palatable than Dante's, yet only because I was an electromagnetic chauvinist, whereas in my teens I had been a Christian mystic, patching a cosmology together out of Bernanos and Mauriac. Now, I suspected, I needed no world picture at all, but simply better world pictures than I'd had. If Swan had known of my purchase, my very first astronomy book, she could have bought a copy too, and then we could have done Paolo and Francesca at a distance. In the end we did, I having told her and she having gone out and bought. We were keeping Mr. Bunsen in clover, but Mr. Shklovsky was perhaps still poorly off in that humdrum, tyrannical country of his. We agreed to compare notes when we reunited; after all, we owned a telescope and lots of star maps; but our interest had so far been mechanical, hobbyistic. Little did we know that many astronomers never used telescopes at all, but contented themselves with binoculars, which struck us as too diffident by half. We were suckers for color, even artificial colors imposed on a drab slide by computer. Shklovsky and Bunsen were preaching to the converted, but we, like so many others, had a touch of vulgarity or garishness in our interest, and this Bunsen knew whereas Shklovsky did not. It was amazing to walk around with a new chapterful in one's head, as if one's brain were a mile wide, brushing distant trains and trees all because, in the context of the vastness of space, size meant nothing at all, and merely to think light-years was to be among them, merely to think neutrinos was to sense them passing through you on their way to Australia. Each night, after a cursory look outside that got my mother looking at the stars too, I read a little sermon to myself from Shklovsky-Bunsen, briefly glimpse-meeting my Swan above the high perimeter.

Averse to a seven-hour bus trip via Williamsport and Elmira, I opted for a three-hour flight via Philadelphia, to get to which I had to take the limousine in front of the Pigskin Hotel and ascend in it to the top of Cold Mushroom Mountain, sawn off and steamrollered in World War Two to create a runway. So here I was, in shorts, with only two flight bags for luggage, looking like a tourist in my own town, or a young man going off to infect a city. Then up the mountain into chillier climes with a better view of the sun and, within, excellent big dishes of mashed potato and sausage while you waited. There was a prewar quiet to that airport; an occasional Lockheed Hudson would growl in, or a Convair like the one I was taking, but otherwise it was birds and tractors, and I wondered where before I had seen that bracing mix of bleached conifers and Finnish-looking lakes. The answer was Newfoundland, where I had waited for planes to Montreal, or from St. John's to Gander and vice versa. In such pale, emaciated places it seemed appropriate to be leaving the land behind as something spent, sapped, woebegone, even in late summer. Arrival at such a place chastened you, making you feel you should have brought it some chlorophyll to get it back on its feet again.

When Swan collected me in Elmira, with only a forty-minute drive ahead of us, she revealed the purple robe she had bought in New York; I have it still, draping it around my shoulders when, naked at the machine, I find the writing tough, but by now it has become a ceremonial garb. What I had for her also has endured: a block of glass smelted into a hollow prism that broke incident light into masses of pale colors depending on where you watched it from. I do believe it was supposed to hold bath oils, but it never did; it was a beaker of light, with a chromatic stopper going deep down. Always, at the bottom of the hole blown into it, there lay this red-hot ingot of light, almost a coiled spring, like all of light assembled and condensed, awaiting further duty. It repeated itself no more than a kaleidoscope did, and if we took the time it rippled again and again, flushing and blanching, a perpetual motion machine of soaring photons. For this we never coined a nickname, though we had one for almost everything else. It arrived and it abided, like a couple of other things I will come to. When we packed again, if ever, we would wrap the glass in the bathrobe, no doubt creating a jubilee of mauve light among the blind. Thanks said, embraces exchanged, we climbed into her VW and sped away to her Coriolis apartment where, I discovered, the dinner candles were already melting, bending down over the candlesticks. It was torrid in that little upstairs hideaway, even with the windows open and the door wafting to and fro. She had moved in; at least she had installed her IBM typewriter and some dresses, a couple of dozen books, a triple pack of paper plates. Had her parents still been living in the northeast, they would somehow have contrived to move her in, with glazed chickens and piles of glossy magazines; but they lived in Florida now and she was free to move at her own speed in her own way, traveling light with an eclectic's viaticum. Perhaps the magic glass would mist up in such confined, oven-like quarters, but no, it gleamed afresh with cascading colors even from what little light was left. When the lamps went on, it changed tint and went on doing its spectral thing. I aired my robe, needlessly, while she warmed up some TV dinners, two very corpses of meals, and produced a huge cold bottle of seltzer.

What an imperfect paradise that was: the bottom of the bath was rough and put your teeth on edge; the landlady's TV in the room below mumbled and squeaked like a wistiti in pain; and nonstop traffic on the road nearby created a shuffle not quite soothing. We resumed our joint life, however, at intervals, I typing on her IBM while she was away at class (taught by a nonwriter who had founded the MFA program), she working on her poems in that up-front cuneiform of hers. We needed to sag backward away from each other before coming together again; we needed to rebound, but we ended up discussing Shklovsky and the chances of there being smart aliens out there. "All aliens are smart," she said, "in their own way." She showed me her brand-new ode to them, to be recited should they show up in need of poetry. What on earth, I wondered, had they made of Earth's TV?

Had they felt as I had felt when, instead of talking literature in office hours in the Sixties, I had discussed life and war with Vietnam vets fresh from the jungle into college and not coping with it at all? Word got out that I, for some years an officer at an Air Force training unit, was willing to listen; I had no war experience, apart from the time when some RAF pilots retracted the undercarriage of their jets when ordered to bomb Israelis during the Suez crisis; but I knew the military mind somewhat and was sympathetic to men who had been dragooned into a war others could avoid. Was that how I gained the name of hawk? I got my vets, as I called them, reading Montaigne, Richard Hillary, and Wilfred Owen, not for literary reasons, but to give them some kind of ballast, some means of comparison. I have no idea if their academic work improved, but my own sense of the world did.

They had come from another planet, an appalling place, and they wanted to know the limits of pain and indifference. In the old days they would have been reading Sartre and Camus, as I had done, or Malraux and T. E. Lawrence, but I did not think existentialism was right for them, not in that form anyway; they had already acted and defined themselves, and I did not see the point of their rationalizing after the fact. To all other students, teenagers themselves, they were aliens, had been to the forbidden place, the unknown region, and done unspeakable things: dogs of war let loose by a benign-sounding government. In truth, as I began to learn, the war in Vietnam had been an instance of the poor being sent to police the poor, a common enough deed on a familiar planet. So I became involved in many a politicist discussion in which literature figured not at all, but money, power, rights, anarchy, and civil disobedience did. Out they went, these conscripts, as familiar minutemen, but they came back barbarously mutated, good for practicing on when you needed to know how an alien might act. I found the sea-change in these men disrupting, as I had found that in my own father, who came back blind from a war he volunteered for because he had been too poor to get into grammar school. I was on familiar turf, never mind anyone else. All vets are aliens, I thought: they know what God permits. Swan, whose account of the Sixties contrasted with mine, spoke of hope, optimism, open-mindedness, joy, serenity, and group enthusiasm, only the last of which occurred to my veterans, who of course bore the brunt of peacelovers when they came home. Wrong or right war, I thought, nobody should abuse a soldier; go after the senior officers, but toss a shred of mercy to the rank and file, who had seen the human animal stretched to its worst. I said these things to my colleagues in the English Department, but they thought I was bluffing, even those like Delray Pepp, our Hemingway man, who as an army captain had flown over the battlefields in Europe in a slow high-wing monoplane: a scout. At one point I suggested forming a little cadre within the department of professors who had held commissions, but the idea fell through when some of them realized I would outrank them all. We could have been useful to those blunted visionaries who, on their return with shattered minds, ran foul of the demons within the castle of literary criticism. It was hard to explain to these young men the need for Empson's *Seven Types of Ambiguity*, yet not impossible, most of all when Empson himself, as indeed happened, was on campus for a whole semester, drenched in cognac and being spun in his office chair by prankish graduate students. I was the man who, realizing he knew nothing about coping with snow, bought for him and slid on to his feet a pair of galoshes, which I do believe he never took off. Empson was another alien, I thought, a man whose thought was Chinese, whose politics were Tory, whose wife, Zeus help her, was the eighth type of ambiguity. Swan, at first despising the war, began to feel sympathy for those sent to wage it, discovering bit by bit the old British idea of the remittance man, which was to say the family black sheep sent off to Australia or Africa with the injunction *Don't come back*, and kept out there by a regular remittance: hush money, I suppose. Of course, some grunts returned, but as often as not they were told they would have done better to stay since aliens such as they no longer belonged in the best of possible worlds. Or dreams.

EIGHT

I examine the record, stripped as it is of days and dates (I being no diary keeper), and exclaim. Look what happened. The temptation is to say *in no time*, which of course is a misnomer; things do have their time of growth and mostly do not happen overnight. I am in two minds about what happened: we played into its hands; it would have happened anyway. No, we played into its hands. There on the worn fitted emerald rug in Swan's apartment sat Raoul Bunsen, whom she had come to know, in a flash it seemed. In his hands was the most used, abused, decrepit address book I had ever seen, with slips of paper pasted or just popped between pages, and cancellations galore with new names and their whereabouts penciled in. Bunsen knew everybody and had risen to eminence in his profession by seizing the microphone at a symposium (or was it a conference?) and making the whole thing go his way by sheer personal pressure and force of personality. Because he was so dominant, everyone had assumed he was right, and the old fogeys had fallen into line behind the young Turks. It had been he who persuaded Shklovsky's American publishers to pay up when they were trying to fob him off without a cent. Clearly, our guest was a man of energetic will. He had trouble with address books, fumbling and cursing under his breath until he at last produced the number he wanted. Then he made a couple of calls and said, yes, it was OK, we could go and watch the *Viking* spacecraft launch themselves from Cape Canaveral to Mars in a couple of weeks' time. It was as if we were going to Mars ourselves. Here was Swan, sucking on the bosom of English studies, already playing footsie with Space Sciences, and to such results. It almost compensated her for not having been chosen by the space program; they didn't need a poet, they said, the poetry was in the spaces and would "eventuate" naturally. What piffle, we said, and so did Bunsen, but he could not sway them on that issue. Indeed, it was almost reassuring that there was something he *couldn't* rig; one had faith again in the old intransigent order as immune to mind as to courtesy. He could accomplish enough, though, and took almost creative delight in upsetting other people's plans and concepts, an astronomical combination of André Breton and Salvador Dalí. He looked like some saturnine Guatemalan *poète maudit*, with brooding dark eyes and big aquiline nose, thick hair in a butcher-boy cut riffling around his head. All he ever wore, it seemed, was a dark blue polo neck sweater and some inherited-looking khaki slacks. The essence of informality, he had a formal-sounding voice that paused elaborately in mellow, poised baritone sorties, very much a produced effect and sedately elegant. Slouched there on Swan's rented rug, he seemed more at home than when standing; as tall men do, he tended to hunch over, not wishing (in this at least) to be too far from terra firma. All we had to do was book our motel at Cocoa Beach and finagle our classes. We would be gone a week.

I had never been involved with any such thing, though it was a suitable reward for devout Shklovskians, not a lunge into outer space, but an excursion into the solar system. There already existed a block booking on the local airline, Allegheny or Mohawk as it was in those days, so we would fly down to Florida with the Coriolis contingent. Who, back in the century, had had the wit to name a university after the Coriolis effect, a fictitious force used mathematically to describe motion—I could not recall the rest, but knew it was named for a nineteenth-century French mathematician named Gaspard G. de. Naming the university after something both scientific and fictitious must have given a lift to those aesthetes and litterateurs who usually whine that science takes over everything. Imagine the cries of outrage if the university had been named for osmosis. Gravity would have been fine, for its generous ambiguity, but not ionization, in spite of Varèse's music entitled that, or surface tension. No, Coriolis, under whose auspices we would travel, had a winsome sound, could be handily abbreviated into Coriol or elongated into Coriolanus, and suggested, to my mind at least, that novelists were welcome. We felt mighty important to be going south as guest of NASA, no doubt to write something rhapsodic. That the two *Viking*s might not make it never occurred to us.

When I asked Swan why she had applied to Coriolis, she said she had no idea; I had suggested it, she told me, and, no, the university's name had had no effect on her except that it was better than Pigskin. No contest. I did not remember suggesting any such thing. True, I had heard of some people who were there, besides Bunsen, that is: an expert on F. Scott Fitzgerald, another on Joyce, an enterprising critic in Russian studies, a Wittgensteinian professor of philosophy, and so forth. The Physics Department, however, had a Nobel Prize winner, Hans Alpha, who had figured out, on a train from Coriol to Princeton, how the sun worked. Now, *he* appealed to me as no expert on Fitzgerald ever would, F. being a shallow flimsy sort of writer. Hans Alpha, whose enormous head tapered at the rear like a teardrop, knew everything; all he had ever to do was take that now nonexistent train again and figure out something else colossal. No, Bunsen would do it by seizing God's microphone, as it were, having already done something similar at Chicago by discovering a chemical called ATP, the prime energy-store for tissue. Not bad, though nobody seemed to trumpet this discovery to the skies. Perhaps if he had been on a train from Chicago to Evanston he would have reached the lumpen public. He was going to find out about Mars anyway, ever arguing the superiority for his purposes of a so-called non-man-rated mission as distinguished from one with astronauts on board. Or were they planetonauts? It was the kind of question that appealed to him. Words attracted him, as they attract many a scientist with their almost algebraic quality, the swerve of their etymology as the word wandered from one meaning to another, ever the same, yet always mutating. This, perhaps, is what had led him to take a developed interest in naming features on Venus and other planets in response to an invitation from an international astronomical body. His zeal was eventually responsible for our compiling for him lists of authors, with, we were told, an emphasis on Japanese and Chinese names. In dozens of other ways we went from the periphery to the startling center, aided and abetted by Bunsen at his most winning. To his credit, he wanted artists to cross the line and get involved with science. He also wanted scientists to cross the line too, but received many a rebuff, not least when he invited SF writers to the Coriolis campus and personally walked them over to the English Department where, he complained, they got the cold shoulder. He had every reason to feel indignant, but he never took his pique out on us; nor did we, in our miscellaneous social round, manage to make deep inroads into the ivory castle of Jane Austen and John Galsworthy. The better known he became, the less they liked him, perhaps for the usual reasons, until he began to recognize that there were indeed two cultures, as the lingo of the time put it, and ne'er the twain would meet except in people such as Swan and me, by now voluptuous zealots of space and stars, more at ease with Bunsen and his wife Nineveh, Cornet Lansberg the painter, Henri Steerforth the science writer, and Shirl Cornwall, Raoul's organizer and secretary, without whom none of us would have been able to function at all. She brought us together for him, at parties and on outings. To be sure, I was neglecting my classes back in New Jersey, but everyone assumed my reasons were sexual only.

"He's got the hots," they'd say, or so Asa Humanas told me.

"She left town and he went after her, dragging his tail." I had always been known, however, for getting out of town as often as possible. No one was being that attentive, however, or they might have noticed in my prose a documentary flavor that consorted awkwardly with fiction; the splendors of space were catching up with the freedom of action a novelist is heir to. The universe as an artifact was too splendid by far to remain a mere metaphor or a background. My head filled with an unusual mix: sex, space, and composite characters as bizarre as those populating the constellations themselves. In truth I pottered about on two campuses now, teaching on one (where my students enjoyed my tales of the hinterland to space at Coriolis) and being a sponge on the other, rapidly getting to know many more Coriolans, as I called them, than Pigskinners. My snobbery got a boost and my imagination an entirely new diet, beginning, I fondly remembered, with Stefan's Quintet. I hardly even noticed, at first, what an appalling Siberian climate Coriolis had in winter, with incessant snow from what locals, with wry distaste, called the lake effect.

The sense that you have become a hybrid being may well distress you and compromise any career you think you have. There is always a decorum of specialty, with guardians posted and spies installed. The sensation of belonging in two places, and especially to two disciplines, becomes both unnerving and intoxicating. Yet, as one scientist said, a nonscientist can go some distance while remaining a math ignoramus, but only so far: beyond that point, no progress at all. So neither Swan nor I reached the holy of holies or could fathom what two thirds of what we overheard was about. We tried, though, astounded at how far toward us these space savants were willing to go, just to share their mystery: a gesture of rapt holism. In later years, much later, I would feel some anger when one famous biologist, asked what he thought humankind's supreme achievement, answered "Science." It wasn't as simple a question as that, I thought, and this fellow did none of the predictable hesitating he might reasonably have done, over Mozart, say, Da Vinci, or Proust. He never said "Literature" or "Music," as almost any reasonable pundit might have done. In my salad days, though, I was bowled over not so much by science's analytical probing side as by its utterly developed sense of wonder, something not often brought into play in discussions of famous texts. Gradually Bunsen became Mr. Astronomy, to the displeasure of some colleagues, but he went on undaunted, crisscrossing the country to plead his cause, virtually teaching his way along the airwaves, mostly without Nineveh.

Ever since those early days of astronomical fervor, I have nonetheless worried that I am not quite the right material for so glorious an undertaking. All the others had their fixation, which meant they loved whatever happened on planets, this one included, whereas I, in whom the very mention of snow produced claustrophobia and panic, yearned always for pink sand and palm trees: a Bajan at heart. Swan, she made clear, adored all kinds of weather, just as a commodity, and most of those specialists adored it too, not in the least concerned with comfort or idyll. What I really adored was air-conditioning, an indoor Arizona, say, or a few days of Indian summer. Was there not, I thought, something hypocritical in becoming a planet freak without the least desire to live on one that did not resemble Bermuda? I escaped this dilemma by convincing myself I was a star person, and that you could never live on a star, whether red giant or white dwarf. The question was beside the point. Therefore, I thought, I was right: these planetary nympholepts really had considered the chances of being on Mars or wherever and wouldn't mind. Knowledge was more important to them than creature comforts. I was a galaxy man too, and of course no one dreamed of inhabiting such a thing as a whole. Why worry? The question was hardly likely to arise. Winter on Earth was bleak enough, certainly in and around Coriolis. I had formed a link between my reinvigorated interest in astronomy and our recent invitation to Cocoa Beach. Astronomy to me *was* tropical, a cult of pastels and warm waves, and so could not be resisted. I could never share, though, Swan's addiction to the worst of weather, during which she told herself this was climate on a planet and therefore of consuming interest. She, Bunsen, and the others had a selfless quality I perhaps aspired to, but would never have. Frozen to death almost, they rejoiced at having a weather specimen, planet-style, on their toes and hands, and almost went out of their way to expose themselves to the harshest moods of our climate, just to be able to rationalize that it was all in the interests of knowledge. I was an escapist to whom hibernation, a treasured concept, recurred again and again, even during summer and spring. What a joy it would be, in November, say, to go underground and stay, as if marooned at one of the Poles, or like a certain Canadian university I had been at, whose campus was subterranean. I had a similar loathing for extreme heat or humidity as well; in fact, my weather phobias kept them all amused while they dealt with weather as if it were some paramount work of art.

I worried about climate and my response to it because, under the spell of Shklovsky, we were essentially relearning the alphabet. Returned to square one, and obliged to integrate so much fresh knowledge with what we thought we already had by heart, we were in a sense infants, gradually assembling a new corpus of concepts, from exobiology to vulcanism. This part of our adventure I didn't mind at all, but I could see how, to be a thoroughgoing astronomer, amateur style, you had to give a lot, setting yourself up not as raw material but as generic human. You had to surrender to things planetary, acknowledging yourself as a planetary product. I could never quite rise to the magic of this, nor could I ever quite fasten to it that later cult of planetary conservation; I would always remain one to whom phrase-making meant more than planet-saving. In other words I was more aesthete than savior and, though I ranked science high, I never ranked it higher than art, though the art I ranked tops—music—might have seemed an odd choice for a novelist. In other words, my moral conscience was hardly up to scratch, and I failed to achieve the highs of outrage my fellow-planetarians did, much happier when I found some pungent phrase in Baudelaire or Rimbaud, or indeed in Delius or Barber. Thus I was compromised, a person of less than true-blue zeal, willing to let fascination lead but not to back it up with Earth-fervor. Had the winter climate in Coriolis, where I spent increasing amounts of time, been less severe, I might have been more of an Earthling. Indeed, peering through binoculars at the winter night sky was a frozen tedium I resorted to less and less, even after I hoicked our telescope Coriolis-ward, stretching my being between two places, neither of which suited me down to the ground. Cocoa Beach was the land of heart's desire, and I could hardly wait for the adventure to begin and that Mohawk jet to thunder off southward to the rocket cathedral, otherwise known as the Vehicle Assembly Building, where launch vehicles and spacecraft were mated and made suave.

My sense of trespass was delicious, akin to that from childhood when, with breath held and stomach muscles contracted, I had climbed down from the top of a wall and invaded an orchard, there to steal just a few russet apples, whose coarse corky exterior belied their internal sweetness. In the old days I might have been thrashed; after all, stealing a sheep was a capital offense, but for a few apples—what? At whose hands? Sneaking into the holy of holies of space science, whose apples were the golden apples of the moon, was that not closer to being a spy, yet a spy they wanted in? We never quite got over the generous, cordial demeanor of the scientists and technologists, who seemed only too pleased to have aliens within their midst, some people to show off their mysteries to. Their own poor welcome in Liberal Arts, thus misnamed, had not soured them, but only made them wish more eagerly for converts from the other nation. Time and again I reviewed, like an amateur general on a podium, the people from Pigskin alongside those of Coriolis, and I marveled at the kvetchy, querulous quality of the former contrasted with the abstruse, genial serenity of the latter. All this in my head made me a bit wobbly at times, most of all when I rode the Greyhound back down to New Jersey or, when I was flush after royalties had come in, the Mohawk via Philly. It was sometimes hard to know which way I was aimed, south or north, and I now and then transplanted the people of one place into the other, installing Raoul Bunsen and his Nineveh in one of Gloria Gluckstein's mortally wounding parties, where of course the majority snubbed them for being uppity and *très* (said tray) Ivy League, don't you know. Less responsibly, I grafted Gloria and her Frank onto one of the Bunsens' own dos. They had recently moved from a tiny apartment on a steep hill (comparable to Swan's own quarters) into a lavish wooden villa with a view of the lake, and this was where Rachel his mother cooked up a storm of potato pancakes, on one occasion turning to Raoul as she loaded up my plate, saying "I've read his books, he's very good. Now *there*'s somebody to take after." Faintly scolding her eminent, productive son, she was elegantly harmless, like brand-new copper wire shining in the wind, and Raoul took her comment in good part, with his customary squeeze and big, ecumenical leer. She had taught him manners, and his social deportment was flawless, especially when he introduced, always saying, with a tremendous surge of discerning affection, "And now I want you to meet this dear friend of mine," getting everyone's attention and guaranteeing goodwill. It was as if he had been saving you up for decades until the exact right occasion, and then he launched you into a social ferment that would never forget your name or face. This, I told Swan, was how he had prospered, through charm; he was a Mario Vargas Llosa with slang, I thought, as expert with folk as with planetary propaganda.

"He introduced us so nicely," Swan was saying.

"With some people," I said, "dealing with the multitude blunts and coarsens them, whereas with him it's always a joyful deployment of his collecting instinct." That made her blink, and she remembered the beguiling tale of his giving a lecture in

Philadelphia and at once converting his check at the university museum into replicas of pre-Columbian artifacts. Again and again I wondered at the openness of this crowd, mathematicians and physicists all, so glad to have a poet and a novelist among them, especially two who had read Shklovsky. "Ah, *Raoul*'s Shklovsky!" they would murmur when we told them. That must have been the key. We could hardly make erudite conversation on technical matters, but often enough our guileless enthusiasm was a sufficient base for considerate response. We picked up all manner of facts and yarns when mingling with Bunsen people. Amazing: astronomers from all over the world showed up at Raoul's and Nineveh's soirées, whisked in by magic carpet. Here was a Yorkshireman talking cricket, a subject I knew well, and it was Fred Hoyle, whom I had once heard giving the Reith lectures on the BBC. He was worried, he said, about writing novels with unattractive heroes, and we at once left cricket behind to discuss the uses of style when handling warty protagonists. I think he was just then writing *The Black Cloud* and feuding with other astronomers at Cambridge. Sometimes Isaac Asimov was there, having stepped out of a cloud, exercising his favorite lines as if they were borzois, informing the group he could recognize Jewish breasts anywhere. This was a headier orbit than that other one.

Observing Bunsen at his travail, I became a good watcher. His face often showed strain, or even pain; there was a rictus, usually followed by a well-groomed smile that quite abolished your memory of what went before. I knew he was unable to swallow much solid food and went off to his office daily on a chocolate milk shake that only Nineveh knew how to mix. There was some hernia, some spasm, obstructing him, which was why he could sometimes be seen making heavy weather of the tiniest morsel, something a canary or a bird of paradise would have devoured in seconds. One sympathized without saying anything; he liked some things to be known, but not saluted in public. He sometimes was a bit creaky too, in that he walked uneasily, perhaps trying to counterbalance that tall-man-stoop of his. Nineveh referred to him as Big Bird, mainly for his nose, which she thought resembled a beak. Her own face was smooth, dimpled, somewhat rosy, wholly given over to the smile when she smiled, and if anything a touch innocent. Sensuous and affable, she was a hugger and a kisser, the image of the wholly undemanding spouse, at least as far as we could see. She didn't seem to get much painting done, but much of her time she gave to their son Ptolemy, locally called Mike, and to Raoul's intensive social life. Backed by Shirl, indefatigable provider at life's and astronomy's feast, she ran a tight enough ship, certainly made a couple of strangers welcome and yet seemed oddly severed; she had no parents, not that one heard about, anyway, and was a devout, traditional Jew, which most of the Jews in the vicinity, Swan included, seemed not to be. At some point I began to feel I had been made an honorary Jew, which was fine by me, since I had already settled for being an honorary Hindu (a status my students conferred upon me, having listened to me too carefully). One could amass theological credentials before feeling them all slide away as one entered the next world, as my Air Force rank slipped away from me when I reentered civilian life. Besides, I needed a counterimage for Gloria Gluckstein who, genial at heart, relied too much on a brusque demeanor that gave her an edge she didn't need. I had seen this sequence in other shy people who, to fight their diffidence in public, made sudden and harsh inroads on people's feelings before they could even say hello. One quick sarcasm to the solar plexus and they were done for. The only way to retort, and fast, was in kind, with comparable asperity or a quietly tooled arrowhead of scorn. She at once construed this as a declaration of love and consanguinity; it was as if Evelyn Waugh, using ear trumpet, had proposed marriage to his hated Stephen Spender. In time we became accustomed to the belligerence in her amenity, but we wearied of having to counter it rather than simply say good evening. At Coriolis, which includes the town around it, people were utterly laid back, almost to the point of not saying hello, but instead vouchsafing a handclasp as between conspirators in front of other conspirators. The future knew us all.

It did not take long before the people who gathered at the Bunsens' house became more than partygoers; not only were we conspirators, we were a club, a phalanx, marshaled for a noble enigmatic purpose, and gradually merging into one another not so much because we had a common language (we did not) as because our faces had become the emblems of our minds. The talk was not so much scientific as general. We actually had a willing audience for chat about what *we* were working on, something that so-called humanists rarely tolerated, especially if you opened up by asking what *they* were working on and the answer had been obscure or drunken. Ask a scientist that, and the answer overflowed. Humanists, or critics, stared at you as if you had asked them for a sample of their underwear, used at that. So, we learned. Swan and I had joined a highly directed group aiming not at literary perfection, scholarly flawlessness, but at vast lumps of matter about which, in the long run, you could say something precise. Either there was water on Mars now, or there was not. Unaccustomed to such certitudes, we began to become double agents; our lives filled with vicarious thrills and our imagery, bit by bit, became tendentious. We ate and drank space.

Each day we harped on how far from our usual experience this excitement was, far from Swan's routine days with MFA work, my own classes on modern literature. The people looked different, the vocabulary was unfamiliar, the aims were grand, and the social repercussion was huge. Our emphasis on individualism, though still there from sentence to sentence in what we wrote, had given way to group fervor, the kind of thing unconsciously parodied in Soviet socialist realism's hymns to hydroelectric stations: *The Dawn of a Great Project* by Galaktionov and Agronovsky, a formulation I had discovered years ago in a Soviet propaganda magazine and memorized, just so as to have an example at hand of totalitarian vacuity. What we were involved with was more like capitalist realism (these were the good old days when NASA was not a military satellite). To watch Bunsen and his allies, their faces all calcified supremacy, was to be in touch with a new era, for which, it seemed, permission had already been given.

"Walking on water," I told Swan. "Like that."

"Prometheus stealing fire from the gods," she said, passing water by.

"What I like is, they have to imagine it all first. They just don't just reach out into space and doodle."

"All very calculating," she answered after a long poetic pause. "It would be, wouldn't it?"

"I still feel like an infidel," I said. "But I won't once it's happened. The success of the *Viking*s will somehow justify us, if you see."

She saw, but vouchsafed no comment I could use against her. Sometimes the mystery overwhelmed her, and she assumed that look of luminous discernment, aiming her mind skyward but usually only as far as a revered planet. She was working on her planetary pastoral with, even, in the Jupiter section a roving red spot that was going to drive typographers crazy—but no crazier than my own proposal once, to a publisher of mine, that a certain book should be printed on pages that ran in order through the spectrum; in other words, as after the popular mnemonic, Richard Of York Gave Battle In Vain, Red, Orange, Yellow, Green, Blue, Indigo, Violet. The first thirty pages would be red. If you flicked the entire book, the tops of the pages would generate a fused white. To say that this idea got pooh-poohed would be understatement, but I had at least tried, and now I was perched on the very lip of marvels, willing to take photographs but more than willing to imprint my mind with images just about unprecedented in human history. The grave obligation remained: to craft unforgettable sentences, if I could, but for once about something colossal yet, in a way, man-made. Something would soon be added to the universe. I remembered an old German philosopher, Professor Eucken, often quoted, who, lecturing, asked "*Was ist Geist?*" and answered himself "*Geist ist.*" Existence rather than essence, if you ask me. Swan agreed, we were safely on the way to Mars. I wondered at my effrontery in including us in the team, or was this the more-than-royal we, open to just about any hanger-on who could tell the Moon from Venus? We suffered, I supposed, from the ecstasy of premature association, wanting so much to be part of the group that we forgot how new we were to space science in the first place.

It all seemed easier and more natural when we watched Raoul Bunsen, clad in yellow swim shorts of a fabric so stiff they rattled, walk into the surf on Cocoa Beach and dive headlong into the waves, reminding ourselves that here was an astronomer who never used telescopes or made notes. Well, he took notes by holding a small tape recorder to his mouth, and that machine and he seemed to have been fused at the jaw. He even kept it in place while talking to you, which created the curious effect that he was having a conversation within a conversation. I had seen him enter the men's john with it going, and reappear urgently dictating something vital, perhaps because Pendennis Cleveland, escaped from Pigskin, had been there before him and smashed the seat. No, what we witnessed, more at Cocoa Beach than anywhere, was the unceasing activity of his mind, and, presumably, the fallibility of his memory. There was just too much to remember. I had never pictured him as a strong swimmer, though, or in any way in athletic gear.

It was most off-putting to be chatting with Bunsen only to find him switching on: you were saying something he wanted to capture, or you were boring him so much he wanted to do some dictating while you spoke. You never quite knew which; he spoke into the microphone in a secretive mumble and, presumably, had Shirl type up the tapes each night—that was why she never seemed to eat dinner with the rest of us, scurrying to please her lord and master with faultless transcription. I had never before realized the uses to which the spoken word could be put. Swan, who later came to use just such a little tape recorder, allowed as how it had its advantages: no more stubs of pencil (the kind once provided by glossy magazines that wanted you to make a checkmark in the little box that said SEND ME (far too much pencil, far too much wood massacred, for so trivial a mark). And no more greasy little notebooks to grapple with in a high wind. I would consider Bunsenizing, I said, but not yet: when I was older. I would rather learn to swim, I told her, but promptly forgot. I even on one occasion forgot I couldn't swim: out there I was with the gang in a dozen feet of water, floating easily among them, buoyed by sociability and defiance, but awed by the waves, while Swan on the beach waved frantically to me to come back. I kept still and the waves washed me ashore just like one of those empty square plastic milk bottles that adorn our shores. Bunsen was *our* coach, of course, and I should have been making notes about him for later use; but that had never been my way of doing things, I always having believed that the stuff you forget wasn't worth remembering, and the stuff that stays with you is the stuff to use, provided of course there's any at all. I responded poorly to coaches anyway.

At first I had shrunk from Bunsen lest he regale me with hubris, but Nineveh kept him sweet and spent her time watering his courtly, civil side, so even when he tape-recorded in your face he seemed to be doing you a favor. In any event, he had lovely brains; indeed, he was a brains trust in one, as willing to answer stupid elementary questions as to formulate, almost as masochistic exercise, questions nobody could answer. I liked him too because he was a late riser and unashamed of it. If he, I reasoned, could find time to snooze the morning away, with all that vied for his attention, then a novelist could afford to goof off too, awaiting inspiration or a hot cup of something. He may even be said to have rehabilitated chocolate among those who had turned against it; men, mainly, wishing to boost their brains to Bunsen level, went back to Hershey bars and risked the nicotine.

NINE

Arrival in Florida put me at once into climatic delight; one view of those clean straight roads, in this case from Orlando to Cocoa, was enough to do it. The roads were almost white, pristine-looking, and I had that old feeling of let it be a cultural wasteland as everyone said it was, it remained my weather paradise, even in summer. Besides, the ocean, having stewed for months, was shockingly warm; we had waded only minutes after checking in, and it had not made us flinch. Now it was morning, much too early for the likes of me, but the siren call of light had awakened me, so there we were again on the littoral, basking and spanieling while, some distance away, the Bunsens, holding their little son between them, dunked him like a teabag in the faint waves, exclaiming hard to reassure him as he went up and down. This family vignette heartened us no end, convincing us that the day's lectures, from nine to five, would not be too tedious; I had already missed a couple that morning, but Swan had sampled them, emerging into the sunlight with a sheaf of handouts that made the lectures redundant. What the lectures were for, I thought, was to have the astronomers all see one another, making a congregation for massive acts of faith that would ensue. Here we are was the mood: we're going to get it right, so let's go over all the preparations we have made.

It was clear that the dominant persons at this event were in the business of inventing and using a new language. Exobiology was the big in-word, but there were others such as *nitrozine* and *man-rated.* All these and many others we copied down, determined to be the first with the new space vocabulary. Imagine letting loose such words in the pampered ambit of literary criticism or aloof scholarship! This was the Ellis Island of scientific initiation, and you could easily make a fool of yourself by being no more than an invited outsider. One lecturer, a woman of severe mien and hefty spectacles, began in a monotone that belied her brains, and then advanced into a slide show that had its merits, at least until Swan nudged me and told me to watch her as best I could. There in the darkness, which she thought darker than it was, she plunged one hand inside her skirt and began to rummage around in the intimate hinterland, surely not hunting something lost (or at least not lost that afternoon) but doing her best to rectify a frontal wedgie, which resisted her, and we imagined an acre of cotton frock stranded and choking off her blood supply. It was not a moment of adjustment, there in the semi-dark, but a cautious onslaught designed to fix a chronic problem. Perhaps only in front of an audience, with slides on show, could she achieve the right blend of excitement and embarrassment. Heaven knew, she might just have been feeling herself up for the fun of it, stimulated to frenzy by the thought of two stilettos standing on their ends not far away on the Cape. Lectures, after all, were going to be fun.

So we ate in an atmosphere of refined gossip into which we ventured whenever we heard a phrase that made sense to us, picking up on an allusion and being gently invited in. After all, we were there, with nameplates saying VIP on our chests, and we had a right to eavesdrop, and then to indulge in whatever it is that follows eavesdropping: partly informed unanimity, always reminding ourselves that this was a human event, not just a technological auto-da-fé. We fueled up, then, and hurried off to the next lecture.

One speaker had an almost marsupial face while another, the

program said, played the trombone in a brass quintet at the University of Arizona. These were not specialists but Renaissance polymaths with such exotic names as Arvydas Kliore and Gerry Soffen, and you just knew that Bunsen and his friends had combed the world for geniuses. The nation as a whole had no idea what was going on at Cocoa Beach, but it was an enormous gamble, using taxpayers' money, of course, with at its highest anticipated end a revelation that we were not alone, or had not always been alone, in the solar system. I thought it worth finding out, even if the finding had only to do with water; with water there, many things could follow. Was this how Columbus and Captain Cook felt among the natives among whom they had landed? One word that circled fast among us, shining and refined, was *spacefaring;* it had the right tinge of neologism and devoutness. Something holy and historically sanctioned was going on, and we, in our marginal way, were going along with it, amazed by even the sometimes awkward preliminaries.

"Are you glad we came?" Swan seemed calmed, beatified, at peace amid the rituals and the burgers. Was this her land of heart's desire, and not Africa, Peru?

My only answer was with a voice almost disused. "We're going to miss this stuff when it's all over. It's an intellectual coronation or jubilee. I should be taking notes." There on my lap lay my yellow pad, bearing a dozen words at most, as when I was an undergraduate. I listened well, but took no notes.

En route to the Vehicle Assembly Building, which was Cape Canaveral's Cheops, we paused to inspect the steel trussed tower of a mobile service structure which, the driver said, was for sale. Even now, he said, people were bidding on it. Like some dun red oil rig trailing one black umbilical cable and two white ones, it looked forlorn, nerveless, dead, its winches dangling in the breeze that could not stir them, like kidneys in an old-style butcher's window. It belonged beside a disused railroad or in a museum of constructivist art, and I couldn't connect it intimately with rockets or blockhouse consoles, which proved only that I was not a utility pipeline. There it stood or reared, part of nothing, awaiting the dismantler, with, on the second-up of its five platforms, something rusty and inert (a bit of iron crane or parapet) that looked just like a marooned corgi dog waiting to be taken down and home.

The dog's image remained even as we arrived at the toe of the fabled VAB, plunked there next to Banana Creek like some titanic cruciform bathroom fitting overflown by vultures and equipped (as the driver said) with a gravity ventilation system that changed the air hourly lest fog or clouds formed in the vast interior. In the fill beneath this building there were pieces of historic mammoth bones (how fitting) and petrified wood 25,000 years old, resting on 4,425 steel pipe pilings which, driven to bearing on the limestone rock, went through to a salty chemical solution beneath. The VAB just might have become the biggest wet cell battery in the world; electrolysis began, and cathodic protection had to be affixed to neutralize the current and prevent the foundation from corroding. The VAB might also, had it not been settled firm, have blown over (or even away) in high winds, a Paul Bunyanesque kite; the wind-tunnel test model did.

So that a completely assembled rocket could be removed, the VAB's narrowest two sides lifted up in seven stages: seven doors that ascended one behind the other until all seven packed into the black balustrade at the top of the tapered runway that extended from the roof to the top runner of bottom leaves that parted and rolled aside. Either wall had two sets of, all told, eight doors, so the VAB had four ways in and out, twenty-eight vertical and four horizontal doors. It retracted its doors as planes their wheels, as conjurers palm cards, an open sesame of sequence that converted itself into a squat Stonehenge with four tall black slots. As our driver said, in his diffidently jubilant way, a jubilance that later wore out, some days you could see a complete rocket, mounted on a giant trestle and held rigid by a launch tower that had a hammerhead on top, being inched out for its debut, the whole assembly on the white platform of the dun-blue crawler-transporter. It was almost too much to take in in anything like a glimpse or one long steady gaze.

I had seen pictures of launch preparation, and astounding they were, as if a monolith that was troll and lighthouse in one were being spirited away by a strip-mining shovel out of which a bass groaning leaked. Ah, the macro-magic of four bulldozers in unison! The earth ached. The gulls went mad. The caterpillar engines churned. The loose Alabama Riverstone Crawlerway, about the width of the New Jersey Turnpike, creaked and spat while the rough green grass of the median went unscathed. It was an event for Jonathan Swift's Brobdingnagians, a slowness you could hardly stand, an ingenious displacement of eighteen million pounds that seemed so high, so precarious, the move evoked a Spanish religious procession in which this, the pièce de résistance, was the victim already nailed to the stake and being towed at a sadistic dawdle to where the fire would be. If a rocket on-the-move was meant to summon up images, all of which pertain yet only in part, it succeeded; but of course it was meant to do nothing of the kind, any more than the lander was. I couldn't fend off, though, overtones from half the rites in history: Ku Klux Klan; totem poles from as far apart as British Columbia and New Guinea; skyscrapers and the Eiffel Tower; wizards in conical hats and condemned men lashed to stretchers borne upright to the execution wall; the Colossus of Rhodes; Jack and the Beanstalk; druid, dust devil, and tornado. A plinthed obelisk crept away at something like the speed of Beckett's Bom who, in *How It Is*, worms his way across the intergalactic wastes at a mere ten or fifteen yards an eon. Something Mayan eased a new Simon Stylites to the brink of the solar system. Who on earth could watch unmoved, with mind unplucked-at, with imagination calm and wise?

"Right through the door, folks," called the driver, his face akin to that of "Ed" (acronym for electric dummy, the half-robot used in tests at the manned spacecraft center in Houston). Anemically impassive, he motioned at a dark slot punched in the flank of the

VAB ziggurat: a dwarf door, or so it seemed, even at a distance of only twenty yards. But I stayed put, catching a glimpse of orange-brown roof on the lowest block of the VAB. It was the color of Mediterranean walls, whereas the entire southern face, at least in that day's harsh light, was black and white, the exact color scheme of Tudor cottages. Then I noticed something else about the VAB: the western pair of upsliding doors faced only a parking lot (or what was being used as such) and a stretch of Banana Creek, whereas the other pair opened to the crawlerway. What the nearest fifty or sixty cars were parked upon didn't look at all like the groomed mineral that led to complex 39. Were the west doors, I wondered, a vertical false bottom? They concealed, as I discovered on entering, an enormous Navy balloon, yellow and finless, roped like an animal in a clamming house.

On my right, shining fit to beat the band, were *Apollo* and *Soyuz*, perched on struts: mock-ups, of course, but arrestingly frozen on the point of clinch, *Apollo* sepia, *Soyuz* white with tan solar panels extended and a bright yellow stripe on its wasp waist. They hovered in a vast granary like insects preparing to mate. You could see into the tunnel protruding from *Apollo*, and *Soyuz*'s rear end had seven symmetrically arranged holes, like a certain kind of vase. Looking upward along the blatant taper of perspective, I stared into serried arc lamps mounted on successive iron galleries reminiscent of jails. If you situated yourself so as to peer up through one of *Soyuz*'s panels, you saw yourself reflected. Every echo clanged. Light strayed in through high glass crisscrossed with girders whose pattern reappeared on each gallery, much enlarged. End toward us, the big balloon had dark seams that furnished it with lines of latitude and a polar circle. Except for a triangular green patch over what otherwise might have been Greenland, or Ford Range if you were geocentric, Thule I or Ortygia if you doted on Mars. A gymnasium for Atlas, this, with props to match, ponderable only in the presence of mild guards who might have been waiting all their lives for just such a job to come along. I was glad to reenter the fog outside, where I strolled fifty yards to look into the five nozzles of a discarded Saturn V at rest like a giant rolling pin, in each of which I could stand up, from each of which an F-1 engine vented 1.5 million pounds of thrust made by mixing kerosene with liquid oxygen. I heard the thunder in that tunnel assembled by Boeing in New Orleans: a shell caching a sea on fire. Then I found I had no idea which bus of six or seven was ours, aboard which, as instructed, I would keep on sitting in the same seat once I had located it.

The launch control center was connected to the VAB by a corridor six floors above ground, but the tour omitted it, so I missed making corroborations I hardly needed. "Not so much a building as an almost living brain," as Max Urbahn described it, the LCC had huge louver-like windows in the east wall, through which the firing crews could watch the liftoff (whereas inside the old-style blockhouses they saw it only via periscope or closed-circuit TV). It looked like a brand-new bank or an ultra-white contemporary sideboard with concertina drawers.

Ink-black clouds had gathered above the VAB, whereas over the sea the sky was total blue. Sprinting to the Vega as outsize raindrops began to fall, I realized I hadn't seen the piece of lunar rock on display inside, but I passed it up. I would be back, but without notebook. Meanwhile I was glad to be dry in the clammy vinyl interior of a car named after one of the stars that make up the summer triangle, so called, which makes the night sky less blank than the sight and sound of the VAB—that drab slab of a lab—itself.

I had not been long at Cocoa Beach, but I had begun to resent the amount of the daily round given over to astronomy, and I began arguing, to myself at first, that nobody on the premises was paying any attention to the novel, or gave any sign of ever having done so. I resolved to force the novel—its past, its present, its prospects—into every *Viking*-oriented conversation, to utterly futile results. No one even knew what it was: a new kind of accumulator battery, maybe, or something to weed the garden with. I began to wonder about such things as Was there more money invested in the novel than in the *Vikings*? I had no idea, but I knew the *Vikings* weren't supposed to make a profit, their purpose being knowledge for its own sake. Anything that altruistic would make most publishers vomit, of course, as anyone who has negotiated a contract knows. Truth told, the smartest minds among the astronomers were hoping that someone would eventually write about them and their machines some kind of a book. We novelists were so self-important, or so impoverished, we could not resist.

So I switched from gratitude to NASA for having invited us along to what would conceivably become one of the high points of the century, technologically speaking, to the usual old resentment felt by the artist in the commercial, materialistic world. Poets felt these emotions more keenly than novelists, but Swan had taken care not to feel the predicted way; she was willing to go along, not dig up old hatreds.

I badly needed diversion, which was forthcoming; it is possible to move into a place and easily miss its peculiar excitements just because you are new and uninitiated, rather like a beetle crawling over the convexity of a safety helmet worn by a roadhog motor biker. You do not have to burrow but only be swept from the surface by a genial wind, and then you are in the underneath, catered to and regaled, as happy with your lot as a child with a sandcastle and a gallon of slop.

"Divert me," I said to her.

"My, you're a bloody handful today," she answered, not at all disposed to play into my hands.

"*You* used to be called the camp clown."

"Only at camp," she said, "and this is not camp. Why don't you go and enjoy the pool?" I couldn't swim, which restricted me somewhat; and, in the pool when I pretended to swim, people could see my feet or my knees on the bottom. I was just a fraud asking for a fraud's succor.

"All these astronomers," I said incompletely.

"Oh, they're not that bad. At least they come up with results." They did, so perhaps that was what converted their joie de vivre into learned euphoria. The far end of their endeavors was not a book but footsteps on a barren planet or the discovery of water in a place nobody could get to.

"Oh," I said, "it's just—well, it's just that I don't always feel at home among them."

"You don't feel at home anywhere," said this paragon of sweetness and light, of devoted sympathy. "Why don't we just agree that you're a bit out of sorts because you haven't been able to write while you've been here. You didn't *come* here to write." It was like teasing the Supreme Court; she so rational I couldn't stand it. Then she drew my attention to the evening's dinner, at a special place, where some fun might be had watching astronomers at play. My mood wilted, then became sunnier. Perhaps all I wanted was distraction after all.

Sure enough, our dinner group met at Bernard's Surf, a seafood Mecca where you could purchase photocopies of a Russian-English menu autographed by the *Apollo-Soyuz* crews (the one-dollar fee went to Cape Canaveral Hospital) and pick up free postcards of a back-toward-you nude brunette out of whose right shoulder limped a handwritten message in cochineal or blood: "You can meet me at"—your eyes descended an inch or two—"BERNARD'S SURF," which was scrawled on the side of the bed she graced. Clad in blue gym tunics and white blouses, rather like fugitives from the farcical movie *The Pure Hell of St. Trinian's*, the waitresses did indeed look like British schoolgirls with oldish faces from among the twenty-year-olds imitating thirteens in that semi-gruesome frolic. As the swing door opened up to the kitchen, you saw full heads of peroxide hair, like dandelions gone to seed and ready to blow. The entire place had a fetching hint of sin. Tempted in a fit of gourmet preciosity to name it Le Surf de Bernard (Bairnah), I refrained, instead helping myself to souvenirs that would bring Bairnah back to me, to eye and ear, when I was a thousand miles farther north among the pell-mell waiters of the Newark Airport Hotel. The menus measured forty-four inches by twenty-nine opened up and could safely be hidden behind whether you were naked or not. I have one by me and I measured it.

"Let's," said Bunsen, roguishly excited, "have dinner here every night! This place is great." We needed no tempting. I looked at him again, seeing a face beneath his public face, sensing I knew him better than I used to, or ever thought I would. If you opened up *The Encyclopedia of Aviation and Space Sciences* (an ambiguous title), Volume 11, there between Bumper Project and Buoyancy you found a black-and-white version of his head, complete with crew cut, Captain Marvel jaw, and on-cue ingenuous, healthy grin. In the flesh, however, he was a charismatic dark owl, in the evenings especially. Observed close, he could be several men in a space of seconds: a dourly Byronic hussar who might just have ridden out of the sea to meet Boris Karloff on the palsied shore of a horror island; a would-be renaissance polymath who was a patron of the arts without ever being patronizing to their practitioners (if you got a bit of science wrong, he let you down with the lightest of bumps); and an ebullient visionary who, dubbed an electromagnetic chauvinist by callow adversaries, welcomed news from responsible adventurers of all kinds, but (in those days—later he changed) never from churches.

Detritus, pronounced *dee-TRY-tuss*, was one of his favorite words, uttered with an antic leer as if it stood for a vile abomination or for what he left on plates after, as was usual with him, picking at his food while talking. He never ate much, even when hungry. He ferried us to and fro in a white rented Ford LTD atop whose hood was a streamlined chrome gunsight which, I told him, was a tool for extracting stones from the hooves of Rolls-Royces. Now I the camp clown. He laughed, descanting into a brief giggle.

As he toyed with a lobster and a roll (both frail specimens culled from an asteroid) he seemed his concisest, most frequent self: Copernicus turned Gatsby, or the Zapata of Arecibo. As he rose to visit the men's room, he walked with the same alternating lope, balanced by his raised long arms. Such was the host, a connoisseur of human variety.

"Some of your best responses in the *Oui* interview," someone is saying, "were backed by a glossy nude's labia. How perverse of the obverse." A sceptical look from Bunsen implied *which* labia? He loathed vagueness. But he did not ask, instead seeming to wonder if anyone could supply the source of a certain quotation I did not hear. Maarten without a pause cited Lewis Carroll's "The Lobster Quadrille"; Mrs. Maarten agreed, and I began to think that everyone at MIT knew Lewis Carroll by heart (Edward Lear as well): festive icing on the sponge cake of deep thought. It was odd that academics, scientific or otherwise, were mostly familiar with the same books, the same music: Mozart, Beethoven, Schubert, Brahms, and so forth, without ever knowing any Scriabin, Delius, Harris, Cowell, Walton, Finzi, Bridge. They knew what they called the classics, which struck me as inconsistent with their zeal to teach the latest twentieth-century books or the latest discoveries in science. Their initiative stopped at 1900, at least as far as the so-called classics were concerned, the sad thing being that they had omitted more than half a century of music and literature. These neophiliacs had stodgy taste, had in their record cabinets no Stravinsky, Hindemith, or Vaughan Williams, having as it were used up their quota of musical interest. And when scientists heard the kind of music I doted on, I being an eclectic amateur devoted to works of the twentieth century, they were amazed, they had no idea that such music existed. Or was allowed to do so. Possibly life is too short for a rounded taste to form, certainly in those teaching the young, but I had heard the theory that it was always those on the cutting edge, in the arts and the sciences, the busiest minds on the planet, who also tuned in to the newest and passed it on to others. Those who have no time for taste have all the taste: thus the maxim as I reconstrued it. I enjoyed our dinners at the Surf because there was scope for the nonspecialist and astronomy no longer ruled the roost.

Now Maarten seemed to be saying "Kansas was stranger than I was." It sounded like an inspired comparison, coming from one of the men who had armed the Fat Man bomb, in spite of his having been crippled by polio. Certain caricatures by Peter Sellers were said to have been based on Maarten's hampered gait. Then I realized that he had said, not "I was," but "Oz." Of course. When, earlier, I had ordered a dry sherry on the rocks, Maarten had looked at me hard, amusedly computing what would be in it and what it would do to my innards, all in precise chemical detail; but he said not a word, given over to the spirit of quizzicality for its own sake. I wondered if the eyes of people accustomed to doing spectral analysis transcended the faces of those around them, seeing through them, recognizing us by some such thing as a sodium line.

Compared to her husband, Nineveh Bunsen was almost staid (she sometimes wore a watch; she drove a Volkswagen, not an orange Porsche with Phobos lettered on the front plate by some bewildered convict in California, which was why she kept her front plate while Raoul kept losing his to souvenir-hunting students at Coriolis, who nailed it to the dorm wall and no doubt muttered incantations to Mars's future). Nineveh watched each evening's doings with even-tempered hazel eyes, contributing thoughtful voluntaries on all the things she was into: politics, espionage, child psychology, and, most of all, photography, painting, and moviemaking. She teased Raoul, sometimes delicately, sometimes with the vehement indignation that accompanies ownership, especially when she felt he had caricatured one of her opinions by overapplying logic to a matter of sympathy or hunch. It had been she who drew the two naked human figures which, along with a schematic version of their spatial whereabouts, occupied half of the gold-anodized aluminum plaques affixed to the antenna support struts of *Pioneers* 10 and 11.

Aimed past Jupiter toward a point between Taurus and Orion, these two earlier spacecraft would not encounter another planetary system for ten billion years, if then. So Nineveh was the first human artist whose work had left the solar system, and then at seven miles per second, going ever deeper into space. She had signed the void and so had a special place in history. Creator of an artifact that would endure for hundreds of millions of years, and probably much longer, she revealed no signs of immortal longings, her main regret being that the design had been a rush job (only three weeks elapsing between the initial presentation of the idea to NASA and the actual engraving process).

Since then, as Raoul said in one of his books, the plaque had been pirated by an engraving company, a distributor of scientific knickknacks, a manufacturer of tapestry, and an Italian mint specializing in silver ingots. It had turned up in graffiti all over the world and must surely be, as well as perdurable in space, famous on Earth, something between Kilroy and the *Mona Lisa.* Copying her male and female from Greek sculptures and drawings by Leonardo da Vinci, Nineveh ran into a cold front of criticism (or at least her figures did): the woman was too passive, it was said, and lacked external genitalia, whereas the man's were complete (although *The Chicago Sun-Times* reproduced three versions on one day—intact, castrated, degenitaled altogether).

"Do-it-yourself mutilation," Nineveh said, looking back on events with the languid smile of one who had fed well, one who had surfed at Bernard's.

"It all makes you wonder," Raoul added, since this had become the subject of the table's talk, "what experience they've had of humans anyway. Blindfolded, maybe."

"Ah, brothels," someone said.

"And secret societies," Raoul added. Nineveh, drawing something on a cocktail napkin, declined to show it. Perhaps she was revising or getting in some practice.

"Both figures," Raoul was saying as he warmed to this well-tried topic yet again, "as well as being generic in a received exoteric mode, were meant to be panracial, if you can say panracial. I see from your expression that we can't." Now he stared right through me. "The woman partly Asian, the man partly African. In the shuffle, though, between final original sketches and final engraving, the woman's hair, shown only in outline, seemed blond, thus making her more Caucasian than intended, while the man's hair, designed as a short Afro, became a Mediterranean shortish back and sides. Thus Caucasianizing him as well." Where, recently, had he said this? It sounded so groomed, so pat.

A more daring creation of Nineveh's, drawn at Raoul's request as part of an experiment to see ourselves as others see us, was a unicorn constellation as seen from a planet of Tau Ceti (just over eleven light-years from the Sun). This beast trotted on two sets of three legs each and sported, sports, at the root of its tail a fourth-magnitude star that happened to be our Sun. The neo-Unicorn's horn was scimitar-shaped, so long in fact as almost to prevent its feeding on anything at hoof-level. "Ah," Raoul said, "it grazes on stars like a giraffe." And it galloped thus: first the two pairs of outside legs went forward, then the two middle legs, at which stage Nineveh's unicorn was as precariously balanced as a hobbyhorse.

Nineveh looked brown-haired to me (who am somewhat color-blind), fairer-haired to others, a shorter Ingrid Bergman, with the same finely modeled nose, whereas Swan looks Persian or Greek, has all that thick black hair, bushbaby eyes, and elegant expressive hands that are rarely still. Swan sits neatly, very ladylike, and at the Surf larded her rapid talk with explosive puns, from Oedipus solving the riddle of the Sphincter to the French novelist, Raymond Queneau, who became a Queneaupener. The word *palindrome*, she claimed, ought to be one itself, like Aga or "A man, a plan, a canal, Panama."

Whatever she was doing, Swan kept in touch with a sophisticated Babel of her own, quite different from mine, in which all the ambiguities of language sought one another out like Doppelgängers at some wailing wall of sense. Word-play suggests but hardly covers what she did, especially when she began an impromptu readout beginning with *barium* and *radium* extracted from Rimbaud, continuing through Rimbaudelaire and Rimbaudelaire-de-lune, and so on this occasion asking the oblivious waitress, who slunk through the gloom like a coquettish panther, "Do you honor American Excrescence cards here?" They did, the waitress said. Under Swan's onslaught; no, too fierce; lovingly stirred by her, the former camp clown, language didn't then, doesn't now, so much disintegrate—though it briefly comes close—as come more closely together around its nucleus. New combinations flow; old ones die natural but sudden deaths; and there she is, like someone handling supercritical helium with her bare hands, at table or wherever, creating in her *bon mot* continuum a metaphor for scalding open-mindedness.

The same back then as now, in this year of grace, the time I am writing in. Our oral lives (in the verbal domain, that is) have always been two interacting Niagaras, opaque and weird to overhearers. There have been no major changes other than what she has added, which I will come to. At Bernard's Surf she gave an adequate sample of her word-hoard, to which the hinterland even then was a host of tenderly guarded and regarded codewords and idiomatic privacies, such as, when she enters the house with the usual armful of the day's mail, she calls "Post Trout," being the trout who has brought in the post. A jubilant, helpful sound, that. I spring from what I am doing and devour the day's incoming. Similarly, depending on what you are carrying, you can be the Coffee Trout, the Bagel Trout, and so on, not that trout are known for their carrying capacity or even for their ability to reduce the portion of daily inconvenience. It just happens to be so. The trout happens to be the epitome-personification of the helpful other, as does the Broadway formula of Tea-Horse of the Augúst Moon, maybe a nimble filly bearing a teapot short and stout down the hallway on a summer night. I don't see how a civilized household that cherishes intimacy can function without these playful oddities, which firm the bond and widen the spectrum of sounds, though what a stranger would make of the little chiming Babel that includes the trout-horse, a certain harvest mouse, the kissel-panther, and (an allusion to one of my novels) the Rat Man (whose only household chore is to replace the plastic liner in the trashcan in her bathroom), I have no idea. Even divulging such a bestiary in the wake of Bernard's Surf must baffle some readers, who may well complain: Why don't they use everyday language, with which they come well supplied? Our creative energy takes its toll of commonplace formulas, making simplicity complex, latching on to the very things that keep other people sane and gussying them up until the mere Adamic act of naming has become choosy bedlam. We love it, indeed are not that conscious of its being different from what other people say since we don't eavesdrop on them any more than they on us, except through books. Was it true that Picasso would paint his penis like a barber's pole and then go sit in the garden with it exposed, waiting for it to be stung? Rituals, these, useless to anyone else, but, to their perpetrators, the gold leaf of tenderness and intimacy; never or rarely revised, they outlive their intoners and then sink into disuse like an exhausted art-form. You would never use them with someone new. Of course. Let it be said that, in and around our regular tables at Bernard's Surf, privacies leaked into the open and beguiled at least this diner. Ours were the only ones that slipped into view, perhaps not even recognized as such, and I wondered at the self-control, the self-proctoring of the other people, dealing with the public world in terms of only the public world. Their most intimate ways were sealed off, I supposed, whereas ours were porous, even in that early phase of living together. The longer you cohabited, the more porous they became because you had begun to think them impervious and unseen.

Of course our fellow diners had never heard the squeaks and warbles with which we populated that tiny apartment on Spencer Road; there is a menagerie streak in all of us, but we two had really learned to exploit it, working at all manner of gradations, with a separate sound for pleading, huff, anger, sympathy, pique, each recognizable by the other. Why, with so many words at our disposal, we needed noises, I will never know, but it must have something to do with our hunting for something nonverbal the instant we stop work for the day—the worst Late Late Show, perhaps, the tackiest ice-skating on repeat. Perhaps we were falling in line with various doctrines about biodiversity, harking back to the mental sets of distant ancestors, as all modern people do. That is why we want a lawn, "a nice view," a balcony facing water. Just about the only TV commercial I could abide showed a man having a tropical dream with a buttocky female who purred alongside him on some glorious platform in the sun. "Pinch me," he murmured; she did, and he began shrieking because the pinch restored him to a room full of cubicles and boxes, no doubt in midwinter Cleveland, with no windows, and certainly Minnesota-type black ice outside. We long for an inward pastoral and will accept an external one in lieu. Once, when I almost accepted a job in Boston, a friend who lived there said uncomprehendingly "What? Are you sick of trees?" I could almost make the case for our encoded privacies being versions of interior pastoral, into which, amid which, to sink and repine. We took possession of conventional language too, calling *asparagus aspar-Á-gus*, saying *beautely* for *beauty*, *garbaggiones* for *garbage*, and Rent-A-Fuck ever after first misreading Rent-A-Flick from a distance at an angle. Legs were *legumes.* As I squeezed past her in the kitchen, she would "present" her rear for a tender pat or "potch." For her birthday or Valentine's Day I would make for her "floppy" greeting cards crowded with soft, warped planes that had long, beanstalky legs. To cool out, she lay on the couch with her feet toward me and I separated her toes, again and again, my mind sometimes on how the passage of time split the plastic cleats on the underside of toilet seats.

To say or do these unheard-of things, with loving brio, gave us a caricatural version of serious creativity, loosened us up, and somehow braced us for the hard graft of the morrow. In some less tolerant or heedful society, the thought police would have arrested us for oral graffiti, or worse; but we only sauntered off into miniature delirium because we knew we could always come back. Childish by-play filled up the well for us. How lucky we felt, each, to have found someone else with the same reckless mental habits. What we said in our off-moments was, too, the argot of love, improvised then sealed with a kiss, conjured at and floated into our private atmosphere with the faintest effort.

TEN

As I sat there, delighted by wit, but less than entranced by astronomical shoptalk, I began to feel something else, almost a form of pleasure, but more a recognition of something beyond: a pressure, a tug, an onus, all reassuring me that everything was all right, that I was responding to the visible end of something altogether more magnificent. How can a more or less rational person deal with such a sensation? A parallel experience would have been that, much as I took pleasure in literature, there was something allied to it but previous that surpassed it. What, then? What could possibly arrive, if it were going to arrive, unless say the beginning of literature by aliens, all translated and adapted for our consumption? Maybe alien literature, if any, would be no better than Arnold Bennett and John Galsworthy, Sir Philip Sidney and Rudyard Kipling. Just because they were sensational at math didn't mean they were good at art, not at our kind anyway. I, though I had used the genetic code as framework in a book of my own, shuddered at the thought of the novel of calculus. It was so depressing. What, then, was there beyond astronomy and wit? Something heaving into my presence had begun to please me, perhaps only an acknowledgment that the universe was full of wonders, that there were many things no astronomer could possibly discover. I was willing to believe that, but I wasn't willing to talk about it. What I had decided to name the riviera of the visible world was invisible, a poor thing to be brooding about. If it were invisible, why did it please so much? Or why had it begun to do so? A lonely trekker through the woods might sense the presence of a grizzly that kept pace with him as he advanced, but would that give him pleasure? Perhaps all I had done was hit on the theory of the double again; what I felt was just not company, but a thorough sense of joy that incalculable resplendence surrounded us—not just in the exquisite details of nature from bombardier beetle to earthworm, from kingfisher to eagle; all that was the visible world, open to any assiduous contemplative, especially one with an electron microscope. What was lifting and fortifying me at Bernard's Surf was nebulous, maybe even an impression without an impressor, with the whole thing cooked up involuntarily in my own mind, Wordsworth-style. *He* sensed a mighty being (or Mighty Being) behind everything, but I was going through something else. Without being in the least attentive or transcendent, I was receiving a huge billow of reassurance from somewhere, far beyond *Viking*s and local planets. Was it merely a gourmandise of good cheer or an extension of my feelings about Swan, whose perfect manners and genial openness had won everyone over: nothing cantankerous in her, nothing kvetchy or unruly. More agitated than she most of the time (maybe the novelist's fidget), I was perhaps entitled to encouragement that told me something glamorous, exotic, ineffable coiled around and above us. I had heard that, at writers' conferences, it was the poets who got up early while the novelists slept till noon, where I would have thought it was the other way around. What prompted poets to fit the copybook maxims and novelists to act up? I had no idea if my sudden awareness of the riviera was mine alone or if hundreds were aware of it. Was it mystical? Not really, though metaphors for it would have been an abrupt rise in temperature, a slackening in the breeze, a slight almost obtuse variation in colors, with all blues gone greener, all pinks redder. I felt uneasy but unfrightened. Were we simply being invigilated and was I feeling the abstruse warmth of that cosmic glance? There I was, troughing and gabbing, my mind slowly being made to respond to a different drummer no doubt having nothing to do with planetary science and rockets. *Viking* was merely the occasion for this acute, overwhelming—I paused for the right word, starting with *impetus*, ending with *glow*.

"What's going on?" I asked the table at large, provoking merriment at my baffled, imprecise face. They could tell I had been out of it, as we say, and still had not come back, so no one answered, leaving it to me to glean what I could from their expressions. It would have all been more plausible if I had been listening to music, not Holst, say, or even Harris, but Finzi or Vaughan Williams, those ace manipulators of unknown regions and immortal intimations. Under the spell of certain music, one might imagine anything, but the only music at the time was the not so subdued soft rock dished out by Bernard's Surf: a bankrupt, drumbeaten whine all of whose words were lost. No, this cloud of unknowing had not come from the heart of local syncopation.

"What's wrong?" Swan was looking worried, no doubt because I seemed like a man who'd had a mild stroke. I was confounded, dumbfounded, flummoxed, but by what?

"Everything's fine," I answered, thinking I might have said hunky-dory, whatever that meant, and lamenting the fewness of phrases we have for something as complex and intractable as what I'd experienced. It was almost as if the dismal formulae of a newspaper death notice had filled in with glorious life-forms, from *Passed away suddenly* to *Predeceased by* and *Leaving to mourn* to *Resting at ———'s Funeral Home.* Radiant and tender vines like blood vessels wound their way through these phrases and gave them uncanny life. That was one way of putting it. Another version, homely as bread-and-butter on a plate, was to say that, in the bathroom, on top of the toilet tank, there sat a brush, a comb, a tube of toothpaste, a roll of dental floss, and a pumice heel buffer, at peace and passive as objects can be (whereas if you fill a tray with marbles, some of them are actually in minor motion), the trouble being that, as a household initiate would know, these objects were skeined together by long Swan hairs that clung to the brush. Move the brush or the comb and you would disarrange all the other things as long hairs tugged at them. The barely seen ruled the roost quite without intending to. All I had encountered, then, was an increased connectedness of things, hardly worth the price of admission when you had read authors who claimed that, if you bit into a persimmon in Nantucket, the teeth of a beggar in Katmandu were put on edge. Something such. I let my new-minted simile fade away, one of the many called, none of the chosen. Some writers, Chaucer included, had written of a day of unusual heat, and that might have served better, although hardly in Florida; *that* image, to be suasive, had to live in a cooler clime. In the end, while struggling to recover my poise in front of a dozen decreasingly interested diners, I went back to my invisible riviera and the visible world opposing it, doubtful about the gaudy connotations of riviera (too flashy, too glitzy?), yet unable to come up with anything better. Perhaps my idea of riviera was wrong to begin with: uninspected, parochial, not even etymologically appropriate. All I knew was that the sensation causing all this furor in my mind had not gone away but curled, a sublime coverlet, about me, hemming me in with delicious cabinetry—drawers and cupboards for everything, alcoves and cubbyholes. There would be always more space than I needed, never mind how much I jammed into the openings. The mystics of old would have made short work of such an image, as too mundane, too humdrum, but perhaps not—the more mundane, humdrum, the image the vaster the disproportion between the vision and its token. The essence of capture was the incommensurate, as when, in much more minor affairs, one says *compare to* when things are truly out of proportion to one another, and *compare with* when they seem truly comparable. I wonder, though, if the indiscriminate use nowadays of both terms doesn't reveal that people no longer feel any need to worry about decorum of comparisons. That little switch from *to* to *with*, clue to a person's adroit discernment, has gone by the board, and for the life of me I do not know which has the upper hand in the speech of our day.

From the ridiculous to the sublime: so the phrase might go, although it's usually the other way around; a descent is always preferable, it seems. We like to achieve the heights first. Those days at Cocoa Beach, on the fringe of a big adventure, took their toll of language in many ways, not least because witnesses arrived unable to express the wonder of what was going on. The word *sublime* evoked science itself, for us at least, in our semi-initiated way. Even ice sublimed, we told ourselves, and snow; which was to say that, when other factors were absent, such as thawing, both would to some degree sublime, i.e., go to nothing. Certain molecules went to nothing, and that was that. Intent upon such processes, we felt like experts, knowing not only that the sublime came from a verb *to raise*, hence all those lofty concepts: grand, majestic, noble, supreme, impressive, awesome, and so forth, while the scientific version meant to make a solid or a gas change state without becoming a liquid. Poof, and it was gone. Mastering (as we thought) both senses of the overused word, we felt even-handed, balanced, doing justice to both sides of our ambiguous heritage. All we asked was that the *Viking*s would not themselves sublime, leaving only, as the poet said, the air signed with their honor.

Swan and I were not entirely at one about science, as is no doubt obvious. For her, composing a suite of poems about the planets was the conceptual big league, and I did not think she had set up the ultimate tournament—art versus science—in her head. I, on the other hand, saw science, still do, as yet another human circus; eager to know and profit from the latest in cardiology, but ever on the watch for a brilliant phrase, in comparison with which something like the discovery of penicillin faded into another category altogether. Penicillin was always there, lurking in the planetary woodwork, whereas such a line as Shakespeare's "Keep up your bright swords, for the dew will rust them" came into being on the spur of the moment. On the sperm of the moment, as we sometimes said. Always, then, the difference between A and B nagged away at me: scientific finds were always there in the texture of nature, needing only to be found, whereas superb phrases were never anywhere save in the dictionary, and their creation was as much mathematical as anything. This distinction did not bother Swan, not then, not now, and she a conspicuous phrasemaker. Certainly she was more hospitable to the myth of a scientist as a supreme being, she more of a Frankensteinian than I, I more of a technology-lover (airplane engines, for example) than she. Perhaps that was just a boy's preference. I was open to the romance of science, as to the romance of language, knowing there were people who believed in what they called the well of English undefiled, whatever that meant (no foreign words, no loan words, maybe), whereas the truth about English was the well of English *long* defiled: the most mongrel lingo of them all.

Such no doubt extraneous factors as these entered into our regard for astronomy as it was being practiced on the nerves at Cocoa Beach. This, for once, was not some highbrow mathematical game played without telescopes; here the hardware was on view, and predominated, so the erector-set side of our mentality came to the fore and was recognized. Had it all been, like so much of Bunsen's science, done with computers, we might never have taken an interest at all. I wasn't sure, knowing that he with others had actually reproduced the primordial soup from which the planet had evolved, once lightning had struck the mixture. You could actually drop croutons into that stuff and slurp it. How abstract was that? The soup had come through pipes and tubing in the laboratory, ending up in a dish, so it qualified as hands-on science akin to what I had practiced with my chemistry set as a child. No doubt of it, we were amateurs, I more of a technologist, more of an aesthete, than she, whereas Swan trusted them more, the savants, perhaps out of some suppressed religious impulse. I was as interested in their social antics as in their discoveries, which only proves that the novelist at heart remains a novelist at heart, eager ever for the social caper, the domestic stance (how do they comb their hair? how do they eat their peas?). I don't think our newfound pals the scientists found our brain-patterns half as interesting as we found theirs. True, now and then they seemed thunderstruck to have a poet and a novelist among them, saying and writing wild things, and there was that brief moment of Columbus-like astonishment, after which they got on with their work. They saw us, alas, as hobbyists dealing with the arbitrary, not with the Nature-given, though you could make a case that a great sonnet was as much Nature-given as penicillin. Nothing, I argued, sometimes quite strenuously, comes out of nothing; only the universe did that. Nothing else is underived, hence all Creation is derivative. Shakespeare's plays did not exist until he invented them, unlike sulfur, cork, and salt. Yet even the word *invent* troubled me since it used to mean, in the Latin, to stumble upon something, to happen upon it, a far cry or a mean stoop from its modern meaning of devise from the outset as completely new. In a sense the word's history epitomized what concerned me: old sense—science; new sense—art.

What any of this had to do with some of our behavior, I had no idea. Quite often, after we had encountered the superb double star in Cygnus (to her topaz yellow and sapphire blue, to me golden and azure), we would improvisationally say to each other on parting, or going to sleep, "Albireo" instead of "Arrivederci" or "Arrivederla," responding to the star's sound, best almost sung with a long sustained RAY on the third syllable. Thus, even as appropriated and borrowed, we used the nomenclature of science, though it would be more accurate to say we started using Arabic, like the skygazers of old. Some of those old words really got us going, from Zubeneschamali to Alnilam, Alnitak, and Mintaka, the three stars in Orion's Belt. Swan had even concocted a jazzy song that began "Zubeneschamali, you've got me on the go," but it died out, and she never sang it to our friendly astronomers at Cocoa Beach. Instead of numbers, the more common modern practice, these stars' names had meanings, and I must confess this fact appealed to the anthropomorphic side of me (maybe the anthropomorbid too), and I formed the habit of drawing the constellations so as to apply to them the original meanings of the names therein. This was at least a change from Greek myth. We had acquired a book, new at the time, about star-names and their meaning, and this I devoured, getting a whole new slant on those join-the-dot exercises in the sky. It impressed me no end that the Milky Way had also been Watling Street, the River of Heaven, the Dove of Paradise, the Silver River, the Milky Footpath, the Path of Noah's Ark, the Path of the Snake, Bil-Idun's Way, Winter Street, the Straw Stalks Lying in the Road, and, perhaps best of all, from Polynesia, the Long, Blue, Cloud-Eating Shark. I wondered, of this last, if those awestruck Polynesians had used the same commas as the book we had. All I had to do was recite this list of names, by no means a complete one, and the bewildered men of yesteryear would come before me, racking their brains and their word-hoards in an almost vain attempt to domesticate that huge splash in the sky, gradually recognizing that naming, though dictatorial, had no impact on the recipient any more than with newborn children. Seeking to warm up, personify, an uncaring pattern in the heavens was no small enterprise, and I wondered if the most alert of those forebears had not wondered about the futility of being underneath the big show, doomed to an impotent mind-game while the component stars went about their appointed business. To mitigate their indifference only drove you back upon yourself, converting burly Orion, say, into a tricky hodgepodge of Giant, Golden Nuts, Snake, Pearls, Barley God, Stag, the Armpit of the Central One *(Ibt al Jauzah)*, the Left Leg of the Jauzah, the Roaring Lion, the Belt, the Pearls, the Girdle. Like anyone else of my careless but honest generation, I cite these from memory, awed by the resolve of the ancients to make sense of everything, even if, over the centuries, non-sense piled up on non-sense, and nobody apparently came into the open and challenged the notion that a star was obliged, anecdotally or figuratively, to make sense, or to mean anything. We could not take the stars or their con-stellings as *it*s or *ont*s. Thereby always had to hang a tale, some of which ended up as literature. After all, literature had to derive from something, and why not?

ELEVEN

I always thought women had a more processive view of life than men; they had an in-built respect for life as a process whereas we men saw it mainly as a visitation, a permanent dirty weekend. To this idea I had held on with the kind of honorable bigotry we bring to what serves but is not quite good enough. Men, I thought, or allowed myself to think, were always in the act of discovering what women took for granted. *They* made no fuss about discovering the invisible riviera, which for them was no doubt implanted in a placenta, cached away in a used sanitary pad. Hence their lack of pomposity, I supposed. It was one thing to be the sperm-bearing visitant, but through that particular prism one was apt to see the universe askew, although I sometimes wondered if Earth had indeed been populated by directed panspermia: a well-aimed ejaculation floating through the vacuum of space until implanted. In that case, men were not far, in procedural method, from the universe itself. Was it Hoyle, when I met him, who confessed to beginning to think along those lines, or was he then still a proponent of steady state? For him for a long time the universe had had no beginning, no end, no cause, almost like one of those malfunctioning toilets that flush for days. Anyway, I told myself I was groping after what women took for granted, and that was why Swan took all the astronomy in her stride (no levity intended).

"Oh," she said, "don't forget you're a guest, and all these smart guys are the hosts. They're not here to celebrate *you*, they're here to launch rockets. Albirayo." She was gone, to some puffing lecture I had decided to skip. Where would we be without the blunt factuality of women who, once they have established the fulcrum of an event, insist on it until the cows come home. Once they have the rules in their pocket, they know how to beat us poor stags into submission. She was going to behave like the perfect guest, and I was going to be a true *Ausländer*, a person from beyond the pale.

She was full of curiosity and wonder, her birthright.

Everything amazed her and must be relayed to others.

Yet the old green-eyed demon of jealousy was rearing his head from underneath the eiderdown. It was much better to be guest of honor than merely a guest, wasn't it? I stewed so much that I dressed up, at least wore a blazer, and trudged off to the latest hypotheses about water on Mars, envisioning a red pissoir devoted to astronomers with roving eyes. I should have stayed put, watching *Combat;* the lecturer did not even grope himself in the dark when showing slides. I could not even see Swan in the lecture hall, so what was she doing? Where had she gone? It was unlike her to walk out on even the most boring speaker, so she must be present. I looked and looked, but not even the lights revealed her, though I found her easily enough in the corridor afterward.

"Pure fustian," I said, muting my personal complaint.

"Just coasting," she murmured. "A duty do."

When we walked on the beach by moonlight, she in jeans and I in shorts, the mosquitoes came after me with the tenderest needle touches. Never mind: we were waiting for *Viking*, we were waiting for the next bout of Bernard's Surf. I had become acquainted with the notion of seasonal time, which was time converted into occasion as distinct from mere chronicity: one damned thing after another. We were having a full ration of the latter, manufacturing occasions in lieu of the big one, but tuning ourselves up for the big cheer: two *Viking*s, not just one, as if NASA had offered us one to practice on, to get our decorum right, to rehearse our hugs.

"Are you enjoying it?" she said. "You don't always look as if you are."

"I'm learning," I told her. "I find it hard to be among people who can get from day to day without the merest hint of literature, without a bar of serious music. It's all hardware and bluff. Only the beach works."

"You can't stay on the beach."

Chewing on that fabulous paradox for a while, I decided to have a think about something else, far from my adored beach.

Having a household routine of exquisite little private rituals prepared you for more imposing quarters. Burbling, you moved from small apartment to a bigger one, thence to a house, and soon, because you had your unvarying rituals to fall back on, you moved into your first mansion without the least sense of being a misfit. So long as routine remained the same, of course. Why, you could shift to Mars and domesticate it with a few hey-nonny-noes or Albireos. One should never underestimate the power of the word, even in the desolate reaches of outer space. During certain wars, the Korean and the Vietnam, it was said that American soldiers panicked because they missed the routines and rituals of home; because there was no Coke, no drive-in, no car, no eggs with bacon, they failed to adapt. I doubted this, having picked up nothing of the kind from my veterans, but I could see it happen to astronauts, who might develop what we would have to term vacuum nausea or space blues. Spiritual paralysis might be a better term for being stranded in the middle of nowhere, the back of beyond; I was not too sure I would be able to abide it myself without a sufficiency of books and CDs, not to mention people. I was not among those who wanted to live on Mars, although a brief sortie would attract me. In some ways Earth itself seemed alien: whole stretches of it, especially the water, one day to be taken over and made livable, but possibly not until the colonization of Mars.

I told Swan much of this, but she had little or no response; she was one of those who for the unique privilege of planetary privation was willing to put up with almost anything else. Certainly she was a luxury lover, yet just as happy roughing it; she was adaptable, whereas I knew I was not; I didn't care for weather unless the sun on my back in a ninety-degree pool. She was a lover of luxury and I was a hedonist, hunting always for a greater degree of sweetness. I openly admitted it. Never would I repose among the bony prose of my contemporaries, those latterday puritans who prided themselves on leanness, plainness, and the meager. Less was never more, it was only an index to a failing intellect. I had never fathomed the sameness cult, which insisted that all writers write the same humdrum prose, electing anonymity over style, that unique parading of the personality. It had never worked in the other arts, and there was little reason to suppose it would work in the literary ones. When I told her all this, she agreed; we enjoyed the sumptuous, but I lacked her sense of being among space's elect, being myself more interested in stars, with which you could not really get to physical grips; Hans Alpha of Coriolis got me as close as I needed. Because of a late booking, we were due to change motels. We packed, then the phone rang: we did not have to migrate after all. So we unpacked, and sat giggling on the bed until dinner.

Already Swan was telling Bunsen that scientific romanticism was for the birds. "We've been reared," she told him, "on the mythology rather than the science. Venus as a voluptuous woman, Mars as a god of war, Jupiter or Zeus as the patriarch, and so on. Piffle. Why *not* present Venus as Venus is? A hot spinning ball of sulfuric, hydrochloric, and hydrofluoric clouds, far more bizarre than any myth we have." Bunsen nodded, perhaps recalling, as I was, his quotation from Richard Feynman, something on the lines of it did no harm to a mystery to know a little about it. Far more marvelous, Feynman said, the truth than artists of the past imagined. (I scowled somewhat at this.) Why did the poets of the present day not speak of the truth as the truth was? Who should be bothered to speak of Jupiter as if he were a man, but not an immense spinning sphere of methane and ammonia? Astronomy books, alas, kept relaying the same old anthropomorphic myths, yield of the first cosmic Rorschach inflicted on primeval men. The truth seemed to be that, as T. S. Eliot had said, human kind cannot bear very much reality and would go on putting its faith in astrology (just as inhuman as astronomy but with humanized pretensions), in myth and mumbo-jumbo. Someone picked up the last word and did a Sanders of the River Paul Robeson imitation: "Muhumbo JumBO, MuhumBO JumBO." It was that kind of interruptible continuum.

"You might almost think," Swan went on as she nibbled crab-stuffed shrimp done up in flaky patties, "humanity confronted with so much Creation still needs to make something up. To add even more. As if inspired. Isn't that fascinating?"

"So as not to feel," I said as I began to tackle mullet on a plank, "insignificantly at the mercy of a great big buzzing blooming chemistry set. But you can have it both ways, I mean, be scientifically accurate and still achieve articulate highs. Elegant precision, such as Nabokov manages when he's writing about butterflies. Like those essays in *Speak, Memory.* Like Thomas Gray's journal, when he reports the day-by-day growth of the flowers in the college courtyard. Like, oh, Linnaeus, sometimes, or Paul Valéry on the seashell, or that guy Bunsen, in the new *Britannica*, on Life!" My mullet was cooling off. Bunsen had a Doc Stahl Special in front of him: shrimp, rice, crabmeat, mushrooms, and garlic butter, costing $7.95: quite a lot for a picky eater. He looked at it as if waiting for it to make the first move. "Sure," he said. "You have a myth called Science. It's as precise, sometimes, as we can make it for now. And some of it's pretty elegant as well." His jaw advanced toward his plate.

Swan then raced into a terse voluntary about myth as public property, about poetry's residing in awe-inspired impiety. "You shuck off the societal lip service, what they *want* you to say—insipid waffle about branches beside babbling brooks—and you mouth your own universe." What had she said? What language was that? I had a painful feeling that we were on the brink of a massive misunderstanding. She was talking against an old-fashioned notion of poetry whipped up out of Tennyson by Matthew Arnold. She was against the received and artificial tropes of nineteenth-century poetry, which was supposed to be dainty and sedate, like one of Queen Victoria's handkerchiefs. I could see that she was returning to her plea, hardly an attack. "I don't think of poetry as an act against society, against what they supposedly want me to say. For me, folks, it's an at times terrifyingly intimate relationship with the universe, and always an attempt to throw light into the dark corners of existence, always an attempt to understand what being alive on the planet looks, tastes like. Being hurt, thrilled, sorrowed, angered—what that feels like. It's what *you* say," she said directly to me, "when you talk about what it feels like to be alive. Just as scientists believe that truth resides in things, I believe that poetry too resides in things." Looking deep into her eyes I could not decide between the dazzling light therein or the fathomless dark browns: an old problem of mine; what she saw with looked intenser than usual. Myself, I thought art resided in emotion, in the presence of things. I had never been able to forget how things ignored us, did not return our befuddled gaze.

Masticating, with eyes aimed clean through the wall, Bunsen did not respond. His own space-truth, lyrical as some of Swan's poems, included a place with four suns (red, white, blue, yellow) and starstuff flowing between them; an Earth-sized sun made of diamond; atomic nuclei the size of Brooklyn that rotate thirty times a second. And a snowball a mile across, otherwise known as a comet. He had declared himself already, all over the place, quite rightly never hesitating to repeat his most famous formulations, such as his not-so-poetic but telling "We are in the galactic boondocks, where the action isn't." Nineveh had just asked Swan about rya rugs that were portraits of amino acids; Swan had made several of these, accurate and colorful. "I'll never do more than a dozen," she was answering, "but it's always the same impulse, really, done with the hands more than with the mind. I've never gotten over the plain shock of living. I mean being here at all, in the midst of lichens and macrophagi, aromatic grasses, and golden-shouldered parakeets. You've heard that before, I'm sure! I feel the same way about amino acids, I suppose. They're beautiful to look at. To have on the wall—you almost forget their function."

She smiled demure apology for appearing to catechize herself. To make herself look bad, she confessed to never cooking proper meals, but eating canned or frozen foods. "Off," she winced, histrionically self-condemned, "paper plates, but only of the best quality." I knew what she meant, though; you could always scribble new ideas, or even old ones, around the edge while you ate. Another part of my mind, triggered by what she said about amino acids, was remembering an old song: *heaven to kiss, delightful to know*, or something such. The erotics of amino, Thirties-style, had occupied my memory just when I was trying to remember what her rya rugs had been of. One was a cross-section of a deer's bladder. So, not an acid. Tryptophan! Score one. Leucine another. Score two. And—what oh what? All I can remember is a Brain Cell in the Act of Imagining. Our discussion should have been wider since her works on the wall dealt with other things than amino acids. But it was too late to go back, she was already chatting in another direction.

The words, the quotations, the quips, flew. So did the time. We overate. The kitchen sounds came louder. Which night was which, which dinner which? Bernard's Surf was a pocket of panspermia in Cocoa Beach, which was a charismatic suburb of a system cradled more or less in the Orion arm of the Milky Way.

Above the ceiling, in the Cocoa Beaches on planets orbiting Barnard's Star, Lalande 21185, and 61 Cygni (all of them likely candidates), other Uranians must be toasting launches of their own, or even quietly celebrating their acceptance into the Galactic Union after thousands of years of application ("When you are ready, you will hear from us"). Perhaps they would resemble raccoons, dolphins, or colossal haggises of superintelligent slime, whose music never had to be composed because it surrounded them from the start (imagine being born with all of Beethoven in your head right off), whose literature was an azure ointment smeared from open wells on a transparent spur of silicon fiber (known there as a literature-receiver), whose food was an algebraic form of magnetism (monopoles like tadpoles washed down, according to formula, with photographic emulsion). My imagination wanted out of there, free to devise its own universe, unobliged to astronomers and physicists.

Anything could happen, I told myself, and not rationally, when you used physics to describe a universe: a set of general laws for one unique particular. Or when you made a composite dinner out of several at the Surf, as I was doing now. Against a background of increasing buzz, I heard someone tout the star Betelgeuse reproduced in "pseudo-color" (it revealed areas of convection), Arvydas Kliore telling Bunsen that the Xerox machines in Lithuania were no longer locked away. In Leningrad they were, said Bunsen, lest clandestine literature got printed (*Samizdat* in the bad old days). Henri Steerforth of *The New Yorker* (which published a lot of water poems), who talked an American English anglicized at Yale and whose mode of speech reminded me of Merleau-Ponty's notion of walking as a series of recovered falls, said he had learned to speed-read. He said this slowly. It worked, he said, especially with such a writer as Proust. He said the thing was surely to get through Proust as fast as possible. Should it really take twenty pages to describe a man getting out of bed? But what, I asked him, about texture, style, nuance, echo, rhythm, all those honorable old literary windmills? "He has a point," said Bunsen. Henri's rejoinder, spoken fast, got lost in badinage about the Coudé room in certain observatories. This, the room which received light at a fixed point regardless of the telescope's position, was where the interferometers were. A scrambled laugh began amid the din. *Coudétat*, said Swan the ever-ready, and this time the laugh was all together. Proust had been slandered, but nobody cared. Tell them, my mind urged me, that the precise effect of long sentences is to make you speed up. Tell them. I did not, however, reluctant to have such oafs read Proust at all, even correctly. I would deny them him.

"I just don't know why yew-all bother with me," said the worldliest girl at the Ramada desk to a persistent astronomer around midnight, "with all these beautiful young girls about." He went on persisting. Tomorrow we would be complaining that, back home on Spencer Road, this month's *Astronomy* would not have arrived. "*Science News*'s the best," Swan would say. The Bunsens' son, Ptolemy, was asleep in the Ramada, all the words in his mind at rest, but with jumpable waves forever ahead, whose salt he had us "blow" off his closed eyes daily.

On a few occasions the astronomers, having exhausted the subject of *Viking*, asked me why I turned to writing fiction, the novel especially, but I never gave them the real answer, instead talking generally about ontological and historical trauma, the need for penetration into history, the need for documentary, even for gratuitous historical impersonations. The truth, valid for all creative people and so obvious that I was amazed when people asked, was that you felt too much emotion: events that ruffled others drove you around the bend, and happiness was almost always extreme. I had heard that tests had been done on people watching TV, and shows that cheered them up did them as much harm as those that depressed them; both raised their blood pressure and reduced their immunity to infection. It was more useful, apparently, to invest in a dog and stroke it. So there seemed to me ample reason to shed the emotional surplus into a book or to lose oneself in painting canvas (like Winston Churchill, who had many military débâcles to reproach himself with). It did not always work of course; no matter how much emotion I purged, I spent some hours with my heart in my mouth or my head pounding with joy (quite often migraine announced itself with a euphoric prelude). Some said artistic folk had more energy than others, and I could see that; but the more convincing explanation had to do with feelings, and it was almost as if the artist had a chunk of his/her emotion reserved outright for shapeliness. The bigger you could make the chunk, the better off you were. Siphon it off. Pour it through the drain into the backyard. Catharsis, I had been taught, was purification or purgation, but I called it venting. Out went the perilous, dark stuff, shaped en route into something bizarre and lasting, or so you hoped. Whether it appealed to anyone else, or fulfilled any similar function for them, I never knew; just perhaps what you vented became another's escape device, a magic carpet. Swan felt much the same, but differed in that she felt a strong need to celebrate the universe—the Almighty's ingenuity, whereas the ingenuity that appealed to me was within the creative artist's own gift and thus, for me, exclusively verbal. She tended to keep things to herself, whereas I got them out of my system. When she was under stress, her bottom twitched, a not unappealing erotic wobble noticed only by me, whose interest in it was a private matter. Sometimes, when lying down, again under stress, she jactitated, unable to control the flickering of her feet, and this phenomenon we fondly named "jackie." Sometimes her hands quivered too, and I sometimes thought she had made a secret pact with motion, paying it her tribute from week to week in exchange for superlative phrasing. We got accustomed to each other's oddities and became almost intoxicated with them: love me, love my clubfoot, my tic, my shimmy. It was as naked as that.

Her work was never twitchy, though, even if at times it developed an intellectual tremor I had never seen in anyone else's. She doted on homophones, echoes, and had a deep sense of the oneness of things, the connectedness through atoms and language, a view I think she shared with her Huron mentor Starchief Ammonite, who supervised her from the first. She invoked him in an astonishing poem called "Starchief Ammonite Amid the Fungi," which implicated the man in an entire fresco of uncanny natural history. Lapidary, vivid, and scientifically accurate (thanks mainly to Raoul), her poetry, as I saw it, appointed her the instant Muse of the solar system, at once visionary and specific, awed and irreverent, flamboyant and strict, words colliding and fusing like particles in an accelerator. She believed in poetry as phrasemaking, panache, and highly wrought individual texture, but also as a blast furnace of dreams. I thought this from the first, amazed even at Cocoa Beach how fast that romp had receded from us, how steady a performer she had remained in the interim. And she read aloud well, too: her soft-spoken, alert cadences wove a spell even while she seemed to be gabbing impromptu about a walking tour of the senses she undertook daily. If there was, as we thought there was, an audience for space writing that wanted not so much SF as scientific art, she was custom-made for it. The only thing was that, writing about planets in a department of English made her feel lonely, a freak, but the Coriolis astronomers in particular urged her on, and on, with results that surprised Swan herself. Somehow she managed to balance that well of English well-defiled with the discoveries that Bunsen and his cohorts were producing monthly and the renegade sensuous streak in her that never went away and took her ever toward tapestries, Turkish rugs, precious stones, the work of Wallace Stevens, Dylan Thomas, Neruda, Rilke, and others. I knew I would never forget her ability to quote *The Notebooks of Malte Laurids Brigge*, in the German, without the least hitch or pause, not as if she had memorized it but as if it had forced its way outward through her compatible being, demanding to be voiced, nearly as if she were speaking in tongues. This could also be her party piece, though try as I did to talk her into doing it she would not recite it at Cocoa Beach. Maybe its being German put her off. Needless to say, it was she who honed my own appetite for the physical world, I especially in the early days a bit liquor-blunted (though never to words).

One Saturday while she was at Coriolis (prelude to hundreds of Saturdays there, in fact), we sauntered out in the early wind-flicked spring and entered a jewelry store, there to browse, but we came out with the first of a series of things we referred to as "bizarre little items": a garnet ring that seemed almost medieval in its mellow, rufous glow within tiny golden claws whose filigree brought to mind the frosted breath and humbly gleaming lamps of Keats's "The Eve of St. Agnes":

> . . . and diamonded with panes of quaint device,
> Innumerable of stains and splendid dyes,
> As are the tiger-moth's deep-damasked wings . . .

The second so-named object was a tiny bookshelf that went at once to her side of the bed. It would hold maybe thirty books of medium heft, but she never filled it, instead made it into her vertical bedside table, with, early on, her framed photograph of Jean Marais as the Beast in Cocteau's *La Belle et la Bête*, a movie she sometimes liked to quote from—"All men are beasts when they don't have love," for instance—which I had always taken to be my own school report for early bad behavior. Jean Marais and she *knew*. Since then, other bizarre little items came and never went, assuming in our lives a mythological force we rather doted on. To see them in a store was to acknowledge their power over us, so we began to cram that small apartment almost as if preparing to hibernate. What with books and pictures, there was scarcely room for us, and we had loosely promised each other that, on our return from Cape Canaveral, we would discuss moving to a house or a yert: something more capacious, with a room we did not need, just for the anticipated overflow. All this time, of course, I had been commuting to and fro from Pigskin, a permanent presence to stewardesses and airline agents, almost like an insurance salesman although they never saw me in a suit, or short-haired like an executive. Did I qualify for special cheap rates? If I did, I rarely got them. I was a steady to my travel agent and the local limo drivers, a man with an acute need to be somewhere else, where the air was brisker and the mental climate more dynamic. In some ways out of date, mostly in the humanities, Coriolis nonetheless had intellectual vigor; there were always readings and concerts, lectures and seminars. It was a hive of work and Swan had begun to thrive within it, somehow finding the corporate attitude congenial. In fact, whatever it protested to be, it was a university that favored research over teaching, as my own students told me indignantly when I taught there: the genius of the place was the quiet room or lab drenched in the advancement of learning. The quiet scratch of the pen, the oily glide of the ballpoint, the creak of the chair or the sigh as yet another brilliant hypothesis bit the dust, related all the ponderers and scribblers there to Hans Alpha, who had worked out our star almost as if besting some colossal crossword puzzle. After that, a university had nowhere to go but down. What problem was huger? Well, how the universe began? Someone surely was at work on that in a dingy little attic somewhere on campus, even while the hungry sheep, the students, looked up and were not fed. They complained because their parents, some of them anyway, had paid bundles to get their kids to that windy eminence above Lake Cuyahoga, and all they got in return, these kids, was a good place in which to hear the sound of a savant scratching his head. Swan did her required term papers, mostly for lit-critters who, qua editor, liked to get their names on other people's books, and in larger print; but she put her best energy into her poems, into *Solar System*, as she called the book, storming past page one hundred well into the second hundred, with little sign of fatigue. The vision sustained her to report it.

Peering south through the little window that graced the alcove in her apartment, I sometimes wondered where Lou Vielis, Asa Humanas, Frank Foxpasta and Gloria Gluckstein,

Delray Pepp, and Pendennis Cleveland had gone. When I went back, they had become exotic to me, more enjoyable than ever, but I had become almost a stranger, a fellow who lived in a different ocean full of shiny fish. I had got above myself, I supposed, commuting not just for love but for oxygen, life in the Ivy League, leisure among the well-to-do, dreams of ascendancy. I had given in to the restlessness that had always motivated me as I shuffled from England to Canada to America, not so much a lover of foreign places as chronic flotsam living the life of the mind and therefore not really being anywhere at all. What had Swan said only yesterday, alluding to yet another dinnertime conversation at the Surf (and hence hardly to be disentangled from sundry ambient noises)?

"They just called us romantics. Somebody did."

"Who's qualified to say any such thing?"

"Those who aren't romantics, I suppose. Screw them."

"Jesus, we haven't even got over the shock of being together."

She had blinked at that, miffed or stunned. "Why must people pass out labels like that?" Again she flinched and mopped her eyes, really hurt by being categorized.

"It means," I said, "people don't want to take you as individuals. If they can see you in terms of A Relationship, they feel more at ease. It happens when someone takes a toucan into a restaurant and has dinner with it. They can't work out how the two live together."

"Quite simple," she told me. "You treat the bird as a bird. I'm not talking about that. The way we talk about writing, when we talk about it at all to strangers, or even friends, isn't the way *they* talk about astronomy."

"You've just discovered that."

"Are you being sarcastic?"

I didn't answer. Insult or affront was in the air, and I knew better. There was an entire tendency in America to take critics, or anyway those who opined about writing, more seriously than those who did the writing. Never believe an eyewitness, never trust those who have been in the fiery furnace. I wanted to get off the topic; after ten at night, she changed demeanor, seeming sullen when she said she was only tired, whereas I, when up too late, got giddy, did everything slowly and untidily. At the dinner table she was at her best, almost as if having husbanded her brio for the occasion, yet she often talked of feeling shy, of stage fright, although I had never seen the signs in her. Her mind thought naturally in terms of dinner parties, those funeral plots where you were trapped for several hours, sometimes with appalling partners, whereas, at a buffet, say, there was merciful escape. I had actually, in the early days when Gloria Gluckstein had been an insatiable host, witnessed a dinner party at which, when a person at one end of the table wanted to swap seats with a person at the other, the second person refused, he having discerned at the far end the cause of the panic, the old Kenya hand and breeder of cut-price bulldogs Keyser Cryxton Sössli. This incessant ex-Hungarian dictated his autobiography all night wherever he went. He had many times promised to leave town, heading north, he said, "towartz ze Vinger Lachen," as he put it, intending to buy a vineyard, but he never went, so condemning a certain stratum of Pigskinners to prandial misery. In their kindness and masochistic curiosity they invited him out to witness him in the act, blathering at speed about the Masai and their diet, the local doctors, the genial ways of British Air with old Kenya hands, and so on. He was like a goat that could read provided he had glasses on. After every dinner party I had been to, I vowed I'd never go to one again, but I always ended up being cajoled out once more, I having surrendered because of my faith in humankind: surely, not every guest at every party was a dithering nincompoop who said such things as "Ah, what's *your* hobby?" or "What do you think of the water here, now you've got used to it?" Perhaps things were better in Kenya. The great leavener in Bernard's Surf was the hubbub, the gradual slither into alcohol, the finale that saw hundred-dollar bills being flashed about like tickets to an orgy.

TWELVE

Each night the Surf party got larger, through an osmosis of talk, and I began to wonder if what we had come south for would ever happen. There was talk of delays. Of course, delays are one thing when they begin on cue, but when people began predicting delays that was something else: futurity pawnbroked and bright aspiration scotched. The huge menus increased your chances of not noticing someone who was present for the first time, sucked in by the uproar and the ammoniac scent of lion meat. Partitioned from others by boastful placards that offered not only various kinds of fish but also such cosmopolitan specialties as chocolate-coated caterpillars, roasted caterpillars (Japan), fried silkworms (also Japan), fried grasshoppers (Japan again), Bristol Farm elephant meat in provincial sauce (South Africa), French fried ants, quail eggs, squid pieces in pepper sauce (Spain), we hovered above the photogravure surface of the tables like gnats over a lake. There was even more. Japan took over again:

Smoked Frog Legs
Smoked Baby Clams
Brood of Eel (which at least one of us misread as Blood)
Smoked Petite Oysters
Broiled Octopus on Squers (skewers?)

After pondering the longest entry—Chocolate Covered Giant Ants ("The genuine ants from South America which have been eaten there many years as the finest delicacy"), we wondered about lark and buffalo and then, unreassured about those genuine ants, wondered why there was nothing from space. Panspermia sausage, say. We tried to order, some of us distantly aware of trying to work our way through the menu but rebounding to old favorites, then making a valiant effort to adapt ourselves to the outrageousness of the place. So we opted for the nonexistent: aphid septum (in an amino acid sauce), coelecanth roe volcano-cooked, polar bear goulash, and so forth, but we finally settled for fish, fish, and fish, proud of having made nightmarish efforts to be different. A cannibal might find fulfillment here, I thought, provided he/she gave the management sufficient warning. Perhaps cannibals were what we were, troughing until launch-time, devouring one another's minds, or at least lapping the froth that sat on top. We met (*foregathered*, even), but without the ponderous creak of that little-used word, not just to have a good time, but to create a conversational gauntlet, which we then ran. Achieving at worst triumphs of educated levity, we sometimes arrived at mellow chain reactions of wound-up wit, as when Swan mentioned the large lemur of Madagascar called *indri*, so named because the French naturalist Pierre Sonnerat mistook the Malagasy imperative, *indri!*, meaning Look!, for the animal's name. A romp of analogies followed; we filled the zoos of the world with bizarre relatives of the *indri*, from the *Upyours* bird to the *Dropdead* ox, from the *Nuts* monkey to the *Uptheassofyourancientoldmother* worm (a Russian variant from the steppes). Almost logically the talk moved to how (in what wise, moaned someone) one learned to give the finger, through exactly what ordonnance of digits and knuckles we erected the middle finger in barbaric retort. Everyone there flexed a hand before settling into the correct position, no one looking at anyone else. It might have been a séance of perverse hitchhikers. An unusual silence came over Bernard's Surf. The very surf of conversational mastication whispered to a halt. The entire dining room was looking at us, wondering at whom we were directing this multiple, juvenile affront. The silence was almost as palpable as it had been, months ago, when the unself-conscious talk of a few of us hit the topic of remote-control dildoes advertised for males. That was in an egregiously chic restaurant poised between Trimalchio (too much to eat) and Barmecide (nothing at all). This was the South, though, and down came our fingers. The Surf resumed. What we had established was that each of us lifts a finger, crooks the others, differently: a matter of regional style, Boston, Brooklyn, Baltimore, Lithuania, England, and other centers of civilization. Each person launched a rocket from the palm.

Surf birds, surf perch, surfer's knobs on the knees, all entered and left our excesses at what I had come to call Bernard's Surfeit. My head was full of enervated glow. Someone vowed to take a sabbatical leave of his or her senses. Then Swan declared, "I consider sweet wines merely in between. I like extremes." Bunsen identified the *or dur*, the hard gold, in *ordure*. Like Mithridates, getting used to poison, we became almost inured to puns, so that a Nathalie Sarrautisserie, or presuming to look for Doctor Livingstone in a Stanley Steamer, won a ripple of indulgent approval, but scarcely more. Things more constructive ensued, even as Swan was indulging in one of her and my favorite chants: "Golden baby owls," chanted for reasons unknown, perhaps to make a meal of the vowels. *Rum, sodomy, and the lash:* Bunsen quoted Winston Churchill's motto for the Royal Navy. I improvised Scotch, incest, and feather boas for the Army; lager, leather, and French fries for the Air Force. Bunsen mused on the time he attended an Achievement Banquet, seated next to Colonel Sanders the chicken merchant, whose speech-notes read: "Commies—Jew joke—sonofabitch." What drove us into ecstasies of bittersweet mirth came from the strangest places. Next thing, Bunsen, quite unprompted, was telling me about his salary at Coriolis and how much lower astronomers' salaries were than those of professors in business administration and law.

* * *

Bernard's Surf had many mansions. I think we dined in all of them: high rooms, low rooms, long rooms, round rooms, rooms amorphous and rooms invisible. Even other eateries began to merge into the one we favored, which was why I couldn't remember the name, or accept the autonomous reality, of the one we ate in last, for some reason having no reservation at the Surfeit. So, we arrived, full of misgiving, to find at the door a tousled Italian-looking child who said we would have to wait; his father ran the place and sometimes didn't have enough fish, but his father hated to turn people away. We had a reservation for nine people, so maybe this kid was a booby-trap. We filed in eventually, past strewn nets and consumptive-looking lanterns, and a twelve-year-old exclaimed to his parents "That's Bunsen! That's McElroy!" "Ah," Bunsen sighed, overwhelmed. McElroy was stunned. Was this lad, I wondered, at the lectures? Was he there when Dr. Donald Hunten, native Montrealer and bassoonist-flautist builder of harpsichords who also played recorders and krummhorns, held forth on thermal and nonthermal escape processes? Would he be there at the launch, discerning human stars at a distance with his telescope and a *Who's Who in Astrophysics*? I dwelled in his enthusiast's mind for a moment as he discovered that Bunsen, McElroy, *et al.*, were real, ate food, had complexions and hands. Could he but see Ptolemy Bunsen wrestle his dad, who had a bad back. Deskwork, said Swan: sedentary bookishness. A sick dependence on sitting down. Then that quick-eyed *Viking* fan reminded me of my own drift: the human side of *Viking*.

Now Swan suggested we play musical chairs after each course so that, in spite of the long narrow table, we all met. It nearly worked out. Peering across a net-coated red lantern like a bloodshot aquarium, Swan looked more Persian than ever, a maned *houri* trimmed with gold. *Houri*, I thought, but she didn't like that word at all. I withdrew it and said *odalisque* though she wasn't lying down. This was not *our* restaurant anyway. On my right, Nineveh was looking peachily serene, but her mind was on the handicapped, extermination camps, the very old, and I realized she had withdrawn from astronomy and art alike into some test tube of the soul, a black-dog fit brought on by who knew what—reading a newspaper, maybe, or thinking too hard about ancestors. She was certainly not off in some verbal or mathematical tropopause.

We had to go away from the Surfeit to appreciate it and to recognize its significance. It was a letting-loose, of course; a rigmarole of urgent swank by means of which intense, high-spirited people made a counterweight to their otherworldly yearnings. But it was also a celebration of affability inasmuch as *affable* meant "speakable to." Friends across the disciplines (except for short spells of rarefied expertise or everyday math, with the scientists' language always better than our math), we regaled one another with verbal emblems of ourselves. And, profane, scurrilous, cerebrally perverse in a score of ways, we nonetheless were venting exhilaration at the act—the buildup, the nerve, the hubris—of sending two literal feelers to Mars. So much beyond our everyday selves, in imagination at least, we arrived time and again at a giddiness, a doodling bravado, that were not quite human; and our keen but feverish exchanges had both an elegiac and a brave-new-world aura, especially for cultural transplants such as Swan and myself, who had never been at a launch in our lives, not even like voiceful Margaret Truman the naming of a ship. We were enthralled. The dish ran away with the spoon. Those two stilettos out there in their housings on the Cape took us beyond the tradition of the new, past even the imaginable, into depths that might impair the notion that humankind was unique. Or alone. I, who had stared endlessly at the trapezium of bright stars in the Great Nebula in Orion, seeing the green glow of doubly ionized oxygen (which Bunsen told me I wasn't seeing at all because it wasn't really there), I ought to be thrilled less than this with something still inside the solar system, not even one of the galaxies in Berenice's Hair, nor the Southern Coalsack, nor the black hole called Cygnus X-1. Even with Mars, though, in spite of my aesthetic resentment, I was captivated beyond measure. This Cape, this state of mind, was the lip of Otherness, the outpost for submissive alienation. I felt cravings not immortal but extraterritorial. Those not so big orbiters and landers, tricked out with wands and vanes and cups and cosmic distilleries, and staying on course among the planets (things that wander, as the Greeks put it), were *our* galleons, half a thousand years after Columbus.

Some of our galleons had, so to speak, sunk: lost radio contact; been destroyed when a malfunctioning rocket slewed them off course; crashed on target or melted; but many more had done unprecedented things—first flown by another planet (*Mariner* 2: Venus), first landed on another planet (*Venera* 3: Venus), first orbited another planet (*Mariner* 9: Mars), first departed from the solar system (*Pioneer* 10). As Bunsen said, in less than twenty years of space exploration human beings had learned more about the Sun, the Moon, and the planets than in all the preceding centuries of earthbound observation. Obviously we were awed by the colossal amount there was to know, as by humankind's slowness to start; but what stirred me most, as it would any writer, is that this was the beginning of communication, a word that meant *making common* or *making known.* Contact with context, whether toward a halting dialogue or just a nature walk, was the name of the endeavor. Not Renaissance Two, perhaps, which sounded more like a real estate agency, but the first Ekumenikon, the Whole World, it was overdue from the best minds of a civilization that had just marketed Baby Alive, a doll that swallowed yellow goo and then voided it into a diaper.

So when Veronica McElroy, in the juicily rhetorical brogue of her native Ireland, talked of the hell that Northern Ireland had become, but in the same breath recalled a BBC radio program, *The Brains Trust*, in which Jacob Bronowski had taken part, I was glad we had a multiple iron in the cosmic fire. If we waited for perfection here before venturing out there, we would never begin, or not until the horse-reptile brain had died its natural death.

I began wondering about the effect on all well-wishers of the spacecraft's being unmanned. Because there would be no one aboard either *Viking*, had we all involuntarily behaved with extreme levity? Was that why we were so intense? If there had been astronauts going up, would we have been even wilder? I doubted it. We had been filling in the histrionic gap; the launch, the mission, had proved too abstract for us, lacking the danger, the melodrama, of the manned version.

"Don't you think so?" Swan yawned, two hours past her bedtime, whereas I, I was just beginning to rev up. She did not answer, soaring off in that closed-door trance of hers. Yet as I moved past her, there on the bed, she tweaked my jeans in her usual way and tugged them down half an inch: just a friendly touch to report that all was well, no major overture. "We needed our circus," I went on, "all through. What on earth would we have done if we'd all been introverts?" The curious pattern of the prelaunch days—in and out of the Ramada or the Atlantis, solidly in the Surfeit except for one night—suggested the prancing of the cygnets in *Swan Lake*.

It was dismal to think our *Viking* enterprise would soon be over, entailing a return to two kinds of academe, whose groves, to be sure, held buoyant girls for skin-watchers, but whose office windows gave no view of Mars. All of a sudden I wanted to have had a different career, one leading up to Cape Canaveral but not from teaching this or that course. I wanted to be full-blown otherworldly from the first, not eking out a hunch from Shklovsky's book, developing an intuition from the table talk of Raoul Edward Bunsen, kind as he was. I wanted to have had inspiration from the first, to have been undergoing the photosynthesis of knowledge. Truly, as the dons said, it was like being a young prince deprived of his inheritance, and I could just about see, back in my early teens, how various factors had conspired to deflect me: no flair for math, a passion for airplanes, a hunger for languages. Only lately had I seen how my love of planes almost led through to the grand highway of space exploration. It is possible, especially if you happen to be a child who came of age during war, to cheat yourself of certain delights, especially if the war left you with a yearning for something fixed where everything else is moving, something intact where all else has disintegrated. I was only just catching up with myself, letting such concepts or images as Stefan's Quintet occupy me almost to the point of obsession. Again and again I told myself that, to switch from aeronautics to astronomy (these my clandestine religions), I would have to go to stars, with Mars only a stepping stone. This meant, of course, gratification infinitely delayed, a waiting period I would not survive. I wanted to look Betelgeuse in the face in the 1970s, which only became possible in the 1990s. I was out of synch, and my telescope, which I had always thought of as an intro, a howdy-do to constellations, now looked like being the be-all and end-all. Even success with Mars would remind me of all I was not getting, though the two spacecraft themselves would drift away into the universe never to be seen again. Coming to terms with this disappointment was hard; I did not mention it to Swan, the long-suffering, the empathetic enabler par excellence, because we were already enough years apart (seventeen), and it was no use reminding her of the different clocks we two observed. Asa Humanas's old point about, if not January and May, then April and July, remained to torment me with the difference between eld, as the poet had it, and youth. Always the gulf would get worse. I had somehow backed into a situation not recommended, but rather the other way around: the young man and the aging woman. Yet when two people plunge at each other, shocked by the unanimity of their feelings, it is almost impossible to push the doctrine of self-denial. The *lest*s do not come to mind. The future is always a promise, the full bloom of a crescent ecstasy, and the whole thing happens under the auspices of reckless tradition: a feeling in the heart as the source of right.

THIRTEEN

But the *Viking* did not go. Bunsen's face wore an antagonized bleariness. Everyone looked paler, as if acquired tans had been revoked. *Viking* II would go up in *Viking* I's place; the pad would have to be cleared, then recharged. Anticlimax said we had been here all this time for mere festivity, highbrow schmoozing. Somehow the magical sequence of acclimatization–preliminary–launch would never happen again and our lives elsewhere would suffer a sea change into something tawdry and drab. It was not anticlimax alone; it was the lack of vindication, as if, say, being quizzed by the scholars and antiquarians of the universities we had left behind, all of them wagging the finger, murmuring Stick to books, dote on the classics, eschew the new. We had been made to look vulgar, or so I thought as I perused Swan's face: crestfallen, sapped from within, defeated by the vacuum of it all. Even an extra trip to the Surf would not help, and we stayed away, making do with anonymous burgers and reach-me-down milk shakes. We spoke endlessly to the airlines, all trying to get on the same flight to make up a *contingent* of disappointed people, but we went back scattered, routed, our thoughts on the shuffle taking place on the Cape as first became second and vice versa. Caught in mid-step, we hardly dared put the other foot down lest it crash clean through the topsoil and anchor us forever. We were not emotionally agile enough to make the substitution in our minds; *Viking* I, "our" *Viking* as we thought, could never be *Viking* II.

So much for preconceptions veneered with time. *Viking* II went up in I's stead, becoming a brief newspaper item while we were busily doing humanities and literature chores, our minds reattuned to business. We met and conferred as survivors of something once splendid and fabulous, unable to shake the old state of mind, indelibly bound up with the Ramada and Bernard's Surf, the white roads and the vulgar store-window signs. What was it like? Having your current friends cut you dead, only to be replaced by friends you thought you had lost and hadn't heard from in years. Something, somebody, always turned up, and you went through ancient obeisances to prove how grateful you were that time's inroads were not yet complete and you and your old friends could survive to lose one another again. In recent years, within the time of writing, old friends from the period penned in the sentences have popped up from Canada and France, even from Chevy Chase, Maryland, not without a sense of triumph on their part (look, we managed to get through the intervening years) that induces a similar feeling in you. We must have been rigid-minded, we *Viking* fans, to have such trouble swapping spacecraft, unable to accept that II had already gone, virtually unwatched, and that we would have to wait. That slight dislocation in schedule had given us more than a shiver in the night; it had delivered all over again the old warnings about chickens and eggs, hatching and being previous.

In order to launch *Viking* II by September 1st, NASA had already bent one of its rules by permitting the spacecraft to be interchanged without first removing the half million pounds of fuel from the rocket. The urgency was celestial as well as bicentennial: early in November, the Sun would come between Earth and Mars, severing communications for about a month, and the *Viking* team wanted the critical part of the mission accomplished by then. But in vain. *Viking* II did not take off on September 1st; the signal from the principal Earth-aimed antenna aboard the

Orbiter had proved strangely weak, and engineers had to overhaul it once again. The next attempt to launch would be September 9th or 10th; if the former, *Viking* II would achieve Mars orbit on August 7, 1976, the same day as if launched on September 1; if the latter, the modified mutual positions of Earth and Mars would delay Mars orbit until August 10. Such were the calculable hazards of celestial marksmanship. Both launch base and target were in constant motion. Hit or miss, you knew what the heavens were going to do, but not the box of tricks atop the Titan III/Centaur rocket. The whole enterprise might have come out of a drunken conversazione held in Bernard's Surf.

Tempted to return to the Cape for the September 1 launch, we heeded intuition instead, sensing a flaw from afar, but unable to prove it. There was by then almost a tradition of delay for *Viking* II. The names were always confusing; it would have been easier to call one *Viking* and the other Noël Coward. We had become connoisseurs, almost epicures, of anticlimax, so we preempted the big let-down with a minor one. Raoul Bunsen, however, on the Sunday before the Monday launch, phoned the Ramada, thinking we were already there, to relay the bad news, and was relieved when he drew a blank. "We decided against it," I eventually told him, "zealous as we both are. We both decided not to go, but only a bit more than we didn't. We kept thinking it over even after it was too late to go. Otherwise known as tendentious stalling." Raoul himself, having figured the odds very finely, wondered if the witch at the Ramada desk had had anything to do with all this, according to her own electromagnetic black arts (she not the one whom the midnight cowboys among the astronomers hit upon). On the last day, she had asked Raoul, "Are you the father of *Viking*?"

"Yes and no," he had answered, semantically confounded.

"We have an expression in French," she then said with a trace of easy malice: "*Maman, oui; papa peut-être.*"

Not only was it one of the Frenchest of French expressions; it may well have been, I suggested to him, the *first* French expression. I adapted it, he recalled, into "*Mars, oui; Viking peut-être.*" We needed something—a motto, a bon mot, a bon motto, a vituperative rune, anything—to compress frustration into sense while calculating (he), guessing (I), what would happen next. Our *Viking* was already three weeks late and would soon be four.

What did happen next occurred in Uris Hall on the Coriolis campus, where he and I, Swan and Nineveh, had gone to see François Truffaut's movie *The Wild Child.* It was due to start at 8 P.M. At ten to eight, Raoul put on a teasing face and asked me if I was game to try for September 9, the newly announced date. We both were, Swan and I decided, and to hell with classes, airline tickets, good behavior, and the rest. The other two laughed unnervedly as the vista unfolded once again of becoming slaves to the whims (or at any rate the malfunctions) of *Viking* II, now *known* to be Noël Coward. This time, however, we would fly down (if we could) the day before, returning immediately after launch. There was no room for delays; we all *had* to be back on time, he to appear Wednesday on TV in New York at seven in the morning, a gruesome thought, although I had not long ago done it myself, on first at NBC with the beguiling Aline Saarinen. It was almost as if we were coercing *Viking-Coward* to do its stuff. Put on its already suspect mettle, would it oblige, or get even more contrary? I thought this was how we should approach it under any circumstances, even if we had loads of time. This was its last chance, after which we would go back to routine living. So: it would be 2:39 P.M. on Tuesday, September 9, or bust.

As if to chide my foolhardiness, but really to show that she had a transatlantic eye on the launch, my mother sent me a clipping from the London *Daily Mail:* "Launch of the *Viking* Mars Probe has been delayed a further ten days at a cost of 357,000 pounds because two battery switches were accidentally left on." By the time the news reached Brest Litovsk it would be three. Of course, there had been two more hitches since that second one, but I briefly relived it: in pounds it sounded worse, as if Dr. Johnson were magistrally scolding a hunk of overpriced halibut. We must all four of us have been out of our minds to persist: rocket-watching could be ruinous in all kinds of ways, especially to one's nerves. Yet enthusiasm, plus optimistic doggedness, ruled us still. It had become almost a point of honor to see a *Viking* lift off for Mars and, seeing it go, to relish it even more for where it was going. Obstinate for that lyrical send-off, we had already invested too much emotion, yet nowhere near as much as the *Viking* team, who by now were feeling spooked. Truffaut's boy scrambled ferally through French undergrowth. The movie gathered momentum. And, with Truffaut himself playing the part of the doctor, there was an image before us of zealous, invasive commitment to at least the possible image of the impossible feat. "Communication," Raoul sighed, moved by the succession of poignant frames. The wild child had begun to learn. We were hoping *Viking* had learned an ABZ of good manners at least. In fact, the more flawed our rocket seemed, the more human too, and so, in a nastily paradoxical way, frustration endeared it to us.

FOURTEEN

So there we were again, fanatical addicts, obsessed dreamers, just a few of us, over a month later, having almost given in to the assumption that technology had ended, but there for one day only: a grab, a snatch, a last sortie. Our reunion dinner at Bernard's Surf should have sedated me, especially after a day's traveling, but no: after four hours of restless air-conditioned sleep in the almost empty Ramada, I got up about dawn and trudged down to the beach in moccasins and shorts, keenly aware of how an empty stomach makes you off-balance, in the physical sense at least. A distant man clad in waders was fishing in the surf. Any minute, I thought, it would rain from the bruise-blue lumps of cloud drifting from inland. Drained and tense, I viewed the space cape, where the day's mysteries would perhaps enact themselves at long last. Only the VAB showed, like a concrete valise dumped on the neighbor shore by some absconding giant. The rank smell of North Atlantic decay (fish, feces, and ammonia) wafted in, smothering the aroma of my pencil-thin cigarillo, then went, a bovine perfume from a distant cattle boat. For a mesmerized half hour I sat there on a stump, plucking dune burrs off my slippers, puffing smoke at the skyline, and willing today not to be another fiasco. It was time our *Viking* did its best.

With a faint crash, the driver of a newspaper truck stacked the day's issue into the serve-yourself machine by the Ramada. I decided to buy one (I had dimes and quarters on me), but not quite yet. I lingered there on the afternoon's coming launch, on our being back on Cocoa Beach as an act of faith, and on the explosive charge that would pound upon land that held Indian burial mounds, ancient middens, and artifacts from the time of Christ. Some of the boosters were only, as the idiom had it, "strapped on" to the launch vehicles, which made them sound awfully frail and vulnerable. Some of the fuels ignited as soon as they touched each other (hypergolic), as people sometimes do. After what was called "shroud jettison," a phrase I liked for its clinical morbidity, the first of two "Centaur burns" would begin, which sounded like some ardent, mythic hybrid, wholly compatible with my photograph of a rocket stage being recovered by whaleboat out in the Atlantic. It looked like an enormous gauntlet, creamy beige and with the hand-part ripped away. How deciduous these rockets or launch vehicles were. They ascended only to come apart. The light stainless steel Centaur, for example, went up loaded with sixteen tons of liquid hydrogen and liquid oxygen, then came tumbling down again, a two-ton husk, with virtually no internal framework at all, its fiberglass nose cone gone, the dragon's breakfast of liquid hydrogen having combined with the much smaller amount of "lox" into something rich and strange called energy. When "coasting," a Centaur was steered by hydrogen peroxide engines, and after separation "ullage" rockets pushed it away from the payload to prevent it from following. Something poignant in this—the rejected workhorse's blind impulsion to go after its master, even as far as Mars—once again humanized those chunks of metal full of chemicals. Perhaps this was how Robert Goddard, the rocket pioneer, felt. Think of all the launches at the Cape, blasting up rockets that split apart like successive nutshells while the seed, or something such, headed on into space under its own slight power. While waiting for the original *Viking* I to perform, I had boned up on the jargon, mainly for lack of something to do, but also to enact voodoo on the rocket, hoping that if I muttered the right formulas I would tip the balance between launch and scrub.

To go from the approximately sublime to the banal cost only twenty cents. In the top right-hand corner of *Today*, "Florida's Space Age Newspaper," it said "Next Space Shot: Second *Viking* Mars probe aboard Titan-Centaur rocket today from Cape Canaveral. Launch window: 2:39 P.M.–4 P.M." As if it were a coming attraction at a local pier. And I was already there, like someone who had waited in line all night for a concert. But *Today*'s weather brought dismal promises of widely scattered thundershowers, with a high in the upper 80s to the lower 90s, winds 8–13 m.p.h. diminishing at night. The U.S. Weather Service map showed all of Florida covered with choppy lines that stood for showers, but it was clear in Berlin and Rio and many other places, raining only in Moscow. Seeing a surfers' and boaters' forecast, I was half-surprised there wasn't one for rocketeers, but all I found, in the five column inches devoted to *Viking* at the bottom of the front page, was "sky and upper atmosphere conditions should be favorable for the afternoon launch." I felt just a bit relieved, enough anyway to heed the paper's lead story on this day of days. Hardly sublime, the headline read "Topless Dance on Sub's Deck Sinks Skipper." I read how a topless dancer called Cat Futch ("34-23-35"), a regular at the Evil People's Lounge in Fort Pierce, did her thing on deck as tugs moved the nuclear-powered submarine toward the open sea. Crewmen wired up some music. She returned to port in a pilot boat, saying "It really boosted the men's morale," continuing on the back page where, in G-string, cuffs, choker, and skimpy bra, she looked almost overdressed. Her unformed, pulpy face was chanting a snatch or a shanty. "I've never before," she added, "seen such a bunch of smiling men go out to sea." There was to be an inquiry, of course, and no doubt one type of booster was going to be clearly differentiated from another.

Such as Cat Futch (was ever a name so loaded with venereal

hints?) performed only for man-rated missions, which *Viking* was not, and certainly not at Jetty Park and Playalinda Beach, the two viewing sites the newspaper listed as having live NASA commentary on the PA system. Nor at the press site, where I would be today. After breakfast we mooned around in the lobby and bought cards and *Viking* T-shirts. Raoul Bunsen spent half the morning on the phone, checking; he had been disappointed before and had become a connoisseur of the hitches that could afflict even the finest space hardware.

"You won't," said the Frenchwoman at the desk as we checked out, "be back. It's go today." Our press badges, issued for both *Viking*s, now designated A and B, were once again signed on the back by Charles L. Buckley Jr., security officer, beneath appropriate warnings sweetened by permission to keep the badge as a souvenir. The *Viking* Science Symposium badge was white, however, whereas this keepsake happened to be salmon-pink and gray, with at top right a new logo consisting of a quartered shield crossed by smaller capital Ts (like studs) beneath which an Earth, vertically halved, divided along an equatorial zigzag on the left, where three nose cones and a half-moon soared, while on the right it almost vanished beneath a mesh of lines blotted out along the equator by an elongated island chain. What mythology! These were the armorial bearings of the Air Force Eastern Test Range, as it said in the V-shaped scroll beneath the shield, as if we cared. I wondered if anyone answering an ad for Your Own Coat of Arms had ever received one such as this. Every one I saw had a staple punched aslant the crest, as if to keep it from flying off. In the opposite corner a familiar logo reappeared: the V in the circle, with an arrowhead refracted downward, as it were, from the right-hand line as it cut past the ring into another medium (though the center of the ring was the same gray as the area outside it). **NASA**, NASA's chromosome-like computer printout of itself, was at the top left, and in the opposite corner the number 267. I clipped the badge on, suddenly aware of my membership.

The next hour was dreamlike: a deluge of rain that halted for an uncertain sun, glint-splash, glint-splash, just like that; three drab-blue Air Force buses in front of the Ramada, due to leave at one o'clock; Nineveh Bunsen passing out nuts and potato chips, daring anyone to diet; Raoul fuming because he, of all people, seemed to have neither badge nor windshield sticker (then I realized his face was his badge); a weird conversation piece, as the charcoal sky poured again, about taking the extra day if need be: "Oh," Raoul drawled, "the TV show can wait," as Nineveh agreed, saying he'd then have something to say, at which he stiffened up, thinly amused by the notion of himself at a loss. We fidget-waited in the car to follow the buses to the viewing site. A space fanatic went by, his hat and coat and grip plastered with space logos in several languages. No doubt he was tattooed with the NASA worm as well, in some fine and private place where only he and they embraced.

Now more fans arrived, from cars and neighboring motels, burdened with cameras, telescopic lenses, umbrellas, and even flags. All of a sudden the sky changed to something like a field of iron filings furrowed by a plough. The rain stopped. The buses revved their engines. A plump girl, purse in hand, ran across the Ramada parking lot and tripped full length over the curb into a puddle. Her purse spilled everything. The buses did not go. "I don't"—Raoul was grunting at the sky—"like the look of that at all. *Lightning*, that's the one thing." Off we went up A1A, aching for a subtropical miracle of clemency, past the Serv-Ur-Self sign we'd come to feel an outrageous fondness for. I saw one, two, three twitches of lightning as we crossed over onto Merritt Island and took the Kennedy Parkway northward to Gate 2. It was already ten after two as we cruised past the sign saying "Titan III: World's Most Versatile Booster" and another: "Deer Wild Hogs Crossing Road." My wrists were trembling from too much coffee and not enough sleep. When it rained again, beating itself in front of us into a bran foam, I almost gave up hope, even as Raoul abruptly regained his, saying the more rain the better. It was now 2:15. I opened a window and heard aircraft not very high, up in the cloud, testing the weather with lightning detectors. As we reached the site and parked, I heard the PA loudspeakers and could not believe my ears: the countdown, which seemed to have halted briefly, had resumed. By Jove, it was going to happen after all.

Next I heard an official, tutored voice, which I recognized as that of Gerry Soffen, giving a two-minute lecturette I was too excited to heed. The atmosphere at the site felt heavy and ionized, reminding me of dark, damp Guyana cricket grounds as you inspected the pitch after the rain that halted play had ceased. Here too the grass felt spongy. Banana Creek was a sluggish graphite hue. Gulls were yawping. I visited one of the outdoor commodes, shaped like old-fashioned humpbacked refrigerators and lit within by an eerie light that was daytime filtering through bottle-green plastic. We all of us stood at the press barrier, a long shelf lined with telephones. We might have been taking communion. Raoul stayed there with Nineveh, aiming his camera, while Swan and I wandered over to the bleachers. For once, Raoul had no tape recorder next to his chin. We borrowed a cloth from the provident local press corps and mopped down a couple of seating spaces. On went the count. There would soon be a decision, announced a monstrously sedate voice, whether or not to switch to automatic countdown.

Two twenty-three. They decided to launch. The computer took over and the *Viking* had no choice. I was actually shaking with fused astonishment and the accumulated anticlimaxes of a month's delay. What had seemed impossible was happening all too easily. We looked dotingly across at Complex 41, two gray wispy towers between the VAB and Complex 37. A chunk of blue sky shaped like a manta ray came floating across from right to left. I had never before found the inevitable so delicious. There were no distractions now, in the eye or the mind. No fleet of small vessels had chugged out from Port Canaveral to form an emergency safety chain under the rocket's path-to-be. There was no steel chute down which astronauts could plunge from the launcher base into a cave-like room, lined with foam rubber, after descending over three hundred feet by elevator cage. No one was talking now except the manicured icicle voice on the PA. Launch would be on time. Raoul turned around, waved jubilantly at us, and we two pointed across the water to where, almost invisible in the gloom, like a stray part from a train set, "our" *Viking* waited, for all the world as if nothing was going to happen. A tiny H shape, dwarfed by the VAB three miles away, *Viking* II, alias *Viking* I, was at the mercy of the Titan III. All planes had cleared the area, we heard, and now the silence was golden as fire, broken only by marsh birds and a distant mutter of thunder. It was almost a religious pause as we waited for something not to descend, but to catch flame and crawl upward away from its makers.

"Nine-eight-seven," went the reverse crescendo of the count as I thought, Nothing can stop it now. It was going to happen, even if it went wrong. The distant structure twinkled like a Christmas tree, or a photon sprinkler starting up. Not a sound, not even as yellow liquid or lava roamed along the ground on one side of the rocket only. Sky thunder came to us before the Titan's hoarser version, which reached us as yellow blebs and spumes out on the other side. A small sun had broken loose. High on a cone of ivory and gold whose base broadened into smoke second by second, *Viking* II on top of Centaur on top of Titan III began to climb. The cone foreshortened into an incandescent disc so white, so bleached-gold, it seemed chryselephantine. I looked away for relief, with a retina image that gave me two *Viking*s when I looked again, so I tried to fit the one in my eye upon the one in the air. I donned Polaroids just before the seethe of that living blot became a tunneling rasp sundered by crackles as solid propellants collided in too little space and spewed forth the basis of lift. Now *Viking* seemed to tilt at a slight eastward angle, and the full blast of the boosters found us, an iron-hollow, desolate slam-slam pitted with terrible irregular crackings as the combustion went mad. "Go, go!" cried someone behind us. The bleachers trembled in unison. The air pressed down as if thickened. My forehead stabbed with pain. As the rocket munched its way up into the clouds, from which it sounded even louder, I realized this was the clanking tubular noise I'd heard under anesthesia, except for the cracks. Again I heard the V-2 of wartime. Again I reminded myself that this raucous dart had just left on a half-million-mile trip. I could still hear it erupting, mixing clank with snarl in its own lonely echo-chamber, and then fading into a busy chug like any other aerial vehicle. It went, it came back, the same ghostly gnawing throb, its crack-crack fainter, as if the cloud-base were going to fall down on us insulted. I felt I had heard something massive being broken, some core of nature split and ground into a billion shards. But it was only a machine doing no more and no less than it was designed to do, and on time, with that unthinkably instrumental crown of Thor on top of it, intended for Mars.

My eyes were dim, my hands were still locked together. Again, even when it should not have done, came the afterburn of that tall explosion, the vastly amplified frying sound, the volcanic splutter, the doom-laden crack-crack. Again the golden reflection sprawled across Banana Creek, both corrugating and smoothing itself, towering but flat. Already, the lopsided double mound of white-and-orange smoke across the creek had begun to rise toward the black stuff. Something out there, low above the land, had been disemboweled. There was the stomach, there the livid and amorphous small intestine. The patch of blue, no longer manta-shaped but a Lüger in silhouette, was now left of the VAB. The entire event had occupied one minute. I felt lowered, as by bathysphere. A Roman candle in incendiary slow motion had outsoared us all.

No one was up there with it. All through the night, it would stave on through space, night after day after night, for ten months. As the last smoke cleared, one part of the launch tower looked bent slightly inward, an optical illusion surely. Or so I thought at the time, hearing later that *Viking* II set fire to the pad, which *Viking* I did not. Once again, "our" rocket had proved almost too much to handle. In fact, the pad had melted; lusty *Viking* II wanted no imitators in train. I shook Raoul's hand as if his horse had won the Kentucky Derby. "Oh," cried Nineveh, back in voice, as if *Viking*—the whole "stack" of it, as space jargon had it—was only just beginning to move. Swan flung her arms wide in celebration. *Viking* had gone. We felt weirdly deprived. Only abstractly were we human. "Something else," Raoul self-consciously wisecracked as someone photographed our group. "It twinkled," I said. We milled around, exchanging impressions. Here came Gerry Soffen, delighted, but like the rest of us unable to speak. "We *saw* it," sighed Swan. Skeins of lightning lanced the coast. Throats full, we said repeated goodbyes as if, somehow, the word or the phrase no longer worked for us. Now the rain slanted down once more and, all the way to the airport, we marveled at what we had witnessed. The gamble had worked. We even had time to kill. My last sight of Complex 41 was of the safety crew aligning its vehicles at a prudent distance; I hadn't yet realized how much damage *Viking* II had done to the concrete beneath it, or that, had *Viking* I done this, the pad would never have been ready in time for its successor. Humming and smiling, we forged through the rain on empty stomachs. How vibrant the water-strewn air felt with our rocket high above it; the world was bigger and not worse. My rib cage had trembled and almost, it felt, imploded; my skull too; and my hands still did as I thought about that noble, savage eyeful: a trance, an affair, an ingot.

At the airport Nineveh deposited her press badge on the ledge at the Hertz desk and I retrieved it for one of my nephews (who knew the space cape was in some measure a holy of holies and would relish one of its pomps). We devoured crab cakes and big steins of beer, wondering if everyone knew the news. I suspected that not many cared, not Cap'n Grog, out catching mullet and snapper for Bernard's Surf, nor those whose principal contemporary attunement was to Patty Hearst as she teetered on the brink of myth. Against what I called a Cal Tech futurity, too many pitted a querulous fatuity of What earthly *good* was *Viking* to society, compared with, say, Disney World or the Salk Institute? I recurred to an old Galilean or Newtonian view, the one that thrived before people began to worry about knowledge's having no moral sense. I belonged to the tribe of wonder, of knowledge for its own sake. I was, as Raoul said all of us were, an ambulatory collection of 10^{14} cells, mobilized for just a brief integrity in a universe whose elementary particles added up to 10^{80}. There was too little time in the life of any of us to justify precluding knowledge of any kind. As Fred Hoyle had suggested, we had no faith in tomorrow, forever harking back to an aggressive, primitive past that overlapped our present. In his view, it might even be possible that what he called "our moment of 'intelligence' " would not last more than a century or two more, perhaps not more than the next few decades. If so, those of us who could should live that moment of intelligence to the full. I would not mind, I told myself, having it said of me that I wondered as much as I could for as long as I could.

We flew back at much less than *Viking* speed, offered a choice of fish or steak for dinner on Eastern 154 to JFK, when all they had, it seemed, was steak. No matter: given the exultant mood we were in, pretzels would have been ambrosia. We did it, we *did* it. Contrary *Viking* I had at last obliged. I was reminded of the French expression which obliged you, when you wanted to say you'd been present at something, to say you'd "assisted" at it. A week later, on the *Tonight Show*, Raoul mentioned his having been present at liftoff; NBC had cut his wandering hair, so he looked a fraction more all-American, but his passing reference to *Viking* II was crisp with the thrill of having seen and heard it go. Reading aloud some amusing material he'd found in a magazine, about what computers could find out about us, he went on to tell how, when the *Viking*s reached Mars, the two computers aboard each would be given an IQ test, after which the two "dumber" computers would be shut down. Non-man-rated, the mission still seemed intensely human. We had seen it flare.

In later weeks, *Viking* II behaved impeccably, at least until the batteries in the Lander refused to obey the signal that charged them (they were uncharged at launch, so as to prolong their life). All went well with *Viking* I, but II's Lander looked as if it wouldn't be able to switch over to its own power supply just before coming down from Mars orbit; the batteries in question powered a motor-driven switch that effected the changeover from Orbiter solar-panel power to self-sufficient Lander power. After some feverish work at the Jet Propulsion Laboratory and the laboratories of Martin Marietta in Denver, analysts identified the fault as being in the battery charger itself. So they switched to the backup system, which worked right away. There were other, slight problems too, but the *Viking* team at the JPL, some of them veterans of the snag-ridden *Mariner* 10 mission to Venus and Mercury, were still in good spirits. This had been the most expensive unmanned vehicle ever launched and, as one report put it, "no one was asleep at the switch."

How far Swan and I had come from those fat books called survey courses of literature, from the jargon of the intentional fallacy and the complex icon. We had emigrated to a world of fire and fuel, metal and smoke, almost that of fireworks and July-the-Fourth jubilation. It was highly likely that we would never come back. We had a keen sense of having been baptized into a new cult, whose obligations would ever after dog us until we had made our peace with space. We were not, ever again, the same people, having thrust our arms upward in concert with the *Vikings*, aching to make contact with what had so far been only imagined, not that imagination suffered from this launch; but sometimes we wanted to test it against the indelible, brute thing.

FIFTEEN

We had heard, and argued about, the old Calvinist notion that, so long as life was productive, it didn't matter if life was bleak: just the sort of doctrine to appeal to someone morose or severe, or to abbots of monasteries or old-style industrialists. Now, it seemed, life was not only being productive, it was being luxurious: not the lap of luxury, perhaps, but most certainly its armpit or within its nether cheeks. If we were supposed to feel guilty about this, we never did; while people less technically or scientifically inclined were busy manufacturing term papers, treatises of scholiastic aridity, and lectures on structuralism, we were having our own fireworks display in excellent company, trespassing, overreaching, going everyone one better. *Solar System* was coming along well. I had expressed myself on it, at her invitation, and had said things about structure that brought a flush to her beautifully modeled face; the novelist is no miniaturist, has few Swiss watchmakerish tendencies, and suspects that poets do not take the novel seriously as an art form. So novelists sometimes say things sharply, deep down aware of the many novelists, the true mercantile hacks of the calling, who have no more idea of structure than a wasp in custard. She would not ask me about structure again, I suspected; it was no problem, it simply had to be attended to, and she was more than capable of that. In fact her cosmic pastoral was beginning to glow, not least from a textural elegance rare in my reading experience. She was taking off like a rocket, and I just knew the launch had reanimated her, making her take chances as Whitman took them; indeed, the entire experience, from Bernard's Surf to final blast-off, had conferred on her the same belongingness I had sensed in myself. In a way, we had been taken over, reenfranchised.

"Know who I am?" she asked me over lunch one day, after we had discussed leaving the ratty little apartment and moving into a rented house, as Nabokov used to do in those parts, he the one Coriolis eminence who boasted no friends.

"The best lyrical poet writing now." It was no sop; I meant it.

"Arguably," she joshed. "Actually, I am the girl with permanent reservations at the Cocoa Ramada. My life has changed. I am so interdisciplinary now, I can't breathe."

She had been vouchsafed a magic carpet and she was riding it to the back of beyond. She even contemplated, now, an interdisciplinary dissertation and was going to spend the next ten years acquiring degrees, something I'd never bothered to do after the first two. Such was the American way, I knew, and a poet might well contemplate such means of safety.

Thanks to catalytic *Viking*, I had embarked on a huge novel, *Jack Fist*, that re-presented the Faust story, working on it in the little alcove in her apartment, or on planes from everywhere to Coriolis. This mighty text was never to see the light of day, not as a novel anyway, but it would eventually yield a shower of short stories that did, as if the book's motion were centrifugal and what I thought were chapters, each compelling the next into being, were self-sufficient stories set in different countries, the best and best-known of which would be the one set in Africa. I was pounding away at something whose essence was diffuse. I thought of Drake and the Spanish Armada and how it was scattered. After finishing, one day I ripped the book apart and read it for proud pieces, setting the rest aside as so much scuff. I was like a Thomson's gazelle, eating the afterbirth so its aroma would not attract predators to the tiny offspring wobbling beside me. Of course, some afterbirths make you want to throw up, which weakens your chances of keeping people from knowing your novel was never a novel but only a bundle of fasces lashed together with a young man's shoelace. We were both working hard, she to more purpose than I. Then she fell ill, with a kind of bronchitis, coughing miserably, and one day I went out to the local variety store to get her some magazines and I ended up cradling her shuddering head on my thigh and asking her if she would like something less temporary-looking: a house, a nest? She seemed overjoyed at the words, little aware that what we would end up with was another miracle, awaiting us only a mile or two away. But I anticipate, as perhaps someone addicted to rockets that don't go is likely to do. Truth was, I had learned something about writing novels, and the lesson had cost me dear, dearer than structure and its ins and outs had cost Swan. I had learned that, after a certain number of pages, the book develops a momentum, a forward charge, it is hard to resist because you think it the authentic motion of the opus that is going well. The lesson to learn was that even books, novels especially, going badly will develop this same onward lunge and drag you after them, giving you that old Attila the Hun feeling. On you go, to defeat. The only way out of this escapade was to fight the novel all the way, not knowing if it were good or bad, always allowing enough forward momentum to keep the thing from stalling, yet curbing it to keep it honest.

When I told Swan this, she said, simply, "So writing novels and writing poems are much the same thing. Do you still believe in inspiration? Don't tell me. This whole discussion, just begun, is too damned serious. Do we *have* to show each other our everything? Tell me, hon, how do we save ourselves from wasting all that energy? Can we advance without backing down? I sometimes think novelists and poets have to be like those Lipizaner stallions that trot so prettily and get nowhere at minimum speed." I agreed, telling her I didn't see the point of assembling six hundred pages only to extract from them a hundred pages of short fiction. My God, every time I tried to write a novel, it turned into a short story, and every time I tried a short story it turned into a novel. Perhaps the right strategy was somehow to deceive the mind, or the hands, not letting on what you intended. So, you lull the mind into thinking you intend a novel when, really, you intend a story, then at the last moment, or halfway, change from one to the other, thus guaranteeing a novel. Would it work? I doubted it, faintly remembering the philosopher Hume's notion that it was impossible to find the mind without an idea in it. Could one keep secrets from the mind itself? Yes, if somehow you could control both the conscious and the subconscious. Or write without intention, letting the words just happen. It was so much of a problem that perhaps one would better leave the mind to its perverse orientation and learn to live with it as it was. Perhaps the problem was one of age and aging. It was one thing to say to yourself, in 1996 or 1997, say, how long ago the two *Viking* missions seemed, and all the hullabaloo about how much the dickering and shuffling cost. It had become a part of history, rather noble history at that, and one was entitled to regard it as something hard and fast with which to compare more recent events, such as the *Challenger* disaster, contrasting minor bungling with lethal criminality. Trouble began, of course, when you told yourself you were there in 1975, in the first or second flush of your prime, and now you were less than flushed, though still addicted to space. In other words, it was hard to accept the degree of aging your historical involvement proved. You wanted history to age, so to speak, without doing so yourself: not logged in a suffocating parallel column in the account book of the ages.

I wouldn't say I felt *caught up* in the *Viking* process. I felt, rather, an osmosis that tugged various childhood fixations into the open: chemistry, planes, the heavens, and showed them not outgrown. Had there been, in and around the Ramada Inn, a seepage of visionaries who soaked up the Florida sun because of what it stood for, rather than because it browned? I recalled a sense of brimming thrill as the years of talk and work came into focus first for the *Viking*eers, then for such as myself, as we tuned in to it. It was as if everyone, while about the mundanest chores (switching a room reservation or drying out a beach towel on one of the coke-hard lawns), felt on the edge of a territory that went up and out, beyond and beneath. There were children everywhere, even babies, as well as visibly retrogressing adults. I came back to that emotion, its waxings and wanings, wondering if it amounted to ecstasy, in this instance being dispossessed of self by a superior validation embodied in two automated laboratories up the coast. There was a leaving without anyone's going anywhere. There was a union without anyone's joining hands with anyone else. There was an interhuman cell of will that wanted the two *Viking*s to stand on their own tails and fly straight. Back of many minds was Captain X, the range officer, who lived in a bunker miles from the launch site; he it was who, if need arose, pressed the button for destruct. No one wore one, but in every lapel, on every swimsuit, I saw another button, and it said "Instruct."

What I felt, then, was an ecstasy of logic, mediated by the scientists of Martin Marietta, TRW, the Langley Research Center, and the Jet Propulsion Laboratory, Pasadena. Without such knowledge as they hankered after, what forgiveness? Without such knowledge, what ignorance! Some forms of research are dangerous and sometimes we abandon them; and that is a decision out of knowledge.

"Got you," said Swan, peeling an orange and deftly dropping the peel into a plastic bag at my request (I a fruit phobic). "To act as if there were things we ought never to know, or to seek to know, that's a monstrous blackout, isn't it? A decision, and a view, out of the Dark Ages. We might as well lie in bed, embracing each other and weeping nonstop. Humanity has no right to play ostrich, looking in the sands of mumbo jumbo for reasons not to look anywhere else. If our context exists, take the smell of orange peel; we have no intellectual or moral right to ignore it. If we had no context at all, the question would never arise. It just so happens that, among the things our limited brain can conceive of, there is the not-ourselves, meaning at least two things: what we can conceive of, but haven't yet achieved, and what exists but isn't human. I would add what might exist and wouldn't be human either. In thinking about these wonderful things we're accepting some kind of Invitation to the Waltz, some cosmic communiqué undreamed of. Wow, I'm getting sleepy. At bottom, I suspect, it's a raw little credo, mine, saying only that the mind should believe in its own unknowable future." She had consumed the orange and appeared on the point of sleep as I retreated, as ever, from the acrid tang in the air, almost retching. I must once have been frightened by an orange or a pear. She was in good form that day, knowing exactly why she had gone to Cocoa, not for the ride, or to witness the liftoff, but to celebrate her love of life. My own reasons, I thought, were woolier. Dumping the little plastic bag of peel in the trash, she sighed as if it had been full of some heavy metal, and went to rinse her hands, emerging with the full bloom of some nonfruity perfume on her hands: Byzance, perhaps, a gift from me. *Viking* was the ritual event that kept repeating in my mind, an engram refiring until, bless the thought, I had become the event myself, my own rocket and payload, blasted without a rearward glance into the airless empyrean of the knowable. The main point was not to be afraid of learning what was there, no matter how little, how severe. Deep down, you wanted the universe altered. You wanted the poisonous arrow of time to go backward. It did not. So you sought to redefine it: the arrow stood still while the context streamed past.

Was this why, lifelong devotee of airplanes, I now began to interest myself even more in flight, seeking to travel much faster within my given orbit, aping the *Viking* rockets, desirous of sheer speed? We had not long ago met a charming couple, Segundo

Cieli, a painter-professor who taught silk screen and other procedures at Coriolis, and his wife, Janette, who worked in the university publications department. They were not astronomy freaks by any means, but he was a pilot and owned a Piper Apache of enormous well-groomed distinction and she had published several historical novels.

We had seen Segundo do his Pitts aerobatic show above the arts quad at Coriolis, marvelous to behold, describing a perfect parallelogram in pink smoke, then bisecting it, quartering it, enclosing it in a fairly tidy ring, then barreling through it in a death dive that made the ivied buildings shake. He must have been in incomparable health, we thought, subjecting his body to such strain, but the show was stunning: deliberate, precise, and lyrical. Then we saw him on TV, the same stunts, and marveled at the scheming involved in being a sky-artist, as he had so often been billed in Prague, Venice, Paris, and many other places. He was a contented polymath, and I could see how a polymath never had enough of anything, never enough other things at which to excel, and I felt for him, fixed on my one and only thing, determined to master it even if it took me down into the lower depths and left me there whining and airless.

SIXTEEN

There I was, then, not long after returning from Cocoa Beach, sitting in his car holding the pump end while he fed air into the Apache's mainwheel tires. We were going up to keep him current, or his airman's ticket would lapse. It was a coolish, stringently bright day with an increasing wind out of the north; so, if we flew south, we would have a tailwind going, a headwind coming back. The little whirr of the pump, powered from the car's cigarette lighter socket, ceased as he switched off, and we soon parked the car beyond the safety fence, which involved much folderol with plastic cards, and walked back to the plane on the ramp to untie it, remove the gust-lock clamp from the rudder, and unlock the loading door.

Just before the Apache took off, its wheels began to get the jitters, gently thrumming up and down, touching the runway then lifting slightly off it. How slowly we went, even to take off, but never as slowly as we landed, almost without seeming to move at all. I asked, and Segundo Cieli explained that, if he worked at it, he could get the landing speed down to about forty miles an hour. Slow flight had always beguiled me as huge jets just lolled in the air, on the brink of lurching out of control but just tweaked and goaded enough to stay on track, close to stall but never quite going that far. Perhaps some analogy with walking had its hooks into me: to walk so slowly as barely to make headway, inching forward. I liked slow flight because it defied the rules, almost, and suggested the plane that did nothing but hover, Harrier-style.

Southward we plunged, fed extra impetus by that somber wind from Canada, above landscapes increasingly green that would soon be bleaching and fading. Here, in Waverley, was a town half in New York, half in Pennsylvania, whatever that meant in terms of taxes. On we flew with, right in front of us, some half hour's flying distant, ridge after ridge, and a huge flattish mountain over on our right. We were not going that far. There was one enormous thump as we hit turbulent air, and then all was smooth again. I knew what sort of clatter we made as we went over as I had heard it from ground-level as Segundo swooped past. Taken by the phenomenon of horizontal flight compared with the vertical mode of the rocket, I said almost not enough to be polite. I wondered at the two mindless engines hammering away, never faltering unless Segundo made them do so. Today we were high, about three thousand feet, but other days we would be skimming a small lake or a huge one like Ontario. The trick was to lunge sideways with the plane as it banked, not to stiffen your body and try to lean the other way lest, vain thought, you might fall out. All these, unless something went wrong, were round trips, whereas the *Viking*s were just aimed outward, to go on forever and ever through limitless space until they disintegrated. That hyperbolic trajectory stirred me, too much perhaps, reminding me of their automatic, inhuman quality. This was bourgeois, riding the Apache; tracking the *Viking*s was avant-garde, though I doubted if any scientist used such a term.

"Utterly gorgeous," I told Swan on my return. "There's nothing more soothing than going up and watching the map it's all become." She knew, but she wanted to fly herself, not be driven. What intrigued her about flight was that we lived on a planet where things flew: if something were shaped right (or not) and propelled fast enough it *flew*. Sprightly, poetic Swan was young enough to delight in the existentialism of flight, making minute life-or-death decisions, which also taught her weather, topography, and ecology. She was never, like some men, into dominating metal. What intrigued her about flight was how it led to joy, to wonder, whereas what intrigued Segundo and me was the technology; we took the necessary domination of the airship for granted, as men would. "What would you call a neighbor of Jason?" She often asked me these riddles out of the blue, on a whim, and I answered as best I could, but not this time. "Adjacent," she said, and we moved on, just a bit rippling with amusement. "What sort of table talk would you get from a command module?" I had no idea. "Orbiter dicta," she laughed, having a ball. The next riddle would be mine, providing a glitch or a flicker in the even tenor of disciplined conversation. Swan had an extraordinary knack for oral tidbits that gave us a rest before conversing hard again.

Talking, she had a singular grace, and her face seemed luminous no doubt because she had fair skin with an almost Irish sheen (the rain-soaked complexion for which the Irish are famous). Her black hair acted as a shawl, frayed behind her, effectively blotting out the whole world and making you wonder, if you didn't know, how far down to the ground it extended. I knew she washed it daily ("*All* of it?" I used to joke). She was a dab hand at empathy, with an enormous gift for getting inside someone's skin and finding words for them when they lacked them. Not that she found me fathomable; she knew to avoid me for the first two hours each day as I woke up slowly, and then to avoid me again toward midnight, which was when I really got my second wind and could start chattering so much I kept her from her well-earned sleep. In between, I do declare she found me fairly civilized, a fundamentally lazy person who drove himself because he knew how little he would achieve if he followed his natural inclination. I liked to get things right the first time, and this was no doubt why I found a couple of hours' writing exhausting, so much so that all I wanted to do was sleep. It was the effort and strain to do several drafts in one, the first time, because deep inside I believed that, if you knew English properly, you should be able to arrange your sentences in your head before setting them down. Any other kind of revision was mere busywork. She did not buy this, and secretly I believed she was one of those—this no slur on her gift—who liked revision for its own sake, a member of the tribe including Oscar Wilde and Walter Pater, who ascended to their room of an afternoon and descended just before tea, having changed a comma, and did so with a sense of triumph. My own view was that you should adjust the comma in your head before committing anything to paper. Indeed, whenever I spoke in public, which was fairly often, I somehow saw what I was going to say arranged before my mind's eye like a series of banner headlines; in a sense I was reading from an internal script. So who was the greater perfectionist? She, tinkering with paper, or I, composing in toto in the cranium? It did not matter, but truly we both took an interest in the process we had committed our lives to, not with a view to changing anything, but simply in the spirit of someone who compares two colorful butterflies whose minds slunk away to space more often than anyone knew.

Hardly a one of these tender, erudite conversations did not end in a kissing spree, done slowly, lingeringly, with finely calculated placing, almost as if there were a schedule of lips, cheeks, chin, nose, eyes, temple, hands, neck, and so forth, not so much foreplay as pensive fondling in its own right. We would sit, sometimes for half an hour, trysting (if that was the word), or plighting our troth (if that was the phrase), sometimes marveling that we had met and actually gone ahead, advancing from circumspect reconnoiter to a wordless clinch that said it all. "Was I just lucky?" I would ask with a touch of staginess. "Or did I deserve you?"

"Both," she would whisper.

"And you were unlucky, then. You could have done much better than someone such as me. Too old for you, not in good enough health, tricky temperament, and all the other minuses." I knew this plaintive speech by heart, and so did she.

"You can't have everything," she sighed, accepting all my disqualifications in one bouquet, which she then threw bride-style to some other victim across the room.

"That's the heroic view of us," I said. "You deserve better. I sometimes think I'll just vanish and leave you to the rest of your days, not because I don't adore and worship you; I do, but because, as they say, I'm stealing your best years now mine are over. Honest."

"It simply means," she told me, as always, "you will have to mend your ways and take better care of yourself. Get your health back in trim and keep it there. It is possible, you know, if you'll only put your mind to it. You are really quite self-indulgent. I mean, instead of boozing, which thank God you do less of, inhaling the scent of flowers. Become a flower inhaler instead of a Scotch guzzler."

"I could," I said. "So why *don't* I?"

"You promised."

So I did. Was this the great female overture, always made when women were trying to make you over, that would improve you no end and make you a better catch? Was it true that women always tried to perfect you once they had decided you were worth breeding with? Was Charles Darwin speaking through all this reformist zeal? Was my exquisite lady trafficking in the evolution of species? She would sit there, often weary, her face somehow drained by preoccupation with term papers, drafts of *Solar System*, correspondence with editors major and minor, and tug her hair backward as if peeling her face. Then she let it go again, to spray sideways and seem to grow, sucking vigor from the very air, especially if we were seated near one of her plants (she never gave them too much water, she claimed, and that was why they did so well). At school I had always been fighting; small, I had often been bullied, so I had learned to fight, and having learned how I didn't want my skills to go to waste. An adult, I drank because it gave me some euphoric glow that lasted all day and a priceless gift of the gab. Now, with her, I watched my step, tried to behave well (as if I knew), and thought to my most private self how lucky I was to have this good-natured, easy-tempered paragon with the superlative gift. I knew enough to hold her tight whenever I was in doubt, and she would never fail to respond, sometimes teasing me about what she called my spade-shaped rump (the shape suited her) or a certain expanse of my upper thigh, which she thought silky and therefore named cuddleskin, which grew into a nickname with an uppercase *C*. We were always tending each other in this way, both celebrating and teasing, each tempting the other into an inadequate gesture for which she/he would have to make immediate restitution. Ever since *Viking* we had been kissier, lofted temporarily into a region beyond humanity and allowed to descend slowly, at silk-worm speed, while communing in a mysterious unknown language full of totemic animals and special kisses: the eyebrow kiss, the earlobe kiss, the eyelash kiss, the abstract kiss in which the lips hovered in place but never touched, hers mine, and vice versa. Who were we to evolve the poetics of kissing? We did what came naturally and sometimes came up with names, as with the spider cuddle, when a galloping middle finger, leading with its knuckle, scampered up the other's arm and then backtracked to take up station in the palm of a cupped hand. That was all, but it felt like elongated stroking, suffering one of the first abnormal rushes of light, as when, in its journey through interstellar space, a narrow-band signal spreads out and frays as it passes through clouds of electrons, the result being that what would otherwise have arrived as an intact single unit arrives in packets, having traveled along a curved instead of a straight line. And their arrival time varies by as much as several thousandths of a second. Were we like that, so vulnerable, starting out as one, then frayed into two, then reunited after having arrived apart? A simile any more scientific would have lost us en route.

I felt as if Swan and I were the chief performers in some freak show of the defiant; swapping affectionate metaphors to beat down the past. It was odd to find a gifted young woman with few happy memories of her childhood, so much so that, at times, as I discovered without much overdue probing, Swan had grown up with low self-esteem. No matter how well she did, and she had distinguished herself in many things, the achievement meant little to her, did not in any way boost her notion of herself. It was almost as if she remembered nothing that was good. There were gaping rents in her memory. When I said to her, in my ponderous way, "You have to invent your self-confidence; parents can sometimes lay it on you, but few do, only a few special ones like my mother," she stared at me as if I had been discussing crockery from Jupiter. None of this made sense. Somehow she had ended up brainwashed into believing herself an unworthy person who, indeed, had no right or need to invent anything of the kind. How ironic to sit with her and, as if planning a rote, reciting the list of her brilliant accomplishments; I might just as well have been mouthing the names of Lon Chaney Jr.'s favorite golf courses. She took none of this in, bizarrely relegated to a chronic pawnbroking that had begun when she began to speak. She was a winged, bird-like thing, intent on knowing and passionately exploring, precocious and idealistic, only recently a child.

Whenever I praised her work or her wit, I realized I was confronting a slogan that said "Praise does not apply to me, ever," and I recognized I wasn't getting through: only in an abstract sense anyway, and it was no use insisting, or repeating; she would civilly and gently accept the encomium without in any way hugging it to herself. It was something that had happened miles away. She, of all women, was the one who would never suffer the palsy of excessive self-esteem.

I wish that back then I'd had the insight I do today; instead of praising her feats I should have extolled the ontology—the beingness—of all created things, gathering her up in the general swoop, pointing out the miracle of organic life. Perhaps that might have worked. The part of her that wrote seemed unconnected to the part of her that suffered. Yet she, of all poets, had been hurt into poetry. What upset me most of all was to watch her saunter-sleepwalking through the bright savannah of human possibility, aching to do well only to distract herself from the nightmare of not caring. Perhaps she should remove herself, I thought, from me, surely the most wounded of all surgeons plying the steel. And, sometimes, the sound of distress she made was the cry of a baby, or a peewit in a marsh, and it cut me to the heart.

One thing I did was to give her a gift-thick Gentile Christmas. The vision of Too Much cheered her, especially when she awoke on that December 25 to find, wrapped in new brown paper emblazoned with jolly decals, an erector set or a chemistry lab. In helping her have a more ravishing childhood, I relived my own, recognizing there was nothing I loved more than regressing. I who had had a childhood of delight even in a family not well-to-do (one never-to-be-forgotten morning awakening to discover by my bed a huge red model railroad locomotive in which I could sit and whose pedals I could push). That pandemonium of parcels, playful index to the world's plenty, might have soothed her had she had it much earlier. I would gladly have shared my delicious childhood with her—who needs *all* of a chemistry lab or an erector set? She certainly needed a barricade of toys back then with which to deflect any critical, undevoted gaze. A model train buzzing around the living room would surely have cramped the censorious style of all household spies, and fantastic heat engines operated by tiny batteries would have held them back just enough. How many deprivations Swan had been through, I would never know; I no longer tried to single them out from one another, but marveled at the way she had survived and continued to do so, not unscarred, but resolved to do no harm to anyone. How she managed to transcend, I have never found out, but I ascribe the miracle to imagination, not always the savior grace in all lives, but in her case enabling her to perform a curative feat of domestic immigration.

Next thing, an August sun in January, we were having this well-informed, unrehearsed conversation about her erector sets, of which she had three—for, as she said, *a boy's* Christmas. "I noticed," she announced, "how the American one was full of parts that would all join together, a miracle of combinability as if inspired by the carbon ring, but no great colors, just a sort of hodgepodge. Democratic, I suppose. Then there was the English box, *Meccano* I think they called it, and it was a masterpiece of colors: blue, red, yellow, white, gold, so whatever you put together had this chromatic aspect to it. A box for the eye. And the German one, you couldn't build anything unless you consulted a plan; there was no improvising with it. There was a right way and a wrong, and the wrong was freely improvisational. Now I know what little boys around the world go through every December. Is there a Japanese one?"

"Would you like," I asked her, using one of our oldest and most respected formulae, "to split a soda?" It must have been one of the first things she said to me, I who had never heard of splitting a soda. All it meant was sharing, but it became one of our fetishes: never a soda opened without being split. We lived together in a house made of words, custom-made for our own esoteric phrases. People grinned, usually, when they heard us speaking our pidgin out in society; perhaps we inspired some into devising new ways of talking to one another. I doubted it, but words were our defense against things that went bump in the night, crash in the day, slinking up on us while we felt supremely happy. Little wonder, I thought, that we had grown fond of what lay out of reach, was uniquely nonhuman, when so much remained to deal with and put right on the Rialto of the at-hand, where we conducted most of our business. In a way we were both unfit for conventional life, as many artists are; and a good deal of what we thought mutual understanding was mere guesswork. We clung to emblematic saliences, unable to forget the doctor who first hypnotized her (a tiny man with huge compensatory pen), delighted to contemplate at a distance the new file that

Shirl Cornwall had created for Raoul Bunsen, who received many crank letters. "Chipped Terra-Cotta," its label said, and into it went all those letters he didn't answer, and couldn't. We may not have left our berth of liberal or creative arts, but we did have the saving grace of another membership that ran from the Space Sciences Building to Arecibo in Puerto Rico and out there to Mars and beyond, tugging us, making us exult because our world had suddenly become huge, even as we doubted our ability to live securely or traditionally in it. One of the great Victorians, I recalled, had spoken exuberantly of how membership in almost any institution conferred the expansive power of a great experience, not so much a membership as, in Great Victorian terms, incorporation into the dayspring or the godhead: something sherbety and fabulous.

SEVENTEEN

I wondered deeply when Swan went off to take her first flying lesson, but I fobbed off the analytical side of my mind by saying to myself such words as *penumbra*, *atmosphere*, *bird's-eye view*, *deep space*, and Cocteau's old bromide "Man is magnificent." In part, she was putting herself to the test; a superb driver, she was going to adapt her skills to another element, but what drove her in the main was the thrill and mystery of it all, the magic of being up aloft, all that flight could teach her about the planet she lived on. She did it despite the weird danger. Her instructor, whom she called Nagel, or Nail, was one of those jumped-up would-be yuppies who saw themselves, only years hence, in the left-hand seat of a jumbo jet: fond hope. This one would end up making a forced landing in a ploughed field, after which, by dint of slaving as an instructor, he settled into the right-hand seat of a commuter plane of evil reputation. He and Swan did not get on; never having made it to college, he hated intellectuals and spent much of their time aloft raving at her, which in a way played into her hands, since challenge was part of what she was paying for. Week after week she returned bathed in sweat and coated with dried tears. Instruction was going ahead, I decided, amazed she handled the math well. Courage she had in abundance, but she got no technological joy from flying; to her, as she often said, it was a matter of innocent fascination, roller-coastery fun, whereas Nagel, in his pedantic way, believed in horsing the plane around and making it obey. She never got to love planes for themselves, for their preeminence as overgrown toys, their way of getting us away from ourselves. To her, planes were refractory machines, almost like children, and so she spent many hours weekly in, as she freely confessed, naked terror as the machine threatened continually to get away from her. In those days she made herself look graver and at the same time flightier by applying heavy eye makeup and attaching long fake eyelashes. There was even, among her friends, a story about her that said she had once gone to a party with a moth taped to each eyelid, yet I could see nothing but impediments to this and didn't believe it. Fixing a moth in place, you might gouge out your eye, and *I* thought of her in subtler terms, happier to discern in her, say, an attitude that became explicit in her face. At flying, she was slow to learn, so it cost her more than it did most folks, but what she mastered stayed with her as immediate, practical knowledge to be called upon in a trice. Gradually I became accustomed to her on her return from flying: fresh from being plunged in wonder, drenched in awe of the sky, and actually amused by the strange new personality types she ran into at the FBO and on the ramp. She was more high-spirited than any of them; I just hoped she would never take to skydiving, taking on Mother Earth with a vengeance, or bungee-jumping—stretching the umbilical cord to the max, though never too far. She was worth watching as she lurched out of control into this mythic dimension or that, ever intent on pulling the brand Excalibur from the rock within which it was embedded.

So, while holding down an academic job two hundred miles away, I had space friends who gave not a jot for literature, a sweetheart pilot wholly immune to the magic of planes, a pilot friend intent upon a literary career, and all over the place literary friends indifferent to space or aviation. The web of my vocations appeared too scattered; why could it not be compressed and made handier? Why was everything in this country spread over so wide an area? I also cared deeply about the sea, and that was too far away. I felt landlocked, stranded, perched near a campus with which I had as yet no official connection. The simplest chores became major puzzles, as when I had to be ready for my regular parcel of books for review, and then "do" them in record time. Instead of having them sent to Pigskin, I had them sent to Pathica, but the mails were not reliable, and on at least one occasion the books arrived there after I had left for Pigskin, and much confusion resulted. Perhaps I should have given up so menial a chore, but I persisted, much to Swan's amusement, certain I was learning a useful trade and publicizing my own books in my byline. Besides, I already had the foundation of a library (in Pigskin, however, and therefore unuseable), and some of the books though not enough were genuinely worth reading—although whether or not they merited a review longer than three hundred words I wasn't sure. Grub Street the British called this living by one's pen; it had a faintly dishonorable sound, but the honor within it consisted in being able to make do on a pittance. You had no salary, for example, whereas I did. By far the braver thing was to live by the pen only, which usually meant owning only one suit, two shirts, two pairs of socks, a broken brush, a rusty razor, a toothbrush whose bristles long ago rooted themselves in a patient dark mucus several years old. Of these abysmal qualifications, I had all but the toothbrush, and had several times resolved to invest in a new one, well within my income and my walk (being no driver, I just did not go to certain stores).

What *was* I, then? I was a space cadet (that academic term of opprobrium for the empty-headed) who wrote novels while failing to arrive at classes on time—I had even, having begun a new chapter in my office between classes, once neglected to go and teach as the chapter in question had been going quite well. I presented a creative excuse for an academic shortcoming and for the first time saw the head of department, an oily toadstrangler from Fargo, beat his head against the cinderblock wall as if to knock his erring brain back into action. He could—*thump*—only make me understand—*thump*—by damaging—*thump*—himself—*thump thump*. Poor Canth, a former dean already on the slippery slope unless he published three or four books instantly. Once, in the spirit of good comradeship, I had told him how I flew reams of typing paper to Europe just to soften them up, let the hammer sink in deep, and he became ill at the very thought, gazing at me as if I had just done reverse surgery and implanted a cancerous heart.

EIGHTEEN

In those days I tried to write almost as soon as I woke, sitting at the machine with coffee and cigarillo, polluting the tiny apartment (if I was with her, which was usual). The trick was to get from sleep to composing without the subconscious's being in the least disturbed. As I told Swan, the slightest chatter about weather or mail would put my sources out of reach for hours and so would, while I was starting up, the merest rattle or voice. I couldn't help it. As a child I had always done my homework in utter silence; it had been a house rule, and I could no more abide the sounds of another human being than I would delegate to someone else the act of writing. The ideal time to start up, as I discovered later, was midnight, when phones ceased to ring and TVs shut down; noon was inferior, but, since I never surfaced until about then, it was the best I could do for myself. In the end, she went out, to campus, leaving me to wake up in peace; since this waking-up took me a couple of hours, I had often finished that part of the day's writing when I truly woke up, having done it in a beneficial trance—provided I was left alone. Obsessive about silence from childhood, I have profited from it and, I'm afraid, insist on it. Most writers I know don't worry about it, seeming able to function amid the usual flurry of noise associated with the presence of people, cars, buses, and so forth. Classical music does not distract me; it never did, provided it is wordless. I spent long hours in that little alcove of hers, accustomed to the chair, the desk, her IBM, the purr of the refrigerator, the faint rumble from the room below. I was one of the more neurotic writers she had known, and I wasn't getting any better at concentrating amid the madding crowd.

Try, she had said until she realized it was hopeless: I was an earplug maven and, during work, shrank from all human contact. On the other hand, having grown up to the sounds of my mother's piano, I could be lulled by piano music, somehow able to contain myself within the golden horn of that sound, as if some plot were hatching between my imagination and Chopin, Liszt, or Beethoven. Indeed, the sound of a piano would often set me writing, or at least dreaming constructively, so I had been Pavloved with high accuracy, not Pav-loved, but Pavlovized, shall we say. Similarly, if things came to a halt, a little piano would get me through, whereas if I came to a dead stop during music I had no recourse at all. I understood why writers went off to the Yaddo and McDowell colonies, just to get away from folk and write in silence; I have never been to any such place, suspicious of the enforced gregariousness that takes over in the evening, after all that creative solitude all day. After writing, I am in no state to commune with anyone, but most eager to sleep, having been drained by the day's work. Swan was altogether more flexible about work habits, which no doubt meant she was more flexible period. I examine photos of her from that phase and marvel at her beauty: the big harvest of black hair, the pulpy tolerant lips, the high cleavage even in a passport-sized picture. She would get into any country, I told her, on the prominence of her cleavage, which she took as a half-compliment. In one exquisitely composed photograph by the late Tom Victor, she stands beside a grandfather clock, pointing to some passage in an open book, a spinning wheel in front of her, her feet in low heels: so demure and so posed, except for her face, which has a grave, almost truculent look that takes you on. Her hand is saying *for instance* as it rests sideways on the page, and you know she has asked a question and is not going to take any old rope for an answer. In the passport-style photo, a loop of her hair is moving away from her head like some solar prominence gone black, and she looks more out of doors, yet equally relentless. I was glad she never watched me in the act of writing; she was never allowed to, of course, and I never watched her. Even back then, our life together depended on maintained privacies, on agreements to let the other one be, especially when she/he was wrestling with the creative force. Twin lighthouses was surely the answer, but that was not what she went hunting, always turning down what she saw as too bourgeois, too standard, too young-coupleish. The hunt went on for weeks, in the course of which she interrupted many a meal of the Coriolis faculty, including one violinist in full cry. The right house did not exist, and, besides, what were we going to use for money when and if we found it? On she looked, urging me now and then to go see something, one a chalet-style house at a crossroads opposite a fraternity (no land), another a blockish-looking barn with umpteen bedrooms and a huge heating bill. All we saw was stock, fudged up according to some real estate person's idea of the holy grail, and, to use her word, yucksome. All that yucksome made us upchuck and we were just about through with inspecting houses when, while I was away teaching, she went out on a final tour with a young real estate agent who had some glimmering of what would suit. After seeing five duds in a row, she decided to go home, defeated, when he sparkled a little and said: "Well, there *is* this white elephant of a place, with a caboose on the premises, a broken-down swimming pool, in a dead-end, a ranch house with a couple of acres. It's an estate deal. The family want it off their hands." It was going cheap. When she saw it, she fell in love with it, captivated by the six huge picture windows out back, the not-so-bad-looking pool, the furnished caboose (with refrigerator and sleeping quarters). Wholly private because enclosed in woodland, it had been on the market a couple of years, too outrageous for anyone who came to see. He stated the asking price and she recoiled. Then, very much in her right mind, she tried a counter-offer, much below his. Things hung fire for a couple of days, when the owners accepted, and, by emptying our bank accounts and begging from her parents, we bought the dwelling that over the past twenty years, always being extended, has been our bliss and joy, wherever we went, to Pittsburgh or the ends of the earth, our indisputable center, with the pool fixed, the house gradually redecorated, the garden crammed with flowers, the roof replaced, the whole place fitted with improvised and awkward-looking bookshelves. We moved in in a searing July and all I remember is carpentry during incessant perspiration. The house came furnished and, for a while, we lived among other people's predilection for orange rugs and orange drapes, tiny black-and-white TVs scattered about the house like dice, and mattresses on which elephants had hemorrhaged. All this junk went eventually and so did the after-aroma of vomit and formaldehyde. Every now and then during the first year, a disinherited daughter would turn up at the front door with her keys, asking to be let in to roam for old times' sake, to torture herself with what she might have had. But, as the interior changed for the better, she recognized the home less and less, eventually feeling very much the interloper as she stumbled about among our things and wished her father chin-deep in hell. We never saw her again. What a happy summer that was as we painted while listening to radios in the empty-sounding rooms, sipping our Cokes and deciding which books would be bedside and which reference. Swan's mother made us new drapes (she helpful once again) and had the house made shipshape. "Scrub everything!" she said on first entering, and she did; her daughter was living in sin, but, at least, as her father in his worldly way observed, she did not have a cold bed. "I thought not."

The story about the house that Swan told most was that of my response to her phone call informing me she had found the ideal place. I had just finished a three-hour seminar, most enjoyable, on Landolfi's *Words in Commotion*, but was bushed and in not much of a mood to discuss responsibilities. So I let forth with my curmudgeon speech and quite perturbed her, going on at length about money and real estate, quite out of character, really, as I had been the one to propose a house in the first place. But weary nerves falsify us all. So up I went to Pathica to see this masterpiece of housing and was overpowered by its sheer quality, the way the roof shut out the summer sun but allowed the winter one in (the house had been designed by an entomologist), the huge picture windows that brought the entire backyard into the living room, the beams, the fireplace, the trees, and of course the pale blue pool (any pool would have looked good to me). As I sat on the hearth and studied the sloping ceiling, I had an abrupt premonition; I just knew this was the house in which we would spend our lives, more or less, yawning at vermilion flames in winter, glancing complacently at the rippling pool in summer, the water always more lucid than we were. Certainly it needed some fixing up, but there was room for us both: a workroom apiece, a shared bedroom that was really two rooms, and a big kitchen, not to mention the caboose, maroon-red and Heideggerian, almost entirely concealed by greenery: an extra study? Of course I was in a different mood when I first saw 333, as we sometimes called it, and I wondered at the aversion that can build up over distance, supplemented by fatigue and general spring malaise. If we were going to live, as distinct from exist, this would be the ideal site. In fact, we ended up paying rent to Swan's mother, who pretended to be the landlord to recoup some of the money she'd put into it.

News from the Coriolis campus was that an ostensible spaceman had been seen in the hallways of the Space Sciences Building, swathed in aluminum foil, but always vanishing at the crucial moment of seizure. A similar person had been seen on other campuses from Johns Hopkins to Amherst, so maybe there were a dozen, all tramping around to cause alarm. The local personage had been heard to call down the hallway, "I want some answers," before disappearing. My own theory was that he had already presented himself at Raoul Bunsen's door, been identified by Shirl Cornwall, and been documented in the Chipped Terra-Cotta file. Having had short shrift from the local astronomers, he or she was now perambulating, just to see what had happened. Campus police seized and arrested a phonetics professor who happened to be trying out a new raincoat of silvery fabric, but they had to let him go, though resentfully, suspecting him of something or other—being an accomplice or a fifth columnist. Indeed, each department, harassed into it by an overzealous dean, appointed its own interloper patrol, English (the one we knew something about) selecting Mikhail ("Mike") Gamine, the distinguished Rabelais and Restif scholar, an authority on illness and gentility, who also excelled at shaggy-dog stories. He had once told me that, although not "a Byron man," he did not wish to be known as a *non*-Byron man. Fair enough, but why had they selected this uncannily well-preserved Cambridge don who cycled to and fro at noble speed, his mind on *The Bride of Abydos* or Marilyn Monroe's voice? One evening, however, after suggesting to me that the caboose would be an ideal venue for low-budget movies (catalogs of which still came in the mail, a legacy from the previous occupant, a diabetic local collector), he began to reminisce about his days in the service, casually recalling how he had been chosen by the brass to redo the phonetic alphabet, changing it from British to American, presumably culling from his vast vocabulary the right words for American airmen and others. This was back in World War Two, so his influence had been huge and long-term, and he had done this all on his own, introducing such a word as "Poppa" for P (sometimes, later, also "Pops"). What power, I thought, wondering what the British English had been: *pepper* maybe, but he couldn't remember. What was clear was that, if an alien marching around campus were to be communicated with, Mike had invented the very thing and could, conceivably, do a reprise, creating a secret phonetic code which the alien would never learn. If you need a monument, I heard an old quote telling me (Christopher Wren), just look around you.

After learning about Mike's patriotic, linguistic contribution, I went and looked up the changes he had wrought, wondering if this, rather than either country's literature, was the key to the differences between two nations. Able he had turned into Alfa, Baker into Bravo, Charlie he had let stand, Dog had become Delta, Easy had become Echo, Fox he had extended into Foxtrot, George had become Gulf, and so on; surely this was the best word-game to have played in the arena of war, no doubt saving countless lives because low-frequency transmissions had always been fuzzy and pilots' enunciation was often none too clear. The standard phrase for Instrument Flight Rules (flying by instruments) had changed from Item Fox Roger, which had a swishy, effete sound, to India Foxtrot Romeo, which seemed to come from a burlier mythos. I could see how such changes made sense to Americans, who pronounced the Brits' "zebra" differently, anyway, and to whom "Quebec" for "Queen" sounded more like something close to home, but I wondered at Mike for not making more of this, for not converting it into at least one scholarly paper on signs and sounds. Later, I vowed, I would write it up myself, maybe even concocting a piece of fiction in which a squadron of Brits tried to communicate with one of Yanks, each using its own version of the phonetic code and getting into such an awful mix-up they flew into each other. As it was, Mike had left alone only four of the original twenty-six: C-Charlie, V-Victor, X-X-ray, and, predictably, M-Mike. I wondered if a man might win something like the Croix de Guerre for such ingenious service, and how "T-tare" ever got into even the British lingo.

My Coriolis friends were fast outnumbering my Pigskin ones, and, when I returned to the more southern campus, I no longer bothered, in the winter, to respond when the limo driver said his ritual "Those Pigs, hey!" In the old days I confessed to an interest in soccer or, when being perverse, lacrosse or hurling, but it was no fun anymore, so my response usually took the form of a dismal, shell-shocked head-shake, almost the equivalent of a line in Virgil that went *"unum oro: desiste manum committere Teucris,"* meaning "I beg one thing: you must not meet the Trojans," or, in Mike Gamine's phonetic alphabet, "uniform november uniform mike/oscar romeo oscar: delta echo sierra india sierra tango echo/mike alpha november uniform mike . . ." and so on, divulging not a hint of Virgil's greatness. My Latin was wilting on the vine, alas, and I saw no way of keeping it up, not even by transposing *The Aeneid* into phonetic bedlam, new style. There were limits, and I had embarked on yet another novel, my sixth, about the German colonel, Stauffenberg, who had tried to kill Hitler with a briefcase bomb and had been executed for his pains. The one-eyed *mutilé de guerre* Stauffenberg had reminded me of my half-blinded father, who had heard of Stauffenberg, and so I was involved with almost a family concern. I knew about the half-blind from close at hand. It was a slow go, however, as I began all wrong, narrating in the third person a chunk of non-history in which Stauffenberg, like so many of his accomplices, was hanged. Wrong, he was shot. After sixty pages in the third person, done in Swan's cozy alcove, I stopped and began again in the first person, and all went much better. One bungles and learns. Now, most of my Pigskin time I spent in the Pigskin stacks as, for some reason, they had an excellent collection on the Stauffenberg plot, so I would squat there, using my rusty Anglo-Saxon to decipher German with, and occasionally going to the watercooler to retch and drink as I ran into yet another Nazi abomination. Anyone dissatisfied with his lot need only read from those shelves to develop a wholly new, grateful view of life. On I wrote, unaware of forces in New York that would soon send my editor toppling; the day was close on which her phone would ring at Harper & Row and she would be summoned upstairs to be told she must clear out her desk by Friday. "You have lost us so much money," they said. "I," she told them, "have been your poetry editor for many years, as well as editing belletristic fiction." By Friday, they told her; she would comply and go off to Tibet for a year, leaving me in the lurch, as so often happens in publishing. I tried to stay fixed on my book, not as long as *Jack Fist*, the phantom novel, but long enough to silence me for years.

On another front, Swan and I had purchased a model *Viking* Lander, lead encased in silver, almost a piece of jewelry, but accurate in all ways. When we had had enough of the world, we would lie back on the Toadstool and play landing games, mostly the Return of the Lander, in which I set it over her navel and made it gently tremble while she tooted "The Star-Spangled Banner"; then its shudders increased, fireworks began, and it shot away from her upward, back to where it now belonged. A quaint, silly game, it somehow took the solemnity out of our space zest, especially when, during the national anthem, we held up our flat and rigid hands, indicative of the flag that would not flutter, the stiff flag of the Moon. Eventually one of the probes broke off, prey to an extraordinary team of house cleaners, just begun in business, named The Daisy Maids, who when they were finished left a severed daisy in each toilet and folded up the free end of the toilet rolls (and the roll of kitchen towels) into a triangle reminiscent of an envelope. Dressed all in yellow, they labored fast and mightily and, unlike our former cleaners, did not steal. They loved to tidy up, but most of all to arrange objects in order of descending or ascending size, which is how they left the refrigerator, as if some berserk drill sergeant moonlighting as a skivvy had decided to "size" everything, from open pots of mustard to upright sticks of celery. The Daisy Maids went on to greater things, advancing into industry and commerce, but they have always cleaned 333 and no doubt always will, provided the river don't rise. With each bill they left little yellow calling cards that bore proverbs culled from Bartlett, few of them worth reading, never mind saving, but the proverbs' general tenor was reliability and faith, so they were an oblique ad, really, and we threw them away without a qualm. Watching the Maids, I sometimes felt myself sinking into a hypnotized trance; I loved watching people work manually, when the peace of all the ages descended upon me and I ended up taking an early nap, soothed by their polishings, their scourings, their ammonia and pine.

So then, the house had a housely existence, properly loved; a plumber, Pat O'Manion, tended the pool heater, even when, one day, it became visibly red-hot and he had to shut it down and I had to replace it. Pat, a former prisoner of the North Koreans, who had beaten him, had survived by eating roaches in the earth toilet of the prison camp, so he could manage where he lived, high on a hill called Alpine, where it snowed in May. His technique, he said, had been to bully his interrogators, and I asked him how. "Just stand up to them, spit at them, insult them," he said, as if getting me ready for them. One day, he said, he would make me a suit of armor with tin snips. He taught me the nature of electricity, water, and dung, in which last he often had to stand when fixing a broken sewer. By my reckoning, he had done enough to qualify for the next century, but his deep-down craving was to live the life of an author, since he thought he had seen it at 333: up late watching movies on his dish; leisurely brunch; a little typing; a nap and a swim, then another nap; dinner; more TV, then the bottle and a big cigar, with sex thrown in somewhere like a rubber glove into a pipe dream. I disabused him, telling of four- or five-hour writing stints after which you felt dizzy and nauseous, unable to eat or speak, fit only for sleep and an air-conditioned room. He did not believe any of it, knowing how fiction writers *romanced* (his word) and got paid for it. He was, nonetheless, as people say, an education, hardly Ivy League but certainly Crown-of-Thorns Tech.

Swan continued to take me in hand, objecting to my habit of wearing ancient ill-fitting clothes. I had a favorite jumpsuit, now threadbare in the pants, so much so that I could read the newspaper through them, and, as she pointed out, observers could make out my private parts. They were welcome to them, I thought. Why wear something so old? Because it *gave*, did not resist me, I felt at ease in it, and it had gone so far in the direction of the decrepit that it no longer seemed clothing at all. I had never liked clothing much, one reason for preferring summer; I had never liked the idea of being wrapped up, enclosed, so perhaps my latent claustrophobia was speaking to me again. What I said in my defense was arbitrary, she said. Then so was, I countered, the peculiar abject posture in which all professional ice-skaters ended their routines: prostrate and begging. Why didn't they ever stand up when they were done? Why grovel on the ice? She didn't understand, nor did she answer me, but she began to see my point. If I had to watch ice-skating, then surely she should watch some cricket or soccer with me, but she hardly ever did. She liked me best, I thought, when I invented piropos for her: those Latin American exaggerations of a woman's beauty, such as the one I had come up with for supermarketing: "Should I not be able to find you in a supermarket, I would go to the manager and ask him to direct me to the most beautiful woman in the store. It always works." She liked that one a great deal, as she did "Silky Chops" and "Silver Heels" (really her pedals flashing as she cycled away) and "Airy-mouse, fairy-mouse." But her own line of seductive invitation, heard all the way from the bathroom, was better: "I'm all rosy," she would cry, and she was. How informal we had become, with quintuple the old space; we had become outspoken and louder, more inventive in the old hyperbolical art of living in a larger house, where there was room to be foolish, oratorical, or lustful in. Presumably all people went through this phase, spreading themselves out, and then perhaps tightened up again so as to relish the echoes of an even larger manse. Either of us ill was a "sicklamen" (cyclamen?). Her visit to the dermatologist became "a mole patrol" and I mutated sometimes into "Doll-face." We both attempted what we knew as the wren-whistle, this the teeniest, highest-pitched tweet a human could achieve.

"What *is* that lovely song?" I called one day as she sang for the joy of it in the same bathroom, a rather small cubicle stacked high with aromatic soap.

"The dove's adagio," she crooned, and there was nothing else to say. Until I realized what was going on, I had decided she had periods of acute, brilliant phrasemaking, when her mind worked uncommonly well and her thought patterns became stringently concise. I then recognized she was concocting titles for a new book, chanting them to herself here and there, hoping to convince herself, or me, that a certain one was the best. Once she had decided, the phrasemaking binge would end, yet not altogether for that was truly the cast of her mind, as of mine. We were not expositors, but ingot-makers, as impatient with long-winded people as with the educational system, which dealt in definitions. If you used a perfectly acceptable word such as *emollient*, someone was bound to ask you for your definition. Indeed, the system was forever working backward whereas the challenge to the person of intellect was to make the most refined statement in the fewest words. "Jubilant suavity" meant just that, but most students, I had found, wanted it spelled out, and all the brain-racking that had gone into the phrase was wasted. This was why, in the end, I would have to give up teaching writing (literature was a wholly different matter, and some literature students could make impressive verbal combinations once they knew such things were welcome). Most faculty, I found, wherever I went, opted for long-windedness, especially in their own speeches, the main thing being to blot out the time allotted and thus protract it into another meeting.

Swan was advancing well on the aeronautical front, though always rowing with her instructor, a born misogynist. My Nazi or anti-Nazi novel was slowly coming into being, although with forever behind me the phantom of the third-person version full of mistakes. *Viking*, with nothing to impede it, was still en route to Mars (we spoke of *our Viking* only, while of course there were two). The alien (or whoever) in the aluminum-foil suit had attacked a girl in the Coriolis stacks, and it was now clear he could don/doff it in a flash and stow/unstow it as well. Raoul Bunsen was on every TV screen, propagandizing and as the weeks went by looking shaggier again as only NBC, it seemed, had the clout and power to chop his hair.

Two people living together have a better chance of becoming even more different from one another than if they remained apart. Proximity activates the quest for difference. Attempts at self-definition bog down in privacy, but thrive in company. I find this odd because it sounds as if it should be the other way around, but Swan and I, with much in common, took our union as a basis for developing differently, she to a sensory and behavioral view of the world, I to a stylish one. The things we had in common remained the same, and that is no doubt the answer. A couple who can spend half an hour watching a female cardinal sit inside a bird-feeder, in as it were pig heaven, pecking and pondering, can do other things too, such as sitting by a table covered with amaryllises and dahlias, pretending it is already spring, or staring at the curvature and convolutions of a nail clipping. This contemplative savoring was always ours, not something we aspired to or had ever read about, but a natural twitch to be reckoned with, its main implication a simple one: There will always be more to gaze and marvel at, even on the level of the commonplace, than we will ever be able to attend to. For us both, it was always a matter of being plonked down amid an ongoing miracle whose component parts could not be counted. One is not an electron microscope, alas, but such a contraption can be had and used. Staring at stuff, I always called it; the account of this activity needs no fancier phrase. So we could often be spotted staring overlong at sheep, birds, grasses, or a certain harvest mouse, in the spirit of Leonardo, who told his painting students to stare at something—even a splotch on a wall—until it seemed to move, and that was when to begin. To be sure, he was recommending one of the magics of the participating, influencing imagination, but he was also, I always thought, demonstrating how much latent energy the universe contains. Any perception of it has to be kinetic. Perception, surely, has always been an animistic act.

Such were our beliefs in our first years, and they are much the same now. One of our favorite words was *salience*, for how something shoots out at you and "gets" you. We were always surrounded by saliences: the world bristled and sparkled, came out to meet us, and we went toward it, accepting fool's gold along with genuine ore. Swan had always demanded more of the world than I, almost like a medical person insisting phenomena make sense, especially the weird ones, whereas I, while making my obligatory salute to the sanctioned world of logic and common sense, cause and effect, was always willing to live with the absurd, not eager to make it into something else. So, while she responded to the chromatic and the garish, she wanted them to make sense of some kind, as in her hunt for titles. I, on the other hand, was more flamboyant and willing to accept something because it was highly original. Some of Emily Dickinson's phrases I would steal and use just because they were prodigies of language, whereas Swan would let them slide from her hands because, in the long run, they didn't evince the burden of her book. She was not always a risk-taker, which is a stern thing to say of a phrasemaker; she was sometimes a reasoner when I was not. Such differences have driven people apart, as distinct from involving them in regular arguments, but I could never see why. She was a liberal, I a radical, and that was that. We would probably have ended up on the same side of the barricades, although she was much less eager than I to abolish National Public Radio for being obsolete, wimpy, and out of touch. Myself, I always favored the Norwegian radio station that broadcast in Latin, I favoring the idea that the people should not always have what they want.

So you see, although we rarely got into conflict, we roamed our different ways, especially in discussions with our newfound friends from Coriolis, who came to the house almost regularly to swim or sunbathe or crowd into the caboose for gossip. In older days, some of them had squeezed into that little apartment on Spencer Road, but now they spread themselves on the repainted deck or draped themselves on pool ladders or floated around on inflatables, drink in hand. They were all poets, I thought, or would-be ones, from Ashley Thorp who in the end gave it up to write about lurid initiation rites in the military (martial anthropology) to Josh Chotiner, who even back then wrote a poem daily (he never watched TV) and in later years had an odd habit of coming into town, phoning us without saying anything (he breathed hard into the mouthpiece), and then hanging up. Ash brought out a small volume of poems with a picture on it so fetching that men called her up and proposed to her then and there. Joshua fell for a young poopsie who eventually jilted him, and we all spent that night at his place trying to keep him from suicide. We were a gang, I suppose, lotos-eating leisure-devourers who had found somewhere to hang out in total privacy, and we reveled in one another, though there was nobody there to discuss experimental fiction with (York is the closest of my fiction-writing friends to have endured, and in those days we had not met). So I talked with the poets about poetry and marveled how few ideas they had to steer themselves by; one page from an Eliot essay launched more ideas than they would give birth to in a lifetime, and I could not figure out why. Was it because they found analytical thought incompatible with poetry? Surely Rilke and Stevens should have taught them otherwise; Swan had got the point, so why not them? These people were not interested in space and they found our hunger for it somewhat misplaced, as if we were not being responsible earthlings, or were overreachers, trespassers. Nor did they, however, pore over a book of new stamps as we did, or a foreign postmark. In other words they were not fanatical, though for both Thorp and Chotiner that did come as the detail of the world closed its muslin mesh around them. As Swan and I said, our backyard, inspected even cursorily, contained enough saliences to occupy an entire civilization for a thousand years if studied bit by bit, bit of bit by bit of bit until you had found the irreducible minimum of everything.

New friends also provided a fresh context for old ones, who now in my mind's eye developed a faint whiff of lepidoptera: beings worth collecting after all and subjecting to the same strain of conversation as held sway at 333. It would have been hard to get Asa Humanas, Delray Pepp, and Lou Vielis, almost names from another era, into the orbit of Thorp, Chotiner, Raoul and Nineveh Bunsen, Frank Deck, the composer Goldstamm, and the science writers who wafted in and out, the JPL technologists, but they would no more have considered going to Cocoa Beach than to Riker's Island. I had strayed off the reservation in more ways than one, and, unwittingly, had planted a leg in alien soil in order to stay put. I had become a halved being, like the traditional migraine sufferer, and could no longer be counted on for reasonable judgments. Raoul Bunsen was having gallbladder trouble, Swan was unable to sleep because her legs twitched, and I was at the beginning of blood-pressure problems. Our lives were propelling themselves along their time-life curves and the *Viking* spacecraft were cleaving vacuum on the way to Mars. Nothing stood still in that perpetually moving world, and the invisible held us to ransom as if our lives were emblematic.

Even the humblest people sometimes develop a sense that they are leading lives of extraordinary symbolic force. Some power has come along, intercepted them, and made them imposing to all who look upon them, not through their efforts or through any propaganda. A buzz surrounds them and affects those who watch them. Swan and I had this sense from our first launch: not so much for other people, who tended to regard us as freaks or poseurs, but for ourselves, finding our lives somehow of greater consequence, fuller of vibration and majesty. We were no longer living on a narrow plinth, but spreading ourselves so wide we no longer had a precise sense of our lifetimes' map. We had heard that some folk were piped, sucked, snatched up into unidentified flying objects, emptied of data, then sent back again to their mundane enterprises, vainly alluding to some terrific experience that had unfitted them for life in the suburbs. We did not mean that, but rather a sense of extra brainpower, as when a certain drug taken in conjunction with another—aspirin on top of warfarin, say—potentiates it and perhaps makes it lethal. The *Physicians' Desk Reference* lists hundreds of such instances. All we knew was that some initiative of our own, undertaken casually enough, had brought us to the point of expecting more than usual, than hitherto, of ourselves, even if this meant only making more enterprising allusions or comparisons, certainly beyond the ken or tolerance of the average reader. Perhaps this was all we would ever get. Pondering the long journey of the two *Viking*s to Mars and the cold-as-mutton conclusion to come from the Landers, we tried to work out what we would do next. Already invited to observe the two *Voyager*s blast off to Jupiter, we wondered if it was necessary to witness another launch, having already been initiated. Maybe not, but to be present in the Jet Propulsion Laboratory, Pasadena, when the results came in, that would be mind-boggling, like being allowed into the poolroom after squinting into it from outside in the rain. We ought to go, we thought; we owed it to celestial marksmanship, after all that our *Viking* had gone through. We felt like members, anyway, having made, since *Viking* launch, repeated overtures to the air. I in the Apache with Segundo Cieli, she in Cessna or Piper with her raucous coach. We had kept on trying to pass muster, I to retrieve an old Air Force standing, she to break the tape sealing another frontier. So we agreed, said yes, and settled back into our preliminary routines, both writing and air-roving, again sharply aware that we were involved not only for our sakes but as deputies, acolytes, believers, bringing to this physics and chemistry event the assent of imaginers. Once again Raoul Bunsen got us invited, and NASA pursued us with complex mailgrams asking our exact intentions, telling us how to enter the various buildings, which badges to show to whom. Riffling through the big fat file we kept on launches, I found the sheet that depicted the *Viking* science team leaders and marveled how little we knew of these men, although having become accustomed to seeing them at Cocoa Beach. Just to list them gave us an eerie otherworldly feeling:

Gerry Soffen (whom we *had* met), Project Scientist
Dick Young, Chief Prog. Sci. (as it said)
Conway Snyder, Orbiter Scientist
Tim Mutch, Lander Imaging
Harold Klein, Biology (he of the marsupial eyes)
Klaus Biemann, Molecular Anal.
Bo Hargraves, Magnetic Props.

And so on. These named but oddly anonymous men, as unknown to us as critics E. M. W. Tillyard and Northrop Frye to them, had their hands on the twenty-first century; was that what disturbed us, made us feel spooked, gave us the space jitters? Boffins, as the British called them, they were the backroom boys of *Viking*, cousins to the backroom boys of *Voyager*; or maybe all the same. Recalling the idea that someone with little math could go only so far in science, we wondered if the JPL was the ultimate boundary; we would come away with strong memories of suspense, surprise, and disappointment, but having understood little of the astronomers' central mystery. Camp followers in other words, we decided to risk it, for the sake of all the humanist-imaginers who would not be going, and who would spurn the offer if it came. Yet I, for one, wondered if pushing our still-new relationship among the mysteries of the JPL would somehow damage us, weaken our bond.

NINETEEN

Only of summer have I ever been able to keep track in terms of weeks and days; all other seasons go past me in undifferentiated continuum, a molasses of cold and cool, but I can always tell you which day of summer it is and feel thankful for its individual blaze. So, on Wednesday the fifth of June, the house seemed to have been invaded early by young people with no classes to go to, but it had escaped me that Coriolis had closed down and the summer semester had not yet begun. We were in an in-between world, a holiday in which to become reacquainted with wrens and house finches, chickadees and orioles. I could never match Pigskin with Coriolis because Pigskin began its academic year a good month earlier, dragging people back to their studies right after New Year's, which I had always thought a misplaced bit of puritanism. So, why had these charming people not gone home? Why were they lingering over the corpse of yet another academic year? Then I had a sudden, invasive flash of palpable acuteness, telling myself to wake up: I had lingered on at Oxford, among friends, precisely thus, unwilling to embark on a summer's intensified reading, to give up on all those emancipated conversations with contemporaries who wanted to return home no more than I did. I had often wished that the Oxford year, composed of three eight-week terms with religious names, had been the vacation or home year, with all the rest (twenty-*eight* weeks) available for pleasure. Hairsplitting, of course, but joyful of its kind. Anyway, here were Ashley and Joshua, Ellen and Jody, long before I awoke, along with others whom I knew not, frolicking and giggling, sipping and nibbling, all in a circle around Swan, who was swathed in a white wrap-around. It looked like a poetry reading or some hopelessly depraved seminar alongside the shuntling blue water, with high sun beating down on their unshielded heads. Instead of joining the ring, I flopped into the pool with a handful of slit mail and began to read, leaning on the already warm coping. It was a perfect day for bad news, and bad news came.

Looking hard at Swan I thought I saw an additional perplexity creating a line where usually there was none at all in her unblemished face. It was an extra load she could not carry, an incident very much of its period, on a campus anyway. Without much prompting, she explained what had happened. Joachim Huppenkothen, a professor of imperative literature, had offered this past semester a lecture course on Gide, Mann, and Kafka, which Swan had swooped upon to fulfill one of her requirements. A victim of Nazi persecution, Huppenkothen had made a habit, almost a fetish, of checking the door of the lecture hall before he began, making some such wisecrack as "They're late today" or "You never know who's recording you." He always warned them to watch for the telltale sign of the swastika. Then he began, holding his single-spaced notes close to his thick bifocals. Swan found this preamble amusing, and the lectures of more than passing interest, especially those on Gide, with whom she had staged an imaginary interview as soon published as finished. In the last week of classes, Huppenkothen had offered her a ride home since he lived nearby, and she had accepted innocently, but he had driven to a bird sanctuary he cherished and invited her to look at it. More innocent than she is now, she joined him, but they no sooner got inside the sanctuary than he threw himself on his knees in his pin-striped suit and confessed his love for her. She brushed him off somehow, though he said he was going to kill himself. What had rattled her was not so much his effrontery as her gullibility, a weakness she now condemned even more in the aftermath of Silverfoil. Anything could have happened, she said. Huppenkothen might even be the sheathed marauder. She worried about her grade, though she need not have. I worried that Huppenkothen, who was aware of my presence at 333, did not even consider that I might have smashed his genitals with a baseball bat, just to help him get a fix on his future; I had never been known for my blandness. Now, we gathered, he had decamped alone to his apartment in Jamaica, in the hot season, no doubt to cook the libido out of him.

"Not wise," I said, "to go with him, either from the building or into the bird sanctuary. What the hell, though, it's over and done with. Just another German romantic sounding off."

"A German Jewish romantic."

"Well, let him go read his Gide all over again. No doubt he was demonstrating the *acte gratuit.* The whole thing was a literary prank. How about that?"

"Not if you know him," she said.

"A pox on him," I answered, going from smolder to heat. "Forget it. Enjoy the summer. He's pathetic." I could link Huppenkothen to the time when Lou Vielis down at Pigskin had taken Giselle Humanas for a similar country stroll, under God knew what pretext, and had also prostrated himself in the mud, protesting. I was sure the Swiss-Viennese mode varied from the German-Jewish, but I was a hardboiled ex-officer hardened to the ways of the world, wasn't I? These guys were wimps, escapees from the opera. Had Asa gone after *him*? No, he had turned the other cheek and then his side of the bed had filled with books. Was Swan weakening? Of course not; she had been caught off guard, that was all, and my duty was to reassure her that her guard had been momentarily down. "*Look* at the man," I said, "embedded in a department whose other members are Vogel, Grossvogel, Kleinvogel, Vogelsanger, and Hund. What can you expect from such a parrot-like menagerie?" She saw the funny side, thank goodness, and began to exonerate herself, agreeing that this kind of thing happened on campuses all the time and was one of those rites of passage no one ever recorded (test the seventies against the nineties!). I soon had her talking normally again, and we were scampering around the house, she crying as she often did "Feed me!" while I countered with "I want my cake." An effective game, especially to banish all traces of a kneeling Huppenkothen, it also depended on hunger, and we were soon devouring turkey sandwiches under an umbrella outside, marveling at our proximity to Sipsucker Woods, the very site of the event. Why, I could have been over there in a trice to demolish him, he who had once told me "Ah yes, we had the Guggenheim in the same year." Next time I saw him I would spill some scalding tea on his fly, just for old times' sake, and tell him that was what disponibility really meant.

On August 20, the first *Viking* touched down on Mars at the site called Chryse, a miraculous piece of tenderness, to be sure, and we identified it as being between Xanthe and the two features magically named Eden and Arabia. That we had a map at all of *Mars*, cluttered with erudite and classical names, was itself a marvel; you could tell with what voracious interest our species had eyed the planet, yearning to dominate it Adam-style with names—Aeous, Cebrenia, Panchaia, Cecropia, Ortygia, Niliacus Lacus—that had an almost acrid, veteran sound: no Trotsky, no Keller, no Sibelius, for instance. We vowed to look up every name, Swan already deep into Martian myth for her poem on it in her cosmic pastoral, but we giggled instead, perhaps deflected by the fact that *our Viking* had caught up with the first one and touched down on the same day, as if the collective mind of NASA had decided to tidy up its act and infuse a little team spirit into the enterprise. So, *our Viking* landed four thousand miles away at Utopia (what else?), a site not on our map, which, oddly enough, ran from north to south and was then printed left to right; these were the areas photographed by *Mariner* IV in 1965. I could not overpower the feeling that John Milton, a poet I much admired, had gotten his hands on Mars and transferred to it most of the classical allusions he had pillaged for *Paradise Lost;* the very name was like a death knell for Martian exploration. Perhaps once Mars had been more, livelier, than it was now. The wandering planet, as it used to be called, was going to turn out to be a dud: fascinating per se, because there was only one of it, and always worth filming because it was unique, and those ruddy vistas had a truly dream-sequence aspect in which the superb aiming of the NASA team figured to a large extent. There was a let-down, though, inescapable; there was no evidence of life on the surface, and we heard the echoes of the doomsayers arguing that the money could have been put to better use. Even Silverfoil, destructive ogre, seemed abstractly vindicated, at least if you presumed his hooligan ways were a protest. Saddest of all, there came to my mind a sad title for the book I now would never write about life on the red planet: *Blues for a Red Planet,* which I never used and eventually, at his request, donated to Raoul Bunsen for the section on Mars in his best-selling book *Our Universe.* In time I wished I'd kept the title to myself, for something or other, and I kept threatening to use it, for something uncommercial. We could not rid our minds of those exquisite photographs showing *Viking* II stranded like an old radio set thrown out along with a big useless dish into a ruddy wasteland, in the bottom left-hand corner what appeared to be a shoulder with an epaulet bearing three stripes—emblems of a second officer, but of course just a piece of the gear aboard. We clutched at anything that gave Mars a personality, a watery past, a spice of life, but it was not to be, and slowly, as the evidence rolled in, exquisitely tabulated and lovingly recited, we began to look the other way, finally deciding that Mars would rank with the Moon.

"Imagine," Swan wailed with a red popsicle at the ready, "something that big being dead!" The line went instantly into her Moon poem, as if to use it of Mars was a sacrilege. Myself, I couldn't help feeling a certain resentful joy that the most animated aspect of Mars was the names plastered all over it, designing it to appeal to an older generation, like that part of the Finger Lakes consecrated to Ovid, Homer, Tully, Manilius, Seneca, and even Dryden, almost as if that region itself were a planet badly in need of domesticating. It took us months to get over the anticlimax; perhaps we never did, stowing away all our maps and folders. We had really hoped, all of us, that something would show up on that only too familiar, much romanticized planet, maybe to give the lie to so many lies about canals, but no luck: landing on it was a double dry promotion. All we had to sustain us, planetarily, was the twin expedition to Jupiter; indeed, one *Voyager* would go on to Saturn, Uranus, and Neptune, biting off a huge chunk. How could we resist the invitation to go to the JPL and watch them land on Jupiter? True obsessives, we had no more hope of finding life there than anywhere else, but some authentic experimental spirit egged us on, to go boldly as it were, not backing down but knowing that whatever became known was knowledge; there would never be nothing to know, the Landers were always bound to bring something back to us we never knew before. Perhaps, because Swan and I dealt with imagination much more than anyone else in the *Viking-Voyager* retinue, we dealt in a more spellbound manner with anything that surfaced, came through, having no cast-iron preconceptions, so perhaps we relished the reddish Martian landscape more than others because it was more exotic than we could have imagined it was. Disappointment was all on the level of stuff not found, but delight was on the level of Shakespeare's Autolycus, the snapper-up of unconsidered trifles. We snapped them up and forced ourselves into a maturer attitude. It was like allowing someone to put you off *Paradise Lost* for life because, they said, it was dry and dull. I had heard this, but when I got around to reading it at nineteen, it was a treasure trove concocted by someone infatuated with language, all languages, and its great feat to my disabused view was to transform the dimension of the divine, the cosmogonical, into patient technicolor. I have doted on Milton ever since, the man who invented the word we needed: *pandemonium.*

In an odd way, our time with Mars had reinstated our passion for literature, that lay there on shelves, waiting and final, capable of giving each reader an individual thrill paramount for that person. There may have been orthodox, "received" responses to *Paradise Lost*, but there were hundreds of others, wrongheaded or cryptically erratic, but nonetheless valid. If this was the romantic (private) view of reading, then I was all for it over and above the so-called classical (public) version. Swan agreed, and we felt we had come to a new watershed, or back to it: what you saw was what you got, on Mars or in the bowels of world literature. Even if we had had to go figuratively to Mars to find this out, our journey had been worth it, and necessary. Now we felt fortified against whatever so-called disappointment came from the *Voyager*s. True, we had waited ten months for the *Viking*s to arrive at Mars, in the meantime romancing and fantasizing (as I thought the astronomers too were doing). In the end, the result was the result and the component parts of it were phenomena to be appreciated. One day, in that interim, Raoul, a rather chastened bleak-seeming Raoul, had asked me what I hoped to get out of my constant efforts with prose fiction, and I told him I always hoped to create something perfect, or nearly so, even if it could be improved by changing a comma I had not pondered enough.

"Oh," he said, "is that all?" The perfect did not mean that much to him, he who polished his own prose a fair amount of the time. What I meant, and explained to him, was something I created that was not already a given, such as the carbon ring delivered to us by the universe. I wanted the arbitrariness of my own concoction to shine as if no arbitrary human had made it. Such was my dream, such his distance from it.

My past was catching up with me, flashbacks that should have died a natural death, and events I should have remembered earlier than this, the point seeming to be that certain scenes or events only came back to you under a certain emotional stress. You almost had to be in pain to recollect certain things of unquestionable import, as if only while writhing could the soul tune in to heraldic saliences. I knew there were canceled liftoffs that had still not come back to me, though Swan regained them sooner than I. What came to me now was poignant enough to have stood the feeblest memory to attention. We were following Raoul's gleaming Ford LTD to Orlando, at each toll plaza finding that Raoul had paid our way. Only an hour ago, Ptolemy had been collecting up his toys, deciding which to leave for other aspirants; he had seen other rockets, and seen them fail, so this was a less catastrophic occasion for him than for us. We were on our way to Disney World; why fly from Orlando without taking in Disney World? An orange-clad neuter-seeming girl motioned at Raoul and asked me "Haven't I seen him somewhere or something? Isn't he somebody?" Her name, her placard said, was Dayzha View. She no doubt had seen him, I told her. "Raoul," I informed him a moment later, "you are reaching your public, God help you." He gave a sheepish pout, indicating he might not mind as much as I thought he did, and loped off to buy camera film, arranging to meet us at the main gate information booth, where tickets awaited us. But there were no tickets at all. Someone paged him, told him for good measure (as we later discovered) that the tickets bore the wrong names. Finally a call to California set things right. We boarded a monorail train after being misinformed about where to stand when the train came in, and Raoul berated the mutinous flunkey from within the choo-choo to the Magic Kingdom. The flunkey looked away, indifferently muttering.

Toward, then through, the Egyptian wedge-habitat of the Contemporary Hotel we glided, half expecting to find beside us Anubis the jackal-headed god who conducted the dead to judgment. But no, there were only the same uniformed juvenile drones you find everywhere in Disney's world, who counter your questions with rote tangents and cannot be shaken out of their devout, pecuniary dream. Was this, I wondered, where the holy army of infant inquisitors, late of the Khmer Rouge, for whom they divined out intellectuals by pointing little sticks, had finally set up shop? We arrived, took lunch, impressed by the charmless boorish graveness of the Disney light militia wherever we went, whose wooden piety made you think you were only in this Vatican of a Pleasuredrome on trust. Anyone, just anyone, could be excommunicated, for not being or looking happy.

In belated compensation we lined up for *Mission to Mars*, first of all standing outside the glassed-in control room in which life-sized humanoids operated consoles and from time to time addressed us in clinical Missionese. Then we mounted the boarding ramp as announcements began. It might have been O'Hare or JFK International. Seated inside the spaceship, which was a theater in the round with a central panel down below us, we inhaled the mingled smells of air freshener and hot plastic. After a few minutes of bogus astro-palaver, liftoff began. The seats cranked up a few degrees, forcing our rear ends backward and down, while fortissimo thumpings came from the rocket and views of inferno, a diminishing Earth, and a star-mottled sky appeared on the screen. It was colorful at least and the hysterical pumping of the pseudo-propellants almost persuaded before it stopped and we floated in orbit before, with only minor commotion, we began to space-fly for three hundred very compressed days. Our seats eased up, rather late. A new celestial window opened on screens around the walls, here a nebula (the Crab, I thought), there a galaxy (the Great, in Andromeda), and now the big blue wet ball where Disney World happened to be, followed by the rapidly-growing apricot-dumpling face of Mars itself. We began what could only be Mars-Orbit Insertion, then deorbited as the civil tremble of the engines gave way to renewed violent thumps. Our seats pinched us again. Chryse or Cydonia, or something ultra-Martian, appeared on the floor screen, as if in the Ur-TV in Lucian's *A Strange Journey*, and we made our terminal descent with nipped buttocks. All along I had been imagining as if this were a *Viking* mission and not a spaceship, but never mind. With an authentic shiver of the seats and a crooning sigh from the end of retrofire, we touched down on Mars. Not a battery or valve had failed. Rusty, bleak Martian landscape filled the eye. Raoul was talking fluently to Ptolemy; Nineveh looked oblivious; Swan wore a quizzical frown as human-type creatures with bilateral symmetries pranced through coppery dust that did not rise. With such a footling substitute as this, I felt doubly cheated, more so than the distinguished exobiologist on my right. Surely they would have done better running a clip from a *Nova* or one of the epilogues Raoul did for it. I half expected to see him—what was the word?—recrudesce upon the screen, in front of himself, but we returned to Earth faster than we left it. The jaws of my seat relaxed, the lights went on, and ordinariness resumed its fateful sway. You felt closer to Mars out on the Cape when you stared at the Lander. This trip had only been a taunt to our flubbed optimism.

Somewhere in the interim, our little group had gathered in the Smithsonian, to look around while Raoul improvised a *Nova* commentary (he could do this because he knew what he was talking about; I could do it only if I had to improvise from minute to minute, inventing, inventing). At dinner that evening in La

Niçoise, where the waiters wore roller skates, we all got talking about our literary careers, and Raoul confessed he thought he needed a literary agent, had been in touch with one, and was going to bring out next a book of essays. He spoke as if he had only just realized what a packet he could make if his career were run properly; I had been amazed to learn that no agent represented him, but I could see how his career would develop from now on. Curt Vallombrosa was a well-known participatory agent who charged for rewrites, though surely Raoul, who wrote well, was beyond all such maneuver. I told him what a good idea it was. Swan had had several agents, I had had thirteen, mainly the result of disagreement, death, and disease—agents didn't seem to be a healthy lot. Some writers had no agent at all, I told him, and he smiled, already knowing how much labor you give yourself if you delegate.

Over dessert, Swan said she had begun using the telephone more, and writing commissioned prose pieces on all kinds of topics from women-and-horses to soccer, landscape, and such historic locales as Ellis Island. I had noticed the frequency with which the phone at 333 rang, and was glad I'd shifted to after midnight. Rarely did the phone ring for me, whose friends were still moldering in the obsolete sloth of letter-writing; besides, what did they know of my imagination? The imaginative writer was doomed to isolation and had best get on with it; no use waiting for the phone to ring and see you through, or see through you. I was alone at the table in this, I thought, though Nineveh the nonfunctioning painter was a dim ally; the other two were into journalism, and had busy agents to prove it, whereas I lived in dreamland, as vulnerable to the next whim of an engram as they were to their editors' livers. I, I answered when asked those damnable questions by interviewers, tried to add to the sum of created things, derivedly maybe, and reckoned it a lonely way to live, especially if your partner's phone rang all the time. The one place that delightfully plagued me was Paris, where I had the most educated editors; they phoned and then faxed me all the time, sometimes if only to hearten me as I went about my recondite labors of Hercules, sometimes to clinch a deal. Nobody I knew had such an *entente cordiale* with their French publishers; I was the luckiest fellow on Earth, even if I preferred to be on Mars, never mind how briefly.

TWENTY

The silence in our lives we carry with us from place to place like a golden eggshell in whose recesses we pick up the vague bruit of peristalsis, the shuffle of the heart, the silkworm creak of muscle. It comes from us, not from where we are and thus ranks as an imposition, whether we have paused at a bullfight when all other sound has ceased or when we stand and stare at a winter's accumulation of snow and all shovelers have quit. One Saturday morning in midsummer, as I drifted from sleep into yet another phase of blessed silence, good sleep allowing me sleep no longer, I woke with the perfect conviction that something had happened, not near me, but close enough emotionally to register as a pressure, a wobble, a peculiar stroke felt on the forearm. You have no doubt experienced these incongruous sensations yourself, in the midst of a silence that seems more a product of chance than one of will. How could I possibly know anything? Yet I had this post-premonition of something affecting yet good, to which I should respond far beyond the casual admiration of silence. The event, if that, had created a new silence, as when, from a power failure, the air conditioner stops in the night and you think it is your heart that has been subtracted into that abrupt lack of noise. As a result, I sat up, wondering, my breath held, noting that the time was eleven-thirty, a bit earlier than my usual waking time. It was good to wake that way, lurching from one silence to another, as unequipped for the day as a baby moth. No one was there. No note had been tucked into the bathroom mirror or left on the washstand's ivory plateau. No warning of any kind.

I washed my eyes free of crumble and gargled with a caustic blue fluid guaranteed to kill bacteria and marveled at the solids in what I spat out, surely entire viscous colonies of bacteria blasted into kingdom come, the first time those millions had clustered together. No wonder we smell: we wake with mouths full of bacteria droppings. On I pushed, taking pills, drinking the weirdly chlorinated water, having about as much taste as newspaper. So, once again, I told myself, I had awakened to an ordinary day, falsely convinced by the uniqueness of the silence that it was a red-letter day with distinctive sounds and tremors. As I stumbled along the hallway to the kitchen, I saw a shadow approaching from the far end. It was Swan in a highly charged state, even for her, caught between effervescence and jubilation. So, there would be something extraordinary after all; the day was not going to be the raw equivalent of the TV show that said "a can of worms" and, as if language and analogy had broken down all together, depicted exactly that on the screen in fudged-up redundancy.

"What?" I gasped, wondering if it had to do with me. How was my mother, four thousand miles away? No, she would not have been this jubilant. Ah, a publisher had bought her planetary pastoral, Zeus be thanked. No, she was making maneuvers with her hands.

"Guess what I just did, while you were sleeping." I had hardly the energy to make some coffee, and I did not guess. "Can't you see it in my face?" She had sold the house, so recently acquired. Not a bit of it. "I soloed," she said. "They *soloed* me. They sent me up alone in the Warrior and I made three circuits all on my own. They were going to cut a piece off my shirt, but I wouldn't let them. I'm a *pilot.*" All I could think of was her body, with all its *places*, tootling above my sleeping one at twelve hundred feet, "pattern altitude," three times, without my knowing anything.

Rather than subject me to the worry of knowing and watching, she had gone and done it during the dead hours when she was fresh and the sun had not yet whipped up the roiling devil's brew of three o'clock. I was so dazed I omitted to congratulate her. She was a different being now, entitled to soar away at will, plunge and cavort, without snide battery from that appalling instructor, Nagel. My Swan had taken flight with the supreme elegance she brought to every activity, and all I could come up with was a resolution to go downtown as soon as possible and buy her a set of wings to pin on her blouse, hitherto named shirt. She was with Amelia Earhart and Harriet Quimby, reborn as a pioneer, living up to her name.

Now we were both flyers, I the retired one who had flown in the good old, bad old days in a blue uniform, in now obsolete machines called Oxfords and Ansons that took my colleagues and me from the Isle of Man in the middle of the Irish Sea to London for lunch. We were the postwar, post–Battle of Britain boys, the peacetime air force, but most of the men I flew with were war heroes with brightly colored ribbons on their chests to prove it. I had never seen so many Distinguished Flying Crosses, Air Force Crosses, never mind Distinguished Service Orders. Those men were the cream, or rather the surviving cream. At some point soon after this salient Saturday, Swan and I decided to invest in an art deco plane, an Ercoupe with mouse ears and trailing beam undercarriage that straightened you out whichever way you landed. Supposedly it was idiot proof, could not be stalled or spun, and had a neat Kenney cowl thanks to the labors of Aldo Chaff, the best local mechanic. By scraping up the remaining funds after paying for 333, we had managed enough (six thousand dollars), so up we went. Or we were supposed to. First, the starter mechanism fell with a crash into the bottom of the fuselage, then the windshield became covered with gasoline from the safety valve in front. We flew it nevertheless, but with a sickening sense of no future. It was a lovely little doodlebug, maroon and white, with something childish and innocuous in its image, but we turned it down, to be bought by someone else who has happily flown it around the neighborhood until this day. November 86963 was almost ours. Tentative numerologist, I counted it up to 32, which made it a five. Ever since that day, we maintained the myth of the lost Ercoupe, an airplane its designer, the great Fred Weick, used to autograph, he felt so close to it. The planes in which Swan learned how to fly—Cessna 152 and Piper Warrior—never stole her heart in the same way; they were just machines in which to perform. She was already writing her book about flying, *Severe Clear*, and wondering if she should embark on instrument flight. She did not, but for several years she flew and flew, and I flew with her, nudging the ceiling of an even wilder dream. She would say, and has always said, she was often frightened, and I believed her, but she brought to this avocation a fund of extraordinary courage, one day fighting a crosswind that kept blowing her Cessna 172 away from the runway even as she tried to land it; again and again the plane wafted to the left and upward, and she horsed it to the right and down because there was nothing else to do, nowhere else to go. Fortunately we did not run out of runway, and we were soon back on the ground, where, as if fired into action by the stern maneuvering of the last ten minutes, she startled the owner of a brand-new Mooney 201, a sleek low-wing monoplane with a forward-canted vertical tail, by asking him "How do you like your new Mooney, sir?" No one had ever asked him, or anyone else, such a question. Pilots and owners never showed that naked an emotion, but she did, and she profited from her open love of the flying act. It was simple: you controlled the machine or you lost.

Newly qualified pilots are notorious for wanting to air their prowess by taking aloft just about anyone who volunteers. At first you should demur, asking how many others the pilot has taken up, and then relent, especially if the proud owner of the airman's ticket happens to be your sweetheart. Segundo Cieli, our master pilot, perhaps felt Swan had encroached on his private mystery, but he was world class with no real competitors, so his role, while I flew with both him and Swan, gradually became one of avuncular witness, proffering now and then specks of counsel, but keeping his distance, getting anecdotal without quite drawing the moral of his tale. On Swan flew, always renting her plane, lamenting how little money even a book of poems brought in, and hoping to make a bit extra with her flying book. Once again the house changed; we kept living beyond our means, of course, as new owners do, groping for the perfect embodiment of all the home's potential. One table in the living room next to the picture window we loaded with flowers, irises, sunflowers, amaryllises, and tulips, so much so that, even as late summer bulged outside, spring-summer ballooned from the surface of that table, and all you had to do to feel transported as by some floral magic carpet was to sit nearby and listen for the birds of summer. This was a trance within a trance, a little horticultural spaceship that fed our constant yearning to be elsewhere, up toward Mars, say, a yearning that never went away but, as we attended or read about other launches, got severer, plunging us into a vicarious space-sickness that seemed to come from childhood and, oddly enough, seemed driven by the crescendo of love.

We had hardly figured this out; it was bizarre, this wanting to be elsewhere in the teeth of supreme joy, but it worked that way, and we could only conclude it was a variant of ecstasy, the state that throws you out of yourself it is so marvelous, not to anywhere in particular, but just outward, dispossessing you of local balm. Off went the *Voyager*s, on their miscellaneous missions (a Benny Goodman number, "Mission to Moscow," became our music), and we settled down to await their arrival, having accepted NASA's invitation. Then began the habit of always wanting to have in prospect a launch or encounter, something preposterous to cleave to as we went about our academic or literary chores, something that set us apart and made us at least amateur cosmologists. We forgot about the terrorist sheathed in silver foil (perhaps he forgot about us as the furor in the newspapers died down and Raoul Bunsen actually got back to his own academic routine). Perhaps the terrorist would resurface when the two *Voyagers* arrived at their destinations. We had no idea, settling for the light militia of the lower air: aircraft, which included of course trips down to New Jersey although officially I was on leave until January. The bargain struck years ago with Pigskin was still paying off: one semester on, one off, so that I could write, it initially having been through some quirk of hasty negotiation two quarters off for one on. In the years that followed the signing of that agreement, there ensued various attempts to make the contract more mathematical; the original one had taken the summer quarter as time on although I did nothing, and this irked the time-and-motion boys inasmuch as I was getting three fourths of the year off while pretending to do half, and everyone else who, sniffing a bargain, applied for the same deal was turned away point blank. So I lived on with a faint tassel of scandal dangling from me, writing hard and thus fulfilling the terms of that skewed agreement. It was all a matter of deans, and up on their level, where Ab Kettleby and Daunton Snedgeforth reigned, there was no argument: constant maneuvering, yes, but from them both on all occasions what I called the stertorous bicker of the ant. Here, typically for Pigskin, geologists reigned over the careers and applications of creative artists and original thinkers, determined to doom them.

Not only did 333 swarm with flowers, it filled with aviation magazines subscribed to and picked up at random from the downtown newspaper store called the Smoke Shop because it also sold tobacco (and coffee). From these I clipped expensive models I would buy instead of the six-thousand-dollar Ercoupe; I kept an Ercoupe file, of course, for happy memories, but launched another one that rarely saw a cutout priced at below a hundred thousand dollars, including the Paris jet and the Potez. Dreambuying, this, as my yearnings lifted me toward my own spaceship. We ate and drank aviation, and a new bedtime habit formed in which I read out to Swan accident reports culled from the magazines; how strange that accounts of disaster soothed her off. Perhaps it was the sound of my voice that did the trick; off she went, never to dream of accident in that she never thought these things could happen to her. Taking the private pilot examination, she had aced it, with a hundred percent pass, notification of which now reposed in a frame in her study. How thrilling, I thought, to feel so much in command of your skills that thoughts of a mishap never occurred, not even secondhand vicarious. It was no use counseling her, as I sometimes had, about inventing her confidence; she had done so and had propelled it into humblest hubris. Truth told, she had grown up at exponential speed, and my own faintly paternal attitudes were somewhat out of date, a little deficient in that she had bloomed and, like one of our many tulips, had both opened up and opened wide.

This was good; she was off my mind. When, out at the airport, only a mile away, she flew over me in the pattern as I sat on a bench inhaling the aromas of summer, I at first had the jitters, but eventually got used to watching her do touch-and-gos by the dozen, cruising in her 152 time and again, like someone trapped in a slow-motion whirligig, and sometimes following the Mohawk jets as they whined in from Pittsburgh. Now she had a gentler feeling for her poetry, as if it had somehow offended by being too delicate. Actually, her poems were earthy, robust, and colorful, the envy of so many who substituted ass-licking for talent and prospered as ass-lickers do. It was the old academic way, and she would pay dearly for having wandered off the reservation, away from correct fawning into cosmicomical dreamland where her fans were scientists and not poets. To most of these worthies it recommended her not at all that she had a pilot's license and could hold her own with the savants of the JPL. She was making her way with supreme originality, but the going was uphill, and the very thought of a mechanistic pastoral (as they saw her book) dismayed gurus of an older generation. Never mind, she ultimately prevailed, though not without, again and again, mountainous hulks of sheer depression in which those old monsters—lack of self-esteem and so on—reared their vicious heads. Hypersensitive, vulnerable, and unsure of her standing, she plunged ahead, doing her own unique thing, and eventually dominated herself as she had dominated the Cessna and the Piper. They were her rocking horses and she was a winner. As for myself, I had to keep remembering I was getting older, that I was not advancing in the same sense as she; we were not getting older together, not in the qualitative sense. You live together through the same year, but you and your partner have aged in bifurcating ways, you (presumably) to the grace beyond maturity, she to a maturity full of worry. All my life, illnesses apart, I have had this weird sense of growing younger, more irresponsible, more of a jester, perhaps the most frivolous form of denial; I know only that the somber recognitions of aging have not found me, nor I them, so perhaps this is the yield of living with someone eighteen years younger.

Months later, fumbling through old magazines to see what the off-duty world had been up to, I found a new word: *tumblehome*, which meant the curvature of a cockpit canopy as it slanted inward to begin to form the roof. What an odd, semi-cozy word, I thought, to keep you from tumbling out, to shield you from what fluttered down. Or from the sun, although perhaps it had its own greenhouse effect. Perhaps, I thought, there is already a word for everything, could we but find it, as there may be, in the Amazon jungle, say, a cure for every ailment known. Or not known. Was there a condign completeness in the world I had never tuned in to? One day, I happened to set one foot on the welt of my other shoe, and could not move, then simply (as it were) stepped off myself, delighted at the prospect of continuing to be. We had ventured into the realm of David Austin roses, dark blue Siberian irises, and Miss Kim lilacs, ever on the alert for things that would curl the mane of a stone lion. Asking for it, in other words. When I felt more than baffled, I said the word *tumblehome* to myself, intent on something windowlike curled over us that kept us safe while letting us look up and out.

TWENTY-ONE

Grave as togetherness can be, it has its comic aspects too, but only if you stand far enough away to appreciate the automatic puerility that can embody the tenderest emotions. There are our party pieces, for example, or there were; we used to perform them quite regularly in the first years, from Swan's devastatingly accurate rendition of a French ambulance or police car to my own cry of "What about the workers?" filched from some movie or other (no workers ever let forth such a cry). When she was going away on a trip, I, the more demonstrative, used to fetch rope from the garage and pretend to tie her to her desk or to the refrigerator, something she never did, though she was willing to emit a plaintive "Don't take the bus," which I often had to do when teaching down at Pigskin. One theory of eccentricity is that it just boils over from people powerless to preclude it, much as style, as I have always said, is a natural emanation from the sensibility. On the contrary, eccentrics have to make love to their vocation, contributing to it both energy and ingenuity so as to produce deceptive shadows of themselves, so as not to go utterly overboard in some more disastrous direction. A couple may well choreograph their eccentricities as a kind of home entertainment meaningless to intimates and outsiders alike, who often assume they have heard or witnessed no such thing, which is marvelous. One can thus sometimes insinuate a tone, a response, a stance without saying anything overt, not that we went in for that devious means of communication. Our eccentricities remained private. What is more dreadful than, having found and bought your paradise, having to become a traveler from and to it, as if all of life were commuting and you came to cherish a place all the more because you were never in it? During those years, we formed the desire to perfect the place whenever we could, extending it and modernizing it, holding ourselves in imaginary thrall. "Summer at the house" would become the most magical of formulas and a new nightmare would afflict us, me especially (I the pessimist), with acute worry that the empty house had not flooded or burned, been torn apart by gales. We felt we had abandoned someone.

But that was not yet; we had a few years of grace before our wander-years began in earnest, and our reputations—whatever that meant—began to precede us, sucking us after them to go perform. In truth we were very much house people, actually decreeing Sundays "house" days, never to be used for any purpose but each other. In would come an invitation, often a tempting one, and we would exclaim in unison "No, it's a housey day!" and that would be that. Sacrosanct, no, but close. We longed to have eight days a week; in fact we had six, and on the seventh day we opted out of everything save ourselves, orthodox romantics with increasingly too much to do. The only breach in this convention was when we attended Sunday afternoon readings downtown at the Rookery, a bookshop that had been good to us; it not only created the readings series (Off-Campus at the Rookery), it published its own literary newspaper, *The Bookpress*, that went throughout the region, even as far as New York City. Other stores tried to follow suit, but Jennifer and Yann had thought of it first and kept it live. On very rare occasions we went to dinner after the reading, hosting the guest, mustering our politesse, and on exceptionally rare occasions took the guest back home to eat with us because he/she was staying with us, in the caboose, as when the essayist-novelist Willy Gauss blew into town to read on campus, then downtown. On the day before, we put on a literary reception for him at 333, I having forgotten that he had razored Elspeth Laria, the novelist, in a recent essay. And she, I recalled, had written kindly about Segundo Cieli in a little monograph about him. How close the maneuvering was! "Who *is* that man?" she asked me. "*What's he doing here?*" When I confirmed her suspicions, she fixed him with her New England eye and said no more, no doubt hoping to shove a knitting needle into his thorax. But she behaved abominably well and went to the reading too, as if suddenly reapprised of her fame. Out in the caboose that night, Gauss stayed up late reading one of the books thoughtfully provided: *Last Tango in Paris*. Out among the trees and the spiders (he adored spiders) you needed a little stimulus. One other Sunday we might have had an overnight guest from the Parisian newspaper *Libération;* the son of Beckett's publisher, Jérôme Lindon, had come to interview me, and all went well until he saw the caboose. His claustrophobia spoke and he arranged to fly back to New York City that night, saved by the bell; the somewhat shabby caboose with its upstairs bunk had touched a nerve, and he went away dismayed.

Our home was filling up with travel guides for journeys untaken: Mexico, the South Pacific, Sicily, not that we never wanted to go; we just hadn't found the time or the money. A truism says that, once you have read up on your intended destinations, you never want to go to them; they remain pipe dreams forever while you go elsewhere, seduced by lack of knowledge. That, perhaps, was the way to go, via the armchair, especially for those contemplating encounters with Jupiter, whose minds lived part of each day on rusty Mars. We lay in each other's arms and dreamed up perfect places to go to, even Kalopsia, the most perfect destination in the world, and then improvised a guidebook to it, quibbling. We were too heartsick to quibble about Mars, though, too loyal to complain; after all, it had stimulated the minds of authors, look at the walls in the Bunsens' home, with, alongside the Gandhi autograph, Cluke Nerjel's Milky Way and Johann Limberger's Mars-scapes. Ironically, we were both hoping NASA would have many another try, and in the far future they were bound to, maybe even sending a manned mission. How did it feel? Sapping, choking. It was as if someone had told us the Elizabethan-Jacobean period had been a great age of sumptuous poetry and we had time-traveled thither only to find no one at all, not even a lightweight such as Sir Philip Sidney. Trying to quell our disappointment, we occupied ourselves as best we could with the local terrorist, but there was too little to go on; all we came up with were agonized negatives, blow-ups of a battered doll and a hammered head. There was nothing to cleave to, and not even the prospect of Jupiter enlivened us. After all, Mars had always had for us a touch of melodrama and figured in an almost domestic anthology of fabled places, whereas Jupiter—already "Jupe"—had remained more scientific, less glamorous.

So we went back to our writing: different hours, to be sure, but undertaken with revulsed intensity while, in my case, an unoccupied bit of my mind confronted the image of my old friend Asa Humanas now commuting to Baltimore to see his new lady love, and I wondered at him and me, now at full stretch, making that old swap of the circle with one center for the ellipse with two. He drove, I flew. Now and then we both took the bus, he southward, I northward, just to be with women. I wondered at the displaced-person aspect of these trips that took us apart more than ever, he because half a bed had filled with books (not travel books, thank goodness), I because life without my Swan had not seemed endurable. Thus do binding shifts come from random fits. You make a move and, years later, it has become your stronghold, your castle, your rock. Really, I thought, one should beware of ever doing anything, lest. . . . Yet we had both, Swan and I, transferred to a social milieu lusher and more ambitious than that at Pigskin, far from flawless, but at least a place in which many folk were busily doing something of caliber. We had found as hearty, as genial a welcome as we could have wanted, and we now, in a purer sense of that odious term, *belonged*, almost from the first, and without having to adjust radically our ways of doing things. It was delightful to be accepted as we were, without spies tootling after us to see if we said anything hostile about the town. No, Pathica was there to be damned or lauded, and nobody cared; they had too many other things to do than to worry about slandering the place. Eventually we would branch out, mainly to stem the gaping financial wound the purchase of 333 had caused, I to campuses in the Finger Lakes, Swan sometimes much farther afield—Pittsburgh, Ohio, William and Mary, Columbia, and NYU. This meant of course that 333 became even more precious and desirable to us; absence made our hearts idealize, and, when one was there and the other not, the one there tried to reel the other in, by means of imagination anyway, at once adoring the technology of the telephone and deploring its lack of physical continuity. Perhaps what saddened us most in this period, as we waited for Jupiter, was the hunch that these were the easy days before we got scattered again, and we somehow had to fuse inseparably against a rainy day. So we behaved with anticipatory zest, waiting for the ax, determined to stave off the day of parting. Perhaps we were mistaken; I had the fall off, and need not have gone afield to teach; but if I did she might not have to go.

It amazed us how fast the tiny increments of personality had grown in our minds into full-blown portraits of our friends. We had become sensitive to the nuances of their social performance, noting and savoring exact innuendo and tone when, for instance, regal Jennifer indicated her distance from someone's stance or intuition by using the phrase *soi-disant* with just a tincture of banter. It was the only put-down she ever used, and mildly delivered, as befitted one who had starred on TV for years before meeting Yann, our bookman extraordinary, a radical like me, and a lover of "difficult" fiction (what an awful phrase, as if fiction were a dog or a child). Once, when Jennifer was introducing the Rookery readings, Swan and I were late and tiptoed in on her remarks, which she halted to say "Here they are. Now we can begin." When people say things like that, you know you have found the community you deserve, much as you may think you do not need a community at all. Nicest of all was what Elspeth Laria wrote about Swan in those early years when asked for a letter of reference. She began by saying what a glamorous apparition the girl was and then exclaiming that such a looker had those extraordinary brains. This was why a certain professor of imperative literature had kneeled at her feet in Sipsucker Woods and, just maybe, why eventually departments of English offered her jobs, as when Howard Hurtado called her one day and said his department needed her. Alas, she went and almost died the death among that department's uncontained misogynists, Howard's goodwill and decent nature notwithstanding. She kept her looks throughout, as well as her wisdom, and that was the last teaching job she ever took. I anticipate, of course, misled by an entirety of recollection that, instead of doing memory chronologically, does it subject by subject, grouping all of Elspeth Laria together, say.

Dining with the Cielis, we wonder about the terrorist, and I supply the name Gottwald Gimblett, he who used to interfere with our mail at Pigskin and, after a stint in the New Zealand CIA as some kind of major domo, ended up in the Polish Foreign Legion, coming out of that eminent army with several scores to settle. He might well have taken a dislike to Mars, Martians, and Mars lovers. Planting a bashed-in doll and hammering someone's head might well have come from the repertoire of the PFL, I thought, especially if he had been hired by some fiendish underreacher. The Bunsens were giving fewer parties now, as if there were nothing to celebrate, so we decided to throw a party of our own, riskily deciding against bodyguards (it wasn't entirely out of the question that the Bunsens would arrive with their own security people anyway). Raoul's parties were almost a statement, a demonstration, revealing how many people he knew and, just perhaps, how many adored him. He circulated at them uneasily, almost as if commanded to sponsor these gatherings by some higher force, much as the Greek gods, no matter how despotic, remained in thrall to the power known as *anangke*, which as far as I could ascertain was a law unto itself; if so, then brought into being how?

Our own parties, few and far between, at least on the Bunsen scale, were casual affairs, almost always held at lunchtime on Saturday or Sunday, less orgiastic than those thrown by Gloria Gluckstein the bringer-together of young people and the queen of a literary salon. What we aspired to do, at one of our catered affairs, was regale guests with white wine and tiny sandwiches, though sometimes we had gone in for gatherings with flimsy plates and plastic forks which bent as the plates bent, with the result that guests had a double problem of adjusting one bend to the other, dealing in curves rather than straight lines, especially while standing up. The weirdest party we ever gave had been a winter thing, with an actual blizzard on the day clogging the roads and disheartening the faint. In fact, only a third of the invited arrived, rather proud of themselves, and a little swift research revealed that the ones who came were the musicians and psychologists whereas the literati—apart from the poet Ellen Kefauver—were notably absent. My musings that snowy day led me to the conclusion that, if you ever plot against Hitler like von Stauffenberg, exclude the literati from the circle of plotters as having no backbone, but count on the shrinks and music-makers, and always invite a lady poet. In the city of New York, Ellen's daughter was making a name for herself mostly for being in the public eye and so different from her punctilious, gracious mother, who got on with her classes and her office hours while awaiting an invitation to blow up Hitler with a bomb. I sometimes allowed fantasy to play too large a role, standing there that day among my fellow-conspirators, as it were, reckoning the odds of killing him on a snowy day with only sociologists and psychologists, plus two female poets to help me. Might it be done with a hammer and a smashed-up doll? Was that how things had to be done? I even dabbled with the notion of creating a special order of honor that rewarded those who struggled through the snow with a gorgeous ribbon: the Order of Amundsen, or the Scott Medal, with crossed batons and oak leaves for those who had suffered frostbite. This kind of levity was not to be found at Bunsen's Burners (as certain wits called his parties). Scientists were serious and feared being caught out in something farcical; they, who altered the world by revealing it, watched their p's and q's, their pis and gammas. Quite often, as we circulated chez Bunsen, I heard the dialogue from gatherings of ours, relayed to me by who knew what demonic force, and scrambled enough to be the puzzle that occupied me as I edged and backed around. The problem was to unpluck things from one another. Elspeth would really like to come and swim, she said so. Yes, Jennifer said she'd become a fixture on TV and the time had come to move on, up or down, so she took on this position at Coriolis, teaching public speaking. They say he's a very nice man, but he just doesn't answer letters. Who? That Gauss fellow who was here. The one with the long gray hair and the rumpled features. He was once out wheeling one of his twin daughters and someone said to the child How nice of your granny to wheel you about like this! He will answer the phone, but he won't write even to his nearest and dearest. If he ever does, they guard the card with their lives as it may be the only one they ever get. Oh, he's peculiar all right. Oh, the one with the Italian name, he doesn't do parties, maybe a small dinner party, but big affairs put him over the edge, darling. No, that was someone else, you see: he'd heard he wasn't going to win, so he declined to be present. And they all lost their tempers with him; after all, most of *them* were losers too. No, that's not quite right, he just refused to stand in line and become a spectacle of suspense while the judges cranked up the agony. I can't say as I blame him. Wasn't he the character who blew the whistle on American Express for using the homeless and the hungry as a publicity stunt? Was that really what he did? I heard that, one day, at the library, because they'd hit him with a huge overdue fine, he took a supermarket bag of pennies in and dumped it all over the circulation library manager's desk. Bully for him. Clearly this ranks him among the most soi-disant of all time: of rebels, I mean, of the flagrant will-not-serves, don't you think? I know of only one other, at least in this erudite vicinity; they say it's Alzheimer's, he doesn't even know his friends anymore and has to be helped around, he was once so suave and handsome. He, no not him, the other, *Mike*, he has one of the biggest collections in New York State, and he's going to sell it, though it's so extreme he thinks no human besides himself can withstand it. Oh, he's the one who rewrote the phonetic code for the military, isn't he? The what? Oh never mind, he's a man for all reasons. Who? Oh, she's a bit remote, she was in— Where are we? What month is this? Won't it ever stop snowing? Yes, the white-haired man with the tan from Puerto Rico is the one who invented the formula that decides how many intelligent civilizations there are likely to be. They keep getting the answer *One* whatever information they feed into it. God help us. He already did. And they haven't caught anyone yet. I wouldn't credit any such thing, these fiction writers float all kinds of rumors about themselves, just to get sympathy, my love. You watch out for them. Where's Tasha? Over there, I think. She doesn't linger long at these affairs. She liked your piece on Arizona in the *Times*. I wonder who else read it. Please thank her if I haven't. I was comparing her with that other one, the poet who moves from campus to campus as slut in residence and latches on to a young couple, telling the girl she'll make her into a poet all right, which she does by seducing the guy and thus creating the pain without which poetry et cetera. A kind of catalytic vampire she is, needs a placard around her neck. Anyway, please say my thank-yous, I have to run. Oh yes, he even dumped his wife for her. Well. They always do, they give them a reflex test with a rubber hammer and that's that. They always get the young chicks. Then the older chicks become nice ladies but nobody wants to screw them anymore. It's nature's way of shutting up shop. How loathsome. Didn't you know? He's been linked with her for months now, scampering in and out of motels. Orgasm heaven, my dear, mark my words. There'll be hell to pay. Does she know? No, she doesn't know she knows, that's how to put it best. Once they get some money stashed away, they go hunting for poontang. I never thought I'd hear that word in polite society. This isn't polite society, my sweet, this is the bottom rung of the slander mill. And I was shocked, I'd been accustomed to going in there, turning left, and there were all those wonderful French books, a whole room of them, lots of red and white Gallimards, and then another room or subdivision full of German books, and Spanish, it was like a trip, and that's where I bought my Gides and Bernanoses and Malrauxs, replacing books I'd lost over the years. They say Yann had the best collection of foreign books in the state, and then to find it all gone, shipped back to the wholesaler, with only English after all, it was like seeing the Taj Mahal crumble during a buzz-bomb attack. Well, you'll have to go to New York for them now, or use Olin. Screw libraries, they make me nervous. Would you believe it, he ran the whole thing himself for years, the only one allowed to teach it, but after he fell ill the wannabes moved in and at once abolished the essay, created a new seminar on brochure-writing and another on filling out a Schedule C. It all collapsed soon after. I sneeze all the time. Feel nervy. Eyes run, which keeps me from reading. My God, she said, here is the one and and only Hendiadys Thwant, and he straightway snaps: To which, some of us may well say thank God indeed. Yeah they used to play classical music all night, from midnight until dawn with minimum talk. Now it's all talk in the daytime and nothing at all at night. All they do is beg for money. It sends you back to your CDs, like an old love affair revived, not such a bad move, really, and there's no one jabbering at you while you work. And they have all these half-baked interviewers whose taste if any is half a century behind the times. Yes,

Alvin won it, didn't he, for the book about the father? No, that was another one. No, I don't think so. And I actually saw him, no not him, *him*, coming out of the bank on the day he deposited the check and his mouth was open wide, ear to ear, and that was not the day he went to the bank in his boxers. You saw him? I saw him and I said have you received it and he said he'd just handed it in. Well, you must make plenty of loot from the movie sales, what you got to bicker about? He's a highbrow. So am I. You have to prove these things, you can't just go around asserting them as if you'd been appointed by Royal Appointment, like those old Brit johnnies, peppermint maker to the Crown, maker by royal appointment of Pontefract cakes. Yknow. No, I don't know. I have to take things on trust. Think of an anagram for poontang. Pity Nabokov isn't here, he'd have one in a trice, he always did. Those were metagrams, ladders, they weren't anagrams. The gram misled me. A lightweight misprision, sir, you should be flogged. Columbia, the university? I wouldn't give Columbia a dead dog pickled in sperm emeritus. Never mind how many begging letters they send. All they care about is their damned faculty, never about their distinguished graduates. There's nothing like taking it in the tookus. Gordon says take it in quim. Who the hell is Gordon? Did you ever know him? *I*'d say slow guitar, soft trumpet, and a bell, you can't ask more than that. Then make a clean break. No, he never writes. Please move your foot. She doesn't mind really, but I would. One day she'll catch him at it. When he won it, they say, he said he could at long last afford to buy a trash compactor. Lear jet's more like it. Eff *him*. Sure, the pensive person sees the already inbuilt disasters looming ahead in infant form: age, illness, loneliness, the shakes, the itch, the heebie-jeebies, phimosis, carcinoma, Parkinson's. Get him out of here, he just comes to upset us all. Where are the fucking writers today then? Home under a blanket where they belong, the wimps. Please give us two together, will you? I'd gladly sacrifice a leg to get two together. Folk music isn't real music, not until somebody like Bartók or Vaughan Williams has dealt with it and reconceived it. Mars music, well, would be inaudible, so I'm effecting a compromise. Don't you remember that piece of Delius, in was it *A Village Romeo and Juliet*, when they sweep the curtain across the stage and make you just appreciate the music? No I never heard that. I'll look it up. So I may have long silences tinily tampered with. You and who? Don't ask. You have to learn to leave people alone, sweetheart. Well, some we will. How about that self-engrossed one whose sentences all begin with *I*, spoken or written? A born user. Was she the one who kept saying *juvenalia* for *juvenilia*, not having read her Juvenal lately? And *momento* for *memento*. Agh. What was that story you told about Hans Alpha? Oh, at the airport, or the Milky Way one? The airport, please. He was standing there at check-in, in a white raincoat, and he looked like a tourist, very European, though to me he seemed more like a stranded polar bear. *At Pittsburgh*, they told him, *go to Gate 43*, at which he nodded grumpily. *Next to Gate 44*, some oaf added, and he said he had some grasp of arithmetic, yes he could understand that. Away he went, and I went up to the desk and told them he was the man who figured out how the sun worked, but they thought we always knew and were unimpressed. To them he was just another Coriolis crank, if to be taken with any kind of seriousness then with yesterday's leftover variety used to wrap fish. The sun came up, the sun went down, who needed to know more than that? Now someone was wandering around quoting Leibniz, he said, beginning with *We delight in the show of danger*, then getting interrupted by some Brit going on about stumps and bails. On windy days the cricketers keep the bails on top of the stumps by smearing raspberry jam in the little groove, no other kind of jam works. Does it work with all grooves? He keeps young with a paper route, he delivers from his plane, banking it steeply to toss out the rolled-up newspapers, a 1948 Aeronca, imagine that landing on your doorstep while the plane roars over low. At least you know when the paper's come. *That is connected with perfor-*

mances on the tightrope, or sword dancing. Leibniz again. At Oxford, you have your viva-ed First, given to you after the examiners have quizzed you, the unviva-ed First, which is self-explanatory, and the Congratulatory First, which says the examiners are dying to meet you and you will soon, possibly next weekend, become prime minister. Didn't Aldous Huxley take the last Congratulatory? It wouldn't surprise me at all. You know all this at first-hand? University of Chattanooga, Class of. . . . *And we ourselves in jest half let go a little boy, as if about to throw him from us.* What, who? Oh that was Leibniz again, circling for prey. You for a year, what? Love can appear in the flesh, you know. It starts with the second injection. Only a hello, out in the air. I am only a little rent lily. Torn, that is, not rental. How can you rent a lily? My heaven-sent one. Tarry faces aft, oozing white. You will be born for a year. The best things with these come-over Brits is not to let them edit or run anything until they have taken a stiff exam in Americana, the Frontier especially. It's their form of revenge, they think we're so dumb we haven't noticed what they've done. Will you do will you please do your wild man of the woods improvisation? Temblor. Ditzy. Worst of all's a nosebleed while you're writing. Always check with your doctor if you cough up anything like coffee grounds. There's no anagram for *poontang*, it has to remain only its obscene self. So there was this sad day when they took all the French books out in cardboard boxes, their light firmly hidden under that bushel, never to be seen again. Abbas Combe. Abberley. Abberley Common. Abberton. Abbess Roding. All due to be closed thanks to some government edict. It makes you sick, Segundo. So who was this Gottfried van der Gimblett? Gottwald Gimblett, actually. What a fancy name. He was the next great imposter after Tony Curtis, remember that movie? Yes, Madame de Scudéry drew with her brother. Odd, most folk use a pencil. Yes, he's Brazilian or Paraguayan, he writes novels while shaving. I mean he can do a whole novel while shaving his face and he's published eleven hundred so far, they never have time to review him, he's always out with a sequel. Imagine that. Did you hear about that fragorist, Alice Adams, sucked out of a jet over the Everglades? And pray who is Solange the Shoulder Rabbit?

I gave this party, but can no longer understand it. So many extraneous noises blot out what I really want to hear. I retire to a neighbor room where, down in the dungeons of blessed memory, Swan and I exchange the word *token* with loving care, knowing this is one of our main fetishes, a token being a gift, of course, but also a treasured gesture. It is almost as intimate a word as *pitness*, meaning bed, or *chap*, meaning whatever it is we cannot be bothered naming although we rather enjoy its presence. How lovely-surreptitious it was, during a hectic party, to sneak away and stroke her moist, fair complexion, always cool in the most hectic rabbles. Not so true of me, the specialist in overheating because my internal thermostat was off, akin to what happened in the house after a party, when The Daisy Maids cleaned up and, while flicking their dusters, accidentally twirled the only too responsive dial on the wall, freezing or baking us an hour later. We got accustomed to that, inventing the term Daisy-cold or Daisy-hot, which would baffle an outsider, none of whose business it was anyway. Was that prolific Brazilian's name Ennui? Or Inuoye? Nobody knew, so he was a goner already, well advised to acquire a name that people could say and remember. Maybe he smoked a pipe, I having always had a fascination with pipe-smoking men, who seemed to have a complete heating system built into their bodies, a chimney, and constant urgent business. Yes, they looked fatherly, Old Russian or Rumanian style. We decided to stop giving parties; during parties we always decided they were unbearable, but you always had to give another so as to get the end of the Leibniz quotation, even if nothing else. Yet it was quaint to watch the Cielis confronting the Bunsens and finding something to talk about since Raoul knew nothing of Segundo's painting/flying world and Segundo knew precious little of astronomy. Our hope was that they would come away with new prejudices, just like diseases. If only Gloria Gluckstein could have butted through the gathered host, exclaiming "Aren't you Carole Lombard?" until she had misidentified half the room. Too hard to arrange, however. I was certainly missing the other setting of my life, the old one, the unfavored one, as one misses a favorite pair of pajamas, but the people at the Coriolis parties were more enterprising, less addicted to the cult of being company men or women, more inclined to disobey. Perhaps, buried even here, a mild-mannered terrorist sipped his white wine and planned further abominations, wondering in mid-aphorism why he hated the human head and wanted to plunder it. We would get him soon, I resolved, lest he ruin our forthcoming trip to the Jet Propulsion Laboratory. What if he were a Coriolis person, worse even than those who kissed and goosed their students, or who padded expense accounts on distinguished trips? How would they punish him? Would it be a him? Put him in a glass tank naked and let him swim around for the rest of his days, like a seaquarium exhibit. That for starters. Give a big party and have everyone pinch him to death and then hang him upside down like Mussolini. "Your imagination," Swan told me, "is just too violent." One of Mussolini's fascist tortures, I recalled, was force-feeding people with castor oil, evocative of the punitive nurse rather than of the horrors Mussolini copied from Hitler. "I grew up in a violent time," I once more explained. "It comes naturally." Nothing natural about it, she told me; it was a conditioned reflex. Only with terrorists, I said. She looked away, reluctant even to have terrorists mentioned in the house by way of allusion. Somehow all terrorists took off their shoes at the door and ate them. "Don't worry, they'll get him."

"No they won't, he knows when to stop. They need to know his rhythm, and they don't." The very thought of him was eroding her peace and quiet; even his capture would distress her; she had this aquamarine sensitivity, transmitting a ripple to all parts of her being, and I wondered, as ever, how can I protect her from the world? Her parents watch any feature about the Holocaust, with embittered avidity, not as if they didn't know; not Swan, the least Jewish of Jews, but the most vulnerable human being of all. She knows of a world in which there was no tenderness, so she insists that the world of now be full of it. It must be so, she echoes, otherwise I cannot endure it. How far she was from the ancient Greeks, with whose views I was more familiar, they who never forgot the vast mincing machine that accepts us all heedlessly in order to cook up another generation. I respected her desire, but sometimes shrank from the looking-away it entailed. Not that she needed Holocaust movies; she didn't, but her preferred diet of mysteries and sundry comedians (Leslie Nielsen and other farceurs) left me cold, as people calling themselves comedians have always left me cold. I loathe little more than someone whose premise is that he/she is funny. I prefer people to do their thing and let me laugh when I feel like it, which is mostly not when others laugh. Spaniards have written on tragedy and Britishers on comedy, but few know anything about either since we all, vis-à-vis those majestic categories, live in a condition akin to color-blindness. Never mind: if Swan wants peace and quiet, good humor and bland art, so be it. She still loves wit, which tells me she uses her mind for that, but for comedy and so forth her heart. We need so much entertainment because we cannot bear the truth, which never alters unless some metaphysics tells you otherwise. So she did not linger on the terrorist, or his token chain mail; his absence she construed as his better nature having told him to desist. If others wanted to linger on what those old Greeks called *deinosis*, or seeing things at their worst, she did not, knowing that the evil in the world required no assist from her. She did well at the job of fending off the horrors, denying them her energy and manifesting a degree of self-control I envied. Already beset with life-denying devils, she resisted the world's constant invitation to the dance of death. I thought this a true gift and an extraordinary contrast to the depression she could not always master. In the end, she took her stand on biology's ability to renew, not on history's capacity to repeat; myself, born among bombardment and atrocity, I could never quite banish the doomsday feeling I acquired with bombers overhead and my father telling me his own youth had been similar. Swan and I made a formidable team because we had different gifts and contrasting handicaps; we managed to help each other, and, of course, we had literature and space in common.

We could hardly wait for the JPL to switch on its huge TV screens as transmissions came in from Jupiter; we felt that NASA owed us one and could never quite dismiss from our minds the scenes of scratched launches: two anticlimaxes to one blastoff. We kept wanting to rewrite the past in positive terms, which was to say focus on the successful launches, but the failures haunted us, reached out to us and made us wince. With so much to go wrong, how could these missions ever go right?

TWENTY-TWO

Trying to think forward to Jupiter courtesy of the JPL, we found ourselves being thrown back by a riptide of anguished pessimism. What afflicted us was well on the way to becoming the perfect image of the failed launch: not a glimpse or a snippet, not an echo or a retina hang-on, but a full-blown recital from A to Z of all that accompanied a fiasco. It happened and rehappened in our heads, inerasable and fiercely seductive; we had been there before and so should not need this extra visit, but back we went, inveigled by worry, like the dental patient awakening in the small hours and jabbing his tongue into the cavity just to check on the pain, doting on the pain because it was all his. We should have been able to dismiss this nightmare, or at least abridge it, settle its hash by classifying it and looking, mentally, the other way.

"I keep getting this awful total recall," I told Swan. "Maybe it's not just one but a composite image of all the failed missions, rolled into one. Damn them. It's just nerves, isn't it?" She allowed that it might be just that. She too had the jitters that, in the end, remobilized old disappointment and sent it skittering through your nervous system that you thought you'd primed for

Jupiter out on the coast. Because I told her how haunted I was, she felt worse and began receiving miserable playbacks herself; it went to show how intensely we had responded when on the Cape, identifying with the *Viking*s as if there were nothing else in the world to regale ourselves with. Back came the nightmare, moment by moment, sequence by sequence, as if it were prophecy. "We have to remember how to forget," she murmured, but I found my mind murmuring to me, accurate and irresistible. Here it came again, programmed for me, destined to depress me about the gorgeous things to come.

Once again, launch day was a blaze of light; but, forewarned by the NASA brochure about coastal Florida's being subject to sudden summer storms, we hunted out the "light rain gear" recommended. You could enter the space center any time after 1:30 P.M. I remember my mind's moving to an odd, abstract sense of relief that nobody would be aboard *Voyager*, which made the enterprise even more superhuman, especially when we pondered NASA's promise, on the invitation, that "Analysis of all the imagery and telemetry returned will continue for years." Was this a fairy tale? It was as if a sublime, hopelessly distant poem were going to be elucidated by a robot.

The Ramada coffeeshop, always noisy, on that day had an extra throb of haste and excitement. Hitherto-contemplative faces were animated. Those who used to hunch over their pastries were sitting up straight. The waitresses were rushed off their feet. We gabbled on in some chain reaction of worried affability (or of prophetic jubilance). Today, for once, there was somewhere to go, something that compelled, not a symposium or a press briefing, but a fiery node aimed out of sight. And this was just the beginning: the mood would bulge in the postlaunch celebration at poolside, perhaps all the livelier because *Voyager* was a laboratory, a tool, more an example of intellectual beauty than of human appeal. When no one was aboard, except symbolically, the fervor on the ground created its own substitute for vicarious heroism, and it came out—at least in my own determined reading—as an exhilaration death-free and utopian, not whoopee but choked wonderment at one of Pygmalion's statues beginning to move. Above all, this was a knowledge mission, not a propaganda stunt. We were as far from *Star Trek* as could be, more in the realm for which Joshua Lederberg coined "exobiology," which some obtuse folk thought a science without a subject matter.

If, someone said, you spent all the time sighting through a viewfinder, you missed the best of liftoff; you'd be three miles from it in any case. I half expected to see people clutching rectangles of smoked glass, or prisms, or periscopes, but most had cameras. My omelet was sitting none too well with so much coffee on top of it in an already nervous stomach. Perhaps it is the stomach that makes us remember so much. Everyone seemed tense. And I, in a fit of almost infantile impatience, wanted the whole thing to be over, so that I could get out of "seasonal" time back into a chronicity of indistinguishable days on the beach. It was how I felt about Christmas, New Year's, the Fourth of July. The fit soon passed, though, when I realized I wanted the event without the communal rigmaroles that surrounded it: a pillar of fire for me alone. Somehow, looking forward to the liftoff was more private than the event itself, the difference being that you rarely test your own anticipations against those of others whereas witnessing almost obliges you to compare. An event belongs to the public at large.

It was time to go, with green permit scotch-taped to the inside of the windshield. The arrowed V in the circle and NASA's linear self-simplification faced outward and a few degrees to the rear. Number 1126. Would they all be there? Millions would be watching on television, but I wanted to eye the blot of flame and hear the rocketmakers as their metal princeling thundered off: an envoy workshop, also a Norse pirate sneaking up on a god of war once called Mawort and Nergal. Something piratical stirred in me now, not the thought of interfering where we were not entitled to, but this: what if the *Voyagers* found life? What homage would be appropriate to it? "We'd have to do it impromptu," Swan said. What a dreadful thought, I decided, what with all the guns on Earth. Discovered, could such life stay intact? What would theologians make of it? To me, it would be only one of a million exemplifications inside our own galaxy. It would be unique only as the first sample found. One day, would a robot swim for me?

We moved on to Atlantic Avenue, heading north.

As the Vega rolled up the sunbaked autobahn called the Bennett Tollway, then up SR3 toward Gate 2, I was caught up in the shapelessness of things to come, haunted by an old switch from science fiction (what if *they* were going to do this to *us*, with only the vaguest suspicion that we were here?). It was beginning to look as if we had beaten the Martians to the punch, but who knew? Maybe they, or other planetarians, had already come, witnessed, said their *Alas*, and gone, even if only via the proxy of their instruments, whose liftoff Earth-eras ago was observed by Martian astronomers, writers, painters, whose Ramadas were globules a millimeter high, and whose Cocoa Beach was an under-the-surface silicon hideaway, or a hillock of monastic blue. My press pass rhymed with *trespass*, an echo whose ambiguity I couldn't shut out.

The roads were jammed, but just as much traffic was coming out of the space center as was going in. A guard motioned us through. A second guard, a hundred yards farther in, told us the launch had been canceled. "Take the Cape Road out." It was only 2:30 P.M. Swan wailed. I felt hollowed out. We cruised past hunchbacked refrigerators that were really outside toilets, past out-of-state families marooned by their trailers, wondering what to do next, past loudspeakers we now could hear. Hundreds of people with binoculars, or sandwiches in hand, were staring in the ninety-degree heat across the Banana Creek at Launch Site 41, as if trying to establish precisely which bit of machinery had gone wrong, or hoping for a sudden reversal of the decision. Big chunks of slate cloud had begun to cluster inland; but they could hardly be to blame. We hadn't the heart to turn around and go back for a bus tour of the center: we wanted to get away from what had failed us on the day of days, after all the talk, the symposium, the buildup, the fond possessive gazes past the surf to the dumpy castellations on the skyline, and the memory of how Arvydas Kliore, with his palm against his chest, said his rib cage had trembled at a blastoff.

Instead, we had eventless afternoon heat to console us. Swan bought yet another necklace at a boutique while I conversed at the counter with a morosely outgoing Czech who hated both space and New Jersey (he didn't say why). Next door we bought postcards of the rockets that *did* go off, leering at the *Apollo-Soyuz* signs still up, and suddenly realized the car radio might have saved us a journey. The fact was, if there was bad news, we hadn't wanted to hear it until the last moment. On the notice board in the Ramada lobby the news awaited us. A five-thousand-dollar valve had stuck in the open position, no one knew why. It was one of twenty-four that ringed the inside of the rocket nozzle on each of the two Titan III solid-fuel engines. Through its silver-dollar-sized vent, someone said, a chemical called nitrogen tetroxide was squirted under high pressure to deflect the exhaust flame and steer the rocket. It was—weird coincidence—what a bright young boy had urgently asked questions about at the briefing for children in the Ramada last night.

"*Non*-man-rated," Raoul said in a voice heavy with insinuation. Then he cheered up. "More beach!" How wise of him. But I would gladly have surrendered miles of sand for one wisp of Titan flame. I had no excuse for not being in the sea; and now, because we had not taken the tour, the image of the tour refused to go away, a mirage snubbed, otherwise known as the Launch

Control Center, not so much a building as a living brain, as its architect had said. The LCC we had already seen had huge louver-like windows in the east wall, through which the firing crews could watch liftoff (whereas inside the old-style blockhouses they saw it only via periscope or closed-circuit TV). It looked, I recalled, like a brand-new bank or an ultra-white contemporary credenza with concertina drawers.

Was it even worth saying that someone out there had blundered badly? There was a new seven- to ten-day postponement, ruling out our chances of seeing anything at all. We had alter egos and other lives to go back to, to pick up where we had left them. You might wangle a couple of days extra, but ten? Against a date that was anyway far from sure. Life had degenerated into a delay mounted on a postponement that fed an indefinite halt and sired the suspicion that the whole thing was a stunt to finance the motels and the local tourist industry. The gloom in and around the Ramada, even as new storms arrived and hit home, was palpable. We went in disappointed circles from notice board to desk and back again. The printout blamed nobody of course, and in reporting the decision to demote *Voyager* A said "demate," which was poignant enough as the two *Voyager*s were always referred to as sister-craft. Somehow "scientist" had become "scientest." Was language breaking down? Were the PR people joking or just illiterate? Our only solace, if that, was the fact that yesterday someone dangling a leg from a rubber float just up the coast about seventy miles had been bitten by a shark and was now in the hospital, as like as not for amputation. Daytona Beach was closed and Cocoa Beach was jammed with space-indifferent aliens. We folded our towels and prepared to steal away. We too had been bitten.

There was an aesthetic, mythic side to my Cocoa Beach experience, though; I had always associated Florida with what flowered (being literal), with renewal, reprieve, and warm benisons. A childish notion to be sure, this Delius-style reverence had helped me to think of the *Voyager*s as gentle extensions of ourselves, probing, almost seducing, not quite to the point at which Jupe gave in and decided to please, but in the interim between technical accuracy and emotional surge. The planet had always been what we wanted it to be, whereas now it was no more and no less than what it was, though we might be subjective about its hues, contrasts, topography, past and future. There were even people who claimed to have seen a face amid Mars's sands, an idea I found ridiculous. All the same, I found it reasonable to think gently, understandingly, of Mars, our old buddy. Swan let emotion into her account too, as poets do with impunity, importing no more psychology than I, but relating Mars to all those wonderful states of mind we humans took such pride in: response to color, beauty, things fearsome and things exquisite. We still had the old privileges of seeing what we wanted wherever we wished, but we now had to bow to the new, boiler-plated empiricism the spacecraft had made.

Two lovers, looking at each other and then briefly at the spilling Sun, share something they would not have if the Sun went out. They have set their private emotions in the context of something massive, almost punitive. They might achieve a comparable effect by bouncing their mutual gaze off a lily pond, a goldfish pool, or even the exposed intestines of a dead deer. This osmosis of the feelings, likened by some to divine affiliation, just happens to depend on what else you might be peering at. They say a man who has held an elephant at bay for an hour (if), picks up a baby in quite a new way, and I believe it. Whatever we do modifies itself according to our other preoccupations, and so a couple that have been attending to Mars will be a bit Martian, not in any crude sense demanding canals, but otherworldly-ravished. Their sense of wonder at the planet Mars will have increased, and so will their sense of wonder at themselves. Call it retina-imagery, it lingers and propels new feelings into being, so the couple has immutably changed in the interests of further change and will make its way farther and farther, two beings raising themselves to intellectual-spiritual maximum by sheer attention to what is. Art does much the same, but what a wonder to have the effect of art mimicked by a natural object unknown until recently! That, surely, is one of the catalytic magnificences of spacefaring; the result is always the result, and the result will always change its perceiver.

TWENTY-THREE

We were driving through Pasadena at four in the morning to watch a masterpiece of celestial pool. In forty minutes the *Voyager* I spacecraft would have its "historic encounter" with the planet Jupiter, and we had not had enough sleep to bring to this vigil senses as finely attuned as they should have been.

At the fence surrounding the Jet Propulsion Laboratory, a guard stroked his flashlight along the guest pass in the left front windshield and seemed to bring to life its latent yellows and the inset shot of Jupiter: a disk of scumbled stripes against a black ground. After we parked, another guard with an even bigger flashlight (maybe they played a machismo size-game in the quiet hours) escorted us to the edge of an open area. "Over there," he said, floating a strip of light in the rough direction of the San Bernardino mountains. And off we stumbled, over loose-feeling soil as an aroma of horse-droppings got stronger and stronger. A paddock was the last thing you expected alongside the anteroom to deep space, but who could be sure of anything a few hours before dawn, and this tense, this excited, this unbelieving?

Up some steps we lurched, into a blast of light. No horses.

"Are you professors?" someone asked; but, too bleary to

answer any such question with all its hidden pitfalls, we recited our professorial names instead. I heard Swan doing almost an incantation of her own melodic name, then my own voice disembodiedly saying *my* name into the faint predawn breeze heavy with mountain and horse aromas.

Next we were in a reception lobby on whose desk some two hundred name tags gleamed like newly alighted celluloid butterflies with oblong wings, perched on their clips. Haggard-looking visitors shuffled around waiting to be told where to go and, from somewhere, a pang of European memory hit home, reminding me of millions who went to their deaths just as patiently as this, but stripped naked. One man had come all the way from Sweden, he said; his name tag had a green spot, meaning International, whereas ours had an orange one, no doubt meaning Professor. The key to the whole operation was a chart on the clipboard held by a self-assured woman who must have had a good night's sleep. She looked like Bette Davis, with rather hooked nose and heavy round eyelids. Was she going to let it all hang out and say "What a dump"? She must have had a good breakfast too, being in sturdy voice. They called us by colors now: green, red, blue, and yellow. "My God," I said to Swan. "What if we're both color-blind and these aren't orange at all?" But we soon went through a gap, as if at Immigration, receiving a portfolio and a big round Jupiter badge. A chatty hostess conducted us fast across a dark courtyard to a soft-lit hallway rich with the aroma of coffee and motioned us into a brightly lit convivial-looking room adorned with breakfast. "I feel just like a communicant," I told Swan as we stepped forward, being ushered into the numinous presence of the planet itself, or even like participants in some secret exchange across the Iron Curtain. We turned right and turned again, sleepwalkers on the magical brink.

And there it was: a small square classroom with a chart on an easel, a big color TV across one corner, and maybe a dozen people on chairs in the avalanche of light. The rug was soft, lulling. The manicured tones of Al Hibbs, the Voice of *Voyager*, added something crisp. All the way along the back of the room, under carefully aimed lights that gave off heat, a smorgasbord breakfast tempted us with cold cuts, doughnuts, and glazed cookies. We heaped our plastic plates with more than we would ever eat and, feeling oddly weightless, swayed to our chairs near the front as the lights went down, our eyes on the screen lest we miss anything.

It was almost like watching the Late Late Show just before the birds began to chirp, and it certainly felt illicit. In fact, however, as soon as we focused our lagging eyes we were joined to a telescope flying toward Jupiter at colossal speed, and all that was slow was the relay of images via Australia, which to my caffeine-fuzzy head sounded much farther away than Jupiter itself. Now, with almost no warning, the first image peeled downscreen and I forgot to chew my ham on rye. I was *flying.* The Great Red Spot came into view, in black and white like all of the night's images, a swirl of linguini ramparts unthinkably vast. My eye was only five Earth-circumferences from Big Jupe, as Swan and I called it, and something akin to horizontal vertigo hit me as I peered at what no one had ever, until now, seen this close: ovals, hot spots, plumes, and stripes broad and bold as those on an admiral's sleeve. Each signal was taking forty minutes to cross space at the speed of light, and I felt a sudden panic. How could we be both this near and yet this far? Visually intimate at such a distance? I let my mind attune to farness, let my eyes become greedy.

As the night wore into dawn, and sunlight filtered into the room through a wall of curtained glass, revealing white styrofoam piles of cups and plates beneath the chairs, I felt overcome by the privilege of being a voyeur in the ghastly hungover glow that seemed to tweak my gritty eyes. My entire body was a model of contorted attention. Jupiter was too vast to apprehend, even in dribs and drabs. I felt ant-like, no longer the amateur who looked at the Great Red Spot through his twelve-inch telescope and said "It's like a dried-up wound." I seemed to have no emotion left.

"Are we really doing this?" Swan whispered, her hand ashake. "Are we *here* or *there*? It's weird." She photographed the screen, seeking not her image of that image but locking away a preposterous bit of time even as Al Hibbs told us, with leprechaun suavity, we were going on now to the south pole of Io, just like that, as if we'd paused at Elmira in the plane to Pathica, and the whole room canted, the left-hand side of the TV screen gulped or nictitated, as the first still of Io's pocks inched in. We marveled in a halted dive. Everyone was exclaiming softly, obscenely. Our NASA compère, seated just in front of me, shook his head in elated wonderment until his quiff sagged loose, down his profile. Io was there with us and we had become primitives in a cave of high technology, gaping with daft easiness at a crater, a caldera—no, something like the deeps of a faraway nostril. Neither of us could speak. If, as I thought, the successive images weren't stills, but formed a continuous movie, zooming closer and closer to the planet-like moon, I would get airsick or space-sick. I was full of cumbersome delight. Io might be more to the human scale than Big Jupe, but it was still so much "out of this world" that you had to invent a special etiquette for viewing it by. A cat may look at a king, as the adage had it, but a human may look at a cosmic secret only with nervously improvised adoration. Anything else was somehow uncouth.

"Have you had enough?" Swan flinched and answered, "Oh no," as if caught doing something forbidden.

As daybreak revealed us to one another in that cozy outpost of a room, and conjecturing experts occupied the screen, we got up and exercised our legs, at last untwisting our knees. This had been the scientific equivalent of shaking Shakespeare's hand. A spell had broken which began in darkling silence and grew with whispered asides. Only the children present seemed awake. I could see gaudy flowers just beyond the window, like a reward for spending a white night with the fastest man-made object to leave Earth. But, of course, we had had the reward already, left on our drained retinas by an ungainly contraption now streaking toward yet another moon, with, attached to its flank, a gold-plated copper LP in a gold and aluminum sleeve, replete with messages for watchers keeping other vigils around other stars. It was like some Golden Fleece in reverse, flung toward the Jasons out there, who themselves had aimed their something at us, ages ago. The spell did not break, I decided; it never breaks. It bends, it flexes, to accommodate breakfast, use of a JPL washroom (to me almost a zero-gravity toilet, such was my excitement), a senior scientist who grumbled to his wife, "At that temperature, it couldn't *flow*, honey, it just couldn't!" And sundry detonations of laughter, almost as if an ordeal were over.

Yet the laughter, the banter, Surfian, had something full-bodied in it, something ripe. The tired faces at the smorgasbord table had an ebullient calm, as if a peace treaty had been signed, and I couldn't help thinking we'd been present at—had assisted at—an almost religious ritual. We were grateful, awed, proud. Once again the superb bull's-eye telemetry had worked, making the vast smaller and the small seem vaster than ever, transporting us into a domain in which ratio—proportion, distance, size—was arbitrary or irrelevant in view of the vision we had just had of something oddly homely at the heart of what was remote.

And soon would come, I told myself, the pageantry that clinched and fixed the images we jitterishly took in. I meant the computer-made color pictures, transforming black-and-white woodcut-like things into chromatic pastures for the eye. I saw myself sitting in another room of the same size, its walls filling with four gigantic blow-ups from *Voyager*'s repertoire of unprecedented sights and scenes. Swan and I were among the last half dozen in the room, watching to the end. Every segment felt historic, at least until the eight o'clock press conference in another building. Out we tottered, with a lame giggle at our newly developed photophobia, into the new day, dazzled by the steady California sun, coaxed along by yet another JPL savant who repeatedly thanked us for coming (even as we thanked him for the whole show). It was as if he was the owner of a prodigious but overlooked museum of unique toys. He was proud it all went off so well, and he kept on giving that almost suppressed NASA smile, but he was gladder, I thought, that we cared enough to stay, and stick around for more, while the imaging went on and on, with closer and closer close-ups flitting across the TV screens we saw through the picture windows of the buildings we went past. Then I realized the JPL was just another campus, to add to our collection. Now, in a dream, we were chatting with Governor Brown of California, nicknamed Governor Moonbeam; his delight in the day's events was unmistakable, and no, he didn't realize the euphoric mob included poets and novelists. His vision of his own state visibly widened. Were we, he asked, going to write about the day's events? How could you not, we said with bleary certainty. Yes, he said, "that's what they said about these missions."

We saw Raoul Bunsen again, seated on a low stone bench, being interviewed; he waved, which the tape recorder could not see, and as we passed by we pulled zany gleeful faces to make him giggle, and succeeded. Later, after some weary hugs and rather self-conscious backslapping, he and Florinda Demetz, who prepared the sounds of Earth for the *Voyager* tapes, asked where we had been. "Just where *were* you guys?" Raoul drawled. "We looked everywhere for you." In unison, as if it were part of an alibi learned by heart, Swan and I huskily said "Room one six seven," but we meant somewhere else, far far away.

Raoul frowned. "But we were there too."

"Then," Swan said, "you still don't know us from the back. You would certainly not recognize us from underneath or even from above. We were on Io, and we didn't see you guys anywhere there either!" It was the same sound as in Bernard's Surf: a triumphant, careless levity, the sound you make when you have aced an examination or when someone tells you you have indigestion and nothing grievous. Such events were a prolongation of life, of cheer, of creative vigor, but most importantly, as I was beginning to apprehend, of human intimacy in a vast arena.

When you had seen wonders, you saw more wonder in your spouse; or so I reasoned, telling myself we lived in a wider context than most people dreamed of, and our heads were full of extraordinary images primed to haunt us as long as we lived. The intoxication of fatigue mixed with consummated hope drove us on into brittle, stagey conversations. "Would you," Raoul asked over omelets in a Howard Johnson's, "say *Ee*-o or Io as in Ohio?" He trusted my knowledge of languages more than I did, and, once again, I felt in the wrong role, as when he looked at the night sky and wasn't sure which star was which, whereas millions of eyeball amateur astronomers did, myself included. What a gulf spread out between us and them.

"Modern Greeks," I said. "Surely *Ee*o. About the ancient Greeks, I'm not so sure. Nobody is." I was more certain of Jovian and Ionian images forever mingled with those of the San Bernardino mountains, in whose foothills the JPL nestled. The tangerine and palomino mottle and that long coronet of snow were Pasadena's own, but *Voyager*'s too, deployed "out there" in shapes and blends that had also come to stay, like emblems of futurity. The entire otherworldly experience remained in the present tense, went on happening again and again, as if to happen were not enough. Bully for our delicate mastery of space; bravo to the nets we used to flirt with time.

The full-blown coda to that excursion brought us back to point-to-point astronomy, the real terrain of *Voyager*'s music (some of it deliberately chosen to evoke the sense of cosmic loneliness). After leaving the solar system, *Voyager* I steered for a point in the constellation Ophiuchus, *Voyager* II for one in Capricorn: here today, gone tomorrow, yet eternally voyaging, touring, eating up the unconsumable distance. If all of that seemed too placeless, too abstract, there remained the comfort of yet another out-of-time, out-of-mind reference, which told us that, in forty thousand years, both *Voyager*s would come reasonably close to a red dwarf star, AC+79 3888, presently in the Big Dipper and seventeen light-years from our Sun. After forty thousand years, though, AC+79 3888 would be within *three* light-years of us, closer to us then than the closest other star—Alpha Centauri—was now. The first *Voyager* would come within 1.7 light-years of it, and the second within 1.1. Cold comfort maybe, to have such certainty, such finality, already on the cards along with that other certainty, that other finality, about what would have become of you in forty thousand years. Yet, to be so thoroughly and intricately wiped out, back into the fund of star stuff, links you tinily to those anonymous-sounding locations in Ophiuchus and Capricorn, to that red dwarf rotating at a speed only a few times greater than that at which the supersonic Concorde crosses the Atlantic Ocean. Haunted by the dread of becoming irreversibly dispersed, we were somehow nearer the *Voyager*s at AC+79 3888, in that far distant time, than to the *Voyager*s as they cruised through the empty backyard of the back of beyond.

Such a sense of the self seemed radically metaphorical, as did the augury of presence in the thought that, with all our music silent in reserve in the grooves on those two gramophone records, we might as well be closer to another star than ever before even if life on our planet by then would have vanished. Present at our own absence, we would still have a presence elsewhere: mute, nominal, with only spiky Stravinsky aboard out of all the twentieth century's serious music, but *there*.

"What? No Villa-Lobos," Swan lamented. "How gross."

"What's missing is an entire century of serious music," I said, cursing Monty Adelaide, who was responsible, along with the musicologists who assisted him. In literary terms, how could you choose Spenser and dump Shakespeare? Or choose Keats over Shelley? I tried to quote:

> . . . Two vast and trunkless legs of stone
> Stand in the desert. Near them, on the sand,

> Half sunk, a shattered visage lies, whose frown,
> And wrinkled lip, and leer of cold command,
> Tell that its sculptor well those passions read.

Shelley the alien. Micrometeors (not micrometeorites until they landed) would pit the outer face of both records, but the inner face would suffer almost no damage at all. I had a last-ditch hope, a hunch: was the inward-facing side on *Voyager* I the outward-facing one on *Voyager* II? Had we covered our bet, as it were, with our sleeves? In Raoul's seemly and exalted biography of the interstellar records fastened to the *Voyagers*, I found a picture of a dense field of stars in the Big Dipper, and then wondered at the caption "One of these may be AC+79 3888." *May?* All of a sudden, my projected self felt nowhere at all; I needed a picture of AC+79 3888 right in front of me, never mind how dim it seemed, and my sense of intimate futurity would not be whole without it.

All those star-giving codas were thanksgivings to people, institutions, places, experiences, that had shone like suns for me: warming, lighting or enlightening, sometimes chafing or searing. To thank a "sun" by offering oneself to it might have been redundant, a misplaced chivalry, an attempt to strike a posture of pointless generosity, giving what was not mine anyway. The giving closed a circle, though, clinched a bond, and the gesture was meant to be huge. After my time at the JPL, I found myself embarrassed with riches; those Jovian savants churned out pictures of superlative quality, whether or not the colors were "false," and might have achieved an all-time high in chronic manipulation in the public interest. If the public wanted colors, they got them in hundreds after every fly-by.

All of us had been haunted ever since by one image, wholly unexpected, from Io, the most volcanically active body yet visited in the solar system. Right up from the limb of that bruised, mottled, maltreated-looking moon there sprang a yellow flame sheathed in green. Someone had struck a match out there—in fact, a mighty plume of debris shooting hundreds of kilometers above the surface. What gushed forth was sulfur which, landing back on the surface of Io, renewed it, alternately tugged and released as it was by the gravity of Jupiter and its other satellites. Amazingly, before *Voyagers* arrived at Io, Stanton Peale had predicted those tides on the surface. And what a surface it was. Reds, oranges, butter yellows, whites, ochers, and black pulsed and mutated with the moon's own skin, like a lacerated canvas. The sulfur itself changed color according to its temperature, yellow when first melted, red when hotter, and finally a cooking-chocolate black. If the sulfur cooled fast enough, the colors "froze in" and became visual features until the next deluge of stuff fell back to the surface. Haemus Mons, a ten-kilometer mountain, was ringed with a sheet of white material which may have sprayed out from fractures in the rind. It was those yellow and green jets, however, that drew us on, something active, something lively, although a mere sideshow to the commotions in and around Jupiter's red spot. I thought what mesmerized us was an analogy with (no pun) a Bunsen burner flame or, grander, a solar prominence. This moon kept popping off as over the next few months the JPL watched it, and we with them via TV. There was Jupiter, Big Jupe, squeezing the little moon like an athlete with a rubber ball in his fist, in a region no human could survive and whose intense radiation pounded even robots into duds. The first human to record the presence of Io, and Europa, Ganymede, and Callisto, was Galileo in 1610; we had at least watched along with him in mind, and vastly augmented eyes. Our retinas had toured some fabled globes, and *we* were the creature we had uncovered, cowering in Room 167. I then realized that the subject drawing me on and on, making the present in which I wrote (and write now), was the field of the cloth of gold, open and cosmic, perfect for humbling you, just the thing to make you care all over again, or where you hadn't cared at all. My subject was both cosmic and sexual, being unable to unstick the mind or the heart from something divine, in all senses of that word. It all made one feel unworthy, of course, not "up" to the experience, and Swan and I suddenly realized, after quite casual talking, that we already had what Raoul was groping for, having turned his back on Nineveh to concentrate on Florinda Demetz, with whom he was seen increasingly, giving the gossip mills what they had wanted all along. How lucky we were, having happened upon each other, not with heavy intentions, but drawn by an electricity that had wandered in out of the sky. It embarrassed Swan if I called her the perfect woman, which she truly was, and she never said anything such about me, with good reason; but, as the saying goes, we clicked, and clicked again, almost amused at so precise an affection we did not disguise in the least. Some couples were restrained in public, Europeans and associate professors especially, but Swan and I just cuddled each other in the open, talking stars and planets, joking that "top copy" as you paid by credit card in restaurants evoked the Topkapi museum in Istanbul, or how, in a steel mill, a heart-attack victim underwent open-hearth surgery. Which country, France or Italy, had made public necking a misdemeanor, technically anyway, because everyone did it, giving either country an amorous patina? In the United States, however, everything was permitted and murder in the street was encouraged as being less surreptitious than when indoors. A drive-by shooting had a frontal, honest air to it. Or so people said.

I countered this thought with one that some would think soppy: I had saved, in a drawer, all the Valentines, birthday cards, and Christmas cards my Swan had sent me or delivered by hand, propped up in the kitchen on a crockery shelf or magneted to the refrigerator. Then I discovered she had done the same, so there we were, two pack-rat elves, each with a sentimental pile of stuff. Ours was a giving house, ours was; she would arrive back from somewhere and march in with the workstopping cry "Token-time!" Heaven only knew what she would bring me next, and I recognized with a smile that she, one of the most articulate women in the world, had resorted to the ways of those who couldn't express themselves, who turned to Hallmark cards and commercial love songs to get their message home. Not as intensive a token-giver myself, I nonetheless brought my own giving up to speed and quantity, knowing I would feel bad if I didn't reciprocate. I marveled at the way she found just the right thing all the time, combing the world of buyable things with her poet's eye as if everything were a final candidate for a concluding stanza. I never ran out of cologne, shaving foam, skin tonic, heel-balm or heel-pumice, nor did she of perfume, hair clips, bath oils, tiny flashlights, or nail polish. We invested in such things, each to possess the world for the other, and of course to symbolize the million tiny strands that held us together. Such tokens never leave the mind's eye, but linger as the heavier confetti of love.

TWENTY-FOUR

Over the ensuing months we tried to formulate exactly what *Voyager* had done to us, as *Viking* had done something to us as well. It was as if, previously, we had been diluted and now we had been brought up to strength, made concentrated or, as I fondly remembered from schooldays, "Conc." as on mysterious oily or fumy bottles with stoppers that grated in their sockets. And of course this concentratedness bled over into our personal life too, making us no less caustic but making us behave with the abandon of privilege. Chattering about our friends, among them Celia the psychologist, we estimated their chances of surviving without going to launches or fly-bys. Or without TV; Celia used her TV for the VCR but had no cable, and therefore no signal. Increasingly we turned against TV and its hidebound ways, deploring the preinterview interview. "Hell," I said, "if they have the right to examine us to see if we can talk, we have a right to examine them to see if they know English."

"Or," she said with exasperation, "have read the bloody book."

We damned TV, then resumed. "Celia seems at ease with me," I suggested, knowing I put some people off with my highbrow ways.

"That's because she's *accustomed* to psychopaths," Swan said with a merry giggle. "Sorry, but you set it up." That was enough of her wit for one afternoon, and I soon heard the *bring-bring* of her bicycle bell as out she went, a sound that stopped my heart in my mouth, as we say, as if all beauty and dearness had been made to reside in it. It was the sound of her generous body compressed in space and time, a warning not to huge trucks and competitive cyclists that she was launching out, but a reminder to me that she existed in a whirr of legs and a spin of wheels. Always, on leaving, I told her, as the garage door swings down behind you because you have the remote, ring your bell for old times' sake and I will register your whereabouts. By the same token, on returning, even at as much as a hundred yards away, she would begin to ring that bell, the dearest most eloquent noise in the world, saying she was available again, announcing the fact like a bird. Muffled somewhat by the low-lying house, the bell's ring dispersed itself, ricocheting from unusual angles, from behind a double hickory or the pool housing; she was approaching from all points with that splintered, tender jingle created by spinning the top cup of the bell as if it were a top; in the old days we rang our bell by pressing a lever, which kept us still remote from the bell proper. Doing as she did, however, demanded a firm grasp of the entire bell. Sometimes, primed by her bicycle bell, I longed for church bells of a summer evening straying over an English meadow, a Bermuda beach, or the scraggy-looking play area in a small town in the South Seas, melodic tintinnabulation enforcing peace.

I even longed, sometimes, for the hearty, no-nonsense bells of Oxford that kept me from work and sleep as they announced the dominance of the Church, but in their instance only a stroke or two in the manner of clocks. I was attuned to bells, I supposed, but owed them no loyalty; Swan's bell was the exception, both intimate and imperious. I rarely failed to race around the house, through the pool gate, to capture her as the garage door swung open and she dismounted with a swift flick of her leg, coming to rest posed as if this were not a bicycle at all but a new style of fence or an apparatus for Mars. Best of all, so far, had been the day she appeared in the distance, riding not a bicycle but an electric cart, maximum speed two miles an hour; she had hurt her foot and this was her way of getting around. In the distance I saw the cart surmounted by a woman in a sari holding an umbrella erect, and it was one of those Cornell Capa photos you see in albums, prepared for at least an hour, then photographed as a still, in this case an enigmatic apparition, tall, swathed, and exotic, inching toward me, and at that moment as I registered who it was I craved her little bell, the confirmation of imminent arrival.

Naturally, I have responded to all the bells of neighborhood children, always disappointed when I reached the other side of the house and found no Swan but someone's progeny mounted and swerving, going round and round the turnaround that announced its human inadequacy with a diamond-shaped metal plate that said Dead End. If she were already out, that is, equipped with lip balm, water, salt tablets, dog spray, insect spray, sunblock, pump, bungee cords, and heaven knew what else, all for a fifteen-minute tour of the area along its stipulated biking paths. Having biked all through boyhood and adolescence, I no longer went in for it, hating how sore it made my rear end; but I rejoiced in her cycling, the special view of *her* rear as she cruised down the driveway en route to regale the rest of the world with it. Dogs had bitten her, mosquitoes and wasps and bees had come after her, but she persisted, on serious occasions riding a good thirty miles with athletic Celia, actually going all the way round a local lake, equipped with maps and guidebooks so they missed nothing en route. They were welcome to it, even to stashing their bikes in the car and driving to the take-off point. She did all this while flying as well, and I wondered that she didn't get confused, at least between handlebars and control column, but her female brain seemed to separate the two acts, which to be sure had nothing in common. The thought of her Cessna or Piper coming in to land with an attached bicycle bell pinging amid the cushioned throb of a slowed engine prompted my heart all over again. Always, a bell rang for her, from her, because she was a delicious, sunny person, happy to ring if it made you happy and thus slowly acquiring a new facet to her personality. *My* only bell was the one I rang for her if I had cooked dinner and it was ready, but this was more a school bell than anything, and *Come and get it* was a long way from *Here I am.* Just perhaps, because my paternal grandfather, reduced to minor roles by tuberculosis, had been a bellrope mender, showing me how to tie and roll the ropes, I had always been into bells, and this latter-day passion for them had traveled right through from childhood without much intervening experience. Doubtless I would have been a good monk, attuning my entire day to bells, fretting not at my narrow room so long as I was left in peace to write. All that praying would have made me wooden, unless writing is praying. Swan the belle, I said in my gross and obvious joke, rang the bell for me, and I was happy to wheel the bike away for her and stand it on its kickstand.

So, no more Nineveh, we said, missing her mellow, even face, her lack of flap, her rueful good humor; she just had not been snazzy enough, intellectual enough, for Raoul. At a certain altitude, we decided, boredom set in and the skin-man deployed his devilish variations, rending sweetheart from sweetheart in the interests of a few mucous membranes. Would memory serve, and keep warm the faces and mannerisms of the departed others, years later after another shower of names had rustled through?

"One list," Swan said, "is worth twenty minutes of anxious remembering. Write them down." I said I would; I did. More soothing than any bell save hers, though, was the sound, in a small university town (virtually the only kind of town outside New York City I'd known), when the typewriters came out at midnight and the term papers and dissertations began to uncoil. Nobody slept, everyone had something to type, and a connoisseur (such as I was not) could distinguish the plastic rattle of the word-processor's keys from the clatter-clash of the older system, not that the results differed much. We had just spent a white night in Pasadena, to our infinite delight, and all we had now was insomnia having nothing to do with Mars, work, or neurosis. In some radiant pavilion of temperate learning, her bicycle bell, the orchestra of nighttime typewriters, and the well-tempered lilt of Al Hibbs's voice came together and kept us awake instead of soothing us off. It had all been too exciting, and here we were to prove it, owl-eyed at dawn.

Apart from those spent in Pasadena, Swan and I had other white nights and spent much of our time explaining their nature to each other. Hers would begin with a jactitation and feeling too hot, so that she would wriggle her toes and ankles and peel off her nightdress while I fetched her a cool drink: not hot milk but cool seltzer and a sliced bagel faintly grazed with diet margarine. If this did not work, on went the TV at the silliest talk show while, sometimes, I lay there holding her arm or hand. Or she would affix a huge triangular cross-sectioned pillow under her raised knees and install a bolster behind her head and shoulders. Some of these maneuvers should have worked, but they rarely did, at least half as well as a sleeping pill administered late or, as in our first years together, my entire bulk flung on top of hers to crush her into somnolence. "I think," she would eventually say, "I'll stay up all night and work." She never did; the threat was an impish tease, but she would lie there for hours reading works of psychology, which by my lights ought to have worked the trick in seconds. My own white nights began with a much too early wake-up, prompted by too much light, but sometimes by the call of a book I was writing, urging me to return to it after only four hours' sleep (I having gone to sleep easily at about five in the morning). Often I got up, had breakfast, and hit the typewriter, knowing that, after three hours or so of exhausted work, I would go back to bed and sleep for half the afternoon. I never took a pill, not permitted such things, and I tried like the plague never to swim too late, as that always kept me from falling asleep. Another, waking destiny wanted us, I told her, and we had to live with it, sleepless or clueless. Some days, after our white nights had coincided, we stumbled around the house pretending to be alert, eventually retreating to bed to repair the damage. One thing we discovered was that a large helping of pasta last thing helped the go-to-sleep process, even if it put an extra two pounds on your girth. Staying asleep was a different matter, and my theory began to be: the imagination wakes you up, twirling and maneuvering things too attractive to be snoozed at. We both can recognize places in our work where the writing was sleepless, not rewritten but installed there like a bad memory, in nostalgic indignation. Swan has not yet acquired the siesta habit, which saves me always, but she has begun to lie there awake in the darkened room, relaxing and repining, for an hour at least. When in that shredded, itchy-eye condition she did not fly, ever, but she tried to write, often on the razor's edge of the frenetic jitters, hoping for the royal way of unclouded, even inspiration to come back. Since she did not write fiction, she had to achieve an almost wholesome balance, especially if writing natural history, in which there was no room for neurotic extremism. I sometimes thought that the serene, unopinionated stance of the natural historian was a bogus thing: antiliterary and righteous, whereas the novelist, especially the first-person narrator, is free to become as tendentious as possible. It was a difference we never quite hashed out, going our own ways to hell, I through evil and violence, she through unfeigned devotion to the planet. Show me your nightmare and I'll show you mine was the tenor of the house.

We had never before considered the vast amount of extraneous work a literary career involved, not to mention the nervous strain, even if agents did the donkeywork for you. It was all very well to have our heads in the clouds one way or another, but the shadowboxing, the durable dumbness encountered on the Rialto, often made us wish we'd become gardeners. And merely keeping up with correspondence, correcting the errors of people who planned readings and such things, sapped energy from vital projects. Friends had died in the midst of all this busyness, unable to cope. It helped to have, as Swan did, an elaborate filing system, whereas I, with no gift for tidiness, dumped things anywhere, then on top of that layer another layer until the layers edged into one another sideways, edge infiltrating into edge until the receipts pile entered the overseas pile and the business letters entered both, not to mention xeroxes, duplicates, postcards, reminders, newspaper clippings that bogged me down. My only gesture in this area, after so many years of torment, was to bundle all postcards together with a rubber band and respond to none of them lest the simple act of opening up the bundle should spill them all; so postcards, read, slid on to the top of the heap and stayed there forever. Finally, unable to manage correspondence, not even through answering on index cards, I gave up and began to use the phone, attracting the rebukes of diligent friends who loved the pen. The fax machine saved me more than once, but nobody liked receiving those coiled, slimy flimsies, and even at once xeroxing them didn't help much; people felt a machine had intervened, and one with a slithery demeanor.

At about five hundred feet, alarming farmers and chickens, Segundo and I are flying toward the girls, Swan and Celia, as they ride around Lake Otsego. After some avid reconnaissance we have identified the only pair of cyclists going around the lake, and we slant down toward them, not to frighten them but to waggle our wings, although how many Piper Apaches could be pursuing them they already know. One-handedly they wave in the midst of a sublime wobble; we see them giggling and Segundo climbs to miss some trees and circles back. The two bicycles have not advanced (we are flying at a hundred miles an hour, anyway) and we repeat the buzz maneuver from behind, perhaps startling them with sheer noise, ourselves waving downward. Perhaps they can see our faces in the cabin. Behind us, Janine, not that well-disposed to flying, certainly not after a recent mishap on coming back from the British Virgin Islands, keeps her peace, looks out briefly, then gets back to her reading, a book on flowers. Surely Segundo does not want to do this all day as the two women nibble away at the circumference road, perhaps hoping to break some record; it was a notable feat of navigation to find them at all, but we do not want to make their lives a hell of smoke and noise, not when they're out for a blithe country ride of twenty to thirty miles. I know full well that Swan will return, compose a dozen pages of notes about the wonders she has seen, and (Apaches apart) the sounds she's heard, and the whole ride will count as useful grist for an ever-turning mill. So we roar away to dive-bomb a prison or a sedate golf course, or to come in low over a lake and rattle a few roofs as if, all this time, they have been waiting for us to come and make their day. Or, with turbochargers on, we fly north to Lake Ontario and go up to ten thousand feet, our favored exercise in the mode of turning lakescape into map. How chilly it gets up here, enough to make us switch on the heater, as if Canada has reached over and swatted us. The girls are a hundred miles behind, pedaling away at their chore, and Janine has gone to sleep, bored by the antics of superannuated boys. Down below, on the graphite blue of the water, something small leaves a wake: no other living sign, most of all as we arrive over the lake's dead center, a moth in its eye, seemingly stationary. We come up here to be up here: no notes, no talk, just an occasional shrug or exclamation, whereas, Swan tells me, she and Celia talk the whole way, sometimes one behind the other, sometimes abreast, saying things that girls can't say over the teacups, as if the gasp and cough of hard pedaling freed them of certain inhibitions. Well, Segundo and I have nothing to say while flying; we let the astonishing downward spectacle overwhelm our minds or we wordlessly scan the vacant sky, now and then just point at a bird or what might be a distant plane coming toward us.

So, women ride around lakes to get things off their chests and men ride their turbochargers to wipe out thought. What about astronauts then? I abandon the notion at once and peer back at Janine, having the best sleep of her week. Not that long ago, after a lovely holiday island-hopping, in and around Tortola and its neighbors, we flew back up the chain of the Bahamas, did Customs, and set course for Pathica by way of Washington, D.C.

As we flew into bad weather, some oaf directed us into a thunderstorm. We were all over the sky as bags and small suitcases flew around the cabin. Segundo called Center for help, specifying severe turbulence. We had actually looped the loop, he said. On we ground, holding on even though we were strapped in firmly, until we managed to pass beyond the thunder cell and make a landing at Kinston, North Carolina, where we stayed the night, speechlessly peering at one another, survivors in disbelief. Since then, Janine had been reluctant to make long trips, and Swan had kept out of the Apache, though our mishap had not been the plane's fault. Segundo and I, however, were now convinced we were born to survive and prevail; after all, the plane had held together, its engines had defied the thundershowers when others would have stopped; and now Segundo had installed the weather radar that showed anything nasty ahead.

The girls are still riding, in their version of pastoral drudgery (as I see it), and they always will be since this is a ritual of fertility and peace, a womanly excursion at which men are allowed to look only from the air above.

When I return to 333, Segundo and Janine having buzzed off to do some shopping, I enter the empty house and, in spite of my somewhat pawnbroking view of the pushbike, break into my forlorn song of loneliness:

> Where is that Swan,
> Where can that Swan have gone?

I already know, but I sing my threnody anyway, wondering how far away she and Celia are, and how exhausted. Often even when she is not in the car, Swan uses her cellular phone to greet me, and usually, on her own, she talks herself right down to the bottom of the driveway, and we have a bell-less preamble to reunion interrupted only by the swoosh of an object's breaking up her signal. I hang up when she presses the button that raises the garage door, and behold, there she is, ever in the present tense, bedewed and begrimed from her cyclic ordeal, but somehow vindicated, even more so than after she has been flying in the pattern, circuits and bumps to make her perfect. In the meantime, all I have done has been to swim or beat the typewriter. The silly thing about these tender memories is that, seasonally speaking, I remember only summer, and I graft summer's memories on to the vacant spaces occupying the other seasons. All American aircraft bear the letter *N*, standing for November, and my memory is similar, often recalling events without the climatic variation with which they have been involved. It is no doubt an idiosyncrasy of aging. "Do you want the big pillow tonight?" She does not and I tug it from beneath her head, then toss it across the room for neater disposition later. "TV off?" "You can leave it on," she says. "Too hot?" No, she is not. "Feet OK?" I am asking if the sheet is too tightly tucked in at the foot of the bed. She has fresh water in her pretty little floral glass, some cough-suppressant lozenges in case the demon hack starts up, the triangular cushion on the floor within easy reach, and the air conditioner on fan for white noise as well as the Hammacher-Schlemmer sea-surf machine on my side. These are the rituals of sleep-invoking, this is the diffident angelus of ten at night. I could do all this in my sleep if I had to. I never latch the door because opening it would make a noise that wakes her, so all night the door wavers between open and shut, trembling in the sucky breeze from the furnace's air pump. These might seem the observances of a quiet, gentle house, but they are more than that; they bribe the night, the light, the echoes, and I keep my music quiet while I work in the room one door down, ever alert for her nocturnal cry, sometimes although close seeming to come from an unthinkable distance. "Are you OK?" I always begin thus. No, she is not, she had a bad dream. No you didn't, I tell her, it was a stanza from a poem you didn't like and didn't write. It was plaguing you for your attention. She agrees and heads for the bathroom opposite, staggering while I remake the bed, turn the pillow cool side outward (as preferred by Winston Churchill too), and check her glass of water. How eerie to enter that room in the dark with my mini-flashlight aimed down, and the bed between the air conditioner and the white-noise machine, a plinth between two winds, two soughs. It seems impossible to hear anything with those two gadgets going, but I recall that I wear earplugs for sleeping in, to blot out even what cannot be heard, to reassure myself that I am a closed system.

Back, she mutters something about a nightmare, and I invent something about flowers, the amaryllises in the living room big as a stand of trees on the African veldt, but then reevoke for her the times the deer, usually eight, come to the brink of the covered pool and peer into the bright-lit house, through the picture windows. She remembers how we pelt them with apples, usually two to each, though the greedier ones get more; they do not budge, except to mime kicks at one another, after a while beginning to gnaw. If you throw the apples high they sink into the snow an inch or two, solidly, and do not roll. I stop. I have remembered something about winter under the pressure of her insomnia, and I want her to go back to sleep at once. Tucked in, she does, leaving a hand above the coverlet for a final clench and pat; I am dealing with precious, frail cargo, I know, and nothing rough will serve.

What did that oaf of a clerk say to her one Sunday in Peekskill (where her family once lived)? She had gone out for her own copy of *The New York Times* only to hear "Isn't that an awfully big newspaper for such a little girl?"

"Yes," she answered, "but I've got a mind just like a grown-up." She was nineteen. That settled him for keeps. If he had ever heard us deliberately mispronouncing words (asparAgus, broccOli, slamon) he would have snatched the newspaper back. Or what would he have done if he had heard her twitting me after I had come up with what she called one of my "clump" phrases, of a certain abstract felicity, but abstract all the same, the yield of many years' teaching? What might I have said? Oh, *devious interstices* or *ethereal epigone*! "Ha, you've been reading that old misogynistic bastard Milton again. You and him, suckled on Latin, eating fried Greek together for breakfast."

Such indignities, these, erased only when, with head lowered to the level of the stainless steel rim, I listened to the seethe of soap bubbles crackling in the sink or watched the tiny snip of cardinals' beaks as they stood in the bird feeder bowl and troughed on seed. While I was doing these things, she might creep up behind me, put a hand on my shoulder, and join in, breath almost held. So inconspicuous to the bubbles or the cardinals, we might have been brown dwarves far away in the constellation Lepus. "Whatchyer doing, Kumquat," she'd ask, and my shrug would tell her.

One downtown diner pained her, but I adored it because it was where the not-too-well-off went: not so much students as laborers and gas-station people. Zanos was either Zano's, as most folk prounced it, or it was Greek, *Zanos*, a singular nominative like *hypnos*. Masculine too. There you troughed on navy bean soup thickened with arrowroot and cornstarch, followed by sliced turkey with thick gravy and big thick cumulus clouds of mashed potato, philistine buns on the side and hearty stuffing under the sliced meat. You went there to get full, to get some soul food before chopping down the next tree or hefting the next barrel. There, amid bright lights and mirrors, in booths with horsehair bursting out of the banquettes, you took in meat-and-potatoes food: no place for gourmets or exquisites, but nostalgia pasture to me once a week before we headed for the supermarket across the road, our bellies squeaking with the load.

How did we talk? "Did you enjoy yourself, shelbst?"

"Like a survivor."

"All over onto yourself?"

"Exactly. You know the verb, *dano* or *danein*? To stuff full with gorgeous stodge. *Dano, daneis, danei, daneimi, dainete* (it now becomes irregular), *danouspikonasthe.*"

Rather than put up with fake Greek fueled by turkeyed mash on top of thickened soup, she hastened into the glorified tunnel opening into Wegman's where we used a little black card instead of money, almost a wafer of polished anthracite.

Going back to her ceremonious bedtimes, with all thought of the rough or hasty banished, I am still levitating between the twin air machines. To go out into the hallway should surely quell that feeling, but it doesn't, not quite, and I walk unsteadily to and fro deprived of some vital component in the inner ear. Where had I last felt this? In here, yes. But also at the launch of our *Viking*, grandly construed in the aphorism "When a great presence goes away, you feel light-headed." It wasn't a bad, meaning inaccurate, idea, but the sensation was unnerving, and it had something in common with a usage I had forgotten about, a relic from my Air Force days when, as the officer in charge of this or that (squadron or toilet paper), you were obliged to heed a convention that required you to begin all letters "Sir, I have the honor to . . ." and end them "Sir, I have the honor to be . . ." and then you signed your name. Whenever doing either, I had this sense of floating away from my own trivial zone toward one of the fattened majestical; I had no right addressing anyone, and there was no honor in what I did or who I was. Odd how these transient recollections hold you by the short hairs and, when the moment is ripe, seize you with greedy loyalty. Clearly, my present and its hinterland were full of stuff I had to master and put away for good. Related to these feelings there was another mental hang-up that now and then grabbed me with the same old yearning; I wanted to be left alone, but some chronic appetite stirred me up with what I had come to call the panic of the divided second. A man formulates to himself that he has only a few years left, so he vows to waste not a second and tries, inasmuch as he can grasp a second at all, to load every rift of living with unique ore, a Keatsian madness no doubt inspired by disease. If you keep spitting blood, then surely you treasure every breath. Anyway, I had this notion that a true sybarite or hedonist, faithful to the doctrine of the divided moment, would split even a divided second and thus go on into dwindling portions until he had reached the *minimum indivisibile*. But how do it? A fancy if unpragmatic idea, it had no place in human experience, yet it haunted me and ran me down, so much so that I would keep on regretting wasted nanoseconds, so wasting even more of them on idle regret, and this process, once embarked on, threatened to destroy whole hours, whole days, and did. Anxious slicer, I sought some means of fixing time, remarking on the absurdity of my predicament: so happy with my so-called love life, I dreaded its end in my own end, therefore aching as above, but unable to escape the mortal trap of, as we say, being so happy as not to notice the passage of time; a whole hour had gone by, say, while you spanieled, and there was no way of getting it back so as to undertake a more disciplined, self-conscious version of the same activity. If I had not been intimately aware of time's elapsing while kissing or hugging (whatever), then I had better not have been doing it at all.

These tiresome frenzies pursued me as I moved from room to room, from toilet to mailbox, telling myself this was the scene of my undoing. I simply had to do better, living extempore (a phrase that cheered me no end because it meant out of time, thus appearing to confer a freedom more to be prized than birth itself). Impossible. No matter how hard I tried to live life as if there were no tomorrow, I knew there was, and the next split second from now drove in upon my mind and amputated it from itself. *Gather ye rosebuds* I had first heard many years ago, but now the whole rose garden was out of reach because, dreading the end of an ecstasy, I refused to begin on one, which was a form of suicide. I may have been looking for mindless spontaneity, but I never found it, instead torturing myself with an old philosophical chestnut, dreaming of Zeno's arrow that, as he proved, never budged; but his proof depended on a fallacy, this being that a straight line, composed of points, had width, or rather its component points had no area. So neither Zeno nor anyone else could go pontificating about getting *from* one point *to* the next; if you were at one, you were also at the next, like one of those solar-driven trains that no sooner depart than they arrive because there is no distance in between. Was that how it went? A smarter soul than I would surely have taken his dubiety and frenzy as the starting point and related all instants to all others, fixing not on the ephemeral but on the way all units of time merged in the head, some visibly, some out of sight. That would have been the ideal way to become the master of elapsing life, not mourning but mingling. I never did it, being too hidebound by my training, but I knew people who could see all other people's instants in their own, through some prodigious feat of gregarious imagination. Beyond the likes of me, amateur stargazer with head in the clouds. The only way not to respond fully to events—death, absence, illness, applause—was to install them in categories, which somehow weakened their individuality, linking this or that particular death or absence to all other deaths and absences until you had the category uppermost and you broke out into the radiant gold of morning having learned that categories do not die, do not go in for absences. In that way you learned to live among the containers of experience only, at one remove from everything that dogged you and threatened to reduce your life to naught. On this whirligig I had spun for many years, unduly afflicted by aging every second in the presence of an aging young woman for whom time seemed to be going more slowly than for me. Perish the thought.

Sir, I began in my mind's ear, I have the honor to be alive and I finished Sir, I have the honor to be myself. End of battle. You couldn't do it like that, sweet and pithy; you had to earn your retreat, your opting-out, listening to *Turandot* until you couldn't stand it anymore. Imagine. It was not a problem I confided to her; it would demoralize her, I thought, and there was no remedy. Better not ever mention it. Time did not stretch like elastic, but sometimes one had the illusion it was doing so, often in the newly waking state: you woke, saw it was noon, and went back to uneasy slumber, yet waking only seconds later thinking you had been asleep for hours and were now hopelessly late, only to realize the truth and laugh at your anxiety. Was there a book *Anxiety and Time*? How could there be? No one would have found the time to write it in, they would have worried themselves into an early grave for fear of not living to finish it. All that palaver: too old to live, too young to die. Death sinks a fang at forty, said a doctor of mine, and the rest of the years go to maintain the body like a defective grandfather clock, tweaking, fudging, maneuvering. It lacked the hard knife-edge of the great and deadly aphorisms, but it said its bit. If you have eighteen years between you and her, the sheer amount of time implied in that phrase gets you down and you waste ages trying to outlive it. The best remedy, I found, if any, was to indulge in entirely boring activity, such as crushing cardboard boxes into two-dimensional flats as required by the tyrannical local garbage collectors, for once finding your weight useful, and then ringing neighbor doorbells to ask if they too needed boxes flattening. "Flattening boxes today," I'd cry, "get your flattening here!" And out would come all the boxes, ripe for their bonecrusher with his beetlecrushers at the ready, a flatlander at heart. The time would go very slowly and the mind would give up in delight.

Swan and I prospered by not discussing matters too bleak to endure; instead we concentrated on the enthralling launches and fly-bys that had come into our lives like some newfangled religion, demanding little of us beyond patience but delivering new optics, new context, almost reinstating us as schoolchildren who, mainly for writing exercise, wrote their address grandly, in perpetual extension, as North America, Western Hemisphere, Earth, the Solar System, the Milky Way, to which ultramodern children nowadays added *the Orion Arm of* the Milky Way, developing a huge precision that would embolden them forever. That was our own mood, simplifying ourselves as humans but devising a complex address. It took a little effort, but we daily imagined ourselves as gliding, soaring amid that solar system, twirling while we circled our star within a system that itself moved toward Hercules at some appalling speed never noticed, but fit to disarrange the greased hair of a youth shot out of his house on a winter morning. Was that a winter memory? I thought not; it was a winter guess, that was all. By now we had tapes of neutron stars and quasars, gramophone records of musical pieces called "Earth's Magnetic Field" and "The Silver Apples of the Moon" and "Fantasy in Space," courtesy of Messrs. Dodge, Feldman, and Luening. We ached deliciously with those frail, disembodied sounds of computer music, hardly robust enough to have a human behind them, yet appropriate to a human so highly evolved as no longer to belong on Earth or to have human-type emotions. Something rarefied, aloof, poignantly gentle tugged on us, drawing us out like filaments, a sensation that lingered even after the music ended and, briefly, we floundered in mid-vacuum awaiting succor, which never came; the spell broke and all we had was an ethereal hangover best relegated, some thought, to the zone of illusion indicated by William James at the end of the nineteenth century, and brought to our minds by Jim McConkey, novelist and wit, as Swan said the worldliest innocent in America, who built his own reflecting telescope. What William James called this zone was that of *specious memory*, using a word that later came to denote some kind of narrative treachery whereas, if you went back farther to the Latin, you recovered (what Swan and I needed) the word *speciosus*, meaning what delighted the eye—without any hint of treachery or deceit. How rarely could we go back again to what a word *used* to mean, or to be, enabling us to speak anciently.

So, we were passionately involved, obsessed, with the circus of airless filigree limned by such as Dodge, Feldman, and Luening, yet confirmed in our esteem for the solid stuff of that new science imposingly called exobiology. This kind of interest, it struck us, called into play more emotions than merely living on Earth thinking of Earth would ever have done, even if we were deceiving ourselves. My inamorata the poet of the planets had become the aviator of a new domain whose thin end she zoomed through because she coveted its thick.

TWENTY-FIVE

The Bunsens' wedding, staged on the top floor of the World Trade Center in New York City, was pagan chic, a crowd scene with hundreds of guests. Because everyone was there, it was as if they all had always been there; nobody even bothered to say hello. Looking out at the ocean from that huge mailbox-like room, with its mighty picture window set well above where the choppers flew, I felt almost airsick, reluctant to lean toward the glass; if you did, you would fall encumbered by the impedimenta of several restaurants, all proffering irresistible samples of lobster, crab, and salmon. The entire Fulton Fish Market was on show and a string quartet was playing. I was amazed how many faces I knew from our excursions to Cocoa and Pasadena, and I envisioned chartered jets full of astronomers ploughing eastward from Los Angeles just to show the flag.

Raoul and Florinda circulated as if in some parody of Brownian motion, he clockwise, she anticlockwise, honestly, at least until things got rather rowdy and untidy, he all bemused geniality as if merely a guest, she like a freshly released frigate bird watching the sad ghost of Nineveh beckon her from the shadows and then depart murmuring an ancient Hebrew curse. No, I was telling someone, "but I'm an *honorary* Jew. Something to do with the Air Force. Good air forces should stick together." Once again my military persona had come to the fore, and I suddenly realized why: this gathering was similar to one of the old dining-in nights when, in dress uniform and wearing black bow ties, we dined, speechified, and mostly got sloshed. I remembered being hazed, as a young officer had to be, commanded to stand on the table and speak to the assembled gentlemen for fifteen minutes about anything at all. I recalled quoting Oscar Wilde's "The Ballad of Reading Gaol," but no more than that. Thereafter I was considered blooded and could assume my place among the tormentors, none of whom went in for the traditional dining-in-night sports of boot-blacking the posteriors of the newest officers, then doing the same to their bare feet with which, held upside down, they had to stamp on the ceiling of the anteroom. Just as ritualistic, this wedding proved how serious and old-fashioned Florinda and Raoul were, not just dating or messing about, but founding a dynasty in a famous public place. Myself, I wondered why they had not staged the do at Cocoa Beach, but that would have been to spurn the Jet Propulsion Laboratory. There was more press coverage here too, and coverage of higher caliber. The Bunsens were making a statement never to be gainsaid until—well, who knew? All the people they had offended were there, patching things up, and all their intimate friends, looking aloof so as to give nothing away.

My old ambivalence about astronomers and other scientists had still not gone away, not quite; I really thought they intended to inherit the Earth, and a few other planets too, as wind-up bathroom toys for the twenty-first century. How wrong I was, at least insofar as only those scientists who joined forces with the military went ahead as space research became a sidebar to Star Wars and the rest. Was it this wedding that symbolized the watershed between the once-holy, somewhat amateurish days of *Viking* and *Voyager* and the impending big-brother stuff of the space shuttle? Something went out of space research at about this time: joie de vivre, perhaps, or the writ-large lovely old idea (often mentioned by Raoul) of the high school boy getting to do for a living what he had always longed to do for fun, with binoculars, and star maps from the Edmund Scientific Company. Certainly this was not the last of the highbrow parties that celebrated an event in exobiology, and it was not the last one that Swan and I attended; our joie de proxy had far from evaporated, and Raoul's sway continued strong, though he smelled politicians at his heels and, talking incessantly to bureaucrats, got nowhere at all. The military-industrial complex had admired his toys from a distance, but his flair for nudging science into social history escaped them altogether. For him, at least in the first ten years of his planetary passion, research was as much a matter of style as it was nose-to-the-grindstone study. His books, his sessions on TV (explaining astronomy to the hoi polloi, who lapped it up), his parties and his wedding all intimated the decent point that science, contrary to what some Britishers said (relegating it to backroom boys or boffins), was like moviemaking, taking a guided tour to Antarctica, relatable to music and literature. Perhaps his emphasis was a little too grand (as you might expect from one who had graduated from the University of Chicago's ecumenical program), but surely he was on the right path, discerning in himself not only a leader but a connoisseur of taste, a space-age Dante's Virgil. Some had called him commercial, money-grubbing, ego-ridden, but nobody else save perhaps Flip Maarten and Frank Deck had done as much not just to popularize astronomy but to initiate the public into the lure and lore of spacefaring. All along, what had drawn Swan and myself into his orbit had been his conviction that an eye on the sky was as civil and humanistic as a stroll through a gallery of art.

There, unbidden, came the image I had been searching for, not as if I had lost it, but rather never having had it, at least not for its present purpose, the one I instantly switched it to. Down in the basement of the Goldwyn Building on Coriolis campus, a gift from a movie producer, there was a gallery called the Dimple of Zeus, full of discarded-looking imitation Greek statues. It was here that the English Department held its prose and poetry readings; I had performed there myself on several occasions, each time right in front of Elspeth Laria's knitting needles held just above her lap. The most cunning listener of all, Starchief Ammonite, always took *his* seat *behind* the reader or speaker so as to sneak out invisibly if he needed to and to make faces at the rest of the audience if he chose. To have him behind you while you tried to decipher the cryptic response to him in the faces before you was hard work, and you could hardly keep turning around to see what he was doing. Much better to read in the so-called Ed Weiss house where the only thing behind you was a blackboard. But it was not the reading ambience of Zeus that fascinated me now, it was the natural way the statues stood, mementoes of obsolete gods, in the offing, just like outer space, ignored for so many hundreds of years but now back in the running, as if Zeus had been reinstated by the constant presence behind the scenes of, not Starchief Ammonite, but Raoul Bunsen, crowd-pleaser, exobiologist, and man of parts. The world was whole again, thanks to Goldwyn and his cellar.

Swan had introduced readers and speakers in that cellar, for some years having been in charge of the Zeus series. It was the only time things ran properly; she was a born and tireless organizer into whose hands the Bunsens might well have entrusted their grandiose wedding, especially such of its component parts as the papier-mâché console within a spaceship at which Raoul and Florinda stood, welcoming the new era and steering *Star Trek* style, Captain Kirk and Lieutenant Uhura in one. It was almost a crèche, though mounted higher and without animals. There they stood, the newlyweds, gleaming with novelty, waving to the wedding guests as they took off into space, almost like leftovers from the Mars ride at Disney World. I hoped some forward-looking school would receive this space icon to play with, to steer all the way to the Septentrional Fires in the galaxy Scotus, or wherever. Weeks later we saw, by invitation, the room in their house by the lake in which the wedding presents had been gathered; enough to start a medium-sized civilization, with enough huge boxes to house half the homeless, and, carefully unwrapped then refolded like funeral flags, the gold and silver that had sheathed most boxes, including the one that had held the pewter globe of Earth we gave, not only able to rotate but to open, halved, and contain some precious substance or even a few vital calling cards. Pewter, we had thought, would be different, and it was beguilingly engraved with all manner of ancient geography and spellings.

One bright morning, Swan went off to fly and encountered a new flying instructor with a manicured, skewed accent she at once learned was Dutch. Why the local FBO had hired him, she had no idea, but there was some talk of a government scheme sponsored by KLM and Pan Am. Erik Voorthuis was six feet tall, had a ready smile, and loved to make puns in English, a big improvement on her current instructor, who at once vanished from the picture as Erik took over. Swan's flying life was going to improve minute by minute, not least because Erik, though mentally sharp, was easygoing, liked women, and was serious: already committed to KLM, one day soon to become the pilot of a 747. He was part of the cream, so why was he slumming at a provincial airport? Building time, and English as well, because English was the language of international aviation, though many foreign pilots mangled it—not those of KLM. After all, Dutch-spoken English was the second-best English spoken, wasn't it? Where had I heard that chauvinistic little quip? Erik was a charmer; Swan let herself be charmed, and she began making notes on him for a new book she was going to write on learning to fly. She cheered up whenever she went to fly with him; indeed, I began to think she was his only pupil and that he had been sent over by KLM to recruit her for the airline. So, she had a brand-new friendship with someone who wasn't an astronomer or a writer, though he was rather well-read.

Where, I wondered, was this man's cantankerous side? Had he no vices at all? Did KLM process its heirs apparent before shipping them out? Perhaps Erik was a diplomat in disguise and would one day appear on the ramp in pinstripe suit, sharply cut-away shirt collar, and polka-dot tie; that was the formal rig of diplomats, wasn't it, or was I out of date? He came from a country so reliable that invading Nazis in World War Two had seized Rotterdam by parachuting in and then taking streetcars to their various destinations. I soothed myself, knowing Erik was a safer pilot than his predecessor; she wouldn't come home in tears, picking furiously at her cuticles and vowing never to fly again. Erik was going to go over the entire course she had already passed, thus equipping her with a foundation that had his stamp on it. If she was willing to pay, he was willing to teach. He even had the approval of Segundo Cieli, a man who had been known to fault Adolf Galland and Chuck Yeager. "Maybe a bit like all Hollanders," Segundo said, "but as flying Dutchmen go, B plus." For him, this was gush. I had watched him grade landings made at our local airport by commercial pilots bringing in DC-9s, BAC 1-11s, Boeing 737s, as well as various propeller-driven aircraft given the oddly sympathetic name of commuters. They rarely passed his neutral inspection, always getting something wrong and extorting from him a derisory comment, sometimes "Hah, balls to the firewall all the way," sometimes "He just don't know what flaps are for." Truth told, Segundo was a flawless pilot, landing the Apache with a slow whisper, letting it feel its way back to Earth, coaxing and gentling it into silky relinquishing of flight. He had never flown for an airline, but I knew that, if he had, all the other pilots would have resigned in envy, or they would have bribed him to go away. Somewhere short of Kinston, he no doubt saved our lives by calling on his aerobatic skills in a moment of acute drama, after which, for all of us, the question had become: either fly with him because he's so good, or don't ever fly with him again because of that inadvertent loop. No matter how well he flew, there was always a chance of something's going wrong; but, if fly I had to, I told myself, and an engine failed, there was no one I'd rather have in the next few vital seconds, arranging asymmetrical flight. If you don't fix it in those few seconds, you enter a roll and a spin. He practiced engine-out procedures over the lake, so much so that emergency became second nature to him. Such a pilot was Erik too (notice the Dutch word order, gleaned from him), though he lacked Segundo's heroic lust for risk, without which Segundo's flying day was never complete. Dapper, debonair, and articulate, Erik was a heartbreaker soon cutting an erotic swath through the airport belles, mostly pupils at the local flying club. He had arrived, they said, and they were lost. "Sure," Segundo had said, "the only place they put their legs together is in the cockpit. Ha. Joke." Erik wasn't quite the Lothario he was cracked up to be, though; the local hangar-flying community loved hyperbole, that was all, saying that when he soloed a girl he clipped not a little square from her shirt but an oval from her underwear. It had even been said that when he said he'd soloed someone it meant something different from the usual. We liked him and shared many a soda pop with him over jabber about Queen Wilhelmina, boys with their fingers in dikes, and the iron-boned, foam-rubber anatomies of voluptuous KLM stewardesses: insatiable, pragmatic, and wry, he told us, boasting. He came from a land whose English was so good that English and American books sold alongside the home-grown product, and virtually no one noticed the difference. He was nineteen, in the first flush, jocular and given to practical joking of a mild order, marking time here until his airline wanted him for serious indoctrination. All he owned went into a little carry-on, and he did his own laundry, even his ironing, in the small apartment complex near the airport. He hung out all the time, getting to know everyone and make himself indispensable, as if he had arrived to represent a brave new world notable for having such creatures as him in it.

Part of his job was to ferry people to and fro, sometimes in a Piper Warrior, sometimes in the smaller, older Piper 140 the Warrior resembled. One day, two burly men showed up, journalists actually, and asked to be flown to a destination half an hour away, so off he went with them, one alongside him in front, the other behind. Not far away from the airport he radioed in that his engine had quit and he had become a glider. Such a mishap would have unnerved him no more than it would Segundo. Find a smooth field and land, that was all: no ploughed fields allowed. Or an empty highway would do. Theoreticians, who abound in hangars, guessed that he embarked on a satisfactory glide, aimed at the right field, and settled down to await the landing, but the man beside him panicked, grabbed the stick, and stalled the 140 into the trees. Both passengers were killed and Erik suffered severe injuries from which he died in the hospital a few hours later.

Swan was devastated, like everyone else. He was too young to die, even to be earning a living. We saw photographs of the crash site in the local newspapers and were appalled to see how little of the plane remained intact: small debris everywhere, unrecognizable and flimsy. Suddenly an implacable and grievous domain to which Swan had paid lip service had enveloped her; she grieved hugely, seeing all that surrounded her as fodder for the reaper, all of it and us ready for dispatch. Young and old received the same favor at the hands of who knew what entity. It was important, she said, to go up flying as often as she could afford, lest Erik's death spook her, and she pressed on with her book, always in tears. Inconsolable was not the word; she became involved with Erik's family and relatives; she dug into funeral conventions as if at last discovering the human race. Her face seemed to shrink and dry, her gaze became opaque (she was seeing horrors) and anonymous, and her hands attained a constant tremor as if she had tried to lift something far too heavy for her, and she had at last put it down. I was amazed that she managed to put word after word, but she did, and she forced herself to go on flying with her former instructor, at least until his tirade about pampered foreign pilots unequal to the simple demands of a 140 wore her out. She had discovered that death, as someone said, does not require you to keep a day free; it moves in like the angel with the sword in the Hasidic parables and enforces silence. Perhaps she had never before considered the absurd, insentient quality of the universe; even to think about it was in part to yield to it. She had shut it out and now it had gone and wiped away her ebullient young instructor, more a friend than an instructor, more a member of her own generation than anything else. The very notion would not fit into her mind. No scream voiced it. No gesture summed it up. Erik was over and done with, no sooner started than stopped. They flew his body overnight to Holland on a KLM 747, ironic echo of all he had planned and all that had been planned for him. He had become cargo instead of, down the line, a four-striper with still youthful looks.

You never get over it, I thought; it is that over which you do not get (Dutch word order again, I fancied). Successful grieving, I had decided, was the recognition that you never got over it; it was too vast, too coarse, for any of us, never mind whom you prayed to, to whom or what you lit a wholly unnecessary candle. Into our bizarre and tender rituals, our absorption with each other and machines of the air, there had entered something we owed no loyalty to, something abstractly omnipotent, an eater of the young and old, an undiscriminating gorgon.

How it happened, I never knew, but the timbre of her bicycle bell, coming or going, altered, muddled by death, as if the fact or the tendency or the promise had leaked into the texture of its metal in a premature blight, changing both pitch and speed just enough to make me wonder if some deviant prankster had attached a bicycle bell to a hearse now approaching the front door. How I ran to check the *bring-bring* of her bell. Nothing, of course, was different, so perhaps what I thought I had heard was a difference in the motion of her wrist, in the little carousel of twirl she applied to the top cup. Erik's death had reanimated all the local forms of death, from the broken-jointed foxglove at the door to our neighbor, the Reverend Mr. Klare, who used to chainsaw trees in the little woodland between our house and his, until the day the chain saw ceased and never ceased ceasing and they bore him away on a steel cot: affability struck down by the destroyer of delight. With renewed horror I heard the sustained shrieks at night of some rabbit trapped by a raccoon, sometimes as much as ten minutes, right there among the trees where the baseballs and cricket balls got lost. When I looked in daylight, there was never a sign, just the everywhereness of an invisible vacancy minus its rabbit.

Nothing swayed her. She had acquired another dismal membership even though she could still speak eloquently about a pilot's having become so proficient that she or he, on landing, could make constant tiny corrections in attitude and pitch without even seeming to calculate. Like Segundo Cieli. It was all in response to the wind, as if the expert read the wind's intent before the wind moved, dipping a wing before a gust began. What was this skill, she wondered, and decided it was constant improvisation bordering on prophecy; a keen pilot sensed what kind of a situation she, he, was in, and which twenty or thirty events might be next. So it was readiness shading over into clairvoyance. We dropped the topic, but I saw her making tiny adjustments with her hands to an invisible stick, which merely brought to mind yet another of our standard utterances: the word *fractionally*, said with thumb and forefinger raised only a millimeter apart. "I'm very fractional today," one of us would groan, and the other would make the thumb-forefinger sign, half an inch apart, and the other would say nothing but just echo the visual and gradually close up finger onto thumb until no light showed between.

TWENTY-SIX

Now and then, in moments of trucial idealism, my mind entertains images of virginal young Australians, all energy, racing across their inhospitable landscape to go fight the Germans in World War One only to be killed in a trice at Gallipoli. What was their haste? I dream that way because my own father volunteered at sixteen for the same carnage, though he came out of it ruined. Something impetuous and heedless comes to life in those images of beardless, inexperienced boys rushing to the slaughter and makes me shudder. I have had no desire to join them, but experience of my father tends to make me feel an initiate, enough to have recognized in Swan some of the same tendencies, minus the war of course. She too raced ahead, to some abrupt destination, like one doomed or appointed, driven forward by some gale of beauty findable nowhere in the wind atlas. My whole career has been other, except when I was a jock, bowling and hitting balls: *my* headlong time, and only then.

That was only one side of her, though, waning as she advanced beyond the clutter of degrees into a career of her own. Her more circumspect side began to emerge as she began writing prose, not that her prose was ever prosaic, any more than mine. In her behavior, certain elements came to the fore, the emblem for which should be the neat basket in her bathroom, loaded with pads and tampons, a whole bundle of blotters, all arranged according to size and length, rather like a hunter's ammunition basket, with the different types of buckshot arranged according to size: the world of phenomena dominated and made easily available. Her evident pride in this basket of hers, the way she ushered me in to appraise and admire it, told me that as well as impetuous she was calculating, a bit finicky almost to the point of indulging a pattern complex. I envisioned her boarding a train or plane with her basket of sanitary goodies, somewhat like Colette with her shopping basket full of groceries, and the welcoming aahs and oohs of the suits in first class, the whole performance trembling on the edge of her offering the contents around as if the basket were a box of cigars. Of course, she never took it with her, but made portable anthologies from it with the same degree of fastidious concern, always tucking in, rolled up tight, two pairs of paper panties, ephemeral garments having, in my book of erotica at least, a certain sexual allure, while clean. Those who design for personal hygiene have little idea how much they delight some watchers for impertinent reasons. When she was away, I would often peep into her bathroom and admire what was left in her basket, all of it—the rump's rump, so to speak—arranged in discrete rows, the tampons erect as grenadier guards, the pads at rest horizontally. She held on to, cosseted, words or phrases in the same fashion, treasuring one she had garnered from the biologist-doctor Lewis Thomas at Sloan-Kettering Hospital where he worked. Handing him a book of mine, she heard him exclaim "Hot dog!" in evident pleasure at receiving something new to read. I could think of no one who responded so eagerly to a book from a stranger, but that was Thomas's avid way; the universe was not something to be stared down and rebuffed. She kept that phrase of his, put it on retainer for any similar situation, so there were then three people hotdogging it in the western hemisphere. So did tiny reflexes build into commanding rituals, easily turning into what more pompously we might have called the texture of our lives. Waltzing off to visit the Lewis Thomases of the world, packing her basket as if heading for six months in the Arctic, were the twin sides of her. I could figure her out fairly easily once I tried, and modulate my tactics accordingly.

Like most people, she could not fathom why I needed to surround myself with classical music every hour of the waking day, even sometimes the same piece by the same composer—Delius, say. It drove them mad but provided me with a place of acoustic safety, a buffer zone, within whose cocoon I could write or think, sometimes both, with a special feeling of luxurious exemption. My weird habits were harder to stomach than hers, I thought; they obtruded more, though I found her constant use of the telephone a punitive cadenza. Miracle gadget as it was, it caused me to begin working even more at night because the ring and the prattle, coming through two doors and a pair of earplugs, proved too much. That bell was the only one I never welcomed, though I have mellowed in that regard. Am I any less compulsive than Swan when, in the course of writing, I take a sheet of good paper (too good for notes and so an extravagance!) and divide it vertically into four or five columns, the widest on the left for main themes, on the right a few narrower ones for *trouvailles.* I fill up the right-hand column first and, when it's been used up and all the bright ideas have been installed in what I'm writing, scissor it off, leaving the next column ready for business. This is no more hidebound than her basket, surely. And no less. On we go, whether like some folk in this universe composing twaddle such as *The Nature of Bad Smells* or inventing a jargon that takes a lifetime to elucidate: we make our marks, wondering if everything we happen upon should fit into our work, nothing refused, nobody turned away, because this is the horn of plenty. There is nowhere else to go. There is no other horn. So, a softly spoken gent called Alan Shawe, who announces classical music for the Coriolis radio station, shows up on another wavelength when the university, yielding to commercial impetus, closes down the station altogether. Surely, we felt all along, he or somebody derived from him has a destiny within our lives; nothing is alien, after all. The problem is to evoke the Alan Shawes accurately without ever mentioning them; it really is. Mostly, you cannot do it, so what was, is, this compulsion to do the impossible, as if a hint were as good as a full-dress habitation and a name? Will the one chosen atom imply all others? Old Jeans (Sir James) exemplified the problem with his box of radium atoms, all identical. Each year, one of those atoms bit the dust; fate knocked on its door, as he said, and that was that. Why that particular atom and none of the others? He did not know. Chance? Maybe. God dithering? Says who?

Far more of our lives was random than it should have been, not that we blamed ourselves, but, with newly biased intensity, we scrutinized our daily behavior and were astounded how much of it had come to us accidentally, and we had settled gladly into it. This unnerved us somewhat because, if you were responsible for all you did, then you should have intended it, whereas to live along in passive poise was less than responsible. Perhaps the same was true for writing, with the best of it coming unbidden, unsought for, but just accepted as it arrived from somewhere like a hot plain bagel. Now Swan and I knew the difference between us and them: we let all manner of things in: a fluke could become an honored piece of our conduct, or a cherished bit of our prose or verse. There was no law banning the fortuitous, whereas most of those we knew dreaded anything unplanned and called an accident an artifact—that old conundrum we abhorred. Did this mean we two were more permissive than others, then, or just surer of ourselves? The more certain you were of who you were, the more accidentals you could assimilate into your intact identity, and the more you could welcome and use brain waves without jeopardizing the nature of your written work. With such puzzles we whiled our lives away, working hard but minus any sense of victimization by the universe we had recently come to know.

TWENTY-SEVEN

By now I had formed the impression that Raoul Bunsen had several birthdays every year. Here came another, duly announced on an ornamental, almost Byzantine card that invited us along to a dinner catered by Etienne, the Italian who cooked French. It had become clear to us that Raoul needed to have his climactic days witnessed; a birthday unheralded by wine and beef for one hundred would not be a birthday at all.

Dining with Raoul was déjà vu; even the same topics came up again and again. Swan sat opposite him, with on her left the editor of a popular magazine. I was glad I was down among the Nobel Prize winners, opposite Hans Alpha, shaggy, sculptured, buoyant, with his transcendental stare working overtime. Now Raoul leaned over and explained to our end of the table that I had written a novel about the Milky Way and had actually built a model of the galaxy in my basement. Alpha cleared his throat and paused, shifting his stare from transcendental to immediate. "A—*working* model?" Was he joking? Of course not. This man, who had figured out our Sun, had a mind that would accommodate the most preposterous notions. Had I said yes, he would no doubt have arranged to come and watch it work, thus exposing himself to fresh humiliation at the Pathica airport. Sadly, I shook my head, and he gave me the nod that said, Well, next time you may be able to get it. Just keep trying.

In the following February, as my own birthday came around, Swan gave me a chirping singing card emblazoned with cutout birds that moved; you opened the card flat and the birds began to sing, activated by a little computer chip built into the center. It reminded me of Respighi. I tucked the card, flattened out, into the front of my shirt and walked about with a chestful of birdsong, a man who was an aviary. Supposedly, birthdays were the epitome of seasonal time, of time made to make sense, but they always made me only too aware of the quiet seepage of moment after moment, banal chronicity having its way with us behind the scenes, and the more the talk was of my birthday the more I felt my being drifting away in a shower of anonymous particles. That, no doubt, was why Raoul needed all those witnesses: they represented seasonal time, falling apart even as they witnessed him, but giving him a constituency not of the airwaves but of the here and now so that whichever way he looked he sensed himself erect among them like statuary. He knew that the quiet recognition at home, among intimates, of a birthday likely to recur was not enough to save you from degeneration; there had to be a ritual populated with strangers who, not loving you or liking you, had lent you their decay for the day, just to make you feel good. I even contemplated writing a book on birthdays and eternal recurrence; I suddenly seemed to know so much about them, to have them on the brain. But I lost interest after the day, as willing to let time sidle over me and through me as to keep count until, with factitious enthusiasm, I arrived at the same day a year later, purring *this is my day* all over again. When she was a little girl, Swan interrupted, they had been so poor that her mother used to send her out at Christmas selling wrapping paper. I had not heard an image so forlorn for years: the little Jewish girl out hawking Christmas wrap was painful and grotesque, bound to hurt her into something; but she said it didn't bother her now and hadn't then. She had not thought about it much. Had there ever been an instance of a Christian child going from door to door with Hanukkah wrap? Of course not. There was something in American culture that didn't balance out, no matter how intense the dream that brought the person to the Statue of Liberty without ever achieving its stature.

Whenever Swan and I needed spiritual refreshment, we went into her bathroom to look at the ingot, that crystal perfume decanter filled only with prismatic light. We lifted its stopper high so that it functioned like a dozen prisms, swift-changing the hues of light with the merest tilt, vouchsafing a tiny glimpse of infinity. The ingot itself, a deep inkless inkwell, burned with the same colors but less gently: one blink and you had varied eye position just enough to change the colors, and always that red-hot coiled spring at the hole's bottom stood for something primal and causal, never going out, on the dullest day standing guardian to the entire specimen. Was this our emblem? Hardly, but we lingered over it, hand in hand, sensing something of a sacrament going on, bolstered by light alone. Here was infinity all over again, in a thicker, less tentative version: the miracle wholesale, as on Jupiter and Mars. There was no need to go whoring away after strange gods; the thing had been here all the time, refracting and dazzling. The universe was remarkably consistent, in this aspect anyway. The armless legless *mutilé de guerre* needed only the ingot to peer into, had been deprived of nothing sacred. It was a matter of doing multiplication, increasing your vision by a big enough number. No perfume or bath oil entered that inkwell of delight, but it sometimes revealed in their paler tints both copper sulfate blue and iron sulfate green, the scarlet of cinnabar and the oily brown of nitric acid. Our sampler of the universe, the ingot gathered the whole house around it, providing a center that human beings cannot be, being so plagued with vagaries. Birthdays and childhood humiliations came and went, but the laws that controlled the ingot had been in at the beginning and were not going to bend. Had the ingot been a figurine, an Aztec or a Hopi god, for instance, our dealings with it might have been more obvious, but that would have been simplistic and vulgar; instead we scooched our awe down to the bottom of the recess and revered the abidingness of light. One twitch of imagination and Hyperion, king of beasts, would be living there next to the red-hot coil, looking to transform all beings into more colorful versions of themselves, complaining that the rugs were too drab, that it was no use clutching stodginess from the very sky. Hail, holy light, we murmured, and got on with life.

Could she have found love in there, love of the kind so often denied a maturing child? She thought not. Then said "You can appreciate the spectrum, or whatever of that kind of thing, only if you have love of the usual kind. Without it the spectrum, the entire magnificence of the universe, is a cold block of steel, a nail file. You can savor it, yes, but the savoring ought to go on in the right context. If not, you get a rather deistic person, closer to a god than to anything, and who wants that?" Numerous dictators, I was going to answer, but I bit my tongue and tried to pursue her point, wondering if it was so poor or bad a thing to approach godhead, even without the least trace of sentiment. If I had been born a god, I wouldn't have demanded praise or awe: none of that, but some rousing songs, some gaudy epic poems, a few bits of pornography to stir the divine prostate now and then. I thought her view of gods unkind; had they no feelings at all? Can a god without feeling produce a human *with*? What an exercise in the singularity of physics and chemistry that was; the answer, I guessed, was yes, anything was permitted if you had the right ID. It was never a matter of working backward from the delivered homuncule to the god that produced us. Creation, I thought, was a gratuitous act, nothing rational, and we had no right expecting a Mother Goose version of the inchoate. Such was my notion of the powers that be, different from hers. Her childhood had unequipped her for pondering gods, and she had survived only by telling herself she could do something to help others, that she was not doomed to feel always as she felt when a child. Gradually she had edged toward an altruistic role, going out of her way to become an ameliorator, an enabler, so much so that, where I once thought she should have been a scientist, she now seemed on the brink of becoming a counselor, a psychologist, intent on improving people's lot, especially those (she found them) whose childhood had been like hers, surrounded by a bodyguard. Compassion as a reflex was what she recommended and enacted. So for a while she became less interested in radiant, ecstatic images, or flying, or soccer, but set out her stall from stuff more prosaic, almost domestically political, with the planet foremost among the ailing patients. It was a holistic vision of ministering to others before they ministered unto you, which put you on the receiving end. In no time she became a far better person than I was, making almost a social policy of what her childhood (and adolescence) had lacked—walking home alone because her parents were too busy working to collect her, eating dinner alone in front of the TV (everyone in the house eating at a different time). When I asked her about her schooldays she could hardly remember them, as if she had not been a witness: hair short and curly, German but no French, English literature her favorite, furtive meetings with Gentile boys (all forbidden), but little else.

TWENTY-EIGHT

That July, on a gorgeous clear-skied summer afternoon, I was treading water with just about minimum skill, trying to do the impossible, which was to think about a novel when not at the machine; I never could do it, but I had always kept trying in hopes that, while disporting myself in one medium, I could soften up the terrain in another. In fact, as soon as I told my mind to work, it went voluptuously blank, no doubt wanting to do the equivalent of tread. Then I saw what I thought was a plane coming over, as usual, since the house lay on the approach to the local airport; but it halted, gleaming and shuntling; it just sat there right over Coriolis campus, and I could make out what seemed window frames and windows: no tail, no wings, no blades. My first and shameful thought on seeing that glossy slotted sphere was Bravo, they have come for us at last. No satellite, no balloon, and certainly not anything else familiar from the world of aviation, it sat there at about seven thousand feet and inspected Coriolis, looking, I facetiously thought, for Raoul Bunsen, surely our leader in this domain. If it found him, I never heard, but would he have told? I had no binoculars, no aids of any kind, but the sky was blue, the object did not move at all, and I had time to improvise an analogy between it and the noses, mated so as to form an egg shape, of two Boeing Stratocruisers all glassed in (the old Boeing-with-the-bar-in-its-belly). Not quite an egg, I thought, but more bulbous. Abruptly it slid toward me, then at unbelievable speed executed a vertical U-turn narrow as a tuning fork, a maneuver I had seen no Cieli perform, not even in a Pitts biplane, and receded faster than I could think. It melted away westward and vanished, flashing in the afternoon sun. It might have become bored, a toy disqualified and ushered off the premises. Had it really come for Raoul, freshly back from the big dish in Arecibo, Puerto Rico, to which and its accompanying apartment we had been invited and never gone. I had never seen anything so ovoid-lustrous cruising the rural air. Since, like a good empiricist, I believed the evidence of my senses, I had seen what my scientific friends thought did not exist, or at least remained merely "unidentifiable," which was all right by me; but, even if you did not presume to identify the thing, you acquired a certain stigma.

My mind's eye has been having a field day ever since, silverly making me a believer against all reason and the crisply registered disbelief of Raoul and other astronomers. What was the thing doing? Were they peeping at my naked body as I trod water midafternoon: one of those enigmatic human activities? Bibbing Cokes at their consoles or puffing grass? Did they sit within that shiny bulb like the passengers in old ads for Northrop's flying wing? Was what they did a quotation of some kind? Like this? Since then, every time I have gone out to the mailbox at night, usually after twelve, and peered up at Orion or Cygnus, old friends, they stammering fuzzy like King Alfred's candles, I've had my best book along, just in case they wanted a sample. Then I'd go back inside feeling oddly deprived, eager to be my untranced self again, anxious to get back to work while waiting for something different.

One doting look at the creature asleep in the huge wide bed, on her stomach amid the billowy waft of the air conditioner, Jean Marais standing guard in his gilt frame on the bedside table, the mane of big hair blotting out my view of her head and back. An interloper who in his day has cooled her pillow in that refrigerated flow while she tripped to piddle, I sneak out, leaving the door perched on its catch; it will not slam or gape, but waver all night in the suck of air from the furnace. I go into Swan's bathroom, put on a feeble light by dimmer switch, and lean over the ingot, half-composing an invocation to it that begins: Inkwell of nothing, in which we dip our eyes. If it is almost enough just to be alive, no wonder I thank my lucky stars for a gift of so much more.

Novels by Paul West available from Overlook

Life with Swan

Terrestrials

Sporting with Amaryllis

The Tent of Orange Mist

Love's Mansion

The Women of Whitechapel and Jack the Ripper

The Universe and Other Fictions

Rat Man of Paris

The Very Rich Hours of Count von Stauffenberg